Lysbeth

1900–2004

Also published by Christian Liberty Press

Pearl Maiden
by H. Rider Haggard

In Freedom's Cause
by G. A. Henty

Lysbeth

A TALE OF THE DUTCH

H. RIDER HAGGARD

REVISED AND EDITED
BY
MICHAEL J. MCHUGH

Christian Liberty Press
Arlington Heights, Illinois

Revised and edited by Michael J. McHugh
Cover painting by Timothy Kou
Original book illustrations by G. P. Jacomb Hood, R.I.
Layout and graphics by Christopher and Timothy Kou at
imagineering studios, inc.

A publication of
Christian Liberty Press
502 West Euclid Avenue
Arlington Heights, IL 60004
www.christianlibertypress.com

ISBN 1-930367-96-1

Printed in The United States of America

Revised Edition

This book is dedicated to the memory of one of the greatest and most noble-hearted beings that the world has ever known; the immortal Prince William, called the Silent, of Nassau. The book that follows tells the tale of the times he shaped and the work that he accomplished on behalf of virtuous liberty, the fruits of which are still present today.

Contents

The Sowing

The Ripening

Book Three
THE HARVESTING

ABOUT THE AUTHOR

Sir Henry Rider Haggard was born in England on June 22, 1856. He was the eighth of ten children and received most of his primary and elementary education at home through private tutors and occasionally at a local grammar school. His parents took him on frequent trips to the Continent during childhood days.

In 1875, when Haggard was nineteen, he traveled to South Africa to work as a secretary for the newly appointed governor of Natal. Three years later, the young Englishman resigned his post at the high court of Pretoria to take up ostrich farming in Natal.

Haggard visited England in 1880 and was married on August 11 to Mariana L. Margitson. The newlyweds soon returned to their farm in Natal to resume the business of farming. In his spare time, Haggard began to work on his first book project and also began to take up the study of law. In 1882, the Haggard family sold their farm in Natal and returned to England.

Henry Haggard completed his law studies in 1884 and accepted a call to the bar of attorneys in London where he worked as an assistant to a chief judge. It was during this time that he made use of what he describes as his "somewhat ample leisure time in chambers" to write his first successful novel *King Solomon's Mines*. This book, as he put it, "finally settled the question of whether to pursue a legal or literary career." Henry Haggard proceeded to write over sixty-six novels and numerous papers, producing nearly one book for each year of his life.

Haggard traveled extensively throughout the world during much of his married life. His knowledge of the culture and terrain of Holland and the Netherlands enabled him to complete one of his grandest novels, *Lysbeth*, in 1900. The recognitions of his contributions as a writer were crowned in the year 1912 when Henry Rider Haggard was knighted.

Sir Haggard died in London on May 14, 1925, at the age of sixty-eight.

INTRODUCTION

There are basically two ways of writing an historical romance—the first is to choose some notable and leading characters of the time to be treated and, by the help of history, attempt to picture them as they were; the other, to make a study of that time and history with the country in which it was enacted, and from it to deduce the necessary characters.

In the case of *Lysbeth*, the author has attempted this second method. By an example of the trials, adventures, and victories of a burgher family of the generation of Philip II (1527–1598) and William the Silent (1533–1584), he strives to set before modern readers something of the life of those who lived through one of the most fearful tyrannies that the Western world has known—the Spanish Inquisition. How did they live, one wonders; how is it that they did not all die from the fierce persecution, those of them who escaped the scaffold, the famine, and the pestilence?

This question and another arises, why were such things permitted to be? I have selected this story, in part, because these issues are worth consideration, especially by young people, who are so apt to take everything for granted, including their own religious freedom and personal security. How often, indeed, do any living folk give a grateful thought to the forefathers who won for us these advantages, and many others with them?

The writer has sometimes heard people who have traveled to the Netherlands express surprise that even in an age of almost universal prosperity its noble churches are permitted to remain smeared with melancholy whitewash. Could they look backward through the centuries and behold with the mind's eye certain scenes that have taken place within these very temples and about their walls, they would marvel no longer. Perhaps that is why in Holland they still love whitewash, which to them is a symbol, a perpetual protest; and remembering stories that have been handed down as heirlooms to this day, frown at the sight of even the most modest sacerdotal vestment. Those who are acquainted with the facts of Dutch history and their great struggle for religious liberty will scarcely wonder why they still fear religious hierarchy that is tied to a bureaucratic power and why many Hollanders still value their right to own a Bible even though many seldom read it.

KEY PERSONALITIES IN THE BATTLE FOR A FREE AND INDEPENDENT DUTCH REPUBLIC

King Charles V (1500-1558)
Ruler of the Holy Roman Empire, including Spain and the Netherlands, from 1516 to 1556. As absolute monarch, he fought to expand and strengthen Spain's control over major portions of Western Europe. His major battles were against Protestant and Jewish strongholds in France and the Netherlands.

King Philip II (1527-1598)
Son of Charles V and ruler of Spain and the Netherlands from 1556 to 1598. Militant Roman Catholic monarch who was intent on exterminating Protestants and Jews in the Netherlands. Philip re-established the system of religious courts in his realm known as the Inquisition, punishing anyone, especially Protestants, who were guilty of heresy by refusing to conform to Roman Catholic teachings.

Alvarez de Toledo, Duke of Alva (1508-?)
Military commander under Philip II. He launched a reign of terror from 1576 to 1582, which resulted in the deaths of over 100,000 men, women, and children in the Netherlands.

Prince William of Orange (1533-1584)
Known in history as William the Silent. Leader of the Dutch Protestants who fought to free themselves from the rule of the tyrannical monarch Philip II. He led the battle for freedom and religious toleration in the Netherlands from the late 1560s until his death in 1584.

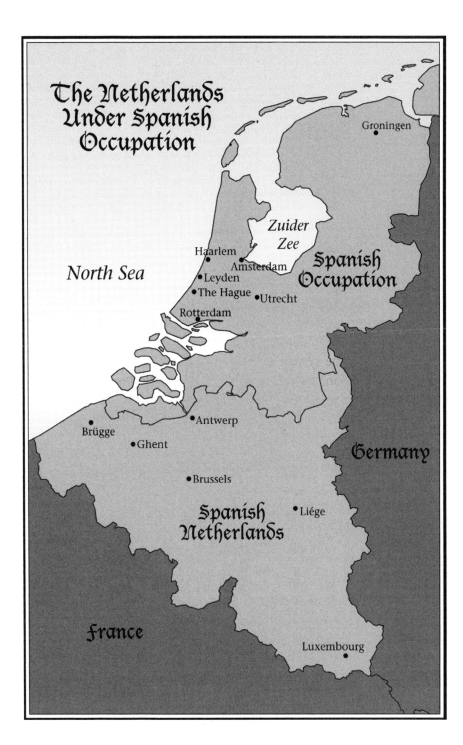

The Netherlands
Under Spanish
Occupation

North Sea

Groningen

Zuider
Zee

Spanish
Occupation

Haarlem
Amsterdam
Leyden
The Hague
Utrecht
Rotterdam

Antwerp

Brügge
Ghent

Germany

Brussels

Spanish
Netherlands

Liége

France

Luxembourg

Book One

THE SOWING

Chapter I
The Wolf and the Badger

The time of our story begins around the year 1544 when Emperor Charles V ruled the Netherlands, and our scene is the city of Leyden.

Anyone who has visited this pleasant town knows that it lies in the midst of wide, flat meadows, and is intersected by many canals filled with water from the Rhine River. But now, as it was winter, near to Christmas indeed, the meadows and the quaint gabled roofs of the city lay buried beneath a dazzling sheet of snow. At this season, instead of boats and barges, skaters glided up and down the frozen surface of the canals, which were swept for their convenience. Outside the walls of the town, not far from the *Morsch poort*, or gate, the surface of the broad moat that surrounded them presented a sight as simple as it was charming. Just here, one of the branches of the Rhine ran into this moat, and down it came the pleasure-seekers in sleigh, on skates, or afoot. They were dressed, most of them, in their best attire, for the day was a holiday set apart for a kind of skating carnival, with sleighing matches, such games as curling, and other amusements.

Among these merry folk might have been seen a young lady about twenty-two years of age, dressed in a coat of dark green cloth trimmed with fur, and close-fitting at the waist. This coat opened in front, showing a broidered woollen skirt, but over the chest it was tightly buttoned and surmounted by a stiff ruff of Brussels lace. Upon her head she wore a high-crowned beaver hat, to which the nodding ostrich feather was fastened by a jeweled ornament of sufficient value to show that she was a person of some means. In fact, this lady was the only child of a sea captain and shipowner named Carolus van Hout, who, whilst still a middle-aged man, had died about a year before, leaving her heiress to a very considerable fortune. This circumstance, with the added advantages of a very pretty face, in which were set two deep and thoughtful gray eyes, and a figure more graceful than was common among the Netherlander women, caused Lysbeth van Hout to be much sought after and admired, especially by the marriageable bachelors of Leyden.

On this occasion, however, she was unescorted except by a serving woman somewhat older than herself, a native of Brussels, Greta by name, who in appearance was as attractive as in manner she was suspiciously discreet.

As Lysbeth skated down the canal towards the moat many of the good burghers of Leyden took off their caps to her, especially the young burghers, one or two of whom had hopes that she would choose them to be her escort for this festival day. Some of the elders, also, asked her if she would care to join their parties, thinking that, as she was an orphan without near male relations, she might be glad to receive their protection in times when it was wise for beautiful young women to be protected. With this excuse and that, however, she escaped from them all, for Lysbeth had already made her own arrangements.

At that date there was living in Leyden a young man around the age of twenty-four, named Dirk van Goorl, a distant cousin of her own. Dirk was a native of the little town of Alkmaar, and the second son of one of its leading citizens, a brass founder by trade. As in the natural course of events the Alkmaar business would descend to his elder brother, therefore, their father apprenticed Dirk to a Leyden firm, in which, after eight or nine years of hard work, he had become a junior partner. While he was still living, Lysbeth's father had taken a liking to the lad, with the result that he grew intimate at the house which, from the first, was open to him as a kinsman. After the death of Carolus van Hout, Dirk had continued to visit there, especially on Sundays, when he was duly and ceremoniously received by Lysbeth's aunt, a childless widow named Clara van Ziel, who acted as her guardian. Thus, by degrees, favored with such ample opportunity, a strong affection had sprung up between these two young people, although as yet they were not engaged, nor indeed had either of them said a word of open love to the other.

This profound timidness may seem strange, but some explanation for their self-restraint was to be found in Dirk's character. In mind he was patient, very deliberate in forming his purposes, and very sure in carrying them out. He felt impulses like other men, but he did not give way to them. For two years or more he had loved Lysbeth; but being somewhat slow at reading the ways of women he was not quite certain that she loved him, and above everything on earth he dreaded a rebuff. Moreover he knew her to be an heiress, and as his own means were still humble, and his expectations from his father small, he did not feel justified in asking her in marriage until his position was more established. Had the Captain Carolus still been living, the case would have been different, for then he could have gone to him. But he was dead, and Dirk's fine and sensitive nature recoiled from the thought that it might be said of him that he had taken advantage of the inexperience of a kinswoman in order to win her fortune. Also, deep down in his mind he had another substantial and quite secret reason for proceeding slowly, whereof more will be said in its proper place.

Thus matters stood between these two. Today, however, though only with diffidence and after some encouragement from the lady, he had asked leave to be his cousin's escort at the ice festival; and when she consented, readily enough, appointed the moat as their place of meeting. This was somewhat less than Lysbeth expected, for she wished him to escort her through the town. But, when she hinted as much, Dirk explained that he would not be able to leave the works before three o'clock, as the metal for a large bell had been poured into the casting, and he must watch it while it cooled.

So, followed only by her maid, Greta, Lysbeth glided lightly as a bird down the ice path on to the moat, and across it, through the narrow cut, to the frozen meer beyond, where the sports were to be held and the races run. The scene at this spot was very beautiful.

Behind her lay the roofs of Leyden, pointed, picturesque, and covered with sheets of snow, while above them towered the bulk of the two great churches of St. Peter and St. Pancras, and standing on a mound known as the Burg, the round tower which is supposed to have been built by the Romans. In front stretched the flat expanse of white meadows broken here and there by windmills with narrow waists and thin, tall sails, and in the distance, by the church towers of other towns and villages.

Immediately before her, in strange contrast to this lifeless landscape, lay the well populated expanse known as the Meer, a frozen body of water fringed around with dead reeds standing so still in the frosty air that they might have been painted things. On this meer half the population of Leyden seemed to be gathered; at least there were thousands of them, shouting, laughing, and skimming to and fro in their bright garments like so many peacocks. Among them, drawn by horses with bells tied to their harness, glided many sleighs of wickerwork and wood mounted upon iron runners, their front ends fashioned into quaint shapes, such as the heads of dogs or bulls, or Tritons. Then there were vendors of cakes and sweetmeats, vendors of spirits also, who did a good trade on this cold day. Beggars too were numerous, and among them a host of crippled souls who slid about in wooden boxes, which they pushed along with crutches. Lastly, many loafers had gathered there with stools for fine ladies to sit on while the skates were bound to their pretty feet, and chapmen with these articles for sale and straps wherewith to fasten them. To complete the picture, the huge red ball of the sun was sinking to the west, and opposite to it the pale full moon began already to gather light and life.

The scene seemed so charming and so happy that Lysbeth, who was young, and now that she had recovered from the shock of her beloved father's death, light-hearted, ceased her forward movement and poised herself upon her skates to watch the interesting scenery. While she stood thus a little apart, a woman came towards her from the throng, not as though she were seeking her, but aimlessly, much as a child's toy boat is driven by light, contrary winds upon the surface of a pond in summer.

She was a remarkable looking woman of about thirty-five

years of age, tall and bony in make, with deep-set eyes, light gray in color, that seemed to flash fiercely and then to waver, as though in memory of some great dread. From beneath a coarse woollen cap a wisp of grizzled hair fell across the forehead, where it lay like the forelock of a horse. Indeed, the high cheekbones, scarred as though by burns, wide-spread nostrils and prominent white teeth, from which the lips had strangely sunk away, gave the whole countenance a more or less equine look which the sunlight seemed to heighten. For her covering, the woman wore a poorly and not too plentifully clad gown of black woollen, torn and stained as though with long use and journeys, while on her feet she wore wooden clogs, to which were strapped skates that were not well matched, one being much longer than the other.

Opposite to Lysbeth this strange, gaunt person stopped, contemplating her with a dreamy eye. Presently she seemed to recognize her, for she said in a quick, low voice, the voice of one who lives in terror of being overheard:

"That's a pretty dress of yours, Van Hout's daughter. Oh, yes, I know you; your father used to play with me when I was a child, and once he kissed me on the ice at just such a festival as this. Think of it! Kissed me, Martha the Mare," and she laughed hoarsely, then went on: "Yes, well-warmed and well-fed, and, without doubt, waiting for a gallant to kiss you"; here she turned and waved her hand towards the people— "all well-warmed and well-fed, and all with lovers and husbands and children to kiss. But I tell you, Van Hout's daughter, as I have dared to creep from my hiding hole in the great lake to tell all of them who will listen, that unless they cast out the cursed Spaniard, a day shall come when the folk of Leyden must perish by thousands of hunger behind those walls. Yes, yes, unless they cast out the cursed Spaniard and his Inquisition. Oh, I know them, I know them, for did they not make me carry my own husband to the stake upon my back? And have you heard why, Van Hout's daughter? Because what I had suffered in their torture dens had made my face—yes, mine that once was so beautiful—like the face of a horse, and they said that 'a horse ought to be ridden.'"

Now, while this poor excited creature, one of a whole group of such people who in those sad days might be found wandering about the Netherlands crazy with their griefs and sufferings, and living only for revenge, poured out these broken sentences, Lysbeth, terrified, shrank back from her. As she shrank the other followed, until presently Lysbeth saw the woman's expression of rage and hate change to one of terror. In another instant, muttering something about a request for alms which she did not wait to receive, the woman had wheeled round and fled away as fast as her skates would carry her, which was very fast indeed.

Turning about to find what had frightened her, Lysbeth saw standing on the bank of the meer, so close that she must have overheard every word, but behind the screen of a leafless bush, a tall, forbidding-looking woman, who held in her hand some broidered caps which apparently she was offering for sale. These caps she began slowly to fold up and place one by one in a leather satchel that was hung about her shoulders. All this while, she was watching Lysbeth with her keen black eyes, except when from time to time she took them off her to follow the flight of that person who had called herself the Mare.

"You keep ill company, lady," said the cap-seller in a harsh voice.

"It was none of my seeking," answered Lysbeth, astonished into making a reply.

"So much the better for you, lady, although she seemed to know you and to know also that you would listen to her song. Unless my eyes deceived me, which is not often, that woman is an evil-doer and a worker of magic like her dead husband Van Muyden; a heretic, a blasphemer of the Holy Church, a traitor to our Lord the Emperor, and one," she added with a snarl, "with a price upon her head that before nightfall will, I hope, be in Black Meg's pocket." Then, walking with long firm steps towards a fat man who seemed to be waiting for her, the tall, black-eyed peddler passed with him into the throng, where Lysbeth lost sight of them.

Lysbeth watched them go, and shivered. To her knowledge she had never seen this woman before, but she knew enough of the times they lived in to be sure that she was a spy of the priests. Already there were such creatures moving about in every gathering, yes, and in many a private place, who were paid to obtain evidence against suspected heretics. Whether they won it by fair means or by foul mattered not, provided they could find something, and it need be little indeed, to justify the Inquisition in getting to its work.

As for the other woman, the Mare, doubtless she was one of those wicked outcasts, accursed by God and man, who were called *heretics*; people who said dreadful things about the Pope and the Church and God's priests, having been misled and stirred up thereto by a certain fiend in human form named Luther. Lysbeth shuddered at the thought and crossed herself, for in those days she was a devout Roman Catholic. Yet the wanderer said that she had known her father, so that she must be as well born as herself—and then that dreadful story—no, she could not bear to think of it. But, of course, heretics deserved all these things; of that there could be no doubt whatever, for had not her father confessor told her that thus alone might their souls be saved from the grasp of the Evil One?

The thought was comforting, still Lysbeth felt upset, and not a little relieved when she saw Dirk van Goorl skating towards her accompanied by another young man, also a cousin of her own on her mother's side who was destined in days to come to earn himself an immortal renown, young Pieter van de Werff. The two took off their caps to her, Dirk van Goorl revealing in the act a head of fair hair beneath which his steady blue eyes shone in a rather thick-set, self-contained face. Lysbeth's temper, always somewhat quick, was ruffled, and she showed it in her manner.

"I thought, cousins, that we were to meet at three, and the kirk clock yonder has just chimed half-past," she said, addressing them both, but looking not too sweetly at Dirk van Goorl.

"That's right, cousin," answered Pieter, a pleasant and alert young man, "look at him, scold him, for he is to blame. Ever since a quarter past two have I—I who must drive a sleigh in the great race and am backed to win, been waiting outside that factory in the snow, but, upon my honor, he did not appear until seven minutes ago. Yes, we have done the whole distance in seven minutes, and I call that very good skating."

"I thought as much," said Lysbeth. "Dirk can only keep an appointment with a church bell or a business partner."

"It was not my fault," broke in Dirk in his slow voice; "I have my business to attend. I promised to wait until the metal had cooled sufficiently, and hot bronze takes no account of ice parties and sleigh races."

"So I suppose that you stopped to blow on it, cousin. Well, the result is that, being quite unescorted, I have been obliged to listen to things which I did not wish to hear."

"What do you mean?" asked Dirk, taking fire at once.

Then she told them something of what the woman who called herself the Mare had said to her, adding, "Doubtless the poor creature is a heretic and deserves all that has happened to her. But it is dreadfully sad, and I came here to enjoy myself, not to be sad."

Between the two young men there passed a glance which was full of meaning. But it was Dirk who spoke. The other, more cautious, remained silent.

"Why do you say that, Cousin Lysbeth?" he asked in a new voice, a voice thick and eager. "Why do you say that she deserves all that can happen to her? I have heard of this poor creature who is called Mother Martha, or the Mare, although I have never seen her myself. She was noble-born, much better born than any of us three, and very fair—once they called her the Lily of Bussels—when she was the Vrouw van Muyden, and she has suffered dreadfully for one reason only, because she and hers did not worship God as you worship Him."

"As we worship Him," broke in Van de Werff with a cough.

"No," answered Dirk sullenly, "as our Cousin Lysbeth van Hout worships Him. For that reason only they killed her husband, and her little son, and drove her mad with torture so that she lives among the reeds of the Haarlemer Meer like a beast in its den; yes, they, the Spaniards and their Spanish priests, as I daresay that they will kill us also."

"Don't you think that it is getting rather cold standing here?"

interrupted Pieter van de Werff before she could answer, "Look the sled races are just beginning. Come, cousin give me your hand," and, taking Lysbeth by the arm, he skated off into the throng, followed at a distance by Dirk and the serving-maid Greta.

"Cousin," he whispered as he went, "this is not my place, it is Dirk's place, but I pray you as you love him—I beg your pardon, as you esteem a worthy relative, do not enter into a religious argument with him here in public, where even the ice and sky are two great ears. It is not safe, little cousin, I swear to you that it is not safe."

In the center of the meer, the great event of the day—the sleigh race—was now in progress. As the competitors were many these must be run in heats, the winners of each heat standing on one side to compete in the final contest. Now each victor had the special honor and duty to select a person to carry as a passenger in the little seat in front of him, his own place being on the seat behind where he directed his horse by means of reins. This passenger he could select from among the number of ladies who were present at the games; unless, indeed, the gentleman in charge of her chose to deny him in set form; namely, by stepping forward and saying in the appointed phrase, "No, for this happy hour she is mine."

Among the winners of these heats was a certain Spanish officer, the Count Don Juan de Montalvo who, as it happened, in the absence of his captain who was on leave, was the commander of the garrison at Leyden. He was a man still young, only about thirty indeed, reported to be of noble birth and handsome in the usual Castilian fashion. That is to say, he was tall, of a graceful figure, dark-eyed, strong-featured, with a somewhat humorous expression, and, of very good if exaggerated address. As he had but recently come to Leyden, very little was known there of this attractive cavalier beyond that he was well spoken of by the priests, and, according to report, a favorite with the Emperor. Many of the high born ladies admired him much as well.

For the rest everything about him was handsome like his per-

son, as might be expected, in the case of a man reputed to be
as rich as he was noble. Thus his sleigh was shaped and colored
to resemble a great black wolf rearing itself up to charge. The
wooden head was covered in wolf skin and adorned by eyes of
yellow glass and great fangs of ivory. Round the neck also ran a
gilded collar hung with a silver shield, whereon were painted the
arms of its owner, a knight striking the chains from off a captive
Christian saint, and the motto of the Montalvos, "Trust to God
and me." His black horse was of the best breed, imported from
Spain, complete with a harness decorated with gilding, and a
splendid plume of dyed feathers rising from the headband.

Lysbeth happened to be standing near to the spot where this
conspicuous driver had halted after his first victory. She was in
the company of Dirk van Goorl alone—for as her other cousin,
Pieter van de Werff was the driver of one of the competing sleds,
he had now been summoned away. Having nothing else to do at
the moment, she approached and not unnaturally admired this
brilliant equipage, although in truth it was the sleigh and the
horse rather than their driver which attracted her attention. As
for the Count himself she knew him slightly, having been introduced to and danced a measure with him at a festival given by a
grandee of the town. On that occasion, he was courteous to her
in the Spanish fashion, rather too courteous, she thought, but as
this was the manner of Castilian dons when dealing with burgher maidens she paid no more attention to the matter.

The Captain Montalvo saw Lysbeth among the throng and
recognized her, for he lifted his plumed hat and bowed to her
with just that touch of condescension which in those days a
Spaniard showed when greeting one whom he considered his
inferior. In the sixteenth century, it was understood that all the
world were the inferiors to those whom God had granted to be
born in Spain, the English who rated themselves at a valua-
tion of their own, and were careful to announce the fact, alone
excepted.

An hour or so later, after the last heat had been run, the stew-
ard of the ceremonies called aloud to the remaining competitors
to select their passengers and prepare for the final contest.

Accordingly, each driver, leaving his horse in charge of an attendant, stepped up to some young lady who evidently was waiting for him, and led her by the hand to his sled. While Lysbeth was watching this ceremony with amusement—for these selections were always understood to show a strong preference on behalf of the chooser for the chosen—she was astonished to hear a well-trained voice addressing her, and on looking up to see Don Juan de Montalvo bowing almost to the ice.

"Señora," he said in Castilian, a tongue which Lysbeth understood well enough, although she only spoke it when obliged, "unless my ears deceived me, I heard you admiring my horse and sleigh. Now, with the permission of your cavalier," and he bowed courteously to Dirk, "I name you as my passenger for the great race, knowing that you will bring me fortune. Have I your leave, Señor?"

Now if there was a people on earth whom Dirk van Goorl hated, the Spaniards were that people, and if there lived a cavalier whom he preferred should not take his cousin Lysbeth for a lonely drive, that cavalier was the Count Juan de Montalvo. But as a young man, Dirk was singularly diffident and so easily confused that on the spur of the moment it was quite possible for a clever person to make him say what he did not mean. Thus, on the present occasion, when he saw this courtly Spaniard bowing low to him, a humble Dutch tradesman, he was overwhelmed, and mumbled in reply, " Certainly, certainly."

If a glance could have withered him, without doubt Dirk would immediately have shriveled to nothing. To say that Lysbeth was angry is too little, for in truth she was absolutely furious. She did not like this Spaniard, and hated the idea of a long interview with him alone. Moreover, she knew that among her fellow townspeople there was a great desire that the Count should not win this race, which in its own fashion was the event of the year, whereas, if she appeared as his companion it would be supposed that she was anxious for his success. Lastly—and this was the chiefest sore—although in theory the competitors had a right to ask anyone to whom they took a fancy to travel in their sleds, in practice they only sought the company of young women with whom they were on the best of terms, and who were already warned of their intention.

In an instant these thoughts rushed through her mind, but all she did was to murmur something about the Heer van Goorl—

"He has already given his consent, like an unselfish gentleman," broke in Captain Juan tendering her his hand.

Now, without absolutely making a scene, which then, as today, ladies considered an ill-bred thing to do, there was no escape, since half of Leyden gathered at these "sleigh choosings," and many eyes were on her and the Count. Therefore, because she must, Lysbeth took the proffered hand, and was led to the sleigh, catching as she passed to it through the throng, more than one sour look from the men and more than one exclamation of surprise, real or affected, on the lips of the ladies of her acquaintance. These manifestations, however, caused her spirit to quicken. So determining that at least she would not look ridiculous, she began to enter into the spirit of the adventure, and smiled graciously while the Captain Montalvo wrapped a magnificent apron of wolf skins around her knees.

When all was ready, her charioteer took the reins and settled himself upon the little seat behind the sleigh, which was then led into position by a soldier servant.

"Where is the course, Señor?" Lysbeth asked, hoping that it would be a short one.

But in this she was to be disappointed, for he answered:

"Up to the little Quarkel Meer, round the island in the middle of it, and back to this spot, something over a league in all. Now, Señora, speak to me no more at present, but hold fast and have no fear, for at least I drive well, and my horse is sure-footed and roughed for ice. This is a race that I would give a hundred gold pieces to win, since your countrymen, who contend against me, have sworn that I shall lose it, and I tell you at once, Señora, that gray horse will press me hard."

Following the direction of his glance, Lysbeth's eye landed upon the next sleigh. It was small, fashioned and painted to resemble a gray badger, that silent, stubborn, and, if molested, savage brute, which will not loose its grip until the head is hacked from off its body. The horse, which matched it well in color, was a Flemish breed; rather a raw-boned animal, with strong quarters and an ugly head, but renowned in Leyden for its courage and staying power. What interested Lysbeth most, however, was to discover that the charioteer was none other than Pieter van de Werff, though now when she thought of it, she remembered he had told her that his sled was named the Badger. In his choice of passenger she noted, too, not without a smile, that he showed his cautious character, disdainful of any immediate glory, so long as the end in view could be attained. For there in the sleigh sat no fine young lady, decked out in fancy attire, who might be supposed to look at him with tender eyes, but a little fair-haired girl aged nine, who was in fact his sister. As he explained afterwards, the rules provided that a lady passenger must be carried, but said nothing of her age and weight.

Now the competitors, eight of them, were in a line, and coming forward, the master of the course, in a voice that every one might hear, called out the conditions of the race and the prize for which it was to be run, a splendid glass goblet engraved with the cross-keys, the Arms of Leyden. This done, after asking if all were ready, he dropped a little flag, whereon the horses were loosed and away they went.

Before a minute had passed, forgetting all her doubts and annoyances, Lysbeth was lost in the glorious excitement of the moment. Like birds in the heavens, cleaving the keen, crisp air, they sped forward over the smooth ice. The happy throng vanished, the dead reeds and stark bushes seemed to fly away from them, the only sounds in their ears were the rushing of the wind, the swish of the iron runners, and the hollow tapping of the hooves of their galloping horses. Certain sleighs drew ahead in the first burst, but the Wolf and the Badger were not among these. The Count de Montalvo was holding in his black stallion, and as yet the gray Flemish gelding loped along with a constrained and awkward stride. When, passing from the little meer, they entered the strait of the canal, these two were respectively fourth and fifth. Up the course they sped, through a deserted snow-clad country, past the church of the village of

Alkemaade. Now, half a mile or more away appeared the Quarkel Meer, and in the center of it the island around which they must turn. They reached it, they were round it, and when their faces were once more set homewards, Lysbeth noted that the Wolf and the Badger were third and fourth in the race, someone having dropped behind. Half a mile more and they were second and third; another half mile and they were first and second, with perhaps a mile to go. Then the real fight began.

Yard by yard the speed increased, and yard by yard the black stallion drew ahead. Now in front of them lay a furlong or more of bad ice encumbered with lumps of frozen snow that had not been cleared away, which caused the sleigh to shake and jump as it struck. Lysbeth looked round.

"The Badger is coming up," she said.

Montalvo heard, and for the first time laid his whip upon the haunches of his horse, which answered gallantly. But still the Badger came up. The gray was the stronger beast, and had begun to put out his strength. Very soon his ugly head was beside them, for Lysbeth felt the breath from his nostrils blowing on her, and saw their steam. Then it was past, for the steam blew back into her face; yes, and she could see the eager eyes of the child in the gray sled. Now they were neck and neck, as the rough ice turned smooth. Six hundred yards away, not more, lay the goal, and all about them, outside the line of the course, were swift skaters traveling so fast that their heads were bent forward and down to within three feet of the ice.

Van de Werff called to his horse, and the gray began to gain. Montalvo lashed the stallion, and once more they passed him. But the black was failing, and he saw it, for Lysbeth heard him curse in Spanish. A moment later, after a cunning glance at his adversary, the Count pulled upon the right rein, and a shrill voice rose upon the air, the voice of the little girl in the other sleigh.

"Take care, brother," she cried, "he will overthrow us."

True enough, in another moment the black would have struck the gray sideways. Lysbeth saw Van de Werff rise from his seat and throw his weight backward, dragging the gray on to

his haunches. By an inch, not more, the Wolf sleigh missed the gelding. Indeed, one runner of it struck his hoof, and the high woodwork on the side brushed and cut his nostril.

"A foul, a foul!" yelled the skaters, and it was over. Once more they were speeding forward, but now the black had a lead of at least ten yards, for the gray must find his stride again. They were in the strait; the course was lined with hundreds of witnesses, and from the throats of every one of them arose a great cry, or rather two cries.

"The Spaniard, the Spaniard wins!" said the first cry that was answered by another and a deeper roar.

"No, Hollander, the Hollander! The Hollander comes up!"

Then in the midst of that fierce excitement, bred by the excitement perhaps—some curious thoughts fell upon the mind of Lysbeth. The race, its details, its objects, its surroundings faded away; these physical things were gone, and in place of them was present a dream—a spiritual interpretation such as the influences of the times in which she lived might well inspire. What did she seem to see? She saw the Spaniard and the Hollander striving for victory, but not a victory of horses. She saw the black Spanish Wolf, at first triumphant, outmatch the Netherland Badger. Still, the Badger, the dogged Dutch badger, held on.

"Who would win?" The fierce beast or the patient beast? Who would be master in this fight? There was death in it. Look, the whole snow was red, the roofs of Leyden were red, and red the heavens; in the deep hues of the sunset they seemed bathed in blood, while about her the shouts of the hackers and factions transformed themselves into a fierce cry as of battling peoples. All voices mingled in that cry—voices of hope, of agony, and of despair; but she could not interpret them. Something told her that the interpretation and the issue were in the mind of God alone.

Perhaps she swooned, perhaps she slept and dreamed this dream; perhaps the sharp rushing air overcame her. At the least, Lysbeth's eyes closed and her mind gave way. When they opened and it returned again, their sleigh was rushing past the winning post. But in front of it traveled another sled, drawn by a gaunt gray horse, which galloped so hard that its belly seemed to lie upon the ice, a horse driven by a young man whose face was set like steel and whose lips were as the lips of a trap.

As Lysbeth began to come to herself, she wondered, could that be the face of her cousin Pieter van de Werff, and, if so, what passion had stamped that strange seal thereon? She turned herself in her seat and looked at him who drove her.

Was this a man, or was it a spirit released from Hades? Blessed Mary! What a countenance! The eyeballs starting and upturned, nothing but the white of them to be seen; the lips curled, and between, two lines of shining fangs; the lifted points of the mustachio touching the high cheekbones. No—no, it was neither a spirit nor a man, she knew now what it was; it was the very type and incarnation of the Spanish Wolf.

Once more she seemed to faint, while in her ears there rang the cry—"The Hollander! Outstayed! Outstayed! Conquered is the accursed Spaniard!"

Then Lysbeth knew that it was over, and again the faintness overpowered her.

Chapter II
She Who Buys—Pays

When Lysbeth's mind recovered from its confusion, she found herself still in the sleigh and beyond the borders of the crowd that was engaged in rapturously congratulating the winner. Drawn up alongside of the Wolf was another sleigh of plain make, and harnessed to it a heavy Flemish horse. This vehicle was driven by a Spanish soldier, with whom sat a second soldier apparently of the rank of sergeant. There was no one else near; already people in the Netherlands had learnt to keep their distance from Spanish soldiers.

"If your Excellency would come now," the sergeant was saying, "this little matter can be settled without any further trouble."

"Where is she?" asked Montalvo.

"Not more than a mile or so away, near the place called Steene Veld."

"Tie her up in the snow to wait until tomorrow morning. My horse is tired and it may save us trouble," he began. Then he added, after glancing first back at the crowd behind him and then at Lysbeth, "No, I will come."

Perhaps the Count did not wish to listen to condolences on his defeat, or perhaps he desired to prolong the time away with his fair passenger. At any rate, without further hesitation, he struck his weary horse with the whip, causing it to amble forward somewhat stiffly, but at a good pace.

"Where are we going, Señor?" asked Lysbeth anxiously. "The race is over and I must seek my friends."

"Your friends are engaged in congratulating the victor, lady," he answered in his suave and courteous voice, "and I cannot leave you alone upon the ice. Do not be troubled, for this is only a little matter of business which will scarcely take a quarter of an hour," and once more he struck the horse urging it to a better speed.

Lysbeth thought of remonstrating, she thought even of springing from the sleigh, but in the end she did neither. To seem to continue the drive with her cavalier would, she determined, look more natural and less absurd than to attempt a violent escape from him. She was certain that he would not put her down merely at her request. Something in his manner told her so, and though she had no longing for his company, it was better than being made ridiculous before half the inhabitants of Leyden. Moreover, the position was no fault of hers. It was the fault of Dirk van Goorl, who should have been present to take her from the sleigh.

As they drove along the frozen moat, Montalvo leant forward and began to chat about the race, expressing regret at having lost it, but using no angry or bitter words. Could this be the man, wondered Lysbeth as she listened, whom she had seen deliberately attempt to overthrow and injure his adversary in a foul? Could this be the man whose face just minutes before had looked like the face of a devil? Had these things happened, indeed, or was it not possible that her fancy, confused with the excitement and the speed at which they were traveling, had deceived her? Certainly it seemed to have been overcome at last, for she could not remember the actual finish of the race, or how they got clear of the shouting crowd.

While she was still pondering these things, replying from time to time to Montalvo in monosyllables, the sleigh in front of them turned the corner of one of the eastern bastions and came to a halt. The place where it stopped was desolate and lonely, for the town being in a state of peace, no guard was mounted on the wall, nor could any living soul be found upon the snowy waste that lay beyond the moat. At first, indeed, Lysbeth was able to see nobody at all, for by now the sun had gone down, and her eyes were not accustomed to the increasing light of the moon. Presently, however, she caught sight of a group of people standing on the ice in a recess or little bay of the moat and half hidden by a fringe of dead reeds.

Montalvo saw also, and halted his horse within three paces of them. The people were five in number, three Spanish soldiers and two women. Lysbeth looked, and with difficulty stifled a cry of surprise and fear, for she knew the women. The tall, dark person, with lowering eyes, was none other than the cap-seller and Spanish spy, Black Meg. And she who crouched there upon the ice, her arms bound behind her, her grizzled locks torn loose by some rough hand, surely it was the woman who called herself the Mare, who that very afternoon spoke to her and cursed the Spaniards and their Inquisition. What were they doing here? Instantly an answer leapt into her mind, for she remembered Black Meg's words, that there was a price upon this heretic's head, which before nightfall would be in her pocket. And why was there a square hole cut in the ice immediately in front of the captive? Could it be—no, that was too horrible.

"Well, officer," broke in Montalvo, addressing the sergeant in a quiet, wearied voice, "what is all this about? Set out your case."

"Excellency," replied the man, "it is a very simple matter. This creature here, so that woman is ready to take oath," and he pointed to Black Meg, "is a notorious heretic who has already been condemned to death by the Holy Office, and whose husband, a learned man who painted pictures and studied the stars, was burnt on a charge of witchcraft and heresy two years ago at Brussels. But she managed to escape the stake and since then has lived as a vagrant, hiding in the islands of the Haarlemer Meer, and, it is suspected, working murder and robbery on any of Spanish blood whom she can catch. Now she has been caught herself and identified, and, of course, the sentence being in full force against her, can be dealt with at once on your Excellency's command. Indeed, it would not have been necessary that you should be troubled about the thing at all had it not been that this worthy woman," and again he pointed to Black Meg, "who was the one who waylaid her, pulled her down, and held her until we came. She requires your certificate in order that she may claim the reward from the Treasurer of the Holy Inquisition. Therefore, you will be asked to certify that this is, indeed, the notorious heretic commonly known as Martha the Mare, but whose other name I forget, after which, if you will please to withdraw, we will see to the rest."

"You mean that she will be taken to the prison to be dealt with by the Holy Office?" queried Montalvo.

"Not exactly, Excellency," answered the sergeant with a discreet smile and a cough. "The prison, I am told, is quite full, but she may start for the prison and as there seems to be a hole in the ice into which, since Satan leads the footsteps of such people astray, this heretic might chance to fall—or throw herself."

"What is the evidence?" asked Montalvo.

Then Black Meg stood forward, and, with the rapidity and unction of a spy, poured out her tale. She identified the woman with one whom she had known was sentenced to death by the Inquisition and escaped, and, after giving other evidence, ended by repeating the conversation which she had overheard between the accused and Lysbeth that afternoon.

"You accompanied me in a fortunate hour, Señora van Hout" said the captain boldly, "for now, to satisfy myself, as I wish to be just, and do not trust these paid hags," and he nodded towards Black Meg, "I must ask you upon your oath before God whether or not you confirm that woman's tale, and whether or not this very ugly person named the Mare called down curses upon my people and the Holy Office? Answer quickly, if you please, Señora, for it grows cold here and my horse is beginning to shiver."

Then, for the first time, the Mare raised her head, dragging at her hair, which had become frozen to the ice, until she tore it free.

"Lysbeth van Hout," she cried in shrill, piercing tones, "would you to please your Spanish lover bring your father's playmate to her death? The Spanish horse is cold and cannot stay, but the poor Netherland Mare—ah, she may be thrust beneath the blue ice and bide there until her bones rot at the bottom of the moat. You have sought the Spaniards, you, whose blood should have warned you against them, and I tell you that it shall cost you dear. But if you say this word they seek, then it shall cost you everything, not only the body, but the spirit also. Woe to you, Lysbeth van Hout, if you cut me off before my work is done. I fear not death, nay I welcome it, but I tell you I have work to do before I die."

Now, in an agony of mind, Lysbeth turned and looked at Montalvo.

The Count was a man of keen perceptions and understood how best to capitalize on this lady's agony. Leaning forward, his arm resting on the back of the sleigh as though to contemplate the prisoner, he whispered into Lysbeth's ear, so low that no one else could hear his words.

"Señora," he said, "I have no wishes in this matter. I do not desire to drown that poor mad woman, but if you confirm the spy's story, drown she must. At present I am not satisfied, so everything turns upon your evidence. I do not know what passed between you this afternoon, and personally I do not care, only, if you should chance to have no clear recollection of the matter alleged, I must make one or two little stipulations—very little ones.

"Let me see, they are that you will spend the rest of this evening's festival in my company. Further, that whenever I choose to call upon you, your door will be open to me, though I must remind you that on three occasions already, when I have wished to pay my respects, it has been shut."

Lysbeth heard and understood. If she would save this woman's life, she must expose herself to the attentions of the Spaniard, which she desired least of anything in the world. Moreover, speaking upon her oath in the presence of God, she must utter a dreadful lie, which she was reluctant to do. For thirty seconds or more she thought, staring round her with anguished eyes, while the scene on which they fell sank into her soul in such fashion that never until her death's day did she forget its aspect.

The Mare spoke no more, she only knelt searching her face with a stern and wondering glance. A little to the right stood Black Meg, glaring at her sullenly, for the blood-money was in danger. Behind the prisoner were two of the soldiers, one putting his hand to his face to hide a yawn, while the other beat his breast to warm himself. The third soldier, who was somewhat in front, stirred the surface of the hole with the shaft of his halbert to break up the thin film of ice that was forming over it, while Montalvo himself, still leaning sideways and forwards, watched her eyes with an amused and cynical expression. And over all, over the desolate snows and gabled roofs of the town behind, over the smooth blue ice, the martyr and the murderers; over the dark sleigh and the fur-wrapped girl who sat within it, fell the calm light of the moon through a silence broken only by the beating of her heart, and now and again by the sigh of the wind breathing among the rushes.

"Well, Señora," asked Montalvo, "if you have sufficiently reflected, shall I administer the oath in the form provided?"

"Administer it," she said hoarsely.

So, descending from the sleigh, he stood in front of Lysbeth, and, lifting his cap, repeated the oath to her, an oath strong enough to blast her soul if she swore to it with false intent.

"In the name of God the Son and of His Blessed Mother, you swear?" he asked.

"I swear," she answered.

"Good, Señora. Now listen to me. Did you meet that woman this afternoon?"

"Yes, I met her on the ice," was her response.

"And did she in your hearing utter curses upon the government and the Holy Church and call upon you to assist in driving the Spaniards from the land, as the spy, whom I believe is called Black Meg, has borne witness?"

"No," said Lysbeth.

"I am afraid that is not quite enough, Señora. I may have misquoted the exact words. Did the woman say anything of the sort?"

For one second Lysbeth hesitated. Then she caught sight of the victim's watching, speculative eyes, and remembered that this crazed and broken creature once had been a child whom her father kissed and played with, and that the crime of which she was accused was that she had escaped from death at the stake.

"The water is cold to die in!" the Mare said, in a meditative voice, as though she were thinking aloud.

"Then why did you run away from the warm fire, heretic witch?" jeered Black Meg.

Now Lysbeth hesitated no longer, but again answered in a monosyllable, "No."

"Then what did she do or say, Señora?"

"She said she had known my father, who used to play with her when she was a child, and begged for alms, that is all. Then that woman came up, and she ran away, whereon the woman said there was a price upon her head, and that she meant to have the money."

"It is a lie!" screamed Black Meg in fierce, strident notes.

"If that person will not be silent, silence her," said Montalvo, addressing the sergeant. "I am satisfied," he went on, "that there is no evidence at all against the prisoner except the story of a spy, who says she believes her to be a vagrant heretic of bad character who escaped from the stake several years ago in the neighborhood of Brussels, whither it is scarcely worthwhile to inquire about the matter. So that charge may drop. There remains the question as to whether or not the prisoner uttered certain words this afternoon, which, if she did utter them, are undoubtedly worthy of the death that, under my authority as acting commandant of this town, I have power to inflict. This question I foresaw, and that is why I asked the Señora, to whom the woman is alleged to have spoken the words, to accompany me here to give evidence. She has done so, and her evidence on oath as against the statement of a spy woman not under oath, is that no such words were spoken. This being so, as the Señora is a good Catholic whom I have no reason to disbelieve, I order the release of the prisoner, whom for my part I take for nothing more than a crazy and harmless wanderer."

"At least you will detain her until I can prove that she is the heretic who escaped from the stake near Brussels," shouted Black Meg.

"I will do nothing of the sort. The prison here is overfull already. Untie her arms, and let her go."

The soldiers obeyed, wondering somewhat, and the Mare soon scrambled to her feet. For a moment she stood looking at her deliverer. Then crying, "We shall meet again, Lysbeth van Hout" suddenly she turned and sped up a dyke at extraordinary speed. In a few seconds there was nothing to be seen of her but a black spot upon the white landscape, and then she vanished altogether.

"Gallop as you will, Mare, I shall catch you yet," screamed Black Meg after her. "And you too, my pretty little liar, who have cheated me out of a dozen florins. Wait until you end up before the Inquisition as a heretic—for that's where you'll end. No fine Spanish lover will save you then. So you have gone to the Spanish, have you, and thrown over your fat-faced burgher. Well, you will have enough of Spaniards before you have done with them, I can tell you."

Twice had Montalvo tried to stop this flood of furious eloquence, which had become personal and might prove prejudicial to his interests, but without avail. He then adopted other measures.

"Seize her!" he shouted to two of the soldiers. "That's it. Now hold her under water in that hole until I tell you to let her up again."

They obeyed, but it took all three of them to carry out the order, for Black Meg fought and bit like a wild cat, until at last she was thrust into the icy moat head downwards. When at length she was released, soaked and shivering, she crept off silently enough, but the look of fury that she cast at Montalvo and Lysbeth drew from the captain a remark that perhaps it would have been as well to have kept her under water two minutes longer.

"Now, sergeant," he added, in a genial voice, "it is a cold night, and this has been a troublesome business for a feastday, so here's something for you and your watch to warm yourselves with when you go off duty," and he handed him a very handsome present. "By the way," he said, as the men saluted him gratefully, "perhaps you will do me a favor. It is only to take this black horse of mine to his stable and harness that gray trooper nag to the sleigh instead, as I wish to go on my round of the moat, and my beast is tired."

Again the men saluted and set to work to change the horses, whereon Lysbeth, guessing her cavalier's purpose, turned as though to fly away, for her skates were still upon her feet. But he was watching.

"Señora," he said in a quiet voice, "I think that you gave me the promise of your company for the rest of this evening, and I am certain," he added with a slight bow, "that you are a lady whom nothing would induce to tell an untruth. Had I not been sure of that, I should scarcely have accepted your evidence so readily just now."

Lysbeth winced visibly. "I thought, Señor, that you were going to return to the festival."

"I do not remember saying so, Señora, and as a matter of fact I have pickets to visit. Do not be afraid, the drive is charming in this moonlight, and afterwards perhaps you will extend your hospitality so far as to ask me to supper at your house."

Still she hesitated, dismay written on her face.

"Jufvrouw Lysbeth," he said in an altered voice, "in my country we have a homely proverb which says, 'she who buys, pays.' You have bought, and the goods have been delivered. Do you understand? Ah, allow me to have the pleasure of arranging those furs. I knew that you were the soul of honor, and were but—shall we say, teasing me? Otherwise, had you really wished to go, of course you would have skated away just now while you had the opportunity. That is why I gave you time, as naturally I should not desire to detain you against your will."

Lysbeth heard and was aghast, for this man's cleverness overwhelmed her. At every step he contrived to put her in the wrong; moreover, she was crushed by the sense that he had justice on his side. She had bought and she must pay. Why had she bought? Not for any advantage of her own, but from an impulse of human pity—to save a fellow creature's life. And why should she have perjured herself so deeply in order to save that life? She was a Catholic and had no sympathy with such people. Probably this person was an Anabaptist, one of that dreadful sect that practiced nameless immoralities. Was it then because the creature had declared that she had known her father in her childhood? To some extent, yes, but was not there more? Had she not been influenced by the woman's invocation about the Spaniards, of which the true meaning came home to her during that dreadful sleigh race—at the moment, indeed, when she saw the Satanic look upon the face of Montalvo? It seemed to her that this was so, though at the time she had not understood it. In Lysbeth's mind, it seemed that she was not a free agent and that some force pushed her forward that she could neither control nor understand.

Moreover—and this was the worst of it—she felt that little good could come of her sacrifice, or that if good came, at least it would not be to her or hers. Now she was as a fish in a net, though why it was worth this brilliant Spaniard's while to snare her she could not understand, for she forgot that she was beautiful and a woman of property. Well, to save the blood of another she had bought, and in her own blood and happiness, or in that of those dear to her, assuredly she must pay, however cruel and unjust might be the price.

These were the thoughts that passed through Lysbeth's mind as the strong Flemish gelding lumbered forward, dragging the sleigh at the same steady pace over rough ice and smooth. And all the while Montalvo behind her was chatting pleasantly about various subjects, telling her of the orange groves in Spain, of the Court of the Emperor Charles, of adventures in the French wars, and many other things. To this conversation, she made such responses as courtesy alone demanded. What would Dirk think, she was wondering, and her cousin, Pieter van de Werff, whose good opinion she valued, and all the gossips of Leyden? She only prayed that they might not have missed her or, at least, that they took it for granted that she had gone home.

On this point, however, she was soon destined to be undeceived, for presently, trudging over the snow-covered ice and carrying his useless skates in his hand, they met a young man whom she knew as Dirk's fellow apprentice. On seeing them, he stopped in front of the sleigh in such a position that the horse, a steady and a patient animal, pulled up of its own accord.

"Is the Jufvrouw Lysbeth van Hout there?" he asked anxiously.

"Yes," she replied, but before she could say more Montalvo broke in, inquiring what might be the matter.

"Nothing," he answered, "except that she was lost and Dirk van Goorl, my friend, sent me to look for her this way, while he took the other."

"Indeed. Then, noble sir, perhaps you will find the Heer Dirk van Goorl and tell him that the Señora, his cousin, is merely enjoying an evening drive and that, if he comes to her house in an hour's time, he will find her safe and sound, and with her myself, the Count Juan de Montalvo, whom she has honored with an invitation to supper."

Then, before the astonished messenger could respond, indeed, before Lysbeth could offer any explanation of his words, Montalvo lashed up the horse and left him standing on the moat bewildered, his cap off and scratching his head.

After this, they proceeded on a journey that seemed to Lysbeth almost interminable. When the circuit of the walls was finished, Montalvo halted at one of the shut gates, and calling to the guard within, summoned them to open. This caused delay and investigation, for at first the sergeant of the guard would not believe that it was his acting commandant who spoke without.

"Pardon, Excellency," he said when he had inspected him with a lantern, "but I did not think that you would be going the rounds with a lady in your sleigh," and holding up the light the man took a long look at Lysbeth, grinning visibly as he recognized her.

"Ah, he is a wise man, the captain, a very wise man, and it's a pretty Dutch bird he is teaching to pipe now," she heard him call to a comrade as he closed the heavy gates behind their sleigh.

Then followed more visits to other military posts in the town and, with each visit, a further explanation. All this while, the Count Montalvo uttered no word beyond those of ordinary compliment and ventured on no act of familiarity, his conversation and demeanor indeed remaining perfectly courteous and respectful. So far as it went this was satisfactory, but at length there came a moment when Lysbeth felt that she could bear the position no longer.

"Señor," she said briefly, "take me home. I grow faint."

"With hunger doubtless," he interrupted. "Well, by heaven, so do I! But, my dear lady, as you are aware, duty must be attended to, and, after all, you may have found some interest in accompanying me on a tour of the pickets at night. I know your people speak roughly of us Spanish soldiers, but I hope that after this you will be able to bear testimony to their discipline. Although it is a festival day you will be my witness that we have not found a man off duty or the worse for drink. Here, you," he called to a soldier who stood up to salute him, "follow me to the house of the Jufvrouw Lysbeth van Hout, where I sup, and lead this sleigh back to my quarters."

CHAPTER III
MONTALVO WINS A TRICK

Turning up the Bree Straat, perhaps the finest in the town of Leyden, Montalvo halted his horse before a substantial house fronted with three round-headed gables, of which the largest—that over the entrance in the middle—was shaped into two windows with balconies. This was Lysbeth's house that had been left to her by her father, where, until such time as she should please to marry, she dwelt with her aunt, Clara van Ziel. The soldier whom he had summoned having run to the horse's head, Montalvo leapt from his driver's seat to assist the lady to dismount. At the moment, Lysbeth was occupied with wild ideas of swift escape, but even if she could make up her mind to try it, there was an obstacle which her thoughtful cavalier had foreseen.

"Jufvrouw van Hout," he said as he pulled up, "do you remember that you are still wearing skates?"

It was true, though in her agitation she had forgotten all about them, and the fact put sudden flight out of the question. She could not straggle into her own house walking on the sides of her feet like the tame seal that old fisherman Hans had once brought from northern seas. It would be too ridiculous, and the servants would certainly tell the story all about the town. Better for a while longer to put up with the company of this odious Spaniard than to become a laughing stock in an attempt to fly. Besides, even if she found herself on the other side of it, could she shut the door in his face? Would her promise let her, and would he consent?

"Yes," she answered briefly, "I will call my servant."

Then for the first time the Count became complimentary in a dignified Spanish manner.

"Let no base-born menial hold the foot that it is an honor for an hidalgo of Spain to touch. I am your servant," he said, and resting one knee on the snow-covered step he waited.

Again there was nothing to be done, so Lysbeth must needs thrust out her foot from which very delicately and carefully he unstrapped the skate.

"What Jack can bear Jill must put up with," muttered Lysbeth to herself as she advanced the other foot. Just at that moment, however, the door behind them began to open.

"She who buys," murmured Montalvo as he commenced on the second set of straps. Then the door swung wide, and the voice of Dirk van Goorl was heard saying in a tone of relief:

"Yes, sure enough it is she, Tante Clara, and some one is taking off her boots."

"Skates, Señor, skates," interrupted Montalvo, glancing backward over his shoulder, then added in a whisper as he bent once more to his task, "ahem—pays. You will introduce me, is it not so? I think it will be less awkward for you."

So, as flight was impossible, for he held her by the foot, and an instinct told her that, especially to the man she loved, the only thing to do was to make light of the affair, Lysbeth said— "Dirk, Cousin Dirk, I think you know—this is—the Honorable Captain the Count Juan de Montalvo."

"Ah! It is the Señor van Goorl," said Montalvo, pulling off the skate and rising from his knee, which, from his excess of courtesy, was now thoroughly wet. "Señor, allow me to return to you, safe and sound, the fair lady of whom I have robbed you for a while."

"For a while, captain," blurted Dirk, "why, from first to last, she has been gone nearly four hours, and a fine state we have been in about her."

"That will all be explained presently, Señor—at supper, to which the Jufvrouw has been so courteous as to ask me," then, aside and below his breath, again the ominous word of reminder—"pays."

"Most happily, your cousin's presence was the means of saving a fellow-creature's life. But, as I have said, the tale is long.

Señora—permit," and in another second Lysbeth found herself walking down her own hall upon the arm of the Spaniard, while Dirk, her aunt, and some guests followed obediently behind.

Now Montalvo knew that his difficulties were over for that evening at any rate, since he had crossed the threshold and was a guest.

Half unconsciously Lysbeth guided him to the balconied sitting room on the first floor. Here several other of her friends were gathered, for it had been arranged that the ice festival should end with a supper as rich as the house could give. To these, too, she must introduce her cavalier, who bowed courteously to each in turn. Then she escaped, but as she passed him she could swear that she saw his lips shape themselves to the hateful word "pays."

When she reached her chamber, so great was Lysbeth's wrath and indignation that she nearly choked with it, until again reason came to her aid, and with reason a desire to carry the thing off as well as might be. So she told her maid Greta to robe her in her best garment, and to hang about her neck the famous collar of pearls which her father had brought from the East, which was the talk and envy of half the women in Leyden. On her head, too, she placed the cap of lovely lace which had been a wedding gift given to her mother by her grandmother, the old dame who wove it. Then she added such golden ornaments as it was customary for women of her class to wear and descended to the gathering room.

Meanwhile, Montalvo had not been idle. Taking Dirk aside and pleading his travel-worn condition, he had prayed him to lead him to some room where he might order his dress and person. Dirk complied, though with an ill grace, but so pleasant did Montalvo make himself during those few minutes that before he ushered him back to the company, in some way Dirk found himself convinced that this particular Spaniard was not, as the saying went, "as black as his mustachio." He felt almost sure too, although he had not yet found time to tell him the details of it, that there was some excellent reason to account for his having carried off the adorable Lysbeth for an entire afternoon and evening.

It is true that there still remained the strange circumstance of the attempted foul of his cousin Van de Werff's sleigh in the great race, but, after all, why should there not be some explanation of this also? It had happened, if it did happen, at quite a distance from the winning post, when there were few people to see what passed. Indeed, now that he came to think of it, the only real evidence on the matter was that of his cousin, the little girl passenger, since Van de Werff himself had brought no actual accusation against his opponent.

Shortly after they returned to the company, it was announced that supper had been served, whereon ensued a pause. It was broken by Montalvo, who, stepping forward, offered his hand to Lysbeth, saying in a voice that all could hear, "Lady, my companion of the race, permit the humblest representative of the greatest monarch in the world to have the honor to escort you, which doubtless that monarch would be glad to do himself."

That settled the matter, for as the acting commandant of the Spanish garrison of Leyden had chosen to refer to his official position, it was impossible to question his right of precedence over a number of folk, who, although prominent in their way, were but unennobled Netherlander burghers.

Lysbeth, indeed, did find courage to point to a rather flurried and spasmodic lady with gray hair who was fanning herself as though the season were July, and wondering whether the cook would come up to the grand Spaniard's expectations, and to murmur "My aunt." But she got no further, for the Count instantly added in a low voice, "Doubtless your aunt comes next in the direct line, but unless my education has been neglected, the heiress of the house who is of age goes before the collateral—however aged.

By this time they were through the door, so it was useless to argue the point further, and again Lysbeth felt herself overmatched and submitted. In another minute, they had passed down the stairs, entered the dining hall, and were seated side by side at the head of the long table, of which the foot was occupied presently by Dirk van Goorl and her aunt, the widow Clara van

Ziel, who was also his cousin.

There was a silence while the domestics began their service, of which Montalvo took opportunity to study the room, the table and the guests. It was a fine room paneled with German oak and lighted sufficiently, if not brilliantly, by two hanging brass chandeliers of the famous Flemish workmanship, in each of which were fixed eighteen of the best candles, while on the sideboards were branch candlesticks, also of worked brass. The light thus provided was supplemented by that from the great fire of peat and an old ships' timber that burned in a wide, blue-tiled fireplace halfway down the chamber, throwing its reflections upon many a flagon and bowl of cunningly hammered silver that adorned the table.

The company was of the same character as the furniture, handsome and solid; people of means, every man and woman of them, accumulated by themselves or their fathers, in the exercise of the honest and profitable trade whereof the Netherlands had a practical monopoly.

"I have made no mistake," thought Montalvo to himself, as he surveyed the room and its occupants. "My little neighbor's necklace alone is worth more cash than ever I had the handling of, and the plate would add up handsomely. Well, before very long I hope to be in a position to make its inventory." Then, having first crossed himself devoutly, he began a supper that was well worth his attention, even in a land noted for the luxury of its food and the superb appetites of those who consumed them.

It must not be supposed, however, that the gallant captain allowed eating to strangle conversation. On the contrary, finding that his hostess was in no talkative mood, he addressed himself to his fellow guests, chatting with them pleasantly upon every convenient subject. Among these guests was none other than Pieter van de Werff, his conqueror in that afternoon's contest, upon whose watchful and suspicious reserve he brought all his efforts to bear.

First he congratulated Pieter and lamented his own bad luck, and this with great earnestness, for as a matter of fact he had lost much more money on the event than he could afford to pay. Then he praised the gray horse and asked if he was for sale, offering his own black in part exchange.

"A good nag," he said, "but one that I do not wish to conceal has his faults, which must be taken into consideration if it comes to the point of putting a price upon him. For instance, Mynheer van de Werff, you may have noticed the dreadful position in which the brute put me towards the end of the race. There are certain things that this horse always shies at, and one of them is a red cloak. Now I don't know if you saw that a girl in a red cloak suddenly appeared on the bank. In an instant, the beast was round and you may imagine what my feelings were, being in charge of your fair kinswoman, for I thought to a certainty that we should be over. What is more, it quite spoilt my chance in the race, for after he has shied like that, the black turns sulky, and won't let himself go."

When Lysbeth heard this amazing explanation, remembering the facts, she also gasped. And yet now that she came to think of it, a girl in a red cloak did appear near them at the moment, and the horse did whip round as though it had shied violently. Was it possible, she wondered, that the captain had not really intended to foul the Badger sled?

Meanwhile, Van de Werff was answering in his slow voice. Apparently he accepted Montalvo's explanation; at least he said that he, too, saw the red-cloaked girl, and was glad that nothing serious had come of the mishap. In regard to the proposed deal, he should be most happy to go into it upon the lines mentioned, as the gray, although a very good horse, was aged, and he thought the black one of the most beautiful animals that he had ever seen. At this point, as he had not the slightest intention of parting with his valuable charger, on such terms at any rate, Montalvo changed the subject.

At length, when the honored guests had well eaten and the beautiful tall Flemish glasses had been replenished with the best Rhenish or Spanish wines, Montalvo, taking advantage of a pause in the conversation, rose and said that he wished to claim the privilege of a stranger among them and to propose a toast, namely, to the health of his recent adversary, Pieter van de Werff.

At this the audience applauded, for they were all very proud of the young man's success, and some of them had won money over him. Still more did they applaud, being great judges of culinary matters, when the Spaniard began his speech by an eloquent tribute to the surpassing excellence of the supper. Rarely, he assured them, and especially did he assure the honorable widow Van Ziel who blushed all over with pleasure at his compliments, that rarely even in the Courts of Kings and Emperors, or at the tables of Popes and Archbishops, had he eaten food so exquisitely cooked, or drunk wines of a better vintage. In her enthusiasm, the blushing widow again fanned herself, but with such vigor that she upset Dirk's wine over his new tunic.

Then, passing on to the subject of his speech, Van de Werff, he toasted him and his horse and his little sister and his sleigh, in well-chosen and appropriate terms, not by any means over-doing it, for he confessed frankly that his defeat was a bitter disappointment to him, especially as every soldier in the camp had expected him to win and, he was afraid, backed him for more than they could afford. Also, incidentally, so that every one might be well acquainted with it, he retold the story of the girl with the red cloak. Next, suddenly dropping his voice and adopting a quieter manner, he addressed himself to the Aunt Clara and the "well-beloved Heer Dirk," saying that he owed them both an apology, which he must take this opportunity to make, for having detained the lady at his right during so unrea-sonable a time that afternoon. When, however, they had heard the facts they would, he was sure, blame him no longer, espe-cially if he told them that this breach of good manners had been the means of saving a human life.

Immediately after the race, he explained, one of his ser-geants had told him that a woman, suspected of certain crimes against life and property and believed to be a notorious escaped witch or heretic, had been captured. The sergeant requested that someone with proper authority deal with the case at once. This woman also, so said the man, had been heard that very afternoon to make use of the most traitorous and blaspheming language to a lady of Leyden, the Jufvrouw Lysbeth van Hout, indeed, as was stated by a certain spy named Black Meg, who had overheard the conversation.

Now, went on Montalvo, as he knew well, every man and woman in that room would share his horror of traitorous and blasphemous heretics—here most of the company crossed them-selves, especially those who were already secret adherents of the Protestant Reformation. Still, even heretics had a right to a fair trial; at least he, who although a soldier by profession, was a man who honestly detested unnecessary bloodshed, held that opinion. Also, long experience taught him great mistrust of the evidence of informers, who had a money interest in the convic-tion of the accused. Lastly, it did not seem well to him that the name of a young and noble lady should be mixed up in such a business. As they knew under the recent edicts, his powers in these cases were absolute. Indeed, in his official capacity he was ordered at once to consign any suspected of Anabaptism, or other forms of heresy, to be dealt with by the appointed courts; and in the case of people who had escaped, to cause them, on satisfactory proof of their identity, to be executed instantly without any further trial. Under these circumstances—fearing that if the lady had known his purpose, she might become fearful—he had, he confessed, resorted to artifice as he was very anxious both for her sake and, in the interest of justice, that she should bear testimony in the matter. So he asked her to accompany him on a short drive while he attended to a business affair, a request to which she had graciously assented.

"Friends," he went on in a still more solemn voice, "the rest of my story is short. Indeed do I congratulate myself on the decision that I took, for when confronted with the prisoner, your young and honorable hostess was able upon oath to refute the story of the spy with the result that I in my turn was able to save an unfortunate, and, as I believe, a half-crazed creature from an immediate and a cruel death. Is it not so, lady?" and helpless in the net of circumstance, not knowing indeed what else to do, Lysbeth bowed her head in assent.

"I think," concluded Montalvo, "that after this explanation, what may have appeared to be a breach of manners will be forgiven. I have only one other word to add. My position is peculiar. I am an official here, and I speak boldly among friends taking the risk that any of you present may use what I say against me, which for my part I do not believe. Although there is no better Catholic and no truer Spaniard in the Netherlands, I have been accused of showing too great a sympathy with your people, and of dealing too leniently with those who have incurred the displeasure of our Holy Church. In the cause of right and justice I am willing to bear such aspersions, but this is a slanderous world, a world in which truth does not always prevail. Therefore, although I have told you nothing but the bare facts, I do suggest in the interests of your hostess—my own humble interest who might be misrepresented—and I may add in the interest of every one present at this party, that it will perhaps be well that the details of the story which I have had the honor of telling you should not be spread about, that they should in fact find a grave within these walls. Friends, do you agree?"

Then moved by a common impulse, and by a common if a secret fear, with the single exception of Lysbeth, every person present, yes, even the cautious and far-sighted young Van de Werff, echoed "We agree."

"Friends," said Montalvo, "those simple words carry to my mind conviction as deep as did the oath of your hostess, upon the faith of which I felt myself justified in acquitting the poor creature who was alleged to be an escaped heretic." Then with a courteous and all-embracing bow Montalvo sat down.

"What a good man, what a delightful man," murmured Aunt Clara to Dirk in the buzz of conversation which ensued.

"Yes, yes, cousin, but—"

"And what discrimination he has, what taste! Did you notice what he said about the cooking?"

"I heard something, but—"

"It is true that folk have told me that my capon stewed in milk, such as we had tonight— Why, lad, what is the matter with your doublet? You fidget me by continually rubbing at it."

"You have upset the red wine over it, that is all," answered Dirk, sulkily. "It is spoiled."

"And little loss either. To tell you the truth, Dirk, I never saw a coat worse cut. You young men should learn in the matter of clothes from the Spanish gentlemen. Look at his Excellency, the Count Montalvo, for instance—"

"See here, Aunt," broke in Dirk with suppressed fury, "I think I have heard enough about Spaniards and the Captain Montalvo for one night. First of all, he spirits off Lysbeth and is absent with her for four hours; then he invites himself to supper and places himself at the head of the table with her, setting me down to the dullest meal I ever ate at the other end."

"Cousin Dirk," said Aunt Clara with dignity, "your temper has got the better of your manners. Certainly you might learn courtesy as well as dress, even from so humble a person as a Spanish hidalgo and commander." Then she rose from the table, adding—"Come, Lysbeth, if you are ready, let us leave these gentlemen to their chatter."

After the ladies had gone, the supper went on merrily. In those days, nearly everybody drank too much liquor at feasts, and this company was no exception. Even Montalvo, his game being won and the strain on his nerves relaxed, partook pretty freely and began to tell falsehoods on even a larger scale than before. Still, so clever was the man that in his cups he yet showed method, for his conversation revealed a sympathy with Netherlander grievances and a tolerance of view in religious matters rarely displayed by a Spaniard.

From such questions they drifted into a military discussion, and Montalvo, challenged by Van de Werff—who, as it happened, had not drunk too much wine—explained how, were he officer in command, he would defend Leyden from attack by an overwhelming force. Very soon Van de Werff saw that the Count was a capable soldier who had studied his profession, and being himself a capable civilian with a thirst for knowledge pressed the argument from point to point.

"And suppose," he asked at length, "that the city were starving and still untaken, so that its inhabitants must either fall into the hands of the enemy or burn the place over their heads, what would you do then?"

"Then, Mynheer, if I were a small man, I should yield to the clamor of the starving folk and surrender," said Montalvo.

"And if you were a big man, captain?" asked Pieter.

"If I were a big man—ah! If I were a big man, why then, I would let out the dykes and let the sea beat once more against the walls of Leyden. An army cannot live in salt water, Mynheer."

"That would drown out the farmers and ruin the land for twenty years."

"Quite so, Mynheer, but when the corn has to be saved, who thinks of spoiling the straw?"

"I follow you, Señor, your proverb is good, although I have never heard it."

"Many good things come from Spain, Mynheer, including this red wine. I should have but one more glass with you, for, if you will allow me to say it, you are a man worth meeting."

"I hope that you will always retain the same opinion of me," answered Van de Werff as he drank, "at a party or in the trenches."

Then Pieter went home, and before he slept that night made careful notes of all the Spaniard's suggested military dispositions, both of attackers and attacked, writing underneath them the proverb about the corn and the straw. There existed no real reason why he should have done so, as he was only a civilian engaged in business, but Pieter van de Werff was a provident young man who knew many things might happen which could not precisely be foreseen.

As for Dirk van Goorl, he sought his lodging rather tipsy, and arm-in-arm with none other than the Captain, Count Don Juan de Montalvo.

CHAPTER IV
THREE WAKINGS

There were three persons in Leyden whose reflections when they awoke on the morning after the sled race are not without interest. First there was Dirk van Goorl, whose work made an early riser of him—to say nothing of a splitting headache which on this morning called him into consciousness just as the clock in the bell tower was chiming half-past four. Now there are few things more depressing than to be awakened by a bad headache at half-past four in the black frost of a winter dawn. Yet, as Dirk lay on his bed in contemplation, a conviction took hold of him that his depression was not due entirely to the headache or to the cold. The simple truth was that Dirk van Goorl was suffering from a guilty conscience, after failing his Maker and his best earthly love on several accounts.

In fact, for the truth may as well be told at once, Dirk was a Lutheran, having been admitted to that community two years before. To be a Lutheran in the Netherlands meant that you walked the world with a halter round your neck and a vision of the rack and the stake before your eyes. During these times, living for God according to the teachings of the Bible became an earnest and serious thing. Still the dreadful penalties for being labeled a heretic did not prevent many of the burgher and lower classes from worshipping God as they believed the Scriptures demanded. Indeed, if the truth had been known, of those who were present at Lysbeth's supper on the previous night, more than half, including Pieter van de Werff, were adherents of the Protestant Reformation—a Christian faith which called sinful men back to the teaching of Scripture alone for their every belief and practice.

One by one he recalled the depressing events of yesterday. First he had been late for his appointment with Lysbeth, which understandably vexed her. Then the Captain Montalvo had swooped down and carried her away, as a hawk bears off a chicken under the very eyes of the hen-wife, while he, donkey that he was, could find no words of protest. He had been a worthless defender of his beloved's honor. Next, thinking it his duty to back the sleigh wherein Lysbeth rode, although it was driven by a Spaniard, he had foolishly lost ten florins on that event, which, being a thrifty young man, did not at all please him. The rest of the afternoon he had spent hunting for Lysbeth, who mysteriously vanished with the Spaniard, to a destination totally unknown to him. Then came the supper, when once more the Count swooped down on Lysbeth, leaving him to escort his cousin Clara, who, having spoilt his new jacket by spilling wine over it, ended by abusing his taste in dress. Nor was that all, for he had drunk a great deal more strong wine than was godly or wise. And to this, his head certified. Lastly, he had walked home arm in arm with this lady-snatching Spaniard, and by Heaven! yes, he had sworn eternal friendship with him on his doorstep.

Well, there was little doubt in Dirk's cloudy mind that the Count was an uncommonly good fellow, for a Spaniard. As for that story of the foul, he had explained it quite satisfactorily, and he had taken his beating like a gentleman. Could anything be nicer or in better feeling than his allusions to Cousin Pieter in his after-supper speech? Also, and this was a graver matter, the man had shown that he was tolerant and kindly by the way in which he dealt with the poor creature called the Mare. This woman's history Dirk knew quite well. He had been informed that her sufferings had made of her a crazy and rash-tongued wanderer, who, so it was rumored, could use a knife.

Although Dirk permitted his guard and discernment to be let down with his late-evening drinking, he did not have the sense to grasp how miserably he had judged the character of Captain Montalvo. He was even less aware, however, of how costly his poor judgment would be to his dear Lysbeth. Heer van Goorl, at this point in his life, could only manage to fear Montalvo because he recognized that he was much too flirtatious.

Dirk could have wished that this kindly natured Spaniard

was not quite so good-looking or quite so appreciative of the
excellent points of the young Leyden ladies, and especially of
Lysbeth, with whose sterling character, he now remembered,
Montalvo had assured him he was much impressed. What he
feared most of all was that this regard might be reciprocal. After
all, a Spanish hidalgo in command of the garrison was a distinguished person, and, alas, Lysbeth also was a Roman Catholic.
Dirk loved Lysbeth; he loved her with that patient sincerity
which was characteristic of his own temperament, but in addition to and above the reasons that have been given already, it
was this fact of the difference of religion which hitherto had
built a wall between them. Of course, she was unaware of anything of the sort. She did not even know that he belonged to the
Lutheran faith, and without the permission of the elders of his
church, he would not dare to tell her, for the lives of men and
of their families could not be confided lightly to the hazard of a
girl's discretion.

Herein lay the real reason why, although Dirk was so devoted
to Lysbeth, and although he imagined that she was not indifferent to him, as yet no word had passed between them of love or
marriage. How could he who was a Lutheran ask a Catholic to
become his wife when Scripture plainly commanded him to be
equally yoked? And if he told her the truth, and she consented
to leave the Roman Catholic doctrines, would it still be proper
to put her life in danger? To Dirk's mind the whole idea of trying to marry someone of another faith was both unscriptural
and impractical. He often thought of the difficulties of having
to try to convert someone who was already a partner for life, and
if they had any children, what faith could he train them in but
his own. Then, sooner or later, might come the informer, that
dreadful informer whose shadow already lay heavy upon thousands of homes in the Netherlands. Then after the informer the
officer, and after the officer the priest, and after the priest the
judge, and after the judge, the executioner and the stake.

In that case, what would happen to Lysbeth? She might prove
herself innocent of the horrible crime of heresy, if by that time
she was innocent, but what would life become to the loving

young woman whose husband and children, perhaps, had been dragged off to the slaughter chambers of the Papal Inquisition? This was the true first cause why Dirk had remained silent, even when he was sorely tempted to speak; yes, although his instinct told him that his silence had been misinterpreted and set down to overcaution, or indifference, or to unnecessary scruples.

The next to wake that morning was Lysbeth, who, if she was not troubled with headache resulting from sinful indulgence—and in that day women of her class sometimes suffered from it—had pains of her own to overcome. When sifted and classified, these pains resolved themselves into a sense of fiery indignation against Dirk van Goorl. Dirk had been late for his appointment, alleging some ridiculous excuse about the cooling of a bell, as though she cared whether the bell were hot or cold, with the result that she had been thrown into the company of that dreadful Martha the Mare. After the Mare—aggravated by Black Meg—came the Spaniard. Here again Dirk had shown contemptible indifference and insufficiency, for he allowed her to be forced into the Wolf sled against her will. Nay, he had actually consented to the thing. Next, in a sequence that followed all the other incidents of that hideous carnival; the race, the foul, if it was a foul; the dreadful vision of the look upon Montalvo's face; the trial of the Mare, her own unpremeditated but indelible perjury, and the lonely drive with the man who compelled her to it. All this, along with the exhibition of herself before all the world as his willing companion; and the feast in which he appeared as her escort, and was accepted of the simple company almost as an angel.

What did he mean by all his advances? Doubtless, for on that point she could scarcely be mistaken, he meant to win her love, for had he not in practice said as much? And now—this was the terrible thing—she was in his power, since if he chose to do so, without doubt he could prove that she had sworn a false oath for her own purposes. Also, that lie weighed upon her mind, even though it had been spoken in a good cause, though she was not certain that it was good to save a wretched fanatic from a fate that, were the truth known, her crime may well have deserved.

Of course, the Spaniard was a bad man, if an attractive one, and he had behaved wickedly, if with grace and breeding; but who expected anything else from a Spaniard, who only acted after his kind and for his own ends? It was Dirk, Dirk, that was to blame, not so much—and here again came the rub—for his awkwardness and mistakes of yesterday, as for his general conduct. Why had he not spoken to her before, and put her beyond the reach of such accidents as these to which a woman of her position and substance must necessarily be exposed? The saints knew that she had given him opportunity enough. She had gone as far as a maiden might, and not for all the Dirks on earth would she go one inch further. Why had she ever come to care for his foolish face? Why had she refused so-and-so, and so-and-so, and so-and-so—all of them honorable men—with the result that now no other bachelor ever came near her, believing that she was under bond to her cousin? In the past she had persuaded herself that it was because of something she felt but could not see, of a hidden nobility of character that was not very evident upon the surface, that she loved Dirk van Goorl. But where was this something, this nobility? Surely a man who was a man ought to play his part, and not leave her in this false position, especially as there could be no question of means. She would not have come to him empty-handed, very far from it, indeed. Oh! Were it not for the unfortunate fact that she still happened to care about him—to her sorrow—never, never would she speak to him again.

The last to awake on this particular morning, between nine and ten o'clock, indeed, when Dirk had been already two hours at his factory, and Lysbeth was buying provisions in the market place, was that accomplished and excellent officer, Captain the Count Juan de Montalvo. For a few seconds after his dark eyes opened, he stared at the ceiling collecting his thoughts. Then, sitting up in bed, he burst into a prolonged roar of laughter. Really the whole thing was too funny for any man of humor to contemplate without being moved to merriment. That gaby, Dirk van Goorl; the furiously indignant but helpless Lysbeth; the solemn, fat-headed fools of Netherlanders at the supper, and the fashion in which he had played his own tune on the whole pack of them, as though they were the strings of a fiddle—oh, it was delicious!

As the reader by this time may have guessed, Montalvo was not the typical Spaniard of romance, nor, indeed, of history. He was not gloomy and stern; he was not even particularly vengeful or bloodthirsty. On the contrary, he was a clever and utterly unprincipled man with a sense of humor and a gift of *bonhomie* (good nature) that made him popular in many places. Moreover, he was a brave and good soldier; in a certain sense sympathetic and, above all, cunning. Although he lived in a day when men often held staunchly to their religious views, his were so loosely held that he had practically none at all. His conduct, therefore, if from time to time it was affected by passing spasms of acute superstition, was totally uninfluenced by any settled spiritual hopes or fears, a condition which, he believed, gave him great advantages in this life. In fact, had it suited his purpose, Montalvo was prepared, at a moment's notice, to become Lutheran or Mohammedan, or Mystic, or even Anabaptist; on the principle, he would reason, that it is easy for the artist to paint any picture he likes upon a blank canvas.

And yet this curious pliancy of mind born out of a relentless worship of his own self, this lack of conviction, this absolute lack of moral sense, which ought to have given the Count such great advantages in a fallen world, were, in reality, the main source of his weakness. Fortune had made a soldier of the man, and he filled the part as he would have filled any part. But overruling Providence intended him for a play-actor, and from day to day he posed, mimed, mouthed his way through life in this character or in that, though never in his own character, principally because he had none. Still, far down in Montalvo's being there was something solid and genuine, yet that something was not good but bad. It was rarely in plain view; the art of discernment must plunge deep to find it, but it dwelt there; the strong, cruel, Satanic spirit which would sacrifice anything to save, or even to advance itself. It was this spirit that Lysbeth had seen looking out of his eyes on the previous afternoon, which, when he knew that the race was lost, had prompted him to try to kill his adversary, even if he killed himself and her in the process.

In short, although Montalvo was a man who really disliked cruelty, he could upon occasion be cruel to the last degree; although he appreciated friends and desired to have them, he could be the foulest of traitors. Although without a cause, he would do no hurt to a living thing, yet if that cause were sufficient he would cheerfully consign a whole city to death. No, not cheerfully, he would have regretted their end very much, and often afterwards might have thought of it with sympathy and even sorrow. This was where he differed from the majority of his countrymen in that age, who would have done the same thing, and more brutally, from honest principle, and for the rest of their lives rejoiced at the memory of the deed.

Montalvo, like most men, had his ruling passion. It was not war, it was not women, rather it was money. But here again he did not care about the money itself, since he was no miser; and being the most inveterate of gamblers, never saved a single stiver. He wanted it to spend and to stake upon the dice. Thus again, in variance to the taste of most of his countrymen, he cared little for the other sex; he did not even particularly like their company, and as for their passion and the rest he thought it something of a bore. But he did care intensely for their admiration, so much so that if no better game were at hand, he would take enormous pains to fascinate even a serving maid or a fish girl. Wherever he went, it was his ambition to be reported the most admired man of the fair in that city, and to attain this end, he offered himself upon the altar of numerous love affairs that did not amuse him in the least. Of course, the indulgence of this vanity meant expense, since the fair require money and presents, and he who pursues them should be well dressed and horsed and able to do things in the very finest style. Also, their relatives must be entertained and, when they were entertained, impressed with the sense that they had the honor to be guests of a grandee of Spain.

Now that of a grandee has never been a cheap profession; indeed, as many a pauper peer knows today, rank without resources is a terrific burden. Montalvo, had the rank, for he was a well-born man, whose sole heritage was an ancient tower built by some warlike ancestor in a position admirably suited to the purpose of the said ancestor, namely, the pillage of travelers through a neighboring mountain pass. When, however, travelers ceased to use that pass, or for other reasons robbery became no longer productive, the revenues of the Montalvo family declined until at the present date they were practically nil. Thus it came about that the status of the last representative of this ancient stock was that of a soldier of fortune of the common type, endowed, unfortunately for himself, with grand ideas, a gambler's fatal fire, expensive tastes, and more than the usual pride of race.

Although, perhaps, he had never defined them very clearly, even to himself, Juan de Montalvo had two aims in life: first, to indulge his every freak and fancy to the full, and next—but this was secondary and somewhat nebulous—to reestablish the fortunes of his family. Yet so far, at any rate, in spite of many opportunities, he had not succeeded, although he was now a man of more than thirty. The causes of his failure were various, but at the bottom of them lay his lack of stability and genuineness.

A man who is always playing a part amuses every one but convinces few. Montalvo convinced almost nobody. When he discoursed on the mysteries of religion with priests, even priests who were for the most part ignorant, they felt that they assisted in a mere intellectual exercise. When his theme was war, his audience guessed that his object was probably love. When love was his song, an inconvenient instinct was apt to assure the lady immediately concerned that it was love of self and not of her. They were all more or less mistaken, but, as usual, the women went nearest to the mark. Montalvo's real aim was self, but he called it Money. Money in large sums was what he wanted, and what in this way or that he meant to win.

Now even in the sixteenth century, fortunes did not fall into the lap of every adventurer. Military pay was small and not easily recoverable; loot was hard to come by and quickly spent.

Even the ransom of a rich prisoner or two soon disappeared in the payment of such debts of honor as could not be avoided. Of course there remained the possibility of wealthy marriage, which in a country like the Netherlands, which was full of rich heiresses, was not difficult to a high-born, handsome, and agreeable man of the ruling Spanish caste. Indeed, after many opportunities, the time had come when Montalvo must either marry or be ruined. His debts, especially his gaming debts, were enormous; and creditors met him at every turn. Unfortunately for him, also, some of these creditors were persons who had the ear of people in authority. So, at last, it came about that an intimation reached him that this scandal must be abated, or he must go back to Spain—a country which, as it happened, he did not in the least wish to visit. In short, the sorry hour of reckoning, that hour which overtakes all procrastinators, had arrived, and marriage, wealthy marriage, was the only way wherewith it could be defied. It was a sad alternative for a man who had no interest in sharing life goals with any women, but this had to be faced.

Thus it came about that, as the only suitable person in Leyden, the Count Montalvo had sought out the well favored and well endowed Jufvrouw Lysbeth van Hout to be his companion in the great sled race, and taken so much trouble to ensure to himself a friendly reception at her house.

So far, things went well, and, what was more, the opening of the chase had proved distinctly entertaining. Also, the society of the place, after his appropriation of her at a public festival and their long moonlight tour, which by now must be common gossip, would be quite prepared for any amount of attention that he might see fit to pay to Lysbeth. Indeed, why should he not pay attention to an unbetrothed woman whose rank was lower if her means were greater than his own? Of course, he knew that her name had been coupled with that of Dirk van Goorl. He was perfectly aware also that these two young people were attached to each other; for, as they walked home together on the previous night, Dirk, possibly for motives of his own, had favored him with a semi-intoxicated confidence to that effect.

But as they were not betrothed, what did that matter? Indeed, had they been betrothed, what would it matter? Still, Dirk van Goorl was an obstacle, and thus—although he seemed to be a good fellow, and Montalvo was sorry for him—Dirk van Goorl must be removed, since the Count was convinced that Lysbeth was one of those stubborn-natured creatures who would probably decline to marry himself until this young Leyden lout had vanished. And yet, he did not wish to be mixed up with duels, if for no other reason because in a duel the unexpected may always happen, and that would be a poor end. Certainly, also, he did not wish to be mixed up with murder; first, because he disliked the idea of killing anybody, unless he was driven to it; and secondly, because murder has a nasty way of coming out. One could never be quite sure in what light the dispatching of a young Netherlander of respectable family and fortune would be looked at by those in authority.

Also, there was another thing to be considered. If this young man died, it was impossible to know exactly how Lysbeth would take his death. Thus she might elect to refuse to marry or decide to mourn him for four or five years, which for all practical purposes would be just as bad. And yet while Dirk lived how could he possibly persuade her to transfer her affections to himself? It seemed, therefore, that Dirk needed to die. For quite a quarter of an hour, Montalvo thought the matter over. He soon determined to give it up and determined to leave things to chance, for a while at least, until a splendid inspiration came to him.

Dirk must not die, Dirk must live; but his continued existence must be the price of the hand of Lysbeth van Hout. If she was half as fond of the man as he believed, it was probable that she would be delighted to marry anybody else in order to save his precious neck, for that was just the kind of sentimental fluff of which nine women out of ten really enjoyed the indulgence. Moreover, this scheme had other merits; it did every one a good turn. Dirk would be saved from extinction for which he should be grateful. Lysbeth, besides earning the honor of an alliance, perhaps only temporary, with himself, would be able to go through life wrapped in a heavenly glow of virtue arising from the impression that she had really done something very fine and tragic. While he, Montalvo, under Providence, the humble purveyor of these blessings, would also benefit to some small extent. The difficulty was: How could the situation he created? How could the interesting Dirk be brought to a pass that would give the lady an opportunity of exercising her finer feelings on his behalf? If only he were a heretic now! Well, by the Pope, why shouldn't he be a heretic? If ever a fellow had the heretical cut this fellow had; flat-faced, sanctimonious-looking, and with a fancy for dark-colored stockings—he had observed that all heretics, male and female, wore dark-colored stockings, perhaps by way of mortifying the flesh. He could think of only one reason why Dirk may not be a Protestant; the young man had drunk too much last night. But there were certain breeds of heretics who were still capable of drinking too much. Also the best would slip sometimes, for, as he had learned from the old Castilian priest who taught him Latin, *humanum est, etc.*

This, then, was the summary of his reflections. (1) To save the situation, within three months or so he must be united in holy matrimony with Lysbeth van Hout. (2) If it proved impossible to remove the young man, Dirk van Goorl, from his path by overmatching him in the lady's affections, or by playing on her jealousy, stronger measures must be adopted. (3) Such stronger measures should consist of inducing the lady to save her lover from death by uniting herself in marriage with one who, for her sake, would do violence to his conscience and manipulate the business. (4) This plan would be best put into execution by proving the lover to be a heretic, but if unhappily this could not be proved because he was not, still he must figure in that capacity for this occasion only. (5) Meanwhile, it would be well to cultivate the society of Mynheer van Goorl as much as possible, first because he was a person with whom, under the circumstances, he, Montalvo, would naturally wish to become intimate, and secondly, because he was quite certain to be an individual with cash to lend.

Now, these inquiries after heretics invariably cost money, for they involved the services of spies. Obviously, therefore,

friend Dirk, the Dutch Flounder, was a man to provide the butter in which he was going to be fried. Why, if any Hollander
had a spark of humor, he would see the joke of it himself—and
Montalvo ended his reflections as he had begun them, with
a merry peal of laughter, after which he rose and ate a most
excellent breakfast. It was about half-past five o'clock that afternoon before the Captain and Acting-Commandant Montalvo
returned from some duty to which he had been attending, for it
may be explained that he was a zealous officer and a master of
detail. As he entered his lodgings, the soldier who acted as his
servant, a man selected for silence and discretion, saluted and
stood at attention.

"Is the woman here?" he asked.

"Excellency, she is here, though I had difficulty enough
in persuading her to come, for I found her in bed and out of
humor."

"Peace to your difficulties. Where is she?" asked the Captain.

"In the small inner room, Excellency."

"Good, then see that no one disturbs us, and—stay, when she
goes out follow her and note her movements until you trace her
home."

The man saluted, and Montalvo passed upstairs into the
inner room, carefully shutting both doors behind him. The
place was unlighted, but through the large stone-mullioned
window the rays of the full moon poured brightly, and by them,
seated in a straight-backed chair, Montalvo saw a draped form.
There was something forbidding, something almost unnatural,
in the aspect of this somber form perched thus upon a chair
in expectant silence. It reminded him—for he had a touch of
inconvenient imagination—of an evil bird squatted upon the
bough of a dead tree awaiting the dawn that it might go forth to
devour some appointed prey.

"Is that you, Mother Meg?" he asked in tones from which
most of the jovialness had vanished. "Quite like old times at The
Hague—isn't it?"

The moonlit figure turned its head, for he could see the light
shine upon the whites of the eyes.

"Who else, Excellency," said a voice hoarse and thick with

rheum, a voice like the croak of a crow, "though it is little thanks
to your Excellency. Those must be strong who can bathe in
Rhine water through a hole in the ice and take no hurt."

"Don't scold, woman," he answered, "I have no time for it.
If you were dunked yesterday, it served you right for losing your
cursed temper. Could you not see that I had my own game to
play, and you were spoiling it? Must I be flouted before my men,
and listen while you warn a lady with whom I wish to stand well
against me?"

"You generally have a game to play, Excellency, but when it
ends in my being first robbed and then nearly drowned beneath
the ice—well, that is a game which Black Meg does not forget."

"Hush, Mother, you are not the only person with a memory.
What was the reward? Twelve florins? Well, you shall have them,
and five more; that's good pay for a lick of cold water. Are you
satisfied?"

"No, Excellency. I wanted the life, that heretic's life. I wanted
to baste her while she burned, or to tread her down while she
was buried. I have a grudge against the woman because I know,
yes, because I know," she repeated fiercely, " that if I do not kill
her she will try to kill me. Her husband and her young son were

burnt, upon my evidence mostly, but this is the third time she has escaped me."

"Patience, Mother, patience, and I dare say that everything will come right in the end. You have bagged two of the family— Papa heretic and Young Hopeful. Really you should not grumble if the third takes a little hunting, or wonder that in the meanwhile you are not popular with Mama. Now, listen. You know the young woman whom it was necessary that I should humor yesterday. She is rich, is she not?"

"Yes, I know her, and I knew her father. He left her house, furniture, jewelry, and thirty thousand crowns, which are placed out at good interest. A nice fortune for a gallant who wants money, but it will be Dirk van Goorl's, not yours."

"Ah! That is just the point. Now what do you know about Dirk van Goorl?"

"A respectable, hard-working burgher, son of well-to-do parents, brass-workers, who live at Alkmaar. Honest, but not very clever; the kind of man who grows rich, becomes a Burgemeester, founds a hospital for the poor, and has a fine monument put up to his memory."

"Mother, the cold water has dulled your wits. When I ask you about a man, I want to learn what you know against him."

"Naturally, Excellency, naturally, but against this one I can tell you nothing. He has no lovers, he does not gamble, he does not drink except a glass after dinner. He works in his factory all day, goes to bed early, rises early, and calls on the Jufvrouw van Hout on Sundays; that is all."

"Where does he attend Mass?" questioned Montalvo.

"At the Groote Kerke once a week, but he does not take the Sacrament or go to confession."

"That sounds bad, Mother, very bad. You don't mean to say that he is a heretic?"

"Probably he is, Excellency; most of them are around here."

"Dear me, how very shocking. Do you know, I should not like that excellent young woman, a good Catholic too, like you and me, Mother, to become mixed up with one of these dreadful heretics, who might expose her to all sorts of dangers. For, Mother, who can touch dirt and not be defiled?"

"You waste time, Excellency," replied his visitor with a snort. "What do you want?"

"Well, in the interests of this young lady, I want to prove that this man is a heretic, and it has struck me that—as one accustomed to this sort of thing—you might be able to find the evidence."

"Indeed, Excellency, and has it struck you what my face would look like after I had thrust my head into a wasp's nest for your amusement? Do you know what it means to me if I go peering about among the heretics of Leyden? Well, I will tell you; it means that I would be killed. They are a strong lot, and a determined lot, and so long as you leave them alone they will leave you alone, but if you interfere with them, why then it is good night. Oh, yes, I know all about the law and the priests and the edicts and the Emperor. But the Emperor cannot burn a whole people, and though I hate them, I tell you," she added, standing up suddenly and speaking in a fierce, convinced voice, "that, in the end, the law and the edicts and the priests will get the worst of this fight. Yes, these Hollanders will beat them all and cut out the throats of you Spaniards, and thrust those of you who are left alive out of their country, and spit upon your memories and worship God in their own fashion, and be proud and free. Those are not my own words," said Meg in a changed voice as she sat down again. "They are the words of that devil, Martha the Mare, which she spoke in my hearing when we had her on the rack, but somehow I think that they will come true, and that is why I always remember them."

"Indeed, her ladyship the Mare is a more interesting person than I thought, though if she can talk like that, perhaps, after all, it would have been as well to drown her. And now, dropping prophecy and leaving posterity to arrange for itself, let us come to business. How much? For evidence that would suffice to procure his conviction."

"Five hundred florins, not a stiver less. So, Excellency, you need not waste your time trying to beat me down. You want good evidence, evidence on which the Council, or whoever they may appoint, will convict, and that means the unshaken testimony of two witnesses. Well, I tell you, it isn't easy to come by. There is great danger to the honest folk who seek it, for these heretics are desperate people, and if they find a spy while they are engaged in devil-worship at one of their meetings, why— they kill him."

"I know all that, Mother. What are you trying to cover up that you are so talkative? It isn't your usual way of doing business. Well, it is a bargain, you shall have your money when you produce the evidence. And now really, if we talk here much longer people will begin to make remarks, for who shall escape aspersion in this censorious world? So good night, Mother, good night," and he turned to leave the room.

"No, Excellency," she croaked with a snort of indignation, "no pay, no play. I don't work on the faith of your Excellency's word alone."

"How much?" he asked again.

"A hundred florins down."

Then, for a while, they wrangled hideously, their heads held close together in the patch of moonlight, and so loathsome did their faces look, so plainly was the wicked purpose of their hearts written upon them, that in that faint luminous glow they might have been mistaken for emissaries from the underworld chaffering over the price of a human soul. At last, the bargain was struck for fifty florins, and having received it into her hand, Black Meg departed.

"Sixty-seven in all," she commented to herself as she regained the street. "Well, it was no use holding out for any more, for he hasn't got the cash. The man's as poor as Lazarus, but he wants to live like a duke, and, what is more, he gambles, as I learned at The Hague. Also, there's something strange about his past; I have heard as much as that. It must be looked into, and perhaps the bundle of papers to which I helped myself out of his desk while I was waiting"—and she touched the bosom of her dress to make sure that they were safe—"may tell me a thing or two, though likely enough they are only unpaid bills. Ah! Most noble cheat and captain, before you have done with her you may find that Black Meg knows how to pay back hot water for cold!"

CHAPTER V
THE DREAM OF DIRK

On the day following Montalvo's interview with Black Meg, Dirk received a message from that gentleman, sent to his lodging by an orderly, which reminded him that he had promised to dine with him this very night. Now he had no recollection of any such engagement. Remembering with shame, however, that there were various incidents of the evening of the supper whereof his memory was most imperfect, he concluded that this must be one of them. So, much against his own wishes, Dirk sent back an answer to say that he would appear at the time and place appointed.

This was the third thing that had happened to annoy him that day. First he had met Pieter van de Werff, who informed him that all Leyden was talking about Lysbeth and the Captain Montalvo, to whom she was said to have taken a great fancy. When he went to call at the house in the Bree Straat, he was told that both Lysbeth and his cousin Clara had gone out sleighing, a lie that he did not believe, for as a thaw had set in the snow was no longer in a condition suitable to that amusement. Moreover, he could almost have sworn that, as he crossed the street, he caught sight of Cousin Clara's red face peeping at him from between the curtains of the upstairs sitting-room. Indeed he said as much to Greta, who, contrary to custom, had opened the door to him.

"I am sorry if Mynheer sees visions," answered that young woman calmly. "I told Mynheer that the ladies had gone out sleighing."

"I know you did, Greta; but why should they go out sleighing in a wet thaw?"

"I don't know, Mynheer. Ladies do those things that please

them. It is not my place to ask their reasons."

Dirk looked at Greta, and was convinced that she was lying. He put his hand in his pocket, to find to his disgust that he had forgotten his purse. So the end of it was that he merely said, "Oh, indeed," and went away.

"Great soft-head," reflected Greta, as she watched his retreating form, "he knew I was telling lies, why didn't he push past me, or do anything. Ah! Mynheer Dirk, if you are not careful that Spaniard will take your wind. Well, he is more amusing, that's certain. I am tired of these duck-footed Leydeners, who are reluctant to wink at a donkey lest he should bray, and among such holy folk somebody a little wicked is rather a change. Then Greta, who, it may be remembered, came from Brussels, and had French blood in her veins, went upstairs to make a report to her mistress, telling her all that passed.

"I did not ask you to speak falsehoods as to my being out sleighing and the rest. I told you to answer that I was not at home, and mind you say the same to the Captain Montalvo if he calls," said Lysbeth as she dismissed her.

In truth she was very upset and angry, and yet ashamed of herself because her decisions had placed her in the position where she was now using deception to avoid dealing with her problems. But things had gone so horribly wrong, and as for Dirk, he was the most exasperating person in the world. It was owing to his bad management and lack of readiness that her name was coupled with Montalvo's at every table in Leyden. And now what did she hear in a note from the Captain himself, sent to make excuses for not having called upon her after the supper party, but that Dirk was going to dine with him that night? Very well, let him do it; she would know how to pay him back. If necessary, she was ready to respond to any situation he had chosen to create.

Thus thought Lysbeth, stamping her foot with vexation, but all the time her heart was heavy with guilt and remorse. All the time she knew well enough that she loved Dirk, and, however strange might be his backwardness in speaking out his mind, that he loved her. And yet she felt as though a river was running between them. In the beginning it had been a tiny stream, but now it was growing to a torrent. Worse still, the Spaniard was upon her bank of the river.

After he had to some extent conquered his shyness and irritation, Dirk became aware that he was really enjoying his dinner at Montalvo's quarters. There were three guests besides himself, two Spanish officers and a young Netherlander of his own class and age, Brant by name. He was the only son of a noted and very wealthy goldsmith at The Hague, who had sent him to study certain mysteries of the metal worker's art under a Leyden jeweler famous for the exquisite beauty of his designs. The dinner and the service were both of them perfect in style, but better than either proved the conversation, which was of a character that Dirk had never heard at the tables of his own class and people. Not that there was anything even broad about it, as might perhaps have been expected. No, it was the talk of highly accomplished and traveled men of the world who had seen much and been actors in many moving events; men who were, above all things, desirous of making themselves agreeable and instructive to the stranger within their gates. The Heer Brant also, who had but just arrived in Leyden, showed himself an able and polished man, one that had been educated more thoroughly than was usual among his class, and who, at the table of his father, the opulent Burgemeester of The Hague, from his youth had associated with all classes and conditions of men. Indeed, it was there that he made the acquaintance of Montalvo, who recognizing him in the street had asked him to dinner. After the dishes were cleared, one of the Spanish officers rose and begged to be excused, pleading some military duty. When he had saluted his commandant and gone, Montalvo suggested that they should play a game of cards. This was an invitation which Dirk would have liked to decline, but when it came to the point he did not, for fear of seeming peculiar in the eyes of these brilliant men of the world.

So they began to play, and as the game was simple very soon he picked up the points of it, and what is more, found them amusing. At first the stakes were not high, but they doubled themselves in some automatic fashion, until Dirk was astonished to find that he was gambling for considerable sums and winning them. Towards the last his winning streak changed a little, but when the game came to an end he found himself the richer by about three hundred and fifty florins.

"What am I to do with this?" he asked coloring up, as with sighs, which in one instance were genuine enough, the losers pushed the money across to him.

"Do with it?" laughed Montalvo, "did anybody ever hear such an innocent! Why, buy your lady-love, or somebody else's lady-love, a present. No, I'll tell you a better use than this, you give us tomorrow night at your lodging the best dinner that Leyden can produce, and a chance of winning some of this coin back again. Is it agreed?"

"If the other gentlemen wish it," said Dirk, modestly, "though my apartment is but a poor place for such company."

"Of course we wish it," replied the three as with one voice, and the hour for meeting having been fixed, they parted, the Heer Brant walking with Dirk to the door of his lodging.

"I was going to call on you tomorrow," said Brant, "to bring to you a letter of introduction from my father, though that should scarcely be needed as, in fact, our mothers having been first cousins, means that we are second cousins."

"Oh, yes, Brant of The Hague, of whom my mother used to speak, saying that they were kinsmen to be proud of, although she had met them but little. Well, welcome, Cousin; I trust that we shall be friends."

"I am sure of it," answered Brant, and putting his arm through Dirk's, he pressed it in a peculiar fashion that caused him to start and look round. "Hush!" whispered Brant, "not here," and they began to talk of their recent companions and the game of cards which they had played, an amusement as to the propriety of which Dirk intimated that he had doubts.

Young Brant shrugged his shoulders. "Cousin," he said, "we live in the world, so it is as well to understand the world. If the risking of a few pieces at play, which it will not ruin us to lose, helps us to understand it, well, for my part I am ready to risk them, especially as it puts us on good terms with those who, under the circumstances, we need to know. Only, Cousin, if I may venture to say it, be careful not to take more wine than you can carry with discretion. Better lose a thousand florins than let drop one word that you cannot remember."

"I know, I agree," answered Dirk, thinking of Lysbeth's supper, and at the door of his lodgings they parted.

Like most Netherlanders, when Dirk made up his mind to do anything, he did it thoroughly. Thus, having undertaken to give a dinner party, he determined to give a good dinner. In ordinary circumstances his first idea would have been to consult his cousins, Clara and Lysbeth. After that ridiculous story about the sleighing, however, which by inquiry from the coachman of the house whom he happened to meet, he ascertained to be perfectly false, this, he did not feel inclined to do. So, in place of it, he talked first to his landlady, a worthy dame, and by her advice afterwards with the first innkeeper of Leyden, a man of resource and experience. The innkeeper, well knowing that this customer would pay for anything he ordered, threw himself into the affair heartily, with the result that by five o'clock relays of cooks and other attendants were to be seen streaming up Dirk's staircase, carrying every variety of dish that could be supposed to tempt the appetite of high class cavaliers.

Dirk's apartment consisted of two rooms situated upon the first floor of an old house in a street that had ceased to be fashionable. Once, however, it had been a fine house, and the rooms themselves were fine, especially the sitting chamber, which was oak-paneled, low, and spacious, with a handsome fireplace carrying the arms of its builder. Out of it opened his sleeping room—which had no other doorway—likewise oak-paneled, with tall cupboards built into the wall, and a magnificent carved bedstead, not unlike the canopy of a tomb in shape and general appearance.

The hour came, and with it the guests. The feast began, the cooks streamed up and down bearing relays of dishes from the inn. Above the table hung a six-armed brass chandelier, and in each of its sockets glowed a tallow candle furnishing light to the company beneath, although outside of its bright ring there was shadow more or less dense. Towards the end of dinner, a portion of the rush wick of one of these candles fell into the brass saucer beneath, causing the molten grease to burn up fiercely. As it chanced, by the light of this sudden flare, Montalvo, who was sitting opposite to the door, thought that he caught sight of a tall, dark figure gliding along the wall towards the bedroom. For one instant he saw it, then it was gone.

"*Caramba*, my friend," he said, addressing Dirk, whose back was turned towards the figure, "have you any ghosts in this gloomy old room of yours? Because, if so, I think I have just seen one."

"Ghosts!" answered Dirk. "No, I never heard of any. I do not believe in ghosts. Take some more of that pasty."

Montalvo took some more pasty, and washed it down with a glass of wine. But he said no more about ghosts—perhaps an explanation for the phenomenon had occurred to him. At any rate, he decided to leave the subject alone.

After the dinner they gambled, and this evening the stakes began where those of the previous night left off. For the first hour Dirk lost, then the game turned and he won heavily, but always from Montalvo.

"My friend," said the captain at last, throwing down his cards, "certainly you are fated to be successful in your gaming adventures, for the devil lives in your dice-box, and it is time for me to bow out. I pass," and he rose from the table.

"I pass also," said Dirk following him into the window place, for he wished to take no more money. "You have been very unlucky, Count," he said.

"Very, indeed, my young friend," answered Montalvo, yawning, "in fact, for the next six months I must live on—well, well, nothing, except the recollection of your excellent dinner."

"I am sorry," responded Dirk, confusedly, "I did not wish to take your money. It was the turn of those accursed dice. See here, let us say no more about it."

"Sir," said Montalvo, with a sudden sternness, "an officer and a gentleman cannot treat a debt of honor in such a fashion. But," he added with a little laugh, "if another gentleman chances to be good enough to change a debt of honor for a debt of honor, the affair is different. If, for instance, it would suit you to lend me four hundred florins, which, added to the six hundred which I have lost tonight, would make a thousand in all, well, it will be a convenience to me, though should it be any inconvenience to you, pray do not think of such a thing."

"Certainly," answered Dirk, "I have won nearly as much as that, and here at my own table. Take them, I beg of you, captain," and emptying a roll of gold into his hand, he counted it with the skill of a merchant, and held it towards him.

Montalvo hesitated. Then he took the money, pouring it carelessly into his pocket.

"You have not checked the sum," said Dirk.

"My friend, it is needless," answered his guest, "your word is rather better than any bond," and again he yawned, remarking that it was getting late.

Dirk waited a few moments, thinking in his coarse, business-like way that the noble Spaniard might wish to say something about a written acknowledgment. As, however, this did not seem to occur to him, and the matter was not one of ordinary affairs, he led the way back to the table, where the other two were now showing their skill in card tricks.

A few minutes later the two Spaniards took their departure, leaving Dirk and his cousin Brant alone.

"A very successful evening," said Brant, "and, cousin, you won a great deal."

"Yes," answered Dirk, "but all the same I am a poorer man than I was yesterday."

Brant laughed. "Did he borrow from you?" he asked. "Well, I thought he would, and what's more, don't you count on that money. Montalvo is a good sort of fellow in his own fashion, but he is an extravagant man and a desperate gambler with a long history, I also cannot find anyone who knows much about him, not even his brother officers. If you ask them, they shrug their shoulders and say that Spain is a big kettle full of all sorts of fish. One thing I do know, however, that he is over head and ears in debt; indeed, there was trouble about it down at The Hague. So, Cousin, don't you play with him more than you can help, and don't reckon on that thousand florins to pay your bills with. It is a mystery to me how the man gets on, but I am told that a foolish old vrouw in Amsterdam lent him a lot until she discovered—but there, I don't need to say more. And now, he added, changing his voice, "is this place private?"

"Let's see," said Dirk, "they have cleared the things away, and the old housekeeper has tidied up my bedroom. Yes, I think so. Nobody ever comes up here after ten o'clock. What is it?"

Brant touched his arm, and, understanding the touch, Dirk led the way into the window-place. There, standing with his back to the room, and his hands crossed in a peculiar fashion, he uttered the word, "Jesus," and paused. Brant also crossed his hands and answered, or, rather, continued, "wept." It was the password of those of the Reformation Faith.

"You are one of us, Cousin?" said Dirk.

"I and all my house, my father, my mother, my sister, and the maiden whom I am to marry. They told me at The Hague that I must seek of you or the young Heer Pieter van de Werff, knowledge of those things which we of the Faith need to know; who are to be trusted, and who are not to be trusted; where prayer is held, and where we may partake of the pure Sacrament of God the Son."

Dirk took his cousin's hand and pressed it. The pressure was returned, and from that point brother could not have trusted brother more completely, for now between them was the bond of a common and burning faith. To be a member of the Reformation Faith in the Netherlands under the awful rule of Charles the Emperor and Philip the King was to be one of a vast family. It was not "sir" or "mistress" or "madame," it was "my father" and "my mother," or "my sister" and "my brother." Yes, and between people who were of very different status and almost strangers in the flesh, such were still brethren in spirit.

It should come as no surprise that in these circumstances Dirk and Brant, already liking each other, and being already connected by blood, were not slow in coming to a complete understanding and fellowship.

There they sat in the window-place telling each other of their families, their hopes and fears, and even of their ladyloves. In this, as in every other respect, Hendrik Brant's story was one of simple prosperity. He was betrothed to a lady of The Hague, the only daughter of a wealthy wine merchant, who, according to his account, seemed to be as beautiful as she was good and rich, and they were to be married in the spring. But when Dirk told him of his current circumstance, he shook his wise young head.

"You say that both she and her aunt are Catholics? he asked.

"Yes, Cousin, this is the trouble. I think that she is fond of me, or, at any rate, she was until a few days since," he added ruefully, "but how can I, being a 'heretic,' ask her to pledge her hand to me unless I tell her? And that, you know, is against the rule. Indeed, I scarcely dare to do so."

"Had you not best consult with some godly elder who by prayer and words may move your lady's heart until the light shines on her?" asked Brant.

"Cousin, it has been done, but always there is the other in the way, that red-nosed Aunt Clara, who is a mad idolater; also there is the serving-woman, Greta, whom I take for little better than a spy. Therefore, between the two of them I see little chance that Lysbeth will ever hear the truth this side of marriage. And yet how dare I marry her? Is it right that I should marry her and dishonor God's command regarding being equally yoked in the Lord? Can I also risk bringing her to the same dreadful fate that may wait for you or me? Moreover, now since this man Montalvo has crossed my path, all things seem to have gone wrong between me and Lysbeth; indeed but yesterday her door was shut on me."

"Women have their fancies," answered Brant, slowly. "Perhaps he has taken hers. She would not be the first who walked that plank. Or, perhaps, she is vexed with you for not speaking out before this; for, man, not knowing what you are, how can she read your mind?"

"Perhaps, perhaps," said Dirk, "but I know not what to do,"

and in his perplexity he struck his forehead with his hand.

"Then, Brother, in that case what keeps you from asking Him Who can tell you?" said Brant, calmly.

Dirk understood what he meant at once. "It is a wise thought, and a good one, Cousin. I have the Holy Scriptures near at hand, but, first let us pray, and then we can seek wisdom there."

"You are rich, indeed," answered Brant. "Sometime you must tell me how and where you came by it."

"Here in Leyden, if one can afford to pay for them, such goods are not hard to get," said Dirk. "What is hard is to keep them safely, for to be found with a Bible in your pocket is to carry your own death-warrant."

Brant nodded. "Is it safe to show it here?" he asked.

"As safe as anywhere, Cousin; the window is shuttered, the door is, or will be, locked, but who can say that he is safe this side of the stake in a land where the rats and mice carry news and the winds bear witness? Come, I will show you where I keep it," and going to the mantelpiece he took down a candle-stick, made of quaint brass, ornamented on its massive oblong base with two copper snails, and lit the candle. "Do you like the piece?" he asked. "It is my own design, which I cast and filed out in my spare hours," and he gazed at the holder with the affection of an artist. Then without waiting for an answer, he led the way to the door of his sitting-room and paused.

"What is it?" asked Brant.

"I thought I heard a sound, that is all," responded Dirk, "but doubtless the old vrouw moves upon the stairs. Turn the key, Cousin, so that we can get in."

They entered the sleeping chamber, and having glanced round and made sure that it was empty, and the window shut, Dirk went to the head of the bed; which was formed of oak-panels, the center one carved with a magnificent coat-of-arms, similar to the one that was on the fireplace in the sitting-room. At this panel Dirk began to work, until presently it slid aside, revealing a hollow, out of which he took a book bound in boards covered with leather. Then, having closed the panel, the two young men returned to the sitting-room, and placed the volume upon the oak table beneath the chandelier.

"First let us pray," said Brant.

It seems curious, does it not, that two flawed young men, as a finale to a dinner party where a gambling match had taken place, should suggest kneeling side by side to offer prayers to their Maker before they studied the Scriptures? But then, in those days, prayer, now so common (and so neglected) an exercise, was an actual privilege and luxury. To these sincere yet immature men, it was a joy to be able to kneel and offer thanks and petitions to God, believing themselves to be safe from the sword of those who worshipped otherwise. Thus it came about that spiritual communion with their Lord and Savior Jesus Christ, was to them a very real and earnest thing, a thing to be indulged in at every opportunity with solemn and grateful hearts. So there, beneath the light of the flickering candles, they knelt side by side while Brant, speaking for both of them, offered up a prayer—a sight touching enough and in its way beautiful.

The words of his personal and heart-felt petition do not need to be repeated. It is enough to know that he prayed for their Church; he prayed for their country that it might be made strong and free; he even prayed for the Emperor, the carnal, hare-lipped, guzzling, yet able Hapsburg self-seeker. Then he prayed for themselves and all who were dear to them, and lastly, that light might be swiftly granted to Dirk in his present difficulty. No, not quite lastly, for he ended with a petition that their enemies might be forgiven, yes, even those who tortured them and burnt them at the stake, since they knew not what they did. It may be wondered whether any human aspirations could have been more thoroughly steeped in the true spirit of Christianity.

When at length he had finished, they rose from their knees.

"Shall I open the Book at random?" asked Dirk, "and read what my eye falls on?"

"No," answered Brant, "for it savors of superstition, thus did the ancients with the writings of the poet Virgilius, and it is not fitting that we who hold the light should follow the example of those blind heathen. What work of the Book, Brother, are you studying now?"

"The first letter of Paul to the Corinthians, which I had never read before," he answered.

"Then begin where you left off, Brother, and read your chapter. Perhaps we may find instruction in it; if not, no answer is ordained for us tonight."

So from the black-letter volume before him, Dirk began to read the seventh chapter, in which, as it turns out, the great Apostle deals with the marriage state. On he read, in a quiet even voice, until he came to the following verses, of which the last several read:

> But I would have you without carefulness. He that is unmarried careth for the things that belong to the Lord, how he may please the Lord: But he that is married careth for the things that are of the world, how he may please his wife. There is difference also between a wife and a virgin. The unmarried woman careth for the things of the Lord, that she may be holy both in body and in spirit: but she that is married careth for the things of the world, how she may please her husband. And this I speak for your own profit; not that I may cast a snare upon you, but for that which is comely, and that ye may attend upon the Lord without distraction. But if any man think that he behaveth himself uncomely toward his virgin, if she pass the flower of her age, and need so require, let him do what he will, he sinneth not: let them marry. Nevertheless he that standeth stedfast in his heart, having no necessity, but hath power over his own will, and hath so decreed in his heart that he will keep his virgin, doeth well. So then he that giveth her in marriage doeth well; but he that giveth her not in marriage doeth better. The wife is bound by the law as long as her husband liveth; but if her husband be dead she is at liberty to be married to whom she will; only in the Lord.

Dirk's voice trembled, and he paused.

"Continue to the end of the chapter," said Brant, so the reader went on.

As he finished reading, there was a sound. They did not hear it, but the door of the bedchamber behind them opened ever so little. They did not see it, but between door and lintel some-

thing white thrust itself, a woman's white face crowned with black hair, and set in it two evil, staring eyes. Surely, when first he raised his head in Eden, Satan might have worn such a countenance as this. It cranes itself forward until the long, thin neck seems to stretch; then suddenly a stir or a movement alarms it, and back the face draws like the crest of a startled snake. Back it draws, and the door closes again.

The chapter is read, the prayer is prayed, and strange may seem the answer to that prayer, an answer to shake out faith from the hearts of men; men who are impatient, who do not know that as the light takes long in traveling from a distant star, so the answer from the Throne to the supplication of trust may be long in coming. It may not come today or tomorrow. It may not come in this generation or this century; the prayer of today may receive its crown when the children's children of the lips that uttered it have in their turn vanished in the dust. And yet that Divine reply may in no wise be delayed; even as our liberty of this hour may be the fruit of those who died when Dirk van Goorl and Hendrik Brant walked upon the earth; even as the vengeance that but now is falling on the Spaniard may be the reward of the deeds of shame that he worked upon them and upon their kin long generations gone. For the Throne is still the Throne, and the star is still the star; from the one flows justice and from the other light, and to them time and space are naught.

Dirk finished the chapter and closed the Book.

"It seems that you have your answer, brother," said Brant quietly.

"Yes," replied Dirk, "it is written clear enough in verse 39 that marriage is to be only 'in the Lord,' that is, between those who have a common bond of faith. Verses twenty-six and twenty-seven also warn people who are living in times of persecution and civil unrest to refrain, as much as possible, from entering into the covenant of marriage. Had the Apostle foreseen my case he could not have set the matter forth more clearly."

"He, or the Spirit in him, knew all cases, and wrote for every man that ever shall be born," answered Brant. "This is a lesson to us. Had you looked sooner you would have learned sooner, and perhaps much trouble might have been spared. As it is, without doubt you must determine to speak to her regarding her relationship with God before you seek her hand in marriage. Your duty now is to make the gospel of Christ clear to Lysbeth, leaving the rest with God."

"Yes," said Dirk, "so soon as may be, but there is one thing more; ought I tell her all the truth?"

"I should not be careful to hide it, friend, and now, good night. No, do not come to the door with me. Who can tell, there may be watchers without, and it is not wise that we should be seen together so late."

When his cousin and new-found friend had gone, Dirk sat for a while, until the glowing tallow lights overhead burned to the sockets indeed. Then, taking the candle from the snail-adorned holder, he lit it, and, having extinguished those in the chandeliers, went into his bedroom and undressed himself. The Bible he returned to its hiding-place and closed the panel, after which he blew out the light and climbed into the tall bed.

As a rule, Dirk was a most excellent sleeper; when he laid his head on the pillow his eyes closed nor did they open again until the appointed and accustomed hour. But this night he could not sleep. Whether it was the dinner or the wine, or the gambling, or the prayer and the searching of the Scriptures with his cousin Brant, the result remained the same; he was very wakeful, which annoyed him the more as a child of God who knew what it was like to cast all of his cares upon the Lord. Still, as vexation would not make him sleep, he lay awake watching the moonlight flood the chamber and thinking.

Somehow, as Dirk continued to ponder his uneasy spirit, he grew afraid; it seemed to him as though he shared that place with another presence, an evil and malignant presence. Never before in his life had he troubled over or been troubled by tales of spirits, yet now he remembered Montalvo's remark about a ghost, and he certainly felt as though one were with him there. In the midst of his growing fear, he sought for comfort and could think of none save that which an old and simple pastor had recommended to him in all hours of doubt and danger, namely, if it could be had, to clasp a Bible to his heart and pray.

Well, both things were easy. Raising himself in bed, in a moment he had taken the Bible from its hiding-place and closed the panel. Then pressing it against his breast between himself and the mattress he lay down again. It would seem that the method worked, for soon he was asleep.

Yet Dirk dreamt a very evil dream. He dreamed that a tall black figure leaned over him, and that a long white hand was stretched out to his headboard where it wandered to and fro, until at last he heard the panel slide home with a rattling noise. Then it seemed to him that he woke, and that his eyes met two eyes bent down over him, eyes which searched him as though they would read the very secrets of his heart. He did not stir, he could not, but in this dream of his, the figure straightened itself and glided away, appearing and disappearing as it crossed the bars of moonlight until it vanished by the door.

A while later and Dirk woke up in truth, to find that although the night was cold enough the sweat ran in big drops from his brow and body. But now strangely enough his fear was gone, and, knowing that he had but dreamed a dream, he turned over, touched the Bible on his breast, and fell sleeping like a child, to be awakened only by the light of the rising winter sun pouring on his face.

Then Dirk remembered that dream of the bygone night, and his heart grew heavy, for it seemed to him that this vision of a dark woman searching his face with those dreadful eyes was a portent of evil not far away.

CHAPTER VI
THE BETROTHAL OF LYSBETH

On the following morning, when Montalvo entered his private room after breakfast, he found a lady awaiting him, in whom, notwithstanding the long cloak and veil she wore, he had little difficulty in recognizing as Black Meg. In fact, Black Meg had been waiting some while, and being a person of industrious habits, she had not neglected to use her time to the best advantage.

The reader may remember that when Meg visited the cunning Captain Montalvo upon a previous occasion, she had taken the liberty of helping herself to certain papers which she found lying just inside an unlocked desk. These papers on examination, as she feared might be the case, for the most part proved to be quite unimportant—unpaid accounts, military reports, a billet or two from ladies, and so forth. But in thinking the matter over, Black Meg remembered that this desk had another part to it, which seemed to be locked, and, therefore, just in case they should prove useful, she took with her a few skeleton keys and one or two little instruments of steel and visited her noble patron at an hour when she believed that he would be at breakfast in another room. Things went well; he was at breakfast and she was left alone in the chamber with the desk. The rest may be guessed. Replacing the worthless bundle in the unlocked part, by the aid of her keys and instruments she opened the inner half. There sure enough were letters hidden, and in a little drawer two miniatures framed in gold, one of a lady, young and pretty with dark eyes, and the other of two children, a boy and a girl of five or six years of age. Also, there was a curling lock of hair labeled in Montalvo's writing, "Juanita's hair, which she gave me as a keepsake."

Here was treasure, indeed, which Black Meg did not fail to appropriate for herself. Thrusting the letters and other articles into the bosom of her dress to be examined at leisure, she was clever enough, before closing and relocking the desk, to replace them with a dummy bundle, hastily made up from some papers that lay about.

When everything had been satisfactorily arranged, she went outside and chatted for a while with the soldier on guard, only re-entering the room by one door as Montalvo appeared in it through the other.

"Well, my friend," he said, "have you the evidence?"

"I have some evidence, Excellency," she answered. "I was present at the dinner that you ate last night, although none of it came my way, and I was present afterwards."

"Indeed, I thought I saw you slip in, and allow me to congratulate you on that; it was very well thought out and done, just as folk were moving up and down the stairs. Also, when I went home, I believe that I recognized a gentleman in the street whom, I have been given to understand, you honor with your friendship—a short, stout person with a bald head; let me see, he was called the Butcher at The Hague, was he not? No, do not pout, I have no wish to pry into the secrets of ladies, but still in my position here it is my business to know a thing or two. Well, what did you see?"

"Excellency, I saw the young man I was sent to watch and Hendrik Brant, the son of the rich goldsmith at The Hague, praying side by side upon their knees."

"That is bad, very bad," said Montalvo shaking his head, but—

"I saw," she went on in her hoarse voice, "the pair of them read the Bible."

"How shocking!" replied Montalvo with a simulated shudder. "Think of it, my orthodox friend, if you are to be believed, these two persons, hitherto supposed to be respectable, have been discovered in the crime of consulting that work upon which our Faith is founded. Well, those who could read anything so dull must, indeed, as the edicts tell us, be monsters unworthy to live.

But, if you please, your proofs. Of course you have this book?"

Then Black Meg poured forth all her tale—how she had watched and seen something, how she had listened and heard little, how she had gone to the secret panel, bending over the sleeping man, and found nothing.

"You are a poor sort of spy, Mother," commented the captain when she had done, "and, upon my soul, I do not believe that even a Papal inquisitor could hang that young fellow on your evidence. You must go back and get some more."

"No," answered Black Meg with decision, "if you want to force your way into conventicles, you had best do it yourself. As I wish to go on living, this is no job for me. I have proved to you that this young man is a heretic, so now give me my reward."

"Your reward? Ah! Your reward. No, I think not at present, for a reward presupposes services—and I see none."

Black Meg began to storm.

"Be silent," said Montalvo, dropping his bantering tone. "Look, I will be frank with you. I do not want to burn anybody. I am sick of all this nonsense about religion; and for aught I care, every Netherlander in Leyden may read the Bible until he grows tired. I seek to marry the Jufvrouw Lysbeth van Hout, and to do this I desire to prove that the man whom she loves, Dirk van Goorl, is a heretic. What you have told me may or may not be sufficient for my purpose. If it is sufficient, you shall be paid liberally after my marriage; if not, well, you have had enough. As for your evidence, for my part, I may say that I do not believe a word of it, for were it true you would have brought the Bible."

As he spoke he rang a bell which stood upon a table, and before Meg could answer, the soldier appeared.

"Show this good woman out," he said, adding, in a loud voice, "Mother, I will do my best for you and forward your petition to the proper quarter. Meanwhile, take this trifle in charity," and he pressed a florin into her hand. "Now, guard, the prisoners, the prisoners. I have no time to waste—and listen, let me be troubled with no more beggars, or you will hear of it."

That afternoon Dirk, filled with a solemn purpose, and dressed in his best suit, called at the house in the Bree Straat, where the door was again opened by Greta, who looked at him expectantly.

"Is your mistress in?" he stammered. "I have come to see your mistress."

"Alas! Mynheer," answered the young woman, "you are just too late. My mistress and her aunt, the Vrouw Clara, have gone away to stay for a week or ten days as the Vrouw Clara's health required a change."

"Indeed," said Dirk aghast, "and where have they gone?"

"Oh! Mynheer, I do not know that, they did not tell me," and no other answer could he extract from her.

So Dirk went away frustrated and upset. An hour later the Captain Montalvo called, and strange to say proved more fortunate. By hook or by crook, he obtained the address of the ladies, who were visiting, it appeared, at a seaside village within the limits of a ride. By a curious coincidence that very afternoon Montalvo, also seeking rest and change of air, appeared at the inn of this village, giving it out that he proposed to lodge there for a while.

As he walked upon the beach on the next day, whom should he happen to meet but the Vrouw Clara van Ziel, and never did the worthy Clara spend a more pleasant morning. So, at least, she declared to Lysbeth when she brought her escort back to dinner.

The reader may guess the rest. Montalvo eventually sought to propose to Lysbeth, and in due course Montalvo was refused. He bore the blow with a tender resignation.

"Confess, dear lady," he said, "that there is some other man more fortunate."

Lysbeth did not confess, but, on the other hand, neither did she deny.

"If he makes you happy, I shall be more than satisfied," the Count insincerely stated, "but, lady, loving you as I do, I do not wish to see you married to a heretic."

"What do you mean, Señor?" asked Lysbeth, bridling.

"Alas!" he answered, "I mean that, as I fear, the worthy Heer

Dirk van Goorl, a friend of mine for whom I have every respect, although he has outstripped me in your regard, has fallen into that evil net."

"Such accusations should not be made," said Lysbeth sternly, "unless they can be proved. Even then," and she stopped.

"I will inquire further," replied the Count. "For myself, I accept the position, that is until you learn to love me, if such should be my fortune. Meanwhile, I beg of you at least to look upon me as a friend, a true friend who would lay down his life to serve you."

Then, with many a sigh, Montalvo departed home to Leyden upon his beautiful black horse, but not before he had enjoyed a few minutes of earnest conversation with the worthy Tante Clara.

"Now, if only this old lady were concerned," he reflected as he rode away, "the matter might be easy enough, and the Saints know it would be won to me, but unhappily that obstinate pig of a Hollander girl has all the money in her own right. In what labors do not the necessities of rank and station involve a man who by disposition requires only ease and quiet! Well, my young friend Lysbeth, if I do not make you pay for these exertions before you are two months older, my name is not Juan de Montalvo."

Three days later the ladies returned to Leyden. Within an hour of their arrival, the Count called and was admitted. "Stay with me," said Lysbeth to her Aunt Clara, as the visitor was announced, and for a while she stayed. Then, making an excuse, she vanished from the room, and Lysbeth was left face-to-face with her tormentor.

"Why do you come here?" she asked. "I have given you my answer."

"I come for your own sake," he replied, "to give you my reasons for conduct which you may think strange. You remember a certain conversation?"

"Perfectly," broke in Lysbeth.

"A slight mistake, I think, Jufvrouw, I mean a conversation about an excellent friend of yours, whose spiritual affairs seem to interest you."

"What of it, Señor?"

"Only this. I have made inquiries, and—"

Lysbeth looked up unable to conceal her anxiety.

"Oh! Jufvrouw, let me beg of you to learn to control your expression. The open face of childhood is so dangerous in these days."

"He is my cousin," stated Lysbeth in a perturbed tone.

"I know. Were he anything more, I should be so grieved, but we can most of us spare a cousin or two."

"If you would cease amusing yourself, Señor—"

"And come to the point? Of course I will. Well, the result of my inquiries has been to find out that this worthy person is a heretic of the most pernicious sort. I said inquiries, but there was no need for me to make any. He has been—"

"Not denounced," broke in Lysbeth.

"Oh, my dear lady, again that tell-tale emotion from which all sorts of things might be concluded. Yes—denounced, but fortunately to myself as a person appointed under the Edict. It will, I fear, be my sad duty to have him arrested this evening—but I shall not deal with the case myself. Indeed, I propose to pass him over to the worthy Ruard Tapper, the Papal Inquisitor, you know—every one has heard of the unpleasant Tapper—who is to visit Leyden next week, and who, no doubt, will make short work of him."

"What has he done?" asked Lysbeth in a low voice, and bending down her head to hide the working of her features.

"Done? My dear lady, it is almost too dreadful to tell you. This misguided and unfortunate young man, with another person whom the witnesses have not been able to identify, was seen at midnight reading the Bible."

"The Bible! Why should that be wrong?"

"Hush! Are you also a heretic? Do you not know that all this heresy springs from the reading of the Bible? You see, the Bible is a very strange book. It seems that there are many things in it which, when read by an ordinary layman, appear to mean this or that. When read by a consecrated priest, however, they mean something quite different. In the same way, there are many doctrines which the layman cannot find in the Bible that to the consecrated eye are plain as the sun and the moon. The difference between heresy and orthodoxy is, in short, the difference between what can actually be found in the letter of this remarkable work and what is really there—according to their holinesses."

"Almost thou persuadest me—" began Lysbeth bitterly.

There came a long pause.

"What will happen to him?" asked Lysbeth.

"After—after the usual painful preliminaries to discover accomplices, I presume the stake, but possibly, as he has the freedom of Leyden, he might get off with hanging."

"Is there no escape?" questioned the young woman.

Montalvo walked to the window and, looking out of it, remarked that he thought it was going to snow. Then suddenly he wheeled round and, staring hard at Lysbeth, asked, "Are you really interested in this heretic, and do you desire to save him?"

Lysbeth heard and knew at once that this Spanish wolf smelled blood. The bantering, whimsical tone was gone. Now her tormentor's voice was stern and cold, the voice of a man who was playing for great stakes and meant to win them.

She also gave up fencing.

"I am and I do," she answered.

"Then it can be done—at a price."

"What price?"

"Yourself in marriage within three weeks."

Lysbeth quivered slightly, then sat still.

"Would not my fortune do instead?" she asked.

"Oh! What a poor substitute you offer me," Montalvo said, with a return to his hateful banter. Then he added, "That offer might be considered were it not for the abominable laws which you have here. In practice, it would be almost impossible for you to hand over any large sum, much of which is represented by real estate, to a man who is not your husband. Therefore, I am afraid, I must stipulate that you and your possessions shall not be separated."

Again Lysbeth sat silent. Montalvo, watching her with genuine interest, noted signs of rebellion, fueled by her despair. He saw the woman's mental and physical loathing of himself conquering her fears for Dirk. Unless he was much mistaken, she was about to defy him, which, as a matter of fact, would have proved exceedingly awkward, as his financial resources were exhausted. Also, on the very insufficient evidence that he possessed, he would not have dared to touch Dirk, and thus make to himself a thousand powerful enemies.

"It is strange," he said, "that the irony of circumstances should reduce me to pleading for a rival. But, Lysbeth van Hout, before you answer I beg you to think. Upon the next movements of your lips it depends whether that body you love shall be stretched upon the rack, whether those eyes which you find pleasant shall grow blind with agony in the darkness of a dungeon, and whether that flesh which you think desirable shall scorch and wither in the furnace. Or, on the other hand, whether none of these things shall happen, whether this young man shall go free, to be for a month or two a little upset, a little bitter about the inconstancy of women, and then to marry some opulent and respected heretic. Surely you could scarcely hesitate. Oh! Where is the self-sacrificing spirit of the sex of which we hear so much? Choose."

Still there was no answer. Montalvo, playing his trump card, drew from his vest an official-looking document, sealed and signed.

"This," he said, "is the information to be given to the incorruptible Ruard Tapper. Look, here written on it is your cousin's name. My servant waits for me in your kitchen. If you hesitate any longer, I call him and in your presence charge him to hand that paper to the messenger who starts this afternoon for Brussels. Once given, it cannot be recalled and the pious Dirk's doom is sealed."

Lysbeth's spirit began to break. "How can I?" she asked. "It is true that we are not engaged. Perhaps for this very reason that I now learn. But he cares for me and knows that I care for him.

Must I then, in addition to the loss of him, be remembered all his life as little better than a shallow woman caught by the tricks and glitter of such a man as you?"

Again Montalvo went to the window, for this hint of rebellion was most disconcerting. No one can marry a despondent woman, and Lysbeth was scarcely likely to leave a will in his favor. It seemed that what troubled her particularly was the fear lest the young man should think her conduct light. Well, why should she not give him a reason which he would be the first to acknowledge as excellent for breaking with him? Could she, a Catholic, be expected to wed a heretic, and could he not be made to tell her that he was a heretic?

Behold an answer to his question! The Saints themselves, desiring that this pearl of price should continue to rest in the bosom of the true Church, had interfered in his behalf, for there in the street below was Dirk van Goorl approaching Lysbeth's door. Yes, there he was dressed in his best burgher's suit, his brow knit with thought, his step hesitating; a very picture of the timid, doubtful lover.

"Lysbeth van Hout," said the Count, turning to her, "as it chances the Heer Dirk van Goorl is at your door. You will admit him, and this matter can be settled one way or the other. I wish to point out to you how needless it is that the young man should be left believing that you have treated him ill. All that is necessary is that you should ask whether or not he is of your faith. If I know him, he will not lie to you. Then it remains only for you to say—for doubtless the man comes here to seek your hand, that however much it may grieve you to give such an answer, you can take no heretic to be your husband. Do you understand?"

Lysbeth bowed her head.

"Then listen. You will admit your suitor; you will allow him to make his offer to you now, if he is so inclined; you will, before giving any answer, ask him of his faith. If he replies that he is a heretic, you will dismiss him as kindly as you wish. If he replies that he is a true servant of the Church, you will say that you have heard a different tale and must have time to make inquiries. Remember also that if by one jot you do otherwise than I have bid you, when Dirk van Goorl leaves the room you see him for the last time, unless it pleases you to attend his execution. Whereas if you obey and dismiss him finally, as the door shuts behind him, I will put this information in the fire and satisfy you that the evidence upon which it is based is forever gone."

Lysbeth gave him a questioning look.

"I see you are wondering how I should know what you do or do not do. It is simple, I shall be the harmless but observant witness of your interview. Over this doorway hangs a tapestry; you will grant me the privilege—not a great one for a future husband—of stepping behind it."

"Never, never," said Lysbeth, "I cannot be put to such a shame. I defy you."

As she spoke came the sound of knocking at the street door. Glancing up at Montalvo, for the second time she saw that look that he had worn at the crisis of the sled race. All its calmness, its careless *bonhomie*, had vanished. Instead of these appeared a reflection of the last and innermost nature of the man, the rock foundation, as it were, upon which was built the false and decorated superstructure that he showed to the world. There were the glaring eyes, there the grinning teeth of the Spanish wolf; a ravening brute ready to rend and tear, if so he might satisfy himself with the meat his soul desired.

"Don't play tricks with me," he shouted, "and don't argue, for there is no time. Do as I bid you, girl, or on your head will be this psalm-singing fellow's blood. And, look you, don't try setting him on me, for I have my sword and he is unarmed. If need be a heretic may be killed on sight, you know, that is by one clothed with authority. When the servant announces him at the door, then order that he is to be admitted," and picking up his plumed hat, which might have betrayed him, Montalvo stepped behind the hanging carpet.

For a moment Lysbeth stood thinking. Alas! She could see no possible escape. She was in the trap, and the rope was about her throat. Either she must obey or, so she thought, she must give the man she loved to a dreadful death. For his sake she would do it, and then trust God to forgive her and avenge Dirk and her at a later season.

Another instant and there came a knock upon the door. She opened it.

"The Heer van Goorl stands below," said the voice of Greta, "wishing to see you, madam."

"Admit him," answered Lysbeth, and going to a chair almost in the center of the room, she seated herself.

Presently Dirk's step sounded on the stair, that known, beloved step for which so often she had listened eagerly. Again the door opened and Greta announced the Heer van Goorl. That she could not see the Captain Montalvo evidently surprised the woman, for her eyes roamed round the room wonderingly, but she was too well trained, or too well bribed, to show her astonishment. Gentlemen of this kind, as Greta had from time to time remarked, have a faculty for vanishing upon occasion.

So Dirk walked into the fateful chamber as some innocent and unsuspecting creature walks into a bitter snare, little knowing that the lady whom he loved and whom he came to ask forgiveness was set as a bait to ruin him.

"Be seated, Cousin," said Lysbeth, in a voice so forced and strained that it caused him to look up. But he saw nothing, for her head was turned away from him, and for the rest his mind was too preoccupied to be observant. By nature simple and open, it would have taken much to wake Dirk into suspicion in the home and presence of his love and cousin, Lysbeth.

"Good day to you, Lysbeth," he said awkwardly, "why, how cold your hand is! I have been trying to find you for some time, but you have always been out or away, leaving no address."

"I have been to the sea with my Aunt Clara," she answered.

Then for a while, five minutes or more, there followed a strained and stilted conversation.

"Will the booby never come to the point?" reflected Montalvo, surveying him through a seam in the tapestry. By the Saints, what a fool he plays!"

"Lysbeth," said Dirk at last, "I want to speak to you about your relationship with Christ."

"Speak on, Cousin," she answered.

"Lysbeth, I—I—have loved you for a long while, and I—have come to ask you to forgive me. I have put off for far too long my duty to challenge you concerning what the Scriptures say about biblical faith, but I can keep silent no longer. This is especially true now when I see that a much finer gentleman is trying to win you—I mean the Spanish count, Montalvo," he added with a jerk.

She said nothing in reply. So Dirk went on pouring out all his honest passion for the Reformation faith in words that momentarily gathered weight and strength, until at length they were eloquent enough. He told her how since first they met he had loved her and only her, and how his one desire in life was to see her come to trust in the work of Christ alone for her salvation. Pausing at length, he began to speak in more detail concerning his biblical beliefs—then she stopped him.

"Your pardon, Dirk," she said, "but I have a question to ask of you," and her voice died away in a kind of sob. "I have heard rumors about you," she went on plainly, "which now appear to be quite true. I have heard, Dirk, that by faith you are what is called a heretic. Is it true?"

He hesitated before answering, feeling that much depended on that answer. But it was only for an instant, since Dirk was far too honest a man to lie.

"Lysbeth," he said, "I came here for the primary purpose of sharing my faith with you in the hope that you would accept my view of the Gospel. This I have done at great risk, although I know well that I am as safe in speaking to you as when upon my knees I speak to the God I serve. I am indeed what you call a heretic. I am a member of that true faith to which I hope to draw you, but which, if you do not wish it I would never seek to press marriage upon you. It is chiefly because I am what I am that for so long I have hung back from speaking to you, since I did not have peace—things being thus—to ask you to mix your lot with mine. Only the other night I sought counsel of—well, never mind of whom, and we prayed together, and together searched the Word of God. Then everything grew clear to me, and I determined to speak. And now, dear, I have spoken, and it is for you to answer. Can you forgive me, and can you learn to

love my new Reformation faith?"

"Dirk, dear Dirk," she replied almost with a cry, "alas, for the answer which I must give you. I cannot leave my church. Renounce the error of your ways, make confession, and be reconciled to the Church or we have no future together. I cannot abandon my beliefs, no, and although I love you, you and no other man," here she put an energy into her voice that was almost dreadful — "with all my heart and soul and body; I cannot, I cannot, I cannot!"

Dirk heard, and his ruddy face turned ashen gray.

"Cousin," he replied, "you seek of me the one thing which I must not give. Even for your sake I may not renounce my vows and my God as I behold Him. Though it break my heart to bid you farewell and live without you, here I pay you back in your own words—I cannot, I cannot!"

Lysbeth looked at him, and his short, massive form and his square-cut, honest countenance in that ardor of renunciation had undergone a change that was as dignified as it was holy. At that moment, to her sight at least, this homely Hollander wore the aspect of an angel. She ground her teeth and pressed her hands upon her heart. "For his sake—to save him," she muttered to herself, then she spoke.

"I respect you for it, I love you for it more than ever but, Dirk, it is over between us. One day, here or hereafter, you will understand and you will forgive."

"So be it," said Dirk hastily, stretching out his hand to find his hat, for he was too blind to see. "It is a strange answer to my prayer, a very strange answer. Doubtless you are right to follow your church as I am sure that I am right to follow mine. We must carry our cross, dear Lysbeth, each of us; you see that we must carry our cross. Please understand, however, that I don't speak as a jealous man, because the thing has gone further than jealousy—I speak as a friend, and come what may while I live you will always find me faithful. I beg of you, beware of the Spaniard, Montalvo. I know that he followed you to the coast. I have heard too he boasts that he will marry you. The man is wicked, although he took me in at first. I feel it, his presence seems to poison the air, yes, this very air I breathe. But I would like him to hear me say it, because I am sure that he is at the bottom of all this, his hour will come. For whatever he does, he will be paid back. He will be paid back here and hereafter. And now, goodbye. God bless you and protect you, dear Lysbeth. It is right for us to avoid getting married, and I know that you will keep my secret. Goodbye again," and lifting her hand Dirk kissed it. Then he stumbled from the room.

As for Lysbeth, she cast herself on the floor at full length, and in the bitterness of her heart dampened the floor with her tears.

When the front door had shut behind Dirk, but not before, Montalvo emerged from his hiding place and stood over the prostrate Lysbeth. He tried to adopt his airy and sarcastic manner, but he was shaken by the scene that he had overheard, shaken and somewhat frightened also, for he felt that he had called into being passions of which the force and fruits could not be calculated.

"Bravo! My little actress," he began, then gave it up and added in his natural voice, "you had best rise and see me burn this paper."

Lysbeth struggled to her knees and watched him thrust the document between two glowing peats.

"I have fulfilled my promise," he said, "and that evidence is done with, but in case you should think of playing any tricks and not fulfilling yours, please remember that I have fresh evidence infinitely more valuable and convincing. With my own ears I heard this worthy gentleman, who is pleased to think so poorly of me, admit that he is a heretic. That is enough to burn him any day, and I swear that if within three weeks we are not man and wife, burn he shall."

While he was speaking Lysbeth had risen slowly to her feet. Now she confronted him, no longer the Lysbeth he had known, but a new being filled like a cup with fury that was the more awful because it was so quiet.

"Juan de Montalvo," she said in a low voice, "your wickedness has won and for Dirk's sake my person and my goods must pay its price. So be it since so it must be, but listen, I make no prophecies about you. I do not say that this or that shall happen to you, but I call down upon you the curse of God."

Then she threw up her hands and began to pray. "God, Whom it has pleased that I should be given to a fate far worse than death; O God, blast the mind and the soul of this monster. Let him henceforth never know a peaceful hour; let misfortune come upon him through me and mine; let fears haunt his sleep. Let him live in heavy labor and die in blood and misery; and if I bear children to him, let the evil be upon them also."

She ceased. Montalvo looked at her and tried to speak. Again he looked and again he tried to speak, but no words would come.

Then the fear of Lysbeth van Hout fell upon him, that fear which was to haunt him all his life. He turned and crept from the room, and his face was like the face of an old man, nor, notwithstanding the height of his immediate success, could his heart have been more heavy if Lysbeth had been an angel sent straight from Heaven to proclaim to him the unalterable doom of God.

CHAPTER VII
HENDRIK BRANT HAS
A VISITOR

Nine months had gone by, and for more than eight of them Lysbeth had been known as the Countess Juan de Montalvo. Indeed of this there could be no doubt, since she was married with some ceremony by the Bishop in the Groote Kerk before the eyes of all men. Folk had wondered much at these hurried nuptials, though some of the more ill-natured shrugged their shoulders and said that when a young woman had compromised herself by long and lonely drives with a Spanish cavalier, and was in consequence dropped by her own admirer, why the best thing she could do was to marry as soon as possible.

So the pair, who looked handsome enough before the altar, were wed, and went to taste of such marital bliss as was reserved for them in Lysbeth's comfortable house in the Bree Straat. Here they lived almost alone, for Lysbeth's countrymen and women showed their disapproval of her conduct by avoiding her company, and, for reasons of his own, Montalvo did not encourage the visiting of Spaniards at his house. Moreover, the servants were changed, while Tante Clara and the girl Greta had also disappeared. Indeed, Lysbeth, finding out the false part which they had played towards her, dismissed them both before her marriage.

It will be guessed that after the events that led to their union, Lysbeth took little pleasure in her husband's company. She was not one of those women who can acquiesce in marriage by fraud or capture, and even learn to love the hand that snared them. So it came about that to Montalvo she spoke very seldom; indeed after the first week of marriage she only saw him on rare occasions. Very soon he found that his presence was hateful to her, and turned her detestation to account with his usual cleverness. In other words, Lysbeth bought freedom by parting with her property. In fact, a regular tariff was established, so many guilders for a week's liberty, so many for a month's.

This was an arrangement that suited Montalvo well enough, for in his heart he was terrified of this woman, whose beautiful face had frozen into a perpetual mask of watchful hatred. He could not forget that frightful curse which had taken deep root in his superstitious mind, and already seemed to flourish there, for it was true that since she spoke it, he had never known a quiet hour. How could he, when he was haunted night and day by fear lest his wife should murder him?

Surely, if ever revenge looked out of a woman's eyes it looked out of hers, and it seemed to him that such a deed might trouble her conscience little; that she might consider it in the light of an execution, and not as a murder. He could not bear to think of it. What would it be to drink his wine one day and then feel a hand of fire gripping at his vitals because poison had been set within the cup; or, worse still, if anything could be worse, to wake at night and find a stiletto point grating against his backbone? Little wonder that Montalvo slept alone and was always careful to lock his door.

He need not have taken such precautions; whatever her eyes might say, Lysbeth had no intention of killing this man. In that prayer of hers, she had placed the matter in the hand of a higher Power, and there she meant to leave it, feeling quite convinced that although vengeance might tarry, it would fall at last. As for her money, he could have it. From the beginning, her instinct told her that her husband's object was not amorous, but purely mercenary; a fact of which she soon had plentiful proof, and her great, indeed, her only hope was that when the wealth was gone he would go too. "An otter," says the Dutch proverb, "does not nest in a dry dyke."

But oh! What months those were, what dreadful months!

From time to time she saw her husband, when he wanted cash, and every night she heard him returning home, often with unsteady steps. Two or three times a week she also was commanded to prepare a luxurious meal for him and some six or eight companions, to be followed by a gambling party at which the stakes ruled high. Then in the morning, before he was up, strange people would arrive, and wait until they could see him, or catch him as he slipped from the house by a back way. These men, Lysbeth discovered, were creditors seeking payment of old debts. Under such constant calls, her fortune, which if substantial was not great, melted rapidly. Soon the ready money was gone, then the shares in certain ships were sold, then the land and the house itself were mortgaged.

So the time went on.

Almost immediately after his split with Lysbeth, Dirk van Goorl had left Leyden, and returned to Alkmaar, where his father lived. His cousin and friend, however, Hendrik Brant, remained there studying the jeweller's art under the great master of filigree work, who was known as Petrus. One morning, as Hendrik was sitting at breakfast in his lodging, it was announced that a woman who would not give her name, wished to see him. Moved more by curiosity than by any other reason, he ordered her to be admitted. When she entered he was sorry, for in the gaunt person and dark-eyed face he recognised one against whom he had been warned by the elders of his church was a spy, a creature who was employed by the papal inquisitors to get up cases against heretics, and who was known as Black Meg.

"What is your business with me?" Brant asked sternly.

"Nothing to your hurt, worthy Heer, believe me, nothing to your hurt. Oh, yes, I know that tales are told against me, who only earn an honest living in an honest way, to keep my poor husband, who is an imbecile. Once, alas! He followed that mad Anabaptist fool, John of Leyden, the fellow who was set up as a king, and said that men might have as many wives as they wished. That was what sent my husband silly, but, thanks be to the Saints, he has repented of his errors and is reconciled to the Church and Christian marriage, and now, I, who have a forgiving nature, am obliged to support him."

"Your business?" said Brant.

"Mynheer," she answered, dropping her husky voice, "you are a friend of the Countess Montalvo, she who was Lysbeth van Hout?"

"No, I am acquainted with her, that is all."

"At least you are a friend of the Heer Dirk van Goorl who has left this town for Alkmaar; he who was her lover?"

"Yes, I am his cousin, but he is not the lover of any married woman."

"No, no, of course not. Love cannot look through a bridal veil, can it? Still, you are his friend, and, therefore, perhaps, her friend, and—she isn't happy."

"Indeed? I know nothing of her present life. She must reap the field that she has sown. That door is shut."

"Not altogether perhaps. I thought it might interest Dirk van Goorl to learn that it is still ajar."

"I don't see why it should. Fish merchants are not interested in rotten herrings. They write off the loss and send out the fleet for a fresh cargo."

"The first fish we catch is ever the finest, Mynheer, and if we haven't quite caught it, oh, what a fine fish is that."

"I have no time to waste in chopping riddles. What is your errand? Tell it, or leave it untold, but be quick."

Black Meg leant forward, and the hoarse voice sank to a cavernous whisper.

"What will you give me," she asked, "if I prove to you that the Captain Montalvo is not married at all to Lysbeth van Hout?"

"It does not much matter what I would give you, for I saw the thing done in the Groote Kerk yonder."

"Things are not always done that seem to be done."

"Look here, woman, I have had enough of this," and Brant pointed to the door.

Black Meg did not stir, only she produced a packet from the bosom of her dress and laid it on the table.

"A man can't have two wives living at once, can he?"

"No, I suppose not—that is, legally."

"Well, if I show you that Montalvo has two wives, how

much?"

Brant became interested. He hated Montalvo. He guessed, indeed he knew something of the part which the man had played in this infamous affair, and knew also that it would be a true kindness to Lysbeth to rid her of him.

"If you proved it," he said, "let us say two hundred florins."

"It is not enough, Mynheer."

"It is all I have to offer and, mind you, what I promise in pay is always given," responded Brant.

"Ah! Yes, the other promises and doesn't pay—the rogue, the rogue," she added, striking a bony fist upon the table. "Well, I agree, and I ask no bond, for you merchant folk are not like cavaliers, your word is as good as your paper. Now read these," and she opened the packet and pushed its contents towards him.

With the exception of two miniatures, which he placed upon one side, they were letters written in Spanish and in a very delicate hand. Brant knew Spanish well, and in twenty minutes he had read them all. They proved to be epistles from a lady who signed herself Juanita de Montalvo, written to the Count Juan de Montalvo, whom she addressed as her husband. Very piteous documents they were also, telling a tale of heartless desertion, pleading for the writer's sake and for the sake of certain children, that the husband and father would return to them, or at least remit them means to live. For they, his wife and family, were sunk in great poverty.

"All this is sad enough," said Brant with a gesture of disgust as he glanced at the miniature of the lady and her children, "but it proves nothing. How are we to know that she is the man's wife?"

Black Meg put her hand into the bosom of her dress and produced another letter dated not more than three months ago. It was, or purported to be, written by the priest of the village where the lady lived, and was addressed to the Captain the Count Juan de Montalvo at Leyden. In substance this epistle was an earnest appeal to the noble count from one who had a right to speak, as the man who had christened him, taught him, and married him to his wife, either to return to her or to forward her the means to join him.

A dreadful rumor, the letter ended, *has reached us here in Spain that you have taken to wife a Dutch lady at Leyden named Van Hout, but this I do not believe, since never could you have committed such a crime before God and man. Write, write at once, my son, and disperse this black cloud of scandal which is gathering on your honored and ancient name.*

"How did you come by these, woman?" asked Brant.

"The last I had from a priest who brought it from Spain. I met him at The Hague, and offered to deliver the letter, as he had no safe means of sending it to Leyden. The others and the pictures I stole out of Montalvo's room."

"Indeed, most honest merchant, and what might you have been doing in his Excellency's room?"

"I will tell you," she answered, "for, as he never gave me my pay, my tongue is loosed. He wished for evidence that the Heer Dirk van Goorl was a heretic, and employed me to find it."

Brant's face hardened, and he became more watchful.

"Why did he wish such evidence?"

"To use it to prevent the marriage of Jufvrouw Lysbeth with the Heer Dirk van Goorl."

"How?"

Meg shrugged her shoulders. "By telling his secret to her so that she might dismiss him, I suppose, or more likely by threatening that, if she did not, he would hand her lover over to the Inquisitors."

"I see. And did you get the evidence?"

"Well, I hid in the Heer Dirk's bedroom one night, and looking through a door saw him and another young man, whom I did not know, reading the Bible, and praying together."

"Indeed; what a terrible risk you must have run, for had those young men, or either of them, chanced to catch you, it is quite certain that you would not have left that room alive. You know these heretics think that they are justified in killing a spy on sight, and, upon my word, I do not blame them. In fact, my good woman," and he leaned forward and looked her straight in the eyes, "were I in the same position I would have knocked you on the head as readily as though you had been a rat."

Black Meg shrank back, and turned a little blue about the lips.

"Of course, Mynheer, of course, it is a rough game, and the poor agents of God must take their risks. Not that the other young man had any cause to fear. I wasn't paid to watch him, and—as I have said—I neither know nor care who he is."

"Well, who can say, that may be fortunate for you, especially if he should ever come to know or to care who you are. But it is no affair of ours, is it? Now, give me those letters. What, do you want your money first? Very well," and, rising, Brant went to a cupboard and produced a small steel box, which he unlocked; and, having taken from it the appointed sum, locked it again. "There you are," he said; "oh, you needn't stare at the cupboard; that box won't live there after today, or anywhere in this house. By the way, I understand that Montalvo never paid you."

"Not a stiver," she answered with a sudden access of rage; "the low thief, he promised to pay me after his marriage, but instead of rewarding her who put him in that warm nest, I tell you that already he has squandered every florin of the noble lady's money in gambling and satisfying such debts as he was obliged to, so that today I believe that she is almost a beggar."

"I see," said Brant, "and now good morning, and look you, if we should chance to meet in the town, you will understand that I do not know you."

"I understand, Mynheer," said Black Meg with a grin and vanished.

When she had gone Brant rose and opened the window.

"Bah!" he said, "the air is poisoned. But I think I frightened her, I think that I have nothing to fear. Yet who can tell? My God! She saw me reading the Bible, and Montalvo, knows it! Well, it is some time ago now, and I must take my chance."

Then, taking the miniatures and documents with him, Brant started to call upon his friend and fellow Christian, the Heer Pieter van de Werff, Dirk van Goorl's friend, and Lysbeth's cousin, a young man for whose judgment and abilities he had a great respect. As a result of this visit, these two gentlemen left that afternoon for Brussels, the seat of Government, where they had very influential friends.

It will be sufficient to tell the upshot of their visit. Just at that time, the Government of the Netherlands wished for its own reasons to stand well with the citizen class, and when those in authority learned of the dreadful fraud that had been played off upon a lady of note, who was known to be a good Catholic, for the sole object of robbing her of her fortune, there was indignation in high places. Indeed, an order was issued, signed by a hand that could not be resisted—so deeply was one woman moved by the tale of another's wrong—that the Count Montalvo should be seized and brought to trial, just as though he were any common Netherland criminal. Moreover, since he was a man with many enemies, no one was found to stand between him and the Royal decree.

Three days later, Montalvo made an announcement to Lysbeth. For the first time in weeks, he was supping at home alone with his wife, whose presence he had commanded. She obeyed and attended, sitting at the further end of the table, whence she rose from time to time to wait upon him with her own hands. Watching him all the while with her quiet eyes, she noticed that he was ill at ease.

"Cannot you speak?" he asked at last and savagely. "Do you think it is pleasant for a man to sit opposite a woman who looks like a corpse in her coffin until he wishes she were one?"

"I have news, indeed," began Lysbeth, "but I do not think it will make you cheerful. I am with child."

"Another financial burden to bear," answered Montalvo, and again there was silence.

A few moments later, she asked her agitated husband, "What do you want, more money?"

"Of course I want money," he answered furiously.

"Then there is none; everything has gone, and the notary tells me that no one will advance another stiver on the house. All my jewelry is sold also."

He glanced at her hand. "You still have that ring," he said.

She looked at it. It was a hoop of gold set with emeralds of considerable value which her husband had given her before marriage, and always insisted upon her wearing. In fact, it had been bought with the money which he borrowed from Dirk van Goorl.

"Take it," she said, smiling for the first time, and drawing off the ring she passed it over to him. He turned his head aside as he stretched his hand towards the trinket lest his face should betray his shame.

"If your child should be a son," he muttered, "tell him that his father had nothing but a piece of advice to leave him; that he should never touch a dice-box."

"Are you going away then?" she asked.

"For a week or two I must. I have been warned that a difficulty has arisen, about which I need not trouble you. Doubtless you will hear of it soon enough, and though it is not true, I must leave Leyden until the thing blows over. In fact I am going now."

"You are about to desert me," she answered. "Having got all my money, I say that you are going to desert me who am great with child. I see it in your face."

Montalvo turned away and pretended not to hear.

"Well, thank God for it," Lysbeth added, "only I wish that you could take your memory and everything else of yours with you."

As these bitter words passed her lips, the door opened, and there entered one of his own subordinates, followed by four soldiers and a man in a lawyer's robe.

"What is this?" asked Montalvo furiously.

The officer saluted as he entered. "My captain, forgive me, but I act under orders, and they are to arrest you alive, or," he added significantly, "dead."

"Upon what charge?" asked Montalvo.

"Here, notary, you had best read the charge," said the nervous lieutenant, "but perhaps the lady would like to retire first," he added awkwardly.

"No," answered Lysbeth, "it might concern me."

"Alas! Señora, I fear it does," put in the notary. Then he began to read the document, which was long and legal. But she was quick to understand. Before ever it was done, Lysbeth knew that she was not the lawful wife of Count Juan de Montalvo, and that he was to be brought to trial for his betrayal of her and the trick he had played on the Church. So she was free—free, and overcome by that thought she staggered, fell, and swooned away.

When her eyes opened again, Montalvo, officer, notary, and soldiers, all had vanished and only a servant woman was there to assist her.

CHAPTER VIII
THE MARE'S STABLE

When Lysbeth's reason returned to her in that empty room, her first sense was one of wild exultation. She was free, she was not Montalvo's wife, never again could she be obliged to see him, never again could she be forced to endure the contamination of his touch—that was her thought. She was sure that the story was true; were it not true, who could have moved the authorities to take action against him? Moreover, now that she had the key, a thousand things were explained, trivial enough in themselves, each of them, but in their sum amounting to proof positive of his guilt. Had he not spoken of some entanglement in Spain and of children? Had he not in his sleep—but it was needless to remember all these things. She was free! She was free! And there on the table still lay the symbol of her bondage, the emerald ring that was to give him the means of flight, a flight from this charge which he knew was hanging over him. She took it up, dashed it to the ground and stamped upon it. Next she fell upon her knees, praising and blessing God, and then, worn out, crept away to rest.

The morning came, the still and beautiful autumn morning, but now all her exultation had left her, and Lysbeth was depressed and heavy hearted. She rose and assisted the one servant who remained in the house to prepare their breakfast, taking no heed of the sidelong glances that the woman cast at her. Afterwards she went to the market to spend some of her last florins in necessaries. Here and in the streets she became aware that she was the object of remark, for people nudged each other and stared at her. Moreover, as she hurried home appalled, her quick ear caught the conversation of two coarse women while they walked behind her.

"She's got it now," said one.

"Serve her right, too," answered the other, "for running after and marrying a Spanish don."

"Marrying?" broke in the first, "it was the best that she could do. She couldn't stop to ask questions. Some corpses must be buried quickly."

Glancing behind her, Lysbeth saw the creature plug her nostrils with her fingers, as though to shut out an evil smell.

Then she could bear it no longer, and turned upon them.

"You are evil slanderers," she said, and walked away swiftly, pursued by the sound of their loud, insulting laughter.

At the house she was told that two men were waiting to see her. They proved to be creditors clamoring for large sums of money, which she could not pay. Lysbeth told them that she knew nothing of the matter. Thereupon they showed her her own writing at the foot of deeds, and she remembered that she had signed more things than she chose to keep count of, everything indeed that the man who called himself her husband put before her, if only to win an hour of blessed freedom from his presence. At length, the men went away vowing that they would have their money if they had to drag the bed from under her.

After that came loneliness and silence. No friend appeared to cheer her. Indeed, she had no friends left, for by her husband's command, she had broken off her acquaintance with all who after the strange circumstances connected with her marriage were still inclined to know her. He said that he would have no chattering Dutch vrouws about the house, and they said and believed that the Countess de Montalvo had become too proud to associate with those of her own class and people.

Midday came and she could eat no food; indeed, she had touched none for twenty-hours; her nerves rose against it, although in her state she needed food. Now the shame of her position began to come home to Lysbeth. She was a wife and no wife; soon she must bear the burden of motherhood, and oh, what would that child be? And what would she be, its mother? What, too, would Dirk think of her? Dirk, for whom she had done and suffered all these things. Through the long afternoon hours, she lay upon her bed thinking such thoughts as these until at length her mind gave and Lysbeth grew lightheaded. Her brain became a chaos, a perfect hell of distorted imaginations.

Then out of its turmoil and confusion rose a vision and a desire; a vision of peace and a desire for rest. But what rest was there for her inside a home filled with bad memories. She was burning hot and she was thirsty. How cool the water would be on this fevered night. What could be better than to visit the sea and slowly let it close above her poor aching head? She would go out and look at the water; in that, at any rate, there could be no harm.

She wrapped herself in a long cloak and drew its hood over her head. Then she slipped from the house and stole like a ghost through the winding streets and out of the Maren or Sea Poort, where the guard let her pass thinking that she was a country woman returning to her village. Now the moon was rising, and by the light of it Lysbeth recognized the place. Here was the spot where she had stood on the day of the ice carnival, when that woman who was called Martha the Mare, and who said that she had known her father, had spoken to her. On that water she had galloped in Montalvo's sleigh, and up yonder canal the race was run. She followed along its banks, remembering the reedy meer some miles away spotted with islets that were only visited from time to time by fishermen and wild-fowlers; the great Haarlemer Meer which covered many thousands of acres of ground. That meer she felt sure must look very cool and beautiful on such a night as this, and the wind would whisper sweetly among the tall bulrushes that fringed its banks.

On Lysbeth went and on; it was a long, long walk, but at last she came there, and, oh, the place was sweet and vast and lonely. For so far as her eye could reach in the light of the low moon there was nothing but glimmering water broken here and there by the reedwreathed islands. Hark! How the frogs croaked and the bitterns boomed among the rushes. Look where the wild ducks swam leaving behind them broad trails of silver as their breasts broke the surface of the great meer into rippling lines.

There, on an island, not a bowshot from her, grew tufts of a daisy-like marsh bloom, white flowers such as she remembered gathering when she was a child. A desire came upon her to pluck some of these flowers, and the water was shallow; surely she could wade to the island, or if not what did it matter? Then she could turn to the bank again, or she might stay to sleep a while in the water; what did it matter? She stepped from the bank—how sweet and cool it felt to her feet! Now it was up to her knees, now it reached her middle, and now the little wavelets beat against her throat. But she would not go back, for there ahead of her was the island, and the white flowers were so close that she could count them, eight upon one bunch and twelve upon the next. Another step and the water struck her in the face, one more and it closed above her head. She rose, and a low cry broke from her lips.

Then, as in a dream, Lysbeth saw a skiff glide out from among the rushes before her. She saw also a strange, mutilated face, which she remembered dimly, bending over the edge of the boat, and a long, brown hand stretched out to clasp her, while a hoarse voice told her to keep still and fear nothing.

After this came a sound of singing in her ears, and darkness.

When Lysbeth woke again, she found herself lying upon the ground, or rather upon a soft mattress of dry reeds and aromatic grasses. Looking round her she saw that she was in a hut, reed-roofed and plastered with thick mud. In one corner of this hut stood a fireplace with a chimney artfully built of clay, and on the fire of turfs boiled an earthen pot. Hanging from the roof by a string of twisted grass was a fish, fresh caught, a splendid pike, and near to it a bunch of smoked eels. Over her also was thrown a magnificent rug of otter skins. Noting these things, she gathered that she must be in the hovel of some fisherman.

Now by degrees the past came back to Lysbeth, and she remembered her parting with the man who called himself her husband; remembered also her moonlight flight and how she had waded out into the waters of the great mere to pluck the white flowers, and how, as they closed above her head a hand had stretched out to save her. Lysbeth remembered, and remembering, she sighed aloud. The sound of her sighing seemed to attract the attention of someone who was listening outside the hut; at any rate, a rough door was opened or pushed aside and a figure entered. "Are you awake, lady?" asked a hoarse voice.

"Yes," answered Lysbeth, "but tell me, how did I come here, and who are you?"

The figure stepped back so that the light from the open door fell full upon it. "Look, Carolus van Hout's daughter and Juan Montalvo's wife. Those who have seen me once do not forget me."

Lysbeth sat up on the bed and stared at the gaunt, powerful form, the deep-set gray eyes, the wide-spread nostrils, the scarred, high cheek-bones, the teeth made prominent by some devil's work upon the lips, and the grizzled lock of hair that hung across the forehead. In an instant she knew her.

"You are Martha the Mare," she said.

"Yes, I am the Mare, none other, and you are in the Mare's stable. What has he been doing to you, that Spanish dog, that you came last night to ask the Great Water to hide you and your shame?"

Lysbeth made no answer; the story seemed hard to begin with this strange woman. Then Martha went on. "What did I tell you, Lysbeth van Hout? Did I not say that your blood should warn you against the Spaniards? Well, well, you saved me from the ice and I have saved you from the water. Ah! Who was it that led me to row round by that outer isle last night because I could not sleep? But what does it matter; God willed it so, and here you lie in the Mare's stable. Nay, do not answer me, first you must eat."

"Then, going to the pot, she took it from the fire, pouring its contents into an earthen basin, and, at the smell of them, for the first time in days Lysbeth felt hungry. Of what that stew was comprised she never learned, but she ate it to the last spoonful and was thankful, while Martha, seated on the ground beside her, watched her with delight, from time to time stretching out a long, thin hand to touch the brown hair that hung about her

shoulders.

"Come out and look," said Martha when her guest had done eating. And she led her through the doorway of the hut.

Lysbeth gazed round her, but in truth there was not much to see. The hut itself was hidden away in a little clump of swamp willows that grew upon a mound in the midst of a marshy plain, broken here and there by patches of reed and bulrushes. Walking across this plain for a hundred yards or so, they came to more reeds, and in them a boat hidden cunningly, for here was the water of the lake, and, not fifty paces away, what seemed to be the shore of an island. The Mare directed her to get into the boat and rowed her across to this island, then round it to another, and thence to another and yet another.

"Now tell me," she said, "upon which of them is my stable built?"

Lysbeth shook her head helplessly.

"You cannot tell, no, nor any living man. I say that no man lives who could find it, save I myself, who know the path there by night or by day. Look," and she pointed to the vast surface of the meer, on this great sea are thousands of such islets, and before they find me the Spaniards must search them all, for here upon the lonely waters no spies or hound will help them." Then she began to row again without even looking round, and presently they were in the clump of reeds from which they had started.

"I must be going home," faltered Lysbeth.

"No," answered Martha, "it is too late, you have slept long. Look, the sun is sinking fast, this night you must stay with me. Oh! Do not be afraid, my fare is rough, but it is sweet and fresh. I can find plenty of fish from the meer, as much as you will, for who can catch them better than I? And waterfowl that I snare, yes, and their eggs; moreover, dried flesh and bacon which I get from the mainland, for there I have friends who sometimes I meet at night."

So Lysbeth yielded, for the great peace of this lake pleased her. Oh, after all that she had gone through, it was like heaven to watch the sun sinking towards the quiet water, to hear the wild-fowl call, to watch the fish leap and the halcyons flash by, and above all to be sure that by nothing short of a miracle could this divine silence, broken only of nature's voices, be defiled with the sound of the hated accents of the man who had ruined and betrayed her. Yes, she was weary, and a strange unaccustomed fatigue crept over her; she would rest there this night also.

So they went back to the hut and made ready their evening meal, and as she fried the fish over the fire of peats, Lysbeth found herself laughing like a girl again. Then they ate it with appetite, and after it was done, Mother Martha prayed aloud; yes, and without fear, although she knew Lysbeth to be a Catholic, read from her one treasure, a Testament, crouching there in the light of the fire and saying:

"See, lady, what a place this is for a heretic to hide in. Where else may a woman read from the Bible and fear no spy or priest?" Remembering a certain story, Lysbeth shivered at her words.

"Now," said the Mare, when she had finished reading, "tell me before you sleep, what it was that brought you into the waters of the Haarlemer Meer, and what that Spanish man has done to you. Do not be afraid, for though I am mad, or so they say, I can keep counsel, and between you and me are many bonds, Carolus van Hout's daughter, some of which you know and see, and some that you can neither know nor see, but which God will weave in His own season."

Lysbeth looked at the weird countenance, distorted and made unhuman by long torment of body and mind, and found in it something to trust; yes, even signs of that sympathy which she so sorely needed. So she told her all the tale from the first word of it to the last.

The Mare listened in silence, for no story of evil perpetrated by a Spaniard seemed to move or astonish her, only when Lysbeth had done, she said, "Ah, child, had you but known of me, and where to find me, you could have asked my aid."

"Why, Mother, what could you have done?" answered Lysbeth.

"Done? I would have followed him by night until I found my chance in some lonely place, and there I would have—" Then she stretched out her bony hand to the red light of the fire, and Lysbeth saw that in it was a knife.

She sank back aghast.

"Why are you frightened, my pretty lady?" asked the Mare. "I tell you that I live on for only one thing—to kill Spaniards, yes, priests first and then the others. Oh! I have a long count to pay; for every time that he was tortured in life, for every groan he uttered at the stake in life; yes, so many for my dear husband and half as many for the son. Well, I shall live to be old, I know that I shall live to be old, and the count will be discharged, aye, to the last stiver."

As she spoke, the outlawed fugitive had risen, and the flare of the fire struck full upon her. It was an awful face that Lysbeth beheld by the light of it, full of fierceness and energy, the face of an inspired avenger, dread and unnatural, yet not altogether repulsive. Indeed, that countenance was such as an imaginative artist might give to one of the beasts in the Book of Revelation. Amazed and terrified, Lysbeth said nothing.

"I frighten you, gentle one," went on the Mare, "you who, although you have suffered, are still full of the milk of human kindness. Wait, woman, wait until they have murdered the man you love, until your heart is like my heart, and you also live on, not for love's sake, not for life's sake, but to be a Sword, a Sword, a Sword in the hand of God!"

"Cease, I pray you," said Lysbeth in a low voice. "I am faint, and my child stirs strangely within me."

As Lysbeth finished her plea, she soon sank down with pains in her side. Little did she realize, that although she was nearly three weeks before her time, that before morning there, in that lonely hovel on the island of the meer, a black-eyed son would be born to her.

Somewhat slowly, lying there in the island hut, Lysbeth won back her strength. The Mare, or Mother Martha, as Lysbeth had now learned to call her, tended her as few midwives would have done. Food, too, she had in plenty, for Martha snared the fowl and caught the fish, or she made visits to the mainland and thence brought eggs and milk and flesh, which, so she said, the boors of that country gave her as much as she wanted. Also, to while away the hours, she would read to her out of the Scriptures, and from that reading Lysbeth learnt many things that until then she had not known. Indeed, before it was done with, she began to wonder in what lay the wickedness of these heretics, and how it came about that they were worthy of death and torment, since, in this Book she could find no law to which their lives and doctrine seemed to give offence.

Thus it happened that Martha, the fierce, half-crazy water-dweller, sowed the seed in Lysbeth's heart that was to bear spiritual fruit. In the weeks that followed, Lysbeth was drawn by the Holy Spirit into a new and living relationship with Christ, as she sought Him by grace through faith alone.

When three weeks had gone by and Lysbeth was on her feet again, though as yet scarcely strong enough to travel, Martha told her she had business that would keep her from home a night, but what the business was, she refused to say. Accordingly, on a certain afternoon, having left good store of all things to Lysbeth's hand, the Mare departed in her skiff, nor did she return until after midday the following afternoon. Now Lysbeth talked of leaving the island, but Martha would not permit it, saying that if she desired to go she must swim; and indeed, when Lysbeth went to look she found that the boat had been hidden elsewhere. So she stayed on, and in the crisp autumn air her health and beauty came back to her, until she was once more much as she had been before the day when she went on her ride with Juan de Montalvo.

On a November morning, leaving her infant in the hut with Martha, Lysbeth walked to the extremity of the island. During the night the first sharp frost of late autumn had fallen, making a thin film of ice upon the surface of the lake, which melted rapidly as the sun grew high. The air too was very clear and calm, and among the reeds, now turning golden at their tips, the finches flew and chirped, forgetful that winter was at hand. So sweet and peaceful was the scene that Lysbeth, also forgetful of many things, surveyed it with a kind of rapture. She knew not why, but her heart was happy that morning. It was as though a dark cloud had passed from her life, as though the blue skies of peace and joy were spread about her. Doubtless other clouds might appear upon the horizon; doubtless in their season they would appear, but she felt that this horizon was as yet a long way off, and meanwhile above her bent the tender sky, serene and sweet and happy.

Upon the crisp grass behind her suddenly she heard a footstep, a new footstep, not that of the long, stealthy stride of Martha who was called the Mare, and swung round upon her heel to meet it.

Oh, God! Who was this? Oh, God! There before her stood Dirk van Goorl. Dirk, and no other than Dirk, unless she dreamed. Dirk with his kind face wreathed in a happy smile. Dirk with his arms outstretched towards her. Lysbeth said nothing, she could not speak, only she stood still gazing, gazing, gazing, and always he came on, until now his arms were round her. Then she sprang back.

"Do not touch me," she cried, "remember what I am and why I stay here."

"I know well what you are, Lysbeth," he answered slowly. "You are the bravest woman who ever walked this earth. You are an angel upon this earth. You are the woman who gave her honor to save the man she loved. Oh! Be silent, be silent, I have heard the story. I know its every word, and here I kneel before you, and, next to my God, I love you, Lysbeth, I love you."

"But the child," she murmured, "it lives, and it is mine and the man's."

Dirk's face hardened a little, but he only answered, "We must bear our burdens. You have borne yours, I must bear mine," and he seized her hands and kissed them, yes, and the hem of her garment and kissed it also.

So after these two talked of their mutual Christian faith, and what they had learned during their long absence from each other, they decided to marry.

Afterwards Lysbeth heard all the story. Montalvo had been brought to trial, and, as it turned out, things went hard with him. Among his judges one was a great Netherlander lord, who desired to uphold the rights of his countrymen; one was a high ecclesiastic, who was furious because of the fraud that had been played upon the Church, which had been trapped into celebrating a bigamous marriage; and a third was a Spanish grandee, who, as it happened, knew the family of the first wife who had been deserted.

Therefore, for the pathetic Montalvo, when the case had been proved to the hilt against him by the evidence of the priest who brought the letter, of the wife's letters, and of the truculent Black Meg, who now found an opportunity of paying back "hot water for cold," there was little mercy. His character was bad, and it was said, moreover, that because of his cruelties and the shame she had suffered at his hands, Lysbeth van Hout had committed suicide. At least this was certain, that she was seen running at night towards the Haarlemer Meer, and that after this, search as her friends would, not a trace of her could be found.

So, that an example might be made, although he lied to the best of his ability, the Captain Juan de Montalvo, was sent to serve for fourteen years in the galleys as a common slave. And that, for a while, was the end of him.

There was also a happy end to the strange and tragic courtship of Dirk van Goorl and Lysbeth van Hout.

Six months later they were married, and by Dirk's wish they took the child, who was baptized Adrian, to live with them. A few weeks later, Lysbeth formally entered the community of the Protestants connected with the Reformation faith, and less than two years after her marriage another son was born to her, who was named Foy.

Book Two

THE RIPENING

CHAPTER IX
ADRIAN, FOY, AND MARTIN THE RED

Many years had gone by since Lysbeth found her love again upon the island in the Haarlemer Meer. The son that she bore there was now a grown man, as was her second son, Foy, and her own hair showed gray beneath the lappets of her cap.

Fast, fast wove the loom of God during those fateful years, and the web thereof was the story of a people's agony and its woof was dyed red with their blood. Edict had followed edict, crime had been heaped upon crime. General Álvarez de Toledo (Alva), like some inhuman and incarnate vengeance, had marched his army, quiet and harmless as is the tiger when he stalks his prey, across the fields of France. Now he was at Brussels, and already the heads of the Counts Egmont and Hoorn had fallen, already the Blood Council was established and at its work. In the Low Countries, law had ceased to exist; and there anything might happen however monstrous or inhuman. Indeed, with one decree of the Holy Office, confirmed by a proclamation of Philip of Spain, all the inhabitants of the Netherlands, three million of them, had been condemned to death. Men's minds were full of terror, for on every side were burnings and hangings and torturings. Without were terrors, within were fears, and none knew whom they could trust, since the friend of today might be the informer or judge of tomorrow. All this because they chose to worship God in a biblical manner uncluttered by images and priests.

Although so long a time had passed, by the grace of God, those people with whom we have already made acquaintance in this history were still alive. Let us begin with two of them, one of whom we know and one of whom, although we have heard of him before, will require some introduction—Dirk van Goorl and his son Foy.

The opening scene in this part of our story places us in an upper room above a warehouse overlooking the marketplace of Leyden, a room with small windows and approached by two staircases. The time was a summer twilight. The faint light that penetrated into this chamber through the unshuttered windows, for to curtain them would have been to excite suspicion, showed that about twenty people had gathered there, among whom were two women. For the most part they were men of the better class, middle-aged burghers of sober mind, some of whom stood about, while others were seated upon stools and benches. At the end of the room addressing them was a man well on in middle life, with grizzled hair and beard, small and somewhat plain in stature. This was Jan Arentz, the famous preacher, by trade a basket maker, a man who showed himself steadfast to the Reformation faith through all afflictions, and who was gifted with a spirit that could remain unmoved amidst the horrors of perhaps the most terrible persecution that Christians had suffered since the days of the Roman Emperors. He was preaching now and these people were his congregation.

"I came not to bring peace but a sword," was his text, and certainly this night it was most appropriate and one that was easy to illustrate. For there, on the very market place beneath them, guarded by soldiers and surrounded with the rabble of the city, two members of his flock, men who a fortnight before had worshipped in that same room, at this moment were undergoing martyrdom by fire!

Arentz preached patience and fortitude. He went back into recent history and told his hearers how he himself had passed a hundred dangers; how he had been hunted like a wolf, how he had been tried, how he had escaped from prisons and from the swords of soldiers, even as St. Paul had done before him, and how yet he lived to minister to them this night. He told them that they must have no fear, that they must go on quite happy, quite confident, taking what it pleased God to send them, feeling that it would all be for the best; yes, that even the worst would be for the best. What was the worst? Some hours of torment and death. And what lay beyond the death? Ah, let them think of that. The whole world was but a brief and varying shadow, what did it matter how or when they walked out of that shadow into the perfect light? The sky was very dark, but behind it the sun shone. They must look forward with the eye of faith; perhaps the sufferings of the present generation were part of the scheme of things; perhaps from the earth which they watered with their blood would spring the flower of freedom, that glorious freedom in whose day all men would be able to worship their Creator, responsible only to God's law and their own consciences, not to the dogmas or doctrines of other men.

As Arentz spoke, eloquently, sweetly, to the assembly, the twilight deepened and the flare from those sacrificial fires flickered on the window pane, and the mixed murmurs of the crowd of witnesses broke upon his listeners' ears. The preacher paused and looked down upon the dreadful scene below, for from where he stood he could behold it all.

"Mark is dead," he said, "and our dear brother, Andreas Jansen, is dying. The executioners heap the wood round him. You think it cruel, you think it piteous, but I say to you, No. I say that it is a holy and a glorious sight, for we witness the passing of souls to bliss. Brethren, let us pray for those who leave us, and for ourselves who stay behind. Yes, and let us pray for those who slay him that know not what they do. We watch his sufferings, but I tell you that Christ his Lord watches also; Christ who hung upon the Cross, the victim of such men as these. He stands with him in the fire. His hand encompasses him. His voice supports him. Brethren, let us pray."

Then at his bidding every member of that little congregation knelt in prayer for the passing spirit of Andreas Jansen.

Again Arentz looked through the window.

"He dies!" he cried. "A soldier has thrust him through with a pike in mercy, his head falls forward. Oh! God, if it be Thy will, grant to us a sign."

Some strange breeze passed through that upper chamber, a cold breeze which blew upon the brows of the worshippers and stirred their hair, bringing with it a sense of the presence of Andreas Jansen, the martyr. Then, there upon the wall opposite to the window, at the very spot where their brother and companion, Andreas, saint and martyr, had frequently knelt, appeared the sign, or what they took to be a sign. Yes, there upon the whitewashed wall, reflected, perhaps, from the fires below, and showing clearly in the darkened room, shone the vision of a fiery cross. For a second it was seen, then it was gone. But to every soul in this room, the vision of that cross had brought its message; the cross is the way that God has ordained to achieve the crown of life. The cross vanished and there was silence.

"Brethren," said the voice of Arentz, speaking in the darkness, "you have seen. Through the fire and through the shadow, follow the Cross and fear not. Let us still our hearts and read Psalm Two together."

The service was over, and below in the emptied marketplace the executioners collected the poor fragments of the martyrs to cast them carelessly and with filthy jests into the dark waters of the river. Now, one by one and two by two, the worshippers slipped away through some hidden door opening on an alley. Let us look at three of their number, as they crept through the streets back to a house on the Bree Straat with which we are acquainted, two of them walking in front and one behind.

The pair were Dirk van Goorl and his son Foy, there was no mistaking their relationship. Although he had grown somewhat portly and thoughtful, Dirk was the Dirk of twenty-five years ago. He was still gray-eyed, bearded, a handsome man by Dutch standards, whose massive, kindly countenance betrayed the massive, kindly heart within. Very like him was his son Foy, only his eyes were blue instead of gray, and his hair was yellow. Though they seemed sad enough just now, these were merry and pleasant eyes, and the somewhat childlike face was merry also, the face of a person who looked upon the bright side of things.

There was nothing remarkable or distinguished about Foy's appearance, but from it the observer, who met him for the first time, received an impression of energy, honesty, and good nature. In truth, such were prone to think of him as a sailor, just returned from a long journey, in the course of which he had come to the conclusion that this world was a pleasant place, and one well worth exploring. As Foy walked down the street with his quick and nautical gait, it was evident that even the solemn and dreadful scene that he had just experienced had not altogether quenched his cheery and hopeful spirit. Yet of all those who listened to the exhortation of Pastor Arentz, none had laid his burden of faith and hope for the future to heart more entirely than Foy van Goorl.

But of this ability to look on the bright side of things, the credit must be given to his nature and not to his piety, for Foy could not be sad for long. *Dum spiro, spero* ("while I breath, I hope") would have been his motto had he known Latin, and he did not intend to grow sorrowful, that is, over the prospect of being burnt, until he found himself tied to the stake. It was this quality of good spirits in a depressing and melancholy age that made of Foy so extraordinarily popular a character.

Behind these two followed a much more remarkable looking personage, the Frisian, Martin Roos, or Red Martin, so named for his hair and beard, which were red to the verge of flame color, and which hung almost to his chest. There was no other such beard in Leyden; indeed the boys, taking advantage of his good nature, would call to him as he passed, asking him if it was true that the storks nested in it every spring. This strange looking man, who was now perhaps forty years of age, for ten years or more had been the faithful servant of Dirk van Goorl, whose house he had entered under circumstances which shall be told of in their place.

Anyone glancing casually at Martin would not have said that he was a giant, and yet his height was considerable; to be accurate, when he stood upright, something over six feet three inches. The reason he did not appear to be tall was that in truth his great bulk shortened him to the eye, and also because he carried himself poorly, more from a desire to conceal his size than for any other reason. It was in girth of chest and limb that Martin was really remarkable. So much so that a short armed man standing before him could not make his fingers touch behind his back. His face was fair as a girl's and almost as flat as a full moon, for his nose was not pronounce. His Maker had furnished him with one of ordinary, if not excessive size, but certain incidents in Martin's early career as a boxer had caused it to spread about his face in a curious fashion. His eyebrows, however, remained prominent. Beneath them appeared a pair of very large, round, and rather mild blue eyes, covered with thick white lids absolutely devoid of lashes, which eyes had a most unholy trick of occasionally taking fire when their owner was irritated. Then they could burn and blaze like lamps tied to a barge on a dark night, with an effect that was all the more alarming because the rest of his countenance remained absolutely impassive.

Suddenly, while this little company went homewards, a sound arose in the quiet street as of people running. Instantly, all three of them pressed themselves into the doorway of a house and crouched down. Martin lifted his ear and listened.

"Three people," he whispered "a woman who flies and two men who follow."

At that moment, a casement was thrown open forty paces or so away, and a hand bearing a torch thrust out of it. By its light they saw the pale face of a lady speeding towards them, and after her two Spanish soldiers.

"The Vrouw Andreas Jansen," whispered Martin again, fleeing from two of the guards who burned her husband."

The torch was withdrawn, and the casement shut with a snap. In those days, quiet burghers could not afford to be mixed up in street troubles, especially if soldiers were involved. Once more the place was empty and quiet, except for the sound of running feet.

Opposite to the doorway, the lady was overtaken. "Oh! Let me go," she sobbed, "oh, let me go. Is it not enough that you have killed my husband? Why must I be hunted from my house

thus?"

"Because you are so pretty, my dear," answered one of the brutes, "also you are rich. Catch hold of her, friend. Lord! How she kicks."

Foy made a motion as though to start out of the doorway, but Martin pressed him back with the flat of his hand, without apparent effort, and yet so strongly that the young man could not move.

"This is my business, masters," he stated. "You would make noise," and they heard his breath come thick.

Now, moving with curious stealthiness for one of so great a bulk, Martin was out of the porch. By the summer starlight, the watchers could see that Martin had managed to sneak up behind the two soldiers. He then gripped them by the napes of their necks, one in either hand, and began to grind their faces together. This, indeed, was evident, for his great shoulders worked visibly and their breastplates clicked as they touched. But the men themselves made little sound at all. Then Martin seemed to catch them round the middle, and behold, in another second the pair of them had gone headlong into the canal, which ran down the center of the street.

"My God! He has killed them," Dirk gasped.

"And a good job, too, father," said Foy, "only I wish that I had shared in it."

Martin's great form loomed in the doorway. "The Vrouw Jansen has fled away," he said, "and the street is quite quiet now, so I think that we had better be moving before any see us, my masters."

Some days later, the bodies of these Spanish soldiers were found with their faces smashed flat. It was suggested in explanation of this plight, that they had got drunk and while fighting together had fallen from the bridge on to the stonework of a pier. This version of their end found a ready acceptance, as it consorted well with the reputations of the men. So there was no search or inquiry.

"I had to finish the dogs," Martin explained apologetically— "may the Lord Jesus forgive me—because I was afraid that they might know me again by my beard."

"Alas! Alas!" groaned Dirk, "what times are these. Say nothing of this dreadful matter to your mother, Son, or to Adrian either." But Foy nudged Martin in the ribs and commented, "Well done, old fellow, well done!"

After this experience, which the reader must remember was nothing extraordinary in those dark and dreadful days when neither the lives of men nor the safety of women, especially Protestant men and women, were things of much account. The three of them reached home without further incident, and quite unobserved. Arriving at the house, they entered it near the Watergate by a back door that led into the stableyard. It was opened by a woman whom they followed into a little room where a light burned. Here she turned and kissed two of them, Dirk first and then Foy.

"Thank God that I see you safe," she said. "Whenever you go

to the Meeting-place, I tremble until I hear your footsteps at the door."

"What's the use of that, Mother?" said Foy. "Your fretting yourself won't make things better or worse."

"Ah, dear, how can I help it?" she replied softly, "we cannot all be young and cheerful, you know."

"True, Wife, true," broke in Dirk, "though I wish we could. We should be more trusting as Christ's servants," and he looked at her and sighed.

Lysbeth van Goorl could no longer boast the beauty that had been hers when first we met her, but she was still a sweet and graceful woman, her figure remaining almost as slim as it had been in girlhood. The gray eyes also retained their depth and fire, only the face was worn, though more by care and the burden of memories than with years. The lot of the loving wife and mother was hard indeed when Philip the King ruled in Spain and General Álvarez (Alva) was his prophet in the Netherlands.

"Is it done?" she asked.

"Yes, Wife, our brethren are now saints in Paradise, therefore rejoice."

"It is a pity," she answered with a sob, "but I cannot understand. Oh!" she added with a sudden blaze of emotion. "Why does God permit His servants to be killed thus?"

"Perhaps our grandchildren will be able to answer that question," replied Dirk.

"That poor Vrouw Jansen," broke in Lysbeth, "just married, and so young and pretty. I wonder what will become of her."

Dirk and Foy looked at each other, and Martin, who was hovering about near the door, slunk back guiltily into the passage as though he had attempted to injure the Vrouw Jansen.

"Tomorrow we will look to it, Wife. And now let us eat, for we are faint with hunger."

Ten minutes later they were seated at their meal. It was a familiar room, the same location where Montalvo, ex-count and captain, made the speech that charmed all hearers on the night when he had lost the race at the ice festival. The same chandelier hung above them, even some portion of the same plate, repurchased by Dirk, was on the table, but how different were the company and the feast! Aunt Clara was long dead, and with her many of the companions of that occasion, some naturally, some by the hand of the executioner, while others had fled the land. Pieter van de Werff still lived, however, and though regarded with suspicion by the authorities, was a man of weight and honor in the town. On this occasion, however, he was not present there. The food, too, if ample was plain, not on account of the poverty of the household, for Dirk had prospered in his worldly affairs, being hardworking and skillful, and the head of the brass foundry to which in those early days he had been apprenticed, but because in such times people thought little of the refinements of eating. When life itself is so doubtful, its pleasures and amusements become of small importance. The ample waiting service of the maid Greta and her fellow domestics, who long ago had vanished, was now carried on by the man, Martin, and one old woman, since, as every servant might be a spy, even the richest employed few of them. In short, all the lighter and more cheerful parts of life were in abeyance.

"Where is Adrian?" asked Dirk.

"I do not know," answered Lysbeth. "I thought that perhaps—"

"No," replied her husband hastily. "He did not accompany us. He rarely does."

"Brother Adrian likes to stay in his own world," said Foy with his mouth full.

The remark was obscure, but his parents seemed to understand what Foy meant; at least, it was followed by an uncomfortable and acquiescent silence. Just then Adrian came in, and as we have not seen him since, twenty-four years ago, he made his entry into the world on the secret island in the Haarlemer Meer, here it may be as well to describe his appearance.

He was a handsome young man, but of quite a different stamp to his half-brother, Foy, being tall, slight, and very graceful in figure. These features were advantages he had inherited from his mother Lysbeth. In countenance, however, he differed from her so much that none would have guessed him to be her son. Indeed, Adrian's face was pure Spanish, there was nothing of a Netherlander about his dark beauty. Spanish were the eyes of velvet black, set rather close together. Spanish also, the finely chiseled features and the thin, spreading nostrils. Spanish the cold, yet somewhat serious mouth, more apt to sneer than smile; the straight, black hair, the clear, olive skin, and that indifferent half-wearied mindset that fit its wearer well enough, but in a man of his years seemed unnatural.

He took his seat without speaking, nor did the others speak to him until his stepfather Dirk said, "You were not at the works today, Adrian, although we could have used your help in founding the culverin."

"No, Father," he often called him father, answered the young man in a measured and rather melodious voice. "You see we don't quite know who is going to pay for that piece. Or, at any rate, I don't quite know, as nobody seems to take me into confidence, and if it should chance to be the losing side, well, it might be enough to hang me."

Dirk flushed up, but made no answer, only Foy remarked, "That's right, Adrian, look after your own skin."

"Just now I find it more interesting," went on Adrian loftily and disregardful of his brother, "to study those whom the cannon may shoot than to make the cannon which is to shoot them."

"Hope you won't be one of them," interrupted Foy again.

"Where have you been this evening, son?" said Lysbeth hastily, fearing a quarrel.

"I have been mixing with the people, Mother, at the scene on the marketplace yonder," said Adrian.

"Not the martyrdom of our good friend, Jansen, surely?"

"Yes, Mother, why not? It is terrible, it is a crime, no doubt, but the observer of life should study these things. There is nothing more fascinating to the philosopher than the play of human passions. The emotions of the brutal crowd, the passive indifference of the guard, the grief of the sympathizers, the stoical endurance of the victims animated by religious exaltation—"

"And the beautiful logic of the philosopher, with his nose

in the air, while he watches his friend and brother in the Faith being slowly burnt to death," broke out Foy with passion.

"Hush! Hush!" said Dirk, striking his fist upon the table with a blow that caused the glasses to ring, "this is no subject for word-chopping. Adrian, you would have been better with us than down below at that butchery, even though you were less safe," he added, with meaning. "But I wish to run none into danger, and you are of an age to judge for yourself. I beg you, however, to spare us your light talk about scenes that we think dreadful, however interesting you may have found them."

Adrian shrugged his shoulders and called to Martin to bring him some more meat. As the great man approached him, he spread out his fine-drawn nostrils and sniffed.

"You smell, Martin," he said, "and no wonder. Look, there is blood upon your jerkin. Have you been killing pigs and forgotten to change it?"

Martin's round blue eyes flashed, then went pale and dead again.

"Yes, Master," he answered, in his thick voice, "I have been killing pigs. But your dress also smells of blood and fire; perhaps you went too near the stake." At that moment, to put an end to the conversation, Dirk rose and said grace. Then he went out of the room accompanied by his wife and Foy, leaving Adrian to finish his meal alone, which he did reflectively and at leisure.

When he left the eating chamber, Foy followed Martin across the courtyard to the walled-in stables, and up a ladder to the room where the serving man slept. It was a strange place, and filled with an extraordinary collection of odds and ends; the skins of birds, otters, and wolves; weapons of different makes, notably a very large two-handed sword, plain and old-fashioned, but of excellent steel; bits of harness and other things.

There was no bed in this room for the reason that Martin disdained a bed, a few skins upon the floor being all that he needed to lie on. Nor did he ask for much covering, since so hardy was he by nature that, except in the very bitterest weather, his woollen vest was enough for him. Indeed, he had been known to sleep out in it when the frost was so sharp that he rose with his hair and beard covered with icicles.

Martin shut the door and lit three lanterns, which he hung to hooks upon the wall.

"Are you ready for a turn, Master?" he asked.

Foy nodded as he answered, "I want to get the taste of it all out of my mouth, so don't spare me. Lay on until I get angry, it will make me forget," and taking a leathern jerkin off a peg, he pulled it over his head.

"Forget what, Master?" asked Martin.

"Oh! The prayings and the burnings and Vrouw Jansen, and Adrian's sea-lawyer sort of talk."

"Ah, yes, that's the worst of them all for us," and the big man leant forward and whispered. "Keep an eye on him, Master Foy."

"What do you mean?" asked Foy sharply and flushing.

"What I say," responded the red-haired servant.

"You forget. You are talking of my brother, my own mother's son. I will hear no harm of Adrian; his ways are different to ours, but he is good-hearted at bottom. Do you understand me, Martin?"

"But not your father's son, Master. It's the sire sets the strain. I have bred horses, and I know."

Foy looked at him and hesitated.

"No," said Martin, answering the question in his eyes, "I have nothing against him, but he always sees the other side, and that's bad. Also he is Spanish—"

"And you don't like Spaniards," broke in Foy. "Martin, you are pig-headed, and prejudiced."

Martin smiled. "No, Master, I don't like Spaniards, nor will you before you have done with them. But then it is only fair as they don't like me."

"I say, Martin," said Foy, following a new line of thought, "how did you manage that business so quietly, and why didn't you let me do my share?"

"Because you'd have made a noise, master, and we didn't want the watch on us; also, being fully armed, they might have bettered you."

"Good reasons, Martin. How did you do it? I couldn't see much."

"It is a trick I learned up there in Friesland. Some of the Northmen sailors taught it to me. There is a place in a man's neck, here at the back, and if he is squeezed there he loses his senses in a second. Thus, master—" and putting out his great hand he gripped Foy's neck in a fashion that caused him the intensest agony.

"Drop it," said Foy, kicking at his shins.

"I didn't squeeze; I was only showing you," answered Martin, opening his eyes. "Well, when their wits were gone of course it was easy to knock their heads together, so that they mightn't find them again. You see," he added, "if I had left them alive—well, they are dead anyway, and getting a hot supper by now, I expect. Which shall it be, Master? Dutch stick or Spanish point?"

"Stick first, then point," answered Foy.

"Good. We need 'em both nowadays," and Martin reached down into a pair of gloves fitted into old sword hilts to protect the hands of the players.

They stood up to each other on guard, and then against the light of the lanterns it could be seen how huge a man was Martin. Foy, although well-built and sturdy, and like all his race of a stout habit, looked but a child beside the bulk of this great fellow. As for their stick game, which was in fact sword exercise, it is unnecessary to follow its details, for the end of it was what might almost have been expected. Foy sprang to and fro slashing and cutting, while Martin the solid scarcely moved his weapon. Then suddenly there would be a parry and a reach, and the stick would fall with a thud all down the length of Foy's back, causing the dust to fly from his leathern jerkin.

"It's no good," said Foy at last, rubbing himself ruefully. "What's the use of guarding against you, you great brute, when you simply crash through my guard and hit me all the same? That isn't science."

"No, Master," answered Martin, "but it is business. If we had been using swords you would have been in pieces by now. No blame to you and no credit to me; my reach is longer and my arm heavier, that is all."

"At any rate I am beaten," said Foy. "Now take the rapiers and give me a chance."

Then they went at it with the swords, rendered harmless by a disc of lead upon their points, and at this game the tide turned. Foy was active as a cat with the eye of a hawk, and twice he managed to get in under Martin's guard.

"You're dead, old fellow," he said at the second thrust.

"Yes, young Master," answered Martin, "but remember that I killed you long ago, so that you are only a ghost and of no account. Although I have tried to learn its use to please you, I don't mean to fight with a toasting fork. This is my weapon," and, seizing the great sword which stood in the corner, he made it hiss through the air.

Foy took it from his hand and looked at it. It was a long straight blade with a plain iron guard, or cage, for the hands, and on it, in old letters, was engraved one Latin word, *Silentium*, "Silence."

"Why is it called 'Silence,' Martin?"

"Because it makes people silent, I suppose, master."

"What is its history, and how did you come by it?" asked Foy in a malicious voice. He knew that the subject was a sore one with the huge Frisian.

Martin turned red as his own beard and looked uncomfortable. "I believe," he answered, staring upwards, "that it was the ancient Sword of Justice of a little place up in Friesland. As to how I came by it, well, I forget."

"And you call yourself a good Christian," said Foy reproachfully. "Now I have heard that your head was going to be chopped off with this sword, but that somehow you managed to steal it first and got away."

"There was something of the sort," mumbled Martin, "but it is so long ago that it slips my mind. I was so often in broils and drunk in those days—may the dear Lord forgive me—that I can't quite remember things. And now, by your leave, I want to go to sleep."

"You old liar," said Foy shaking his head at him, "you killed that poor executioner and made off with his sword. You know you did, and now you are ashamed to own the truth."

"Maybe, maybe," answered Martin slowly; "so, many things happen in the world that a fallen man cannot remember them all. I want to go to sleep."

"Martin," said Foy, sitting down upon a stool and dragging off his leather jerkin, "what kind of life did you live before you turned to Christ? You have never told me all the story. Come now, speak up. I won't tell Adrian."

"Nothing worth mentioning, Master Foy."

"Out with it, Martin."

"Well, if you wish to know, I am the son of a Friesland boor," began the bearded giant.

"And an Englishwoman from Yarmouth—I know all that," asserted Foy impatiently.

"Yes," repeated Martin, "an Englishwoman from Yarmouth. She was very strong, my mother; she could hold up a cart on her shoulders while my father greased the wheels, that is for a bet; otherwise, she used to make my father hold the cart up while she greased the wheels. Folk would come to see her do the trick. When I grew up, I held the cart and they both greased the wheels. But, at last they died of the plague, the pair of them, God rest their souls! So I inherited the farm—"

"And—" said Foy, fixing him with his eye.

"And," jerked out Martin in an unwilling fashion, "fell into bad habits."

"Drink?" suggested the merciless Foy.

Martin sighed and hung his great head, for he had a tender conscience.

"Then you took to prize-fighting," went on his tormentor. "You can't deny it; look at your nose."

"I did, Master, for the Lord hadn't touched my heart in those days, and," he added, brisking up, "it wasn't such a bad trade, for nobody ever beat me except a Brussels man once when I was drunk. He broke my nose, but afterwards, when I was sober—" and he stopped.

"You killed the Spanish boxer here in Leyden," said Foy

sternly.

"Yes," echoed Martin, "I killed him sure enough, but—oh, it was a pretty fight, and he brought it on himself. He was a fine man, that Spaniard, but the devil wouldn't play fair, so I just had to kill him. I hope that they bear in mind up above that I had to kill him."

"Tell me about it, Martin, for I was at The Hague at the time, and can't remember. Of course I don't approve of such things"— the young rascal clasped his hands and looked pious—"but as it is all done with, one may as well bear the story of the fight. To spin it won't make you more wicked than you are."

For some strange reason, Martin suddenly developed a marvelous memory, and with much wealth of detail set out the exact circumstances of that historic encounter.

"And after he kicked me in the stomach," he ended, "which, Master, you will know he had no right to do, I lost my temper and hit out with all my strength, having first feinted and knocked up his guard with my left arm—"

"And then," said Foy, growing excited, for Martin really told the story very well, "what happened?"

"Oh, his head went back between his shoulders, and when they picked him up, his neck was broken. I was sorry, but I couldn't help it. The Lord knows I couldn't help it; he shouldn't have called me 'a dirty Frisian ox' and kicked me in the stomach."

"No, that was very wrong of him. But they arrested you, didn't they, Martin?"

"Yes, for the second time they condemned me to death as a brawler and a manslayer. You see, the other Friesland business came up against me, and the magistrates here had money on the Spaniard. Then your dear father saved me. He was burgemeester during that year, and he paid the death fine for me—a large sum to be sure. Then, afterwards, he taught me to be sober and think of my soul. It was your father who led me to place my sins under the blood of Christ and to trust Him as my Sovereign Lord and Savior. So you know why Red Martin will serve him and his while there is a drop of blood left in his worthless carcass. And now, Master Foy, I'm going to sleep, and God grant that those dirty Spanish dogs may not haunt me."

"Don't you fear for that, Martin," said Foy as he took his departure, *"absolvo te* for those Spaniards. Through your strength, God smote them who were not ashamed to rob and insult a poor new widowed woman after helping to murder her husband. Yes, Martin, you may enter that on the right side of the ledger, for a change, so they won't haunt you at night. I'm more afraid lest the business should be traced home to us, but I don't think it likely since the street was quite empty."

"Quite empty," echoed Martin nodding his head. "Nobody saw me except the two soldiers and Vrouw Jansen. They can't tell, and I'm sure that she won't. Good night, my young master."

Chapter X
Adrian Goes Out Hawking

In a house down a back street not very far from the Leyden prison, a man and a woman sat at breakfast on the morning following the burning of the Heer Jansen and his fellow martyr. These also we have met before, for they were none other than the estimable Black Meg and her companion, named the Butcher. Time, which had left them both strong and active, had not, it must be admitted, improved their personal appearance. Black Meg, indeed, was much as she had always been, except that her hair was now gray and her features, which seemed to be covered with yellow parchment, had become sharp and hag-like, though her dark eyes still burned with their ancient fire. The man, Hague Simon, or the Butcher, scoundrel by nature and spy and thief by trade, one of the evil spawn of an age of violence and cruelty, boasted a face and form that fit his reputation well. His countenance was villainous, very fat and flabby, with small, pig-like eyes, and framed, as it were, in a fringe of sandy colored whiskers, running from the throat to the temple, where they faded away into the great expanse of an utterly bald head. The figure beneath was heavy, pot-paunched, and supported upon a pair of bowed but sturdy legs.

But if they were no longer young, and such good looks as they ever possessed had vanished, the years had brought them certain compensations. Indeed, it was a period in which spies and all such wretches flourished, since, besides other pickings, by special enactment a good proportion of the realized estates of heretics was paid over to the informers as blood-money. Of course, base tools like the Butcher and his wife did not get the largest joints of the heretic sheep, for whenever one was slaughtered, there were always many influential middlemen of various degree to be satisfied, from the judge down to the executioner, with others who never showed their faces.

Still, when the burnings and torturings were brisk, the amount totaled up very handsomely. Thus, as the pair sat at their meal this morning, they were engaged in figuring out what they might expect to receive from the estate of the late Heer Jansen, or at least Black Meg was so employed with the help of a slate board and a bit of chalk. At last she announced the result, which was satisfactory. Simon held up his fat hands in admiration.

"Clever little dove," he said, "you ought to have been a lawyer's wife with your head for figures. Ah! It grows near, it grows near."

"What grows near, you fool?" asked Meg in her deep masculine voice.

"That farm with an inn attached of which I dream, standing in rich pasture land with a little wood behind it, and in the wood a church. Not too large; no, I am not ambitious; let us say a hundred acres, enough to keep thirty or forty cows, which you would milk while I marketed the butter and the cheeses—"

"And slit the throats of the guests," interjected Meg.

Simon looked shocked. "No, Wife, you misjudge me. It is a rough world, and we must take unusual paths to fortune, but once I get there, respectability is what I desire and a seat in the village church, provided, of course, that it is orthodox. I know that you come of the people, and your instincts are of the people, but I can never forget that my grandfather was a gentleman," bellowed Simon, as he puffed himself out and looked at the ceiling.

"Indeed," sneered Meg, "and what was your grandmother, or, for the matter of that, how do you know who your grandfather was? Country house! The old Red Mill, where you hide goods out there in the swamp, is likely to be your only country house. Village church? Village gallows more likely. No, don't you look nasty at me, for I won't stand it, you dirty little liar. I have done things, I know, but I wouldn't have got my own aunt burned as an Anabaptist, which she wasn't, in order to earn twenty florins, so there."

Simon turned purple with rage for that aunt story was one that pricked even his well-worn and scarred conscience. "Ugly—" he began.

Instantly Meg's hand shot out and grasped the neck of a bottle, at which point he changed his tune.

"The sex, the weaker sex!" he exclaimed, turning aside to mop his bald head with a napkin. "Well, it's only their simple way, they will have their little joke. Hullo, there is someone knocking at the door."

"And mind how you open it," said Meg, becoming alert. "Remember we have plenty of enemies, and a pike blade comes through a small crack."

"Can you live with the wise and remain a greenhorn? Trust me." And placing his arm about his spouse's waist, Simon stood on tiptoe and kissed her gently on the cheek in token of reconciliation, for Meg had a nasty memory in quarrels. Then he skipped away towards the door as fast as his chubby legs would carry him.

The conversation there was long and for the most part carried on through the keyhole, but in the end their visitor was admitted, a beetle-browed brute of much the same character as his host.

"You are nice ones," he said sulkily, "to be so suspicious about an old friend, especially when he comes on a job."

"Don't be angry, dear Hans," interrupted Simon in a pleading voice. "You know how many bad characters are abroad in these rough times; why, for aught we could tell, you might have been one of these desperate Lutherans, who stop at nothing. But about the business?"

"Lutheran, indeed," snarled Hans. "Well, if they are wise they'd poke at your fat stomach; but it is a Lutheran job that I have come from The Hague to talk about."

"Ah!" said Meg, "who sent you?"

"A Spaniard named Ramiro, who has recently turned up there,

a humorous dog connected with the Inquisition, who seems to know everybody and whom nobody knows. However, his money is good enough, and no doubt he has authority behind him. He says that you are old friends of his."

"Ramiro? Ramiro?" repeated Meg reflectively, "that means Oarsman, doesn't it, and sounds like an alias? Well, I've lots of acquaintances in the galleys, and he may be one of them. What does he want, and what are the terms?"

Hans leant forward and whispered for a long while. The other two listened in silence, only nodding from time to time.

"It doesn't seem much for the job," said Simon when Hans had finished.

"Well, friend, it is easy and safe; a fat merchant and his wife and a young girl. Mind you, there is no killing to be done if we can help it, and if we can't help it, the Holy Office will shield us. Also it is only the letter that he thinks the young woman may carry that the noble Ramiro wants. Doubtless it has to do with the sacred affairs of the Church. Any valuables about them we may keep as a bonus over and above the pay."

Simon hesitated, but Meg announced with decision, "It is good enough; these merchant women generally have jewels hidden in their stays."

"My dear," interrupted Simon.

"Don't 'my dear' me," said Meg fiercely. "I have made up my mind, so there's an end. We meet by the Boshhuysen at five o'clock at the big oak in the grove, where we will settle the details."

After this Simon said no more, for he had one virtue so useful in domestic life—he knew when to yield.

On this same morning, Adrian rose late. The talk at the supper table on the previous night, especially Foy's coarse, uneducated sarcasm, had ruffled his temper, and when Adrian's temper was ruffled he generally found it necessary to sleep himself into good humor. As the bookkeeper of the establishment, for his stepfather had never been able to induce him to take an active part in its work, Adrian should have been in the office by nine o'clock. Not having risen before ten, however, nor eaten his breakfast until after eleven, this was clearly impossible. Then he remembered that here was a good chance of finishing a sonnet, of which the last lines were running in his head. It happened that Adrian was a bit of a poet, and like most poets, he found quiet essential to the art of composition. Somehow, when Foy was in the house, singing and talking, and that great Frisian brute, Martin, was tramping to and fro, there was never any quiet, for even when he could not hear them, the sense of their presence exasperated his nerves. So now was his opportunity, especially as his mother was out—marketing, she said—but in all probability engaged upon some wretched and risky business connected with the people whom she called martyrs. Adrian, therefore, determined to avail himself of this opportunity to finish his sonnet.

This took some time. First, as all true artists know, the appropriate mood must be summoned, and this will rarely arrive until the poet spends an hour or two in appropriate and gloomy contemplation of things in general. Then, especially in the case of sonnets or rhymes, which are stubborn and remorseless things, these ingredients must be found and arranged. The pivot and object of this particular poem was a certain notable Spanish beauty, Isabella d'Ovanda by name. She was the wife of a decrepit but exceedingly noble Spaniard, who was old enough to be her grandfather, and who had been sent as one of a commission appointed by King Philip II to inquire into certain financial matters connected with the Netherlands.

This grandee, who as it happened, was a very industrious and conscientious person, had visited Leyden in order to assess the value of the Imperial dues and taxes. The task did not take him long, because the burghers rudely and vehemently declared that under their ancient charter they were free from any Imperial dues or taxes whatsoever, nor could the noble marquis's arguments move them to a more rational view. Still, he argued for a week, and during that time his wife, the lovely Isabella, dazzled the women of the town with her costumes and the men with her exceedingly attractive person.

Especially did she dazzle the romantic Adrian; hence the poetry. On the whole, the rhymes went pretty well, though there were difficulties, but with industry he got round them. Finally the sonnet, a high-flown and very absurd composition, was completed.

By now it was time to eat; indeed, there are few things that make a man hungrier than long-continued poetical exercise, so Adrian ate. In the midst of the meal his mother returned, pale and anxious-faced, for the poor woman had been engaged in making arrangements for the safety of the beggared widow of the martyred Jansen, a sad and even dangerous task. In his own way, Adrian was fond of his mother, but being a selfish puppy he took but little note of her cares or moods. Therefore, seizing the opportunity of an audience he insisted upon reading to her his sonnet, not once but several times.

"Very pretty, my son, very pretty," declared Lysbeth, through whose bewildered brain the stilted and meaningless words buzzed like bees in an empty hive, "though I am sure I cannot guess how you find the heart in such times as these to write poetry to fine ladies whom you do not know."

"Poetry, Mother," said Adrian instructively, "is a great consoler; it lifts the mind from the contemplation of petty and sordid cares."

"Petty and sordid cares!" repeated Lysbeth wonderingly, then she added with a kind of cry, "Oh! Adrian, have you no heart that you can watch a saint burn and come home to philosophize about his agonies? Will you never understand? If you could have seen that poor woman this morning who only three months ago was a happy bride." Then bursting into tears Lysbeth turned and fled from the room, for she remembered that what was the fate of the Vrouw Jansen today, tomorrow might be her own.

This show of emotion quite upset Adrian whose nerves were delicate, and who being honestly attached to his mother did not like to see her weeping.

"Pest on the whole thing," he thought to himself, "why can't we go away and live in some pleasant place where they haven't got any religion, unless it is the worship of Venus? Yes, a place of orange groves, and running streams, and pretty women with guitars, who like having sonnets read to them, and—"

At this moment the door opened and Martin's huge and dusty frame appeared.

"The master wants to know if you are coming to the works, Heer Adrian, and if not will you be so good as to give me the key for the strong-box as he needs the cash book."

With a groan Adrian rose to go, then changed his mind. No, after that perfumed vision of green groves and lovely ladies it was impossible for him to face the malodorous and boring foundry, which he was confident was beneath his dignity.

"Tell them I can't come," he said, drawing the key from his pocket.

"Very good, Heer Adrian, why not?"

"Because I am writing," insisted the young man indignantly.

"Writing what?" queried Martin.

"A sonnet," replied the pompous poet.

"What's a sonnet?" asked Martin blankly.

"Ill-educated clown," murmured Adrian, then—with a sudden inspiration, "I'll show you what a sonnet is. I will read it to you. Come in and shut the door." Martin obeyed, and was duly rewarded with the sonnet, of which he understood nothing at all except the name of the lady, Isabella d'Ovanda.

But Martin was not without the guile of the serpent, and, in the weakness of his flesh insincerely stated: "Beautiful," he said, "beautiful! Read it again, Master."

Adrian did so with much delight, remembering the tale of how the music of Orpheus had charmed the very beasts.

"Ah!" said Martin, "that's a love letter, isn't it, to that splendid, black-eyed marchioness, whom I saw looking at you?"

"Well, not exactly," said Adrian, highly pleased, although to tell the truth he could not recollect upon what occasion the fair Isabella had favored him with her kind glances. "Yet I suppose that you might call it so, an idealized love letter, a letter in which ardent and distant yet tender admiration is wrapped with the veil of verse."

"Quite so. Well, Master Adrian, just you send it to her."

"You don't think that she might be offended?" queried Adrian doubtfully.

"Offended!" said Martin, "if she is, I know nothing of women" (as a matter of fact he didn't). "No, she will be very pleased; she'll take it away and read it by herself, and sleep with it under her pillow until she knows it by heart, and then I daresay, she will ask you to come and see her. Well, I must be off, but thank you for reading me the beautiful poetry letter, Heer Adrian."

"Really," reflected Adrian, as the door closed behind him, "this is another instance of the deceitfulness of appearances. I always thought Martin a great, brutal fool, yet in his breast, uncultured as it is, the sacred spark still smolders." And then and there he made up his mind that he would read Martin a further selection of poems upon the first opportunity.

If only Adrian could have been a witness to the scene which at that very moment was in progress at the works! Martin having delivered the key for the box, sought out Foy, and proceeded to tell him the story. The red-headed giant soon handed Foy a rough draft of the sonnet which he had surreptitiously garnered from the floor. Foy, clad in a leather apron, and seated on the edge of a casting, read it eagerly.

"I told him to send it," went on Martin, "and, by St. Peter, I think he will, and then if he doesn't have old Don Diaz after him with a pistol in one hand and a stiletto in the other, my name isn't Martin Roos."

"Of course, of course," gasped Foy, kicking his legs into the air with delight, "why, they call the old fellow 'Señor jealousy.' Oh! It's capital, and I only hope that he opens the lady's letters."

Thus did Foy, the commonplace and practical, make a mock of the poetic efforts of the lofty and sentimental Adrian.

Meanwhile Adrian, feeling that he required air after his literary labors, fetched his peregrine from its perch, for he was fond of hawking, and, setting it on his wrist, started out to find a quarry on the marshes near the town.

Before he was halfway down the street, he had forgotten all about the sonnet and the lovely Isabella. His was a curious temperament, and this sentimentality, born of vainness and idle hours, by no means expressed it all. That he was what we would nowadays call *pompous* we know, and also that he possessed his father Montalvo's readiness of speech without his father's sense of humor. In him, as Martin had hinted, the heredity of the sire predominated, for in all essentials Adrian was as Spanish in mind as in appearance.

For instance, the sudden and violent passions into which he was apt to fall, if thwarted or overlooked, were purely Spanish; there seemed to be nothing of the patient, logical Netherlander about this side of him. Indeed, it was this temper of his perhaps more than any other desire or tendency that made him so dangerous, for, whereas the impulses of his heart were often relatively good enough, they were always liable to be perverted by some access of suddenly provoked rage.

From his birth, Adrian had mixed little with Spaniards, and every influence about him, especially that of his mother, the being whom he most loved on earth, had been anti-Spanish. Still were he an hidalgo fresh from the Court, at the Escurial, he could scarcely have been more Castilian. Thus he had been brought up in what might be called a Republican atmosphere, yet he was without sympathy for the love of liberty that animated the people of Holland. The sturdy independence of the Netherlanders, their perpetual criticism of kings and established rules, their vulgar and silly assumption that the good things of the world were accessible to all honest and hardworking citizens, and not merely the birthright of blue blood, did not appeal to Adrian. Also, from childhood, he had been a member of the dissenting Church, one of the Protestant community. Yet, at heart, he rejected this faith with its humble professors and pastors, its simple, and sometimes squalid rites; its long and earnest prayers offered to the Almighty in the damp of a cellar or the reek of a cowhouse.

Like thousands of his Spanish fellow countrymen, he was spiritually and constitutionally unable to appreciate the fact that sinful men are given the gift of true faith through the gracious work of the Holy Spirit apart from external trappings and man-made schemes. God is seeking those who will worship Him in spirit and in truth, and the evidence of one who has been brought into a living relationship with Himself are the plain fruits of repentance and faith—an active faith that seeks to abide in regular communion with the Lord.

For safety's sake, like most politic Netherlanders, Adrian was called upon from time to time to attend worship in the Catholic churches. For reasons already explained, he did not find the obligation irksome.

In fact, the forms and rites of that stately ceremonial, the moving picture of the Mass in those marble aisles, the grandeur of the music and the sweet voices of hidden choristers—all these things unsealed a fountain in his bosom and at times moved him well nigh to tears. The system appealed to him also, and he could understand that in it were peace and comfort. For here was to be found forgiveness of sins, not far off in the heavens, but at hand upon the earth; forgiveness to all who bent the head and paid the fee. Here, ready made by the art of princely bishops and lofty Popes, was a Church that was worthy to secure on his behalf the eternal security which, after the death he dreaded (for he was full of spiritual fears and superstitions), would suffice to turn the shafts of Satan from his poor shivering soul, however steeped in crime. Was this not a more serviceable and practical faith than that of these loud-voiced, rude-handed Lutherans among whom he lived; men who elected to cast aside this armor and trust instead to a buckler supported by their faith and prayers—yes, and to trust only and entirely in the substitutionary sacrifice of Christ for salvation and eternal life?

Such were the thoughts of Adrian's secret heart, but as yet he had never acted on them, since, however much he might wish to do so, he had not found the courage to break away from the influence of his surroundings. His surroundings—Ah! How he hated them! How he hated them!

To preserve his dignity in the midst of his discontent, however, he could not live in complete idleness among folk who were always busy, therefore he acted as accountant in his stepfather's business, keeping the books of the foundry in a scanty and inefficient fashion, or writing letters to distant customers, for he was a skilled clerk, to order the raw materials necessary to the craft. But of this occupation he was weary, for he had the true Spanish dislike and contempt of trade. In his heart, he held that war was the only occupation worthy of a man. Successful war, of course, against foes worth plundering, such as Cortes and Pizarro had waged upon the natives of New Spain.

Adrian had read a chronicle of the adventures of these heroes, and bitterly regretted that he had come into the world too late to share them. The tale of heathen foemen slaughtered by thousands, and of the incalculable golden treasures divided among their conquerors, fired his imagination—especially the treasures. At times he would see them in his sleep, baskets full of gems, heaps of barbaric gold and tents filled with fair women slaves, all given by heaven to the true soldier whom it had charged with the sacred work of converting unbelievers by means of massacre and the rack.

Oh, how deeply did he desire such wealth and the power it would bring with it; he who was dependent upon others who looked down upon him as a lazy dreamer, who had never a guilder to spare in his pouch, who had nothing indeed but more debts than he cared to remember. But it never occurred to him to set to work and grow rich like his neighbors by honest toil and commerce. No, that was the task of slaves, like these low Hollander fellows among whom his lot was cast.

Such were the main characteristics of Adrian, surnamed van Goorl. He was the superstitious and unregenerate dreamer, the vain and dull poet, the chopper of false logic, the weak and passionate self-seeker, whose best and deepest cravings, such as his love for his mother were really little more than a reflection of his own passionate need to be flattered and pampered by others. Not that he was completely corrupt; in at least a few areas, God had restrained his evil nature. Thus he was capable of good purposes and of bitter remorse. Under certain circumstances he might even become capable of spiritual exaltation. But for this to become a pattern in his life, he must be in a prison strong enough to protect him from the blows of temptation. Adrian tempted would always be Adrian overcome. He was fashioned by his fallen human nature to be the tool of others or of his own desires.

It may be asked, what part had his mother in him; where in his weak ignoble nature was there a trace of a pure and noble character? Was this lack of godly will to be accounted for by the circumstances connected with his birth, in which she had been so unwilling an agent? Had she given him something of her body but naught of her spirit? This at least is true, that from his mother's stock he had derived nothing beyond a certain Dutch doggedness of purpose that, when added to his other qualities, might in some respects merely serve to make him a more accomplished sinner than may have otherwise been the case.

Adrian reached the Witte Poort, and paused on this side of the moat to reflect about things in general. Like most young men of his time and blood, he had military leanings and was convinced that, given the opportunity, he might become one of the foremost generals of his age. Now he was engaged in imagining himself besieging Leyden at the head of a great army, and in fancy disposing his forces after such fashion as would bring about its fall in the shortest possible time.

As he was thus occupied, a rude voice suddenly called, "Wake up, Spaniard," and a hard object—it was a green apple—struck him on his flat cap nearly knocking out the feather. Adrian leaped round with an oath, to catch sight of two lads, louts of about fifteen, projecting their tongues and jeering at him from behind the angles of the gatehouse. Adrian was not popular with the youth of Leyden, and he knew it well. So, thinking it wisest to take no notice of this affront, he was about to continue on his way when one of the youths, made bold by impunity, stepped from his corner and bowed before him until the ragged cap in his hand touched the dust, saying, in a mocking voice, "Hans, why do you disturb the noble hidalgo? Cannot you see that the noble hidalgo is going for a walk in the country to look for his most high father, the honorable duke of the Golden Fleece, to whom he is taking a cockolly bird as a present?"

Adrian heard and winced at the sting of the insult, as a

high-bred horse winces beneath the lash. In a moment rage boiled in his veins like a fountain of fire, and drawing the dagger from his girdle, he rushed at the boys, dragging the hooded hawk, which had become dislodged from his wrist, fluttering through the air after him. At that moment, indeed, he would have been capable of killing one or both of them if he could have caught them, but, fortunately for himself and them, being prepared for an onslaught, they vanished this way and that up the narrow lanes. Presently he stopped, and, still shaking with wrath, replaced the hawk on his wrist and walked across the bridge.

"They shall pay for it," he shouted. "Oh! I will not forget, I will not forget."

Here it may be explained that of the story of his birth Adrian had heard something, but not all. He knew, for instance, that his father's name was Montalvo, that the marriage with his mother for some reason was had been declared to be illegal, and that this Montalvo had left the Netherlands under a cloud to find his death, so he had been told, abroad. More than this Adrian did not know for certain, since everybody showed a singular reticence in speaking to him of the matter. Twice he had plucked up courage to question his mother on the subject, and on each occasion her face had turned cold and hard as stone, and she answered almost in the same words, "Son, I beg you to be silent. When I am dead, you will find all the story of your birth written down, but if you are wise you will not read."

Once also he had asked the same question of his stepfather, Dirk van Goorl, whereupon Dirk looked ill at ease and answered, "Take my advice, lad, and be content to know that you are here and alive with friends to take care of you. Remember that those who dig in churchyards find bones."

"Indeed," replied Adrian haughtily, "at least, I trust that there is nothing against my mother's reputation."

At these words, to his surprise, Dirk suddenly turned pale as a sheet and stepped towards him as though he were about to fly at his throat.

"You dare to doubt your mother," he began, "that angel out of

Heaven—" then ceased and added quickly, "Go! I beg your pardon; I should have remembered that you at least are innocent, and it is but natural that the matter weighs upon your mind."

So Adrian went, yet that proverb about churchyards and bones made such an impression on him that he did no more digging. In other words, he ceased to ask questions. He tried to console his mind with the knowledge that, however his father might have behaved to his mother, at least he was a man of ancient rank and ancient blood, which blood was his today. The rest would be forgotten, although enough of it was still remembered to permit his being taunted by those street louts, and when all was said and done, that precious blue blood of an hidalgo of Spain, must still remain his heritage.

Chapter XI
Adrian Rescues Beauty in Distress

All that long evening, Adrian wandered about the causeways that pierced the meadowlands and marshes, pondering these things and picturing himself as having attained to the dignity of a grandee of Spain, perhaps even—who could tell—to the proud rank of a Knight of the Golden Fleece entitled to stand covered in the presence of his Sovereign. More than one snipe and other birds such as he had come to hunt rose at his feet, but he was so preoccupied that they were out of range before he could unhood his falcon. At length, after he passed the church of Weddinvliet, Adrian followed the left bank of the Old Vliet River, which flowed opposite to the Boshhuysen wood, named after the half-ruined castle that stood in it. At this point, the young falconeer caught sight of a heron winging its homeward way to the heronry, and quickly unhooded his peregrine. She saw the prey at once and dashed towards it, whereon the heron, becoming aware of the approach of its enemy, began rising high into the air in narrow circles. Swiftly the falcon climbed after it in wider rings until at length she hovered high above and dove, but in vain. With a quick turn of the wings the heron avoided her, and before the falcon could find her pitch again, was far on its path towards the wood.

Once more the peregrine climbed and dove with a similar result. A third time she soared upwards in great circles, and a third time rushed downwards, now striking the heron full and holding on to it. Adrian, who was following their flight as fast as he could run, leaping some of the dykes in his path and splashing through others, soon paused to watch the end. For a moment, falcon and heron hung in the air, two hundred feet above the tallest tree beneath them, then the two birds began to descend to the grove for refuge, a struggling black dot against the glow of sunset. Then, still bound together, they rushed downward head-long, for their tangled fluttering wings did not serve to stay their fall, as they vanished among the tree-tops.

"Now my good falcon will be killed in the boughs—oh, what a fool was I to fly her so near the wood," thought Adrian to him-self as again he started forward.

Pushing on at his best pace, soon he was wandering about among the trees as near as possible to that spot where he had seen the birds fall, calling to the falcon and searching for her with his eyes. But here, in the dense grove, the fading light grew dim, so that he was soon obliged to abandon the quest in despair, and turned to find his way to the Leyden road. When within twenty paces of it, suddenly he came upon falcon and heron. The heron was stone dead, and the brave falcon so injured that it seemed hopeless to try to save her, for as he feared, they had crashed through the boughs of a tree in their fall. Adrian looked at her in dismay, for he loved this bird, which was the best of its kind in the city. He had trained her himself from a nestling. Indeed there had always been a curious sympathy between himself and this fierce creature of which he made a companion, as another man might of a dog. Even now he noted with a sort of pride that broken-winged and shattered though she was, her talons remained fixed in the back of the quarry, and her beak through the neck.

He stroked the falcon's head, whereon the bird, recognising him, loosed her grip of the heron and tried to flutter to her accus-tomed perch upon his wrist, only to fall to the ground, where she lay watching him with her bright eyes. Then, because there was no help for it, although he choked with grief at the deed, Adrian struck her on the head with his staff until she died.

"Goodbye, friend," he whispered, "at least that is the best way to go hence, dying with a dead foe beneath," and, picking up the peregrine, he smoothed her ruffled feathers and placed her ten-derly in his satchel.

Then it was, just as Adrian rose to his feet, standing beneath the shadow of the big oak upon which the birds had fallen, that coming from the road, which was separated from him by a little belt of undergrowth, he heard the sound of men's voices growling and threatening, and with them a woman's cry for help. At any other time he would have hesitated and reconnoitered, or, perhaps, have retreated at once, for he knew well the dangers of mixing himself up in the quarrels of travelers in those rough days. But the loss of his falcon had exasperated his nerves, making any excitement or adventure welcome to him. Therefore, without pausing to think, Adrian pushed forward through the brushwood to find himself in the midst of a curious scene.

Before him ran the grassy road or woodland lane. In the midst of it, sprawling on his back, for he had been pulled from his horse, lay a stout burgher, whose pockets were being rifled by a heavy-browed robber, who from time to time, doubtless to keep him quiet, threatened his victim with a knife. On the pillion of the burgher's thickset Flemish horse, which was peacefully cropping at the grass, sat a middle-aged woman, who seemed to be stricken dumb with terror, while a few paces away a second ruffian and a tall, bony woman were engaged in dragging a girl from the back of a mule.

Acting on the impulse of the moment, Adrian shouted, "Come on, friends, here are the thieves," whereon the robber woman took to flight and the man wheeled round. Moments later, the man pulled a naked knife from his girdle. But before he could lift it, Adrian's heavy staff crashed down upon the point of his shoulder, causing him to drop the dagger with a howl of pain. Again the staff rose and fell, this time upon his head, staggering him and knocking off his cap, so that the light, such as it was, shone full upon his villainous fat face. Adrian recognized at once that the fringe of sandy-colored whisker running from throat to temples, and the bald head above, belonged to the man known as Hague Simon, or the Butcher. Fortunately for him, however, the Butcher was too surprised, or too confused by the blow he had received upon his head, to recognise his assailant. Nor, having lost his knife, and believing doubtless that Adrian was only the first of a troop of rescuers, did he seem inclined to continue the combat. Moments later, calling to his companion to follow him, he began to run away from the woman with a swiftness almost incredible in a man of his build and weight, turning promptly into the brushwood, where he and his two fellow thieves vanished away.

Adrian dropped the point of his stick and looked round him, for the whole affair had been so sudden, and the rout of the enemy so complete, that he was tempted to believe he must be dreaming. Not eighty seconds ago he was hiding the dead falcon in his satchel, and now behold, he was a gallant knight who, unarmed, except for a dagger, which he had forgotten to draw, had conquered two sturdy knaves and a female accomplice, bristling with weapons, rescuing from their clutches Beauty (for doubtless the maiden was beautiful), and, incidentally, her wealthy relatives. Just then the lady, who had been dragged from the mule to the ground, where she still lay, struggled to her knees and looked up, thereby causing the hood of her traveling cloak to fall back from her head.

Thus it was, softened and illuminated by the last pale glow of this summer evening, that Adrian first saw the face of Elsa Brant.

The hero Adrian, overthrower of robbers, looked at the kneeling Elsa and knew that she was lovely, and as under the circumstances was right and fitting, the rescued Elsa, gazing at the hero Adrian, admitted to herself that he was handsome. She also recognized that his appearance on the scene had been opportune, not to mention providential.

Elsa Brant, the only child of that Hendrik Brant, the friend and cousin of Dirk van Goorl, who has already figured in this history, was just nineteen. Her eyes and her curled hair were brown, her complexion was pale, suggesting delicacy of constitution, her mouth small, with a turn of humor about it, and her chin rather large and firm. She was of middle height, if anything somewhat under it, with an exquisitely rounded and graceful figure and perfect hands. Lacking the stateliness of a Spanish beauty and the coarse fullness of outline which has always been

admired in the Netherlands, Elsa was still without doubt a beautiful woman, though how much of her charm was owing to her bodily attractions, and how much to the vibrant spirit which shown out of her clear large eyes when she was thoughtful, it would not be easy to determine. At any rate, her charms were sufficient to make a powerful impression upon Adrian, who, forgetting all about the Marchioness d'Ovanda, inspirer of sonnets, became enamored of her then and there, partly for her own sake and partly because it was the right kind of thing for a rescuer to do.

But it cannot be said, however deep her feelings of gratitude, that Elsa became enamored with Adrian. Undoubtedly, as she had recognised, he was handsome, and she much admired the readiness and force with which he had smitten that singularly loathsome-looking individual who had dragged her from the mule. But as it happened, standing where he did, the shadow of his face lay on the ground beside her. It was a faint shadow, for the light faded, still it was there, and it fascinated her, for seen thus the fine features became sinister and cruel, and their smile of courtesy and admiration was transformed into a most unpleasant sneer. A trivial accident of light, no doubt, and foolish enough that Elsa should notice it under such circumstances. But notice it she did, and what is more, so quickly are the minds of women turned this way or that, and so illogically do they draw a conclusion from some strange event that it nevertheless raised her prejudice against him.

"Oh! Señor," said Elsa clasping her hands, "how can I thank you enough?"

This speech was short and not entirely original. Yet there were two things about it that Adrian noted with satisfaction; first, that it was uttered in a soft and most attractive voice, and secondly, that the speaker supposed him to be a Spaniard of noble birth.

"Do not thank me at all, gracious lady," he replied, making his lowest bow. "To put to flight two robber rogues and a woman was no great feat, although I had but this staff for a weapon," he added, perhaps with a view to impressing upon the maiden's mind that her assailants had been armed while he, the deliverer, was not.

"Ah!" she answered, "I daresay that a brave knight like you thinks nothing of fighting several men at once, but when that wretch with the big hands and the flat face caught hold of me I nearly died of fright. At the best of times, I am a dreadful coward, and—no, I thank you, Señor, I can stand now and alone. See, here comes the Heer van Broekhoven under whose escort I am traveling, and look, see if he is bleeding. Oh! Worthy friend, are you hurt?"

"Not much, Elsa," gasped the Heer, for he was still breathless with fright and exhaustion, "but that ruffian—may the hangman have him—gave me a dig in the shoulder with his knife as he rose to run. However," he added with satisfaction, "he got nothing from me, for I am an old traveler, and he never thought to look in my hat."

"I wonder why they attacked us?" questioned Elsa.

The Heer van Broekhoven rubbed his head thoughtfully.

"To rob us, I suppose, but the strange thing is that they were expecting us, for I heard the woman say, 'Here they are; look for the letter on the girl, Butcher.'"

As he spoke, Elsa's face turned serious, and Adrian saw her glance at the animal she had been riding and slip her arm through its rein.

"Worthy sir," went on Van Broekhoven, "tell us whom we have to thank."

"I am Adrian, called Van Goorl," Adrian replied with dignity.

"Van Goorl!" said the Heer. "Well, this is strange. Providence could not have arranged it better. Listen, Wife," he went on, addressing the stout lady, who all this while had sat still upon the horse, so alarmed and bewildered that she could not speak, "here is a son of Dirk van Goorl, to whom we are charged to deliver Elsa."

"Indeed," answered the good woman, recovering herself somewhat. "I thought from the look of him that he was a Spanish nobleman. But whoever he is I am sure that we are all very much obliged to him, and if he could show us the way out of this dreadful wood, which doubtless is full of robbers, to the house of our kinsfolk, the Broekhovens of Leyden, I should be still more grateful."

"Madam, you have only to accept my escort, and I assure you that you need fear no more robbers. Might I in turn ask this lady's name?"

"Certainly, young sir, she is Elsa Brant, the only child of Hendrik Brant, the famous goldsmith of The Hague, but doubtless now that you know her name you know all that also, for she must be some kind of cousin to you. Husband, help Elsa on to her mule."

"Let that be my duty," said Adrian, and, springing forward, he lifted Elsa to the saddle gracefully enough. Then, taking her mule by the bridle, he walked onwards through the wood praying in his heart that the Butcher and his companions would not find courage to attack them again before they were out of its depths.

"Tell me, sir, are you Foy?" asked Elsa in a puzzled voice.

"No," answered Adrian, shortly, "I am his brother."

"I see that explains it. No wonder I was perplexed, for I remember Foy from the days when I was quite little; a beautiful boy with blue eyes and yellow hair, who was always very kind to me. Once he stopped at my father's house at The Hague with his father."

"Indeed," said Adrian, "I am glad to hear that Foy was ever beautiful. I can only remember that he was very stupid, for I used to try to teach him. At any rate, I am afraid you will not think him beautiful now—that is, unless you admire young men who are almost as broad as they are long."

"Oh! Heer Adrian," she answered, laughing, "I am afraid that fault can be found with most North Holland folk, and myself among the number. You see it is given to very few of us to be tall and noble-looking like high-born Spaniards—not that I should wish to resemble any Spaniard, however lovely she might be," Elsa added, with a slight hardening of her voice and face. "But," she went on hurriedly, as though sorry that the remark had escaped her, "you, sir, and Foy are strangely unlike to be brothers; is it not so?"

"We are half-brothers," said Adrian looking straight before him; "we have the same mother only; but please do not call me 'sir,' call me 'cousin.'"

"No, I cannot do that," she replied with a grin, "for Foy's mother is no relation of mine. I think that I must call you 'Sir Prince,' for, you see, you appeared at exactly the right time; just like the Prince in the fairy tales, you know."

Here was an opening not to be neglected by a young man of Adrian's background.

"Ah!" he said in a tender voice, and looking up at the lady with his dark eyes, "that is a happy name indeed. I would ask no better lot than to be your Prince, now and always charged to defend you from every danger." And Adrian honestly meant what he said, seeing that already he was convinced that to be the husband of the beautiful heiress of one of the wealthiest men in the Netherlands would be a very satisfactory walk in life for a young man in his position.

"Oh! Sir Prince," broke in Elsa hurriedly, for her cavalier's boldness was somewhat embarrassing, "you are telling the story wrong; the tale I mean did not go on like that at all. Don't you remember? The hero rescues the lady and hands her over to her father."

"Of whom I think he comes to claim her afterwards," replied Adrian with another languishing glance, and a smile of conscious vanity at the neatness of his answer. Their glances met, and suddenly Adrian became aware that Elsa's face had undergone a complete change. The playful, half-amused smile had vanished. It was now strained and hard and her eyes were frightened.

"Oh! Now I understand the shadow—how strange," she exclaimed in a new voice.

"What is the matter? What is strange?" he asked.

"Oh, only that your face reminded me so much of a man of whom I am terrified. No, no, I am foolish, it is nothing, those robbers have upset me. Praise be to God that we are out of that dreadful wood! Look, neighbor Broekhoven, here is Leyden before us. Are not those red roofs pretty in the twilight, and how big the churches seem. See, too, there is water all round the walls. It must be a very strong town. I should think that even the Spaniards could not take it, and oh! I am sure that it would be a good thing if we might find a city which we were quite, quite certain the Spaniards could never capture," and she sighed heavily.

"If I were a Spanish general with a proper army," began Adrian pompously, "I would take Leyden easily enough. Only this afternoon I studied its weak spots and made a plan of attack that could scarcely fail, seeing that the place would only be defended by a mob of untrained, half-armed burghers."

Again that curious look returned into Elsa's eyes.

"If you were a Spanish general," she said slowly. "How can you jest about such a thing as the sacking of a town by Spaniards? Do you know what it means? That is how they talk; I have heard them," and she shuddered, then went on. "You are

not a Spaniard, are you, sir, that you can speak like that?" And
without waiting for an answer Elsa urged her mule forward, leaving him a little behind.

Presently, as they passed through the Witte Poort, he was
at her side again and chatting to her, but although she replied
courteously enough, he felt that an invisible barrier had arisen
between them. She had read his secret heart; it was as though she
had been a party to his thoughts when he stood by the bridge
this afternoon designing plans for the taking of Leyden and half
wishing that he might share in its capture. She mistrusted him
and was half afraid of him, and Adrian knew that it was so.

Ten minutes' ride through the quiet town, brought the party
to the van Goorl's house in the Bree Straat. Here Adrian dis-
mounted and tried to open the door, only to find that it was
locked and barred. This seemed to exasperate a temper already
somewhat excited by the various events and experiences of the
day, and more especially by the change in Elsa's manner. At any
rate, he used the knocker with unnecessary energy. After a while,
with much turning of keys and drawing of bolts, the door was
opened, revealing Dirk, his stepfather, standing in the passage,
candle in hand, while behind, as though to be ready for any
emergency, loomed the great stooping shape of Red Martin.

"Is that you, Adrian?" asked Dirk in a voice at once testy
and relieved. "Then why did you not come to the side entrance
instead of forcing us to unbar here?"

"Because I bring a guest," replied Adrian pointing to Elsa and
her companions. "It did not occur to me that you would wish
guests to be smuggled in by a back door as though—as though
they were ministers of our New Religion."

The bow had been drawn at a venture, but the shaft went
home, for Dirk became startled and whispered, "Be silent, fool."
Then he added aloud, "Guest! What guest?"

"It is I, cousin Dirk, I, Elsa, Hendrik Brant's daughter," she
said, sliding from her mule.

"Elsa Brant!" shouted Dirk. "Why, how came you here?"

"I will tell you presently, but," she answered, "I cannot talk
in the street," and she touched her lips with her finger. "These

are my friends, the van Broekhovens, under whose escort I have traveled from The Hague. They wish to go on to the house of their relations, the other Broekhovens, if someone will show them the way."

Then followed greetings and brief explanations. After a few minutes of further discussion, the Broekhovens departed to the house of their relatives under the care of Martin, while Elsa was busy having her saddle removed and carried into the house. At the request of his father, Adrian led the mule round to the stable.

When Dirk had kissed and welcomed his young cousin, he ushered her, still accompanied by the saddle, into the room where his wife and Foy were at supper, and with them Pastor Arentz. He was clergyman who had preached to them on the previous night. Here he found Lysbeth, who had risen from the table, anxiously awaiting his return. So dreadful were the times that a knocking on the door at an unaccustomed hour was enough to throw those within into fear, especially if at the moment they chanced to be harboring a Protestant pastor, a crime punishable with death. That sound might mean nothing more than a visit from a neighbor, or it might be the trump of doom to every soul within the house, signifying the approach of the familiars of the Inquisition and of a martyr's crown. Therefore Lysbeth uttered a sigh of joy when her husband appeared, followed only by a girl.

"Wife," he said, "here is our cousin, Elsa Brant, come to visit us from The Hague, though why I know not as yet. You remember Elsa, the little Elsa, with whom we used to play so many years ago."

"Yes, indeed," answered Lysbeth, as she put her arms about her and embraced her, saying, "welcome, child, though," she added, glancing at her, "you should no longer be called child who have grown into so fair a maid. But look, here is the Pastor Arentz, of whom you may have heard, for he is the friend of your father and of us all."

"In truth, yes," answered Elsa curtsying, a salute which Arentz acknowledged by saying sincerely, "Daughter, I greet you in the name of the Lord, who has brought you to this house safely, for which we give thanks."

"Truly, Pastor, I have need to do so since—" and suddenly she stopped, for her eyes met those of Foy, who was gazing at her with such wonder and admiration stamped upon his open face that Elsa colored at the sight. Then, recovering herself, she held out her hand, saying, "Surely you are my cousin Foy; I should have known you again anywhere by your hair and eyes."

"I am glad," he answered simply, for it flattered him to think that this beautiful young lady remembered her old playmate, whom she had not seen for at least eleven years, adding, "but I do not think I would have recognized you."

"Why?" she asked, "have I changed so much?"

"Yes," Foy answered bluntly, "you used to be a thin little girl with red arms, and now you are the most lovely maiden I ever saw."

At this speech everybody laughed, including the Pastor, while Elsa, reddening still more, replied, "Cousin, I remember that you used to be rude, but now you have learned to flatter, which is worse. Nay, I beg of you, spare me," for Foy showed signs of wishing to argue the point. Then turning from him she slipped off her cloak and sat down on the chair which Dirk had placed for her at the table, reflecting in her heart that she wished it had been Foy who had rescued her from the thieves, and not the more polished Adrian.

Afterwards as the meal went on, she told the tale of their adventure. Scarcely was it done when Adrian entered the room. The first thing he noticed was that Elsa and Foy were seated side by side, engaged in animated talk, and the second, that there was no place for him at the table.

"Have I your permission to sit down, Mother?" he asked in a loud voice, for no one had seen him come in.

"Certainly, Son, why not?" answered Lysbeth, kindly. Adrian's voice warned her that his temper was ruffled.

"Because there is no place for me, Mother, that is all, though doubtless it is more worthily filled by the Rev. Pastor Arentz. Still, after a man has been fighting for his life with armed thieves, well—a bit of food and a place to eat it in would have been welcome."

"Fighting for your life, Son!" said Lysbeth astonished. "Why, from what Elsa has just been telling us, I gathered that the rascals ran away at the first blow which you struck with your staff."

"Indeed, Mother; well, doubtless if the lady says that, it was so. I took no great note, at least they ran and she was saved with the others, a small service barely worth mentioning, still useful in its way."

"Oh, take my chair, Adrian," said Foy rising, "and don't make such a stir about a couple of cowardly robbers and an old hag. You don't want us to think you a hero because you didn't turn tail and leave Elsa and her companions in their hands, do you? "

"What you think, or do not think, Brother, is a matter of indifference to me," replied Adrian, seating himself with an injured air.

"Whatever my cousin Foy may think, Heer Adrian," broke in Elsa anxiously, "I am sure I thank God who sent so brave a gentleman to help us. Yes, yes, I mean it, for it makes me sick to remember what might have happened if you had not rushed at those wicked men like, like—"

"Like David on the army of Philistines," suggested Foy.

"You should study your Bible, lad," put in Arentz with a slight smile. "It was Samson who slew an entire army of Philistines. David conquered the giant Goliath, though it is true that he also was a Philistine."

"Oh! Please, cousin Foy, do not laugh," requested Elsa, "I believe that you might have left me at the mercy of that dreadful man with a flat face and the bald head, who was trying to steal my father's letter. By the way, cousin Dirk, I have not given it to you yet, but it is quite safe, sewn up in the lining of the saddle, and I was to tell you that you must read it by the old cypher."

"Man with a flat face," said Dirk anxiously, as he slit away at the stitches of the saddle to find the letter. "Tell me about him. What was he like, and what makes you think he wished to take the paper from you?"

So Elsa described the appearance of the man and of the black-eyed hag, his companion, and repeated also the words that the Heer van Broekhoven had heard the woman utter before the attack took place.

"That sounds like the spy, Hague Simon, him whom they call the Butcher, and his wife, Black Meg," said Dirk.

"Adrian, you must have seen these people, was it they?" continued the Father.

For a moment Adrian considered whether he should tell the truth; then, for certain reasons of his own, decided that he would not.

"How should I know?" he answered, after a pause; "the place was gloomy, and I have only set eyes upon Hague Simon and his wife about twice in my life."

"Softly, Brother," said Foy, "and stick to the truth, however gloomy the wood may have been. You know Black Meg pretty well at any rate, for I have often seen you—" and he stopped suddenly, as though sorry that the words had slipped from his tongue.

"Adrian, is this so?" asked Dirk in the silence which followed.

"No, Father," answered Adrian.

"You hear," said Dirk addressing Foy. "In the future, son, I trust that you will be more careful with your words. It is no charge to bring lightly against a man that he has been seen in the fellowship of one of the most infamous wretches in Leyden, a creature whose hands are stained red with the blood of innocent men and women, and who, as your mother knows, once brought me near to the scaffold."

Suddenly the laughing boyish look passed out of the face of Foy, and it grew stern.

"I am sorry for my words," he said, "since Black Meg does other things besides spying, and Adrian may have had business of his own with her which is no affair of mine. But, as they are spoken, I can't eat them, so you must decide which of us is—not truthful."

"Nay, Foy, nay," interposed Arentz, "do not put it thus.

Doubtless there is some mistake, and have I not told you before that you are over rash of tongue?"

"Yes, and a great many other things," answered Foy, "everyone of them true, for I am a miserable sinner. Well, all right, there is a mistake, and it is," he added, with an air of radiant innocency that somehow was scarcely calculated to deceive, "that I was merely poking a stick into Adrian's temper. I never saw him talking to Black Meg. Now, are you satisfied?"

Then the storm broke, as Elsa, who had been watching the face of Adrian while he listened to Foy's artless but somewhat satisfactory explanation, saw that it must break.

"There is a conspiracy against me," said Adrian, who had grown white with rage; "yes, everything has conspired against me today. First the ragamuffins in the street make a mock of me, and then my falcon is killed. Next it happens that I rescue this lady and her companions from robbers in the wood. But do I get any thanks for this? No, I come home to find that I am so much forgotten that no place is even laid for me at the table; more, to be jeered at for the humble services that I have done. Lastly, I have a lie spoken of me, and without reproach, by my brother, who, were he not my brother, should answer for it at the sword's point."

"Oh! Adrian, Adrian," broke in Foy, "don't be a fool; stop before you say something you will be sorry for."

"That isn't all," went on Adrian, taking no heed. "Whom do I find at this table? The worthy Heer Arentz, a minister of the New Religion. Well, I protest. I belong to the New Religion myself, having been brought up in that faith, but it must be well known that the presence of a pastor here in our house exposes everybody to the risk of death. If my stepfather and Foy choose to take that risk, well and good, but I maintain that they have no right to lay its consequences upon my mother, whose eldest son I am, nor even upon myself."

Now Dirk rose and tapped Adrian on the shoulder. "Young man," he said coldly and with glittering eyes, "listen to me. The risks that I and my son, Foy, and my wife, your mother, take, we run for conscience sake. You have nothing to do with them, it is our affair. But since you have raised the question, if your faith is not strong enough to support you I acknowledge that I have no right to bring you into danger. Look you, Adrian, you are no son of mine; in you I have neither part nor lot, yet I have cared for you and supported you since you were born under very strange and unhappy circumstances. Yes, you have shared whatever I had to give with my own son, without preference or favor, and should have shared it even after my death. And now, if these are your opinions, I am tempted to say to you that the world is wide and that, instead of idling here upon my bounty, you would do well to win your own way through it as far from Leyden as may please you."

"You throw your benefits in my teeth, and reproach me with my birth," broke in Adrian, who by now was almost raving with passion, "as though it were a crime in me to have other blood running in my veins than that of Netherlander tradesfolk. Well, if so, it would seem that the crime was my mother's, and not mine, who—"

"Adrian, Adrian!" cried Foy, in warning, but the madman heeded not.

"—who," he went on, furiously, "was content to be the companion, for I understand that she was never really married to him who was a noble Spaniard before she became the wife of a Leyden artisan."

He ceased, and at this moment there broke from Lysbeth's lips a low wail of such bitter anguish that it chilled even his mad rage to silence.

"Shame on you, my son," said the wail, "who are not ashamed to speak thus of the mother that bore you."

"Ay," echoed Dirk, in the stillness that followed, "shame on you! Once you were warned, but now I warn no more."

Then he stepped to the door, opened it, and called, "Martin, come here."

Several moments later, still in that heavy silence, which was broken only by the quick breath of Adrian panting like some wild beast in a net, was heard the sound of heavy feet shuffling down the passage. Then Martin entered the room, and stood

there gazing about him with his large blue eyes that were like the eyes of a wondering child.

"Your pleasure, Master," he said as he entered the room.

"Martin Roos," replied Dirk, waving back Arentz who rose to speak, "take that young man, my stepson, the Heer Adrian, and lead him from my house without violence if possible. My order is that henceforth you are not to permit him to set foot within its threshold; see that it is not disobeyed. Go, Adrian, tomorrow your possessions shall be sent to you, and with them such money as shall suffice to start you in the world."

Without comment or any expression of surprise, the huge Martin shuffled forward towards Adrian, his hand outstretched as though to take him by the arm.

"What," exclaimed Adrian, as Martin advanced down the room, "you set your mastiff on me, do you? Then I will show you how a gentleman treats dogs," and suddenly, with a naked dagger shining in his hand, he leaped straight at the Frisian's throat. So quick and fierce was the onslaught that only one result to it seemed possible. Elsa gasped and closed her eyes, thinking when she opened them to see that knife plunged to the hilt in Martin's breast. Yet in this twinkling of an eye the danger soon dissipated, for by some movement too quick to follow, Martin had dealt his assailant such a blow upon the arm that the weapon, jarred from his grasp, flew flashing across the room to fall in Lysbeth's lap. Another second and the iron grip had closed upon Adrian's shoulder, and although he was strong and struggled furiously, yet he could not loose the hold of that single hand.

"Please cease fighting, Mynheer Adrian, for it is quite useless," said Martin to his captive in a voice as calm as though nothing unusual had happened. Then he turned and walked with him towards the door.

On the threshold Martin stopped, and looking over his shoulder said, "Master, I think that the Heer is dead, do you still wish me to put him into the street?"

They crowded round and stared at the pathetic creature. It was true, Adrian appeared to be dead. His face was like that of a corpse, while from the corner of his mouth blood trickled in a thin stream.

Chapter XII
The Summons

"Wretched man!" said Lysbeth wringing her hands, and with a shudder shaking the dagger from her lap as though it had been a serpent, "you have killed my son."

"Your pardon, mistress," replied Martin placidly, "but that is not so. The master ordered me to remove the Heer Adrian, whereon the Heer Adrian very naturally tried to stab me. But I, having been accustomed to such things in my youth," and he looked deprecatingly towards the Pastor Arentz, "struck the Heer Adrian upon the bone of his elbow, causing the knife to jump from his hand, for had I not done so I should have been dead and unable to execute the commands of my master. Then I took the Heer Adrian by the shoulder, gently as I might, and walked away with him, whereupon he died of rage, for which I am very sorry but not to blame."

"You are right, man," said Lysbeth, "it is you who are to blame, Dirk; yes, you have murdered my son. Oh! Never mind what he said, his temper was always fierce, and who pays any heed to the talk of a man in a mad passion."

"Why did you let your brother be thus treated, Cousin Foy?" broke in Elsa quivering with indignation. "It was cowardly of you to stand still and see that great red creature crush the life out of him when you know well that it was because of your taunts that he lost his temper and said things that he did not mean, as I do myself sometimes. No, I will never speak to you again—and only this afternoon he saved me from the robbers!" and she burst into weeping.

"Peace, peace! This is no time for angry words," said the Pastor Arentz, pushing his way through the group of bewildered men and overwrought women. "He can scarcely be dead; let me look at him, I am something of a doctor," and he knelt by the senseless and bleeding Adrian to examine him.

"Take comfort, Vrouw van Goorl," he said cheerfully, "your son is not dead, for his heart beats, nor has his friend Martin injured him in any way by the exercise of his strength, but I think that in his fury he has burst a blood vessel, for he bleeds fast. My counsel is that he should be put to bed and his head cooled with cold water until the surgeon can be fetched to treat him. Lift him in your arms, Martin."

So Martin carried Adrian not to the street, but to his bed, while Foy, glad of an excuse to escape the undeserved reproaches of Elsa and the painful sight of his mother's grief, went to seek the physician. In due course he returned with him, and, to the great relief of all of them, the learned man announced that, notwithstanding the blood which he had lost, he did not think that Adrian would die. The doctor proceeded to recommend that the patient be kept in his bed for some weeks, have skillful nursing, and be cared for in all things.

While Lysbeth and Elsa were attending to Adrian, Dirk and his son Foy, for the Pastor Arentz had gone, sat upstairs talking in the sitting room, that same balconied chamber in which Dirk had once been refused while Montalvo hid behind the curtain. Dirk was much disturbed, for when his wrath had passed he was a tenderhearted man, and his stepson's plight distressed him greatly. Now he was justifying himself to Foy, or, rather, to his own conscience.

"A man who could speak so of his own mother was not fit to stay in the same house with her," he said. "Moreover, you heard his words about the pastor. I tell you, Son, I am afraid of this Adrian."

"Unless that bleeding from his mouth stops soon you will not have cause to fear him much longer," replied Foy sadly, "but if you want my opinion about the business, Father, why here it is— I think that you have made too much of a small matter. Adrian is—Adrian. He is not one of us, and he should not be judged as though he were. You cannot imagine me flying into a fury because the women forgot to set my place at the table, or trying to stab Martin and bursting a blood vessel because you told him to lead me out of the room. No, I should know better, for what is the use of any ordinary man attempting to struggle against Martin? He might as well try to argue with the Inquisition. But then I am I, and Adrian is Adrian."

"But the words he used, Son. Remember the words," insisted Heer van Goorl.

"Yes, and if I had spoken them they would have meant a great deal, but in Adrian's mouth I think no more of them than if they came from some angry Inquisition judge. Why, he is always sulking, or taking offense, or flying into rages over something or other, and when he is like that, it all means—just nothing, except that he wants to use fine talk and show off and play the Don over us. He did not really mean to lie to me when he said that I had not seen him talking to Black Meg, he only meant to contradict, or perhaps to hide something up. As a matter of fact, if you want to know the truth, I believe that the old witch took notes for him to some young lady, and that Hague Simon supplied him with rats for his falcons."

"Yes, Foy, that may be so, but how about his talk regarding the pastor? It makes me suspicious, Son. You know the times we live in, and if he should go that way—remember it is in his blood—the lives of every one of us are in his hand. The father tried to burn me once, and I do not wish the child to finish the work."

"Then if and when Adrian threatens your life, you are at liberty to cut off mine," answered Foy hotly. "I have been brought up with Adrian, and I know what he is; he is vain and pompous, and every time he looks at you and me he thanks God that he was not made like us. Also he has failings and vices, and he is lazy, being too fine a gentleman to work like a common Flemish burgher, and all the rest of it. But, Father, he has a proud heart, and if any man outside this house were to tell me that Adrian is capable of playing the traitor and bringing his own family to the scaffold, well, I would make him swallow his words, or try to, that is all. As regards what he said about my mother's first marriage," and Foy hung his head, "of course, it is a subject on which I have no right to talk, but, Father, speaking as one man to another, he is sadly placed, and I don't wonder that he feels sore about the story."

As Foy finished speaking, the door opened and Lysbeth entered.

"How goes it with Adrian, Wife?" Dirk asked hastily.

"Better, Husband, thank God, though the doctor stays with him for this night. He has lost much blood, and at the best must lie long in bed; above all, none must cross his mood or use him roughly," and she looked at her husband with meaning.

"Peace, Wife," Dirk answered with irritation. "Foy here has just read me one lecture upon my dealings with your son, and I am in no mood to listen to another. I served the man as he deserved, neither less nor more, and if he chose to go mad and vomit blood, why it is no fault of mine. You should have brought him up with a greater understanding of the importance of self-control."

"Adrian is not as other men are, and ought not to be measured by the same rule," said Lysbeth, almost repeating Foy's words.

"So I have been told before, Wife, though I, who acknowledge but one biblical standard of right and wrong, find the saying hard. But so be it. Doubtless the rule for Adrian is that which should be used to measure angels—or Spaniards, and not one suited to us poor Hollanders who do our work, pay our debts, and don't draw knives on unarmed men!"

"Have you read the letter from your cousin Brant?" asked Lysbeth, changing the subject.

"No," answered Dirk, "what with daggers, swoonings, and scoldings it slipped my mind," and drawing the paper from his tunic he cut the silk and broke the seals. "I had forgotten," he went on, looking at the sheets of words interspersed with meaningless figures. "It is in our private cypher, as Elsa said, or at least most of it is. Get the key from my desk, Son, and let us set to work, for our task is likely to be long."

Foy obeyed, returning quickly with an Old Testament of a very scarce edition. With the help of this book and an added vocabulary by slow degrees they deciphered the long epistle,

Foy writing it down until by sentence as they learned their significance. When at length the task was finished, which was not until well after midnight, Dirk read the translation aloud to Lysbeth and his son. It ran thus:

> Well-beloved cousin and old friend, you will be astonished to see my dear child Elsa, who brings you this paper sewn in her saddle, where I trust none will seek it, and wonder why she comes to you without warning. I will tell you.
>
> You know that here the axe and the stake are very busy, for at The Hague the devil walks loose; yes, he is the master in this land. Well, although the blow has not yet fallen on me, since for a while I have bought off the informers, hour by hour the sword hangs over my head, nor can I escape it in the end. That I am suspected of being a Protestant is not my real crime. You can guess it. Cousin, they desire my wealth. Now I have sworn that no Spaniard shall have this, no, not if I must sink it in the sea to save it from them, since it has been heaped up to another end. Yet they desire it sorely, and spies are about my path and about my bed. Worst among them all, and at the head of them, is a certain Ramiro, a one-eyed man, but lately come from Spain, it is said as an agent of the Inquisition, whose manners are those of a person who was once a gentleman, and who seems to know this country well. This fellow has approached me, offering that if I will give him three-parts of my wealth he will secure my escape with the rest. I have told him that I will consider the offer, merely so that I can gain extra time, since he desires that my money should go into his pocket and not into that of the Government. But, by the help of God, neither of them shall touch it.
>
> See you, Dirk, the treasure is not here in the house as they think. It is hidden, but in a spot where it cannot stay.
>
> Therefore, if you love me, and hold that I have been a good friend to you, send your son Foy with one other strong and trusted man, your Frisian servant, Martin, if possible on the morrow after you receive this. When night falls, he should have been in The Hague some hours, and have refreshed himself, but let him not come near me or my house. Half an hour after sunset let him, followed by his serving man, walk up and down the right side of the Broad Street in The Hague, as though seeking adventures, until a girl, also followed by a servant, pushes up against him as if

on purpose, and whispers in his ear, 'Are you from Leyden, sweetheart?' Then he must say 'Yes,' and accompany her until he comes to a place where he will learn what must be done and how to do it. Above all, he must follow no woman who may accost him and who does not repeat these words. The girl who addresses him will be short, dark, pretty, and brightly dressed, with a red bow upon her left shoulder. But let him not be misled by look or dress unless she speaks the words.

If he reaches England or Leyden safely with the stuff let him hide it for the present, friend, until your heart tells you it is needed. I care not where, nor do I wish to know, for if I knew, flesh and blood are weak, and I might give up the secret when they stretch me on the rack.

Already you have my will sent to you three months ago, and enclosed in it a list of goods. Open it now and you will find that under it my possessions pass to you and your heirs absolutely as my executors, for such especial trusts and purposes as are set out therein. Elsa has been ailing, and it is known that the doctor has ordered her a change. Therefore her journey to Leyden will excite no wonder, neither, or so I hope, will even Ramiro guess that I should enclose a letter such as this in so frail a casket. Still, there is danger, for spies are many, but having no choice, and my need being urgent, I must take the risks. If the paper is seized they cannot read it, for they will never make out the cypher, since, even did they know of them, no copies of our books can be found in Holland. Moreover, were this writing all plain Dutch or Spanish, it tells nothing of the whereabouts of the treasure, of its destination, or of the purpose to which it is dedicated. Lastly, should any Spaniard happen to find that wealth, it will vanish, and, perhaps, he with it.

"What can he mean by that?" interrupted Foy.

"I know not," answered Dirk. "My cousin Brant is not a person who speaks at random, so perhaps we have misinterpreted the passage." Then he went on reading:

Now I have little need for the wealth, which must soon be transferred. Only, I pray you—I trust it to your honor and to your love of an old friend to bury it, burn it, cast it to the four winds of heaven before you permit a Spaniard to touch a gem or a piece of gold.

I send to you today Elsa, my only child. You will know my reason. She will be safer with you in Leyden than here at The Hague, since if they take me they might take her also. The priests and their tools do not spare the young, especially if their rights stand between them and money. Also she knows little of my desperate strait; she is ignorant even of the contents of this letter, and I do not wish that she should share these troubles. I am a doomed man, and she loves me, poor child. One day she will hear that it is over, and that will be sad for her, but it would be worse if she knew all from the beginning. When I bid her goodbye tomorrow, it will be for the last time. May God give me strength to bear the blow.

You are her guardian, as you deal with her—nay, I must be crazy with my troubles, for none other would think it needful to remind Dirk van Goorl or his son of their duty to the dead. Farewell, friend and cousin. God guard you and yours in these dreadful times with which it has pleased Him to visit us for a season, that through us perhaps this country and the whole world may be redeemed from priestcraft and tyranny. Greet your honored wife, Lysbeth, from me; also your son Foy, who used to be a merry lad, and whom I hope to see again within a night or two, although it may be God's will that we shall not meet. My blessing on him, especially if he prove faithful in all these things. May the Almighty who guards us give us a happy meeting in the hereafter, which is at hand. Pray for me. Farewell, farewell. —HENDRIK BRANT.

P. S. I beg the dame Lysbeth to see that Elsa wears woollen when the weather turns damp or cold, since her chest is somewhat delicate. This was my wife's last charge, and I pass it on to you. As regards her marriage, should she live, I leave that to your judgment with this command only, that her inclination shall not be forced, beyond what is biblically right and proper. When I am dead, kiss her for me and tell her that I loved her beyond any creature now living on the earth, and that as I rest in God's presence above I will wait to welcome her, as I shall wait to welcome you and yours, Dirk van Goorl. In case these presents miscarry, I will send duplicates of them, also in mixed cypher, whenever the opportunity may offer.

Having finished reading the translation of this cypher document, Dirk bent his head while he folded it, not wishing that his face should be seen. Foy also turned aside to hide the tears which gathered in his eyes, while Lysbeth wept openly.

"A sad letter and sad times!" said Dirk at length.

"Poor Elsa," muttered Foy, then added, with a return of hopefulness, "perhaps he is mistaken, he may escape after all."

Lysbeth shook her head as she answered, "Hendrik Brant is not the man to write like that if there was any hope for him, nor would he part with his daughter unless he knew that the end must be near at hand."

"Why, then, does he not flee to another place?" asked Foy.

"Because the moment he stirred, the Inquisition would pounce upon him, as a cat pounces upon a mouse that tries to run from its corner," replied his father. "While the mouse sits still the cat sits also and purrs; when it moves then the animal springs into action."

There was a silence in which Dirk, having fetched the will of Hendrik Brant from a safe hiding place, where it had lain since it reached his hands some months before, opened the seals and read it aloud.

It proved to be a very short document, under the terms of which Dirk van Goorl and his heirs inherited all the property, real and personal, of Hendrik Brant, upon trust (1) to make such ample provision for his daughter Elsa as might be needful or expedient; (2) to apply the remainder of the money "for the defense of our country, the freedom of the Christian Faith, and the destruction of the Spaniards in such fashion and at such time or times as God should reveal to them, which," added the will, "assuredly He will do."

Enclosed in this document was an inventory of the property that constituted the treasure. At the head came an almost endless list of jewels, all of them carefully scheduled. These were the first three items:

"Item: The necklace of great pearls that I exchanged with the Emperor Charles when he took a love for sapphires, enclosed in a watertight copper box.

"Item: A coronet and stomacher of rubies mounted in my own gold work, the best that ever I did, which three queens have coveted, and none was rich enough to buy.

"Item: The great emerald that my father left me, the biggest known, having magic signs of the ancients engraved upon the back of it, and enclosed in a chased case of gold."

Then came other long lists of precious stones, too numerous to mention, but of less individual value, and after them this entry:

"Item: Four casks filled with gold coin (I know not the exact weight or number)."

At the bottom of this listing was written, "A very great treasure, the greatest in all the Netherlands, a fruit of three generations of honest trading and saving, converted by me for the most part into jewels, that it may be easier to move. This is the prayer of me, Hendrik Brant, who owns it for his life; that this gold may prove the earthly doom of any Spaniard who tries to steal it, and as I write it comes into my mind that God will grant this my petition. Amen. Amen. Amen! So say I, Hendrik Brant, who stand at the Gate of Death."

All of this inventory Dirk read aloud, and when he had finished, Lysbeth gasped with amazement.

"Surely," she said, "this little cousin of ours is richer than many princes. Yes, with such a dowry princes would be glad to take her in marriage."

"The fortune is large enough," answered Dirk. "But, oh, what a burden has Hendrik Brant laid upon our backs, for under this will the wealth is left, not straight to the lawful heiress, Elsa, but to me and to my heirs on the trusts stated, and they are heavy. Look you, Wife, the Spaniards know of this vast hoard, and the priests know of it, and no stone in earth or hell will they leave unturned to win that money. I say that for his own sake, my cousin Hendrik would have done better to accept the offer of the Spanish thief Ramiro and give him three-fourths and escape to England with the rest. But that is not his nature, who was ever stubborn, and who would die ten times over rather than enrich the men he hates. Moreover, he, who is no miser, has saved this fortune that the bulk of it may be spent for his country in the hour of her need, and alas, of that need we are made the judges, since he is called away. I foresee that these gems and gold will breed bloodshed and misery to all our house. But the trust is laid upon us and it must be borne. Foy, tomorrow at dawn you and Martin will start for The Hague to carry out the command of your cousin Brant."

"Why should my son's life be risked on this mad errand?" asked Lysbeth.

"Because it is a duty, Mother," answered Foy cheerfully, although he tried to look depressed. He was young and enterprising; moreover, the adventure promised to be full of novelty.

In spite of himself, Dirk smiled and told his son to summon Martin.

A minute later, Foy was in the great man's den and kicking at his prostrate form. "Wake up, you snoring bull," he said. "Awake!"

Martin sat up, his red head showing like a fire in the shine of the taper. "What is it now, Master Foy?" he asked, yawning. "Are they after us about those two dead soldiers?"

"No, you sleepy lump, it's treasure."

"I don't care about treasure," replied Martin, indifferently.

"It involves Spaniards," said Foy with a smile.

"That sounds better," said Martin, shutting his mouth. "Tell me about it, Master Foy, while I pull on my jerkin."

So Foy told him as much as he could in two minutes.

"Yes, it sounds well," commented Martin, critically. "If I know anything of those Spaniards, we shan't get back to Leyden without something happening. But I don't like that bit about the women; as likely as not, they will spoil everything."

Then he accompanied Foy to the upper room, and there Martin received instructions from his master with a solemn and unmoved countenance.

"Are you listening?" asked Dirk, sharply. "Do you understand?"

"I think so, Master," replied Martin, and then he repeated,

sentence by sentence, every word that had fallen from Dirk's lips. When he chose to use it, Martin's memory was good. "One or two questions, Master," he said. "This stuff must be brought through at all hazards?"

"At all hazards," answered Dirk.

"And if we cannot bring it through, it must be hidden in the best way possible?"

"Yes," indicated Dirk.

"And if people should try to interfere with us, I understand that we must fight?"

"Of course."

"And if in the fighting we happen to kill anybody, I shall not be reproached and called a murderer by the pastor or others?"

"I think not," replied Dirk.

"And if anything should happen to my young master here, his blood will not be laid upon my head?"

Lysbeth groaned. Then she stood up and spoke.

"Martin, why do you ask such foolish questions? Your peril my son must share, and if harm should come to him as may be the Lord's will, we shall know well that it is no fault of yours. You are not a coward or a traitor, Martin."

"Well, I think not, Mistress, at least not often; but you see here are two duties: the first, to get this money through, the second, to protect the Heer Foy. I wish to know which of these is the more important."

It was Dirk who proceeded to answer this difficult question.

"You go to carry out the wishes of my cousin Brant. His treasure must be attended to before anything else."

"Very good," replied Martin "you quite understand, Heer Foy?"

"Oh! Perfectly," replied that young man, grinning.

"Then go to bed for an hour or two, as you may have to keep awake tomorrow night. I will call you at dawn. I am your servant, Master and Mistress. I hope to report myself to you within sixty hours, but if I do not come within eighty, or let us say a hundred, it may be well to make inquiries," and he shuffled back to his den still clad in his leather jerkin.

Youth sleeps well whatever may be behind or before it, and it was not until Martin had called to him thrice the next morning that Foy opened his eyes in the gray light, and, remembering, sprang from his bed.

"There's no hurry," said Martin, "but it will be as well to get out of Leyden before many people are about."

As he spoke, Lysbeth entered the room fully dressed, for she had not slept that night, carrying in her hand a little leathern bag.

"How is Adrian, Mother?" asked Foy, as she stooped down to kiss him.

"He sleeps, and the doctor, who is still with him, says that he does well," she answered. "But see here, Foy, you are about to start upon your first adventure, and this is my present to you— this and my blessing." Then she untied the neck of the bag and poured from it something that lay upon the table in a shining heap no larger than Martin's fist. Foy took hold of the thing and held it up, whereon the little heap stretched itself out marvelously, until it was as large indeed as the body garment of a man.

"Steel shirt!" exclaimed Martin, nodding his head in approval, and adding, "good wear for those who mix with Spaniards."

"Yes," said Lysbeth, "my father brought this from the East on one of his voyages. I remember he told me that he paid for it its weight in gold and silver, and that even then it was sold to him only by the special favor of the king of that country. The shirt, they said, was ancient, and of such work as cannot now be made. It had been worn from father to son in one family for three hundred years, but no man that wore it ever died by body-cut or thrust, since sword or dagger cannot pierce that steel. At least, Son, this is the story, and, strangely enough, when I lost all the rest of my heritage—" and she sighed, "this shirt was left to me, for it lay in its bag in the old oak chest, and none noticed it or thought it worth the taking. So make the most of it, Foy. It is all that remains of your grandfather's fortune, since this house is now your father's."

Beyond kissing his mother in thanks, Foy made no other

answer. He was too engaged in examining the wonders of the shirt, which, as a worker in metals, he could well appreciate. But Martin said: "Better than money, much better than money. God knew that and made them leave the mail."

"I never saw the like of it," broke in Foy. "Look, it runs together like quicksilver, and is light as leather. See, too, it has stood sword and dagger stroke before today," and holding it up to sunlight they perceived in many directions faint lines and spots upon the links caused in past years by the cutting edge of swords and the points of daggers. Yet never a one of those links was severed or broken.

"I pray that it may stand them again if your body be inside of it," said Lysbeth. "Yet, Son, remember always that there is One who can guard you better than any human mail, however perfect," and she left the room.

Then Foy drew on the coat over his woolen jersey, and it fitted him well. Indeed, when his linen shirt and his doublet were over it none could have guessed that he was clothed in body armor.

"It isn't fair, Martin," he said, "that I should be wrapped in steel and you in nothing."

Martin smiled. "Do you take me for a fool, master," he said, "who have seen some fighting in my day, private and public? Look here," and, opening his leathern jerkin, he showed that he was clothed beneath in a strange garment of thick but supple hide.

"Bullskin," said Martin, "tanned as we know how up in Friesland. Not so good as yours, but it will turn most cuts or arrows. I sat up last night making one for you. It was almost finished, but the steel is cooler and better for those who can afford it. Come, let us go and eat. We should be at the gates at eight when they open."

Chapter XIII
Mother's Gifts are Good Gifts

At a few minutes to eight that morning, a small crowd of people had gathered in front of the Witte Poort at Leyden waiting for the gate to be opened. The group was made up of all sorts, but country folk for the most part, returning to their villages, leading mules and donkeys slung with empty panniers, and shouting greetings through the bars of the gate to acquaintances who led in other mules laden with vegetables and provisions. Among these stood some priests, saturnine and silent, doubtless bent upon dark business of their own. A squad of Spanish soldiers waited also, the insolence of the master in their eyes; they were marching to some neighboring city. There, too, appeared Foy van Goorl and Red Martin, who led a pack mule. Foy was dressed in the gray jerkin of a merchant, but was armed with a sword and mounted on a good mare. Martin rode a Flemish gelding that nowadays would only have been thought fit for the plough, since no lighter-boned beast could carry his great weight. Among these moved a dapper little man with sandy whiskers and sly face, asking the business and destination of the various travelers, and under pretence of guarding against the smuggling of forbidden goods, taking count upon his tablets of their merchandise and baggage.

Presently he came to Foy.

"Name?" he said, shortly, although he knew him well enough.

"Foy van Goorl and Martin, my father's servant, traveling to The Hague with specimens of brassware, consigned to the correspondents of our firm," answered Foy, indifferently.

"You are very glib," sneered the sandy-whiskered man. "What is the mule laden with? It may be Bibles for all I know."

"Nothing half so valuable, Master," replied Foy. "It is a church chandelier in pieces."

"Unpack it and show me the pieces," said the officer.

Foy flushed with anger and set his teeth, but Martin, administering to him a warning nudge in the ribs, submitted with prompt obedience.

It was a long business, for each arm of the chandelier had been carefully wrapped in hay bands, and the official would not pass them until every one was undone, after which they must be done up again. While the pair of them were engaged upon this tedious and unnecessary task, two fresh travellers arrived at the gate, a long, bony person, clothed in a priest-like garb with a hood that hid the head, and a fierce, dissolute-looking individual of military appearance who was armed to the teeth. Catching sight of young van Goorl and his servant, the long person, who seemed to ride very awkwardly with legs thrust forward, whispered something to the soldier man, and they passed on through the gate without question.

When Foy and Martin followed them twenty minutes later, they were out of sight, for the pair were well mounted and rode hard.

"Did you recognise them?" asked Martin as soon as they were clear of the crowd.

"No," said Foy, "who are they?"

"The papist witch, Black Meg, dressed like a man, and the fellow who came here yesterday from The Hague, Heer Butcher. They cannot wait to report that the Heer Adrian routed them, and that the Broekhovens with the Jufvrouw Elsa got through unsearched."

"What does it all mean, Martin?" asked Foy.

"It means, Master, that we shall have a warm welcome yonder; it means that someone guesses we know about this treasure, and that we shan't get the stuff away without trouble."

"Will they waylay us?" asked the young man.

Martin shrugged his shoulders as he answered, "It is always

well to be ready, but I think not. Coming back they may waylay us, not going. Our lives are of little use without the money, and our lives cannot be had for the asking."

Martin was right, for traveling slowly they reached the city without molestation, and, riding to the house of Dirk's correspondent, put up their horses, ate, rested, delivered the sample chandelier, and generally transacted the business that appeared to be the object of their journey. In the course of conversation, they learned from their host that things were going very ill here at The Hague, for all who were supposed to favor the Reformation in general or Luther in particular. Tortures, burnings, abductions, and murders were of daily occurrence, nor were any brought to judgment for these crimes. Indeed, soldiery, spies, and government agents were quartered on the citizens, doing what they would, and none dared to lift a hand against them. Hendrik Brant, they heard also, was still at large and carrying on business as usual in his shop, though rumor said that he was a marked man whose time would be short.

Foy announced that they would stay the night, and a little after sunset called to Martin to accompany him, as he wished to walk in the Broad Street to see the sights of the town.

"Be careful, Mynheer Foy," said their host in warning, "for there are many strange characters about, men and women."

"We will be wary," replied Foy, with the cheerful air of a young man eager for excitement.

"I hope so, I hope so," said the host, "still I pray you be careful. You will remember where to find the horses if you want them; they are fed and I will keep them saddled. Your arrival here is known, and for some reason this house is being watched."

Foy nodded and they started out; Foy going first, and Red Martin, staring round him like a bewildered bumpkin, following at his heel, with his great sword, which was called Silence, girt about his middle, and hidden as much as possible beneath his jerkin.

"I wish you wouldn't look so big, Martin," Foy whispered over his shoulder. "Everybody is staring at you and that red beard of yours, which glows like a kitchen fire."

"I can't help it, Master," said Martin, "my back aches with stooping as it is, and, as for the beard, well, God made it so."

"At least you might dye it," answered Foy. "If it were black you would be less like a beacon on a church tower."

"Another day, Master; it is a long business dyeing a beard like mine; I think it would be quicker to cut it off."

Then he stopped, for they were approaching the Broad Street.

Here they found many people moving to and fro, although the people were so numerous it was difficult to distinguish them, for no moon shone, and the place was lighted only by lanterns set up on poles at long distances from each other. Foy could see, however, that they were for the most part folk of bad character, disreputable women, soldiers of the garrison, half-drunken sailors from every country, and gliding in and out among them all, priests and other observers of events. Before they had been long in the crowd, a man stumbled against Foy rudely, at the same time telling him to get out of the path. But although his blood leapt at the insult and his hand went to his sword hilt, Foy checked his anger, for he understood at once that it was intended to coax him into a quarrel. Next a woman accosted him, a well-dressed woman, but she had no bow upon her shoulder, so Foy merely shook his head and smiled. For the rest of that walk, however, he was aware that this woman was watching him, and with her a man whose figure he could not distinguish, for he was wrapped in a black cloak.

Foy, followed by Martin, walked along the right side of the Broad Street three times, until he was heartily weary of the game indeed, and began to wonder if his cousin Brant's plans had not miscarried.

As he turned for the fourth time his doubts were answered, for he found himself face to face with a small woman who wore upon her shoulder a large red bow, and was followed by another woman, a buxom person dressed in a peasant's cap. The lady with the red bow, making pretence to stumble, precipitated herself with an affected scream right into his arms, and as he caught her, whispered, "Are you from Leyden, sweetheart?"

"Yes," replied Foy.

"Then treat me as I treat you, and follow always where I lead. First make pretence to be rid of me."

As she finished whispering, Foy heard a warning stamp from Martin, followed by the footsteps of the pair whom he knew were watching them, which he could distinguish easily, for here at the end of the street there were fewer people. So he began to act as best he could—it was not very convincing, but his awkwardness gave him a certain air of sincerity.

"No, no," he said, "why should I pay for your supper? Come, be going, my good girl, and leave me and my servant to see the town in peace."

"Oh! Mynheer, let me be your guide, I beg you," answered the lady with the red bow clasping her hands and looking up into his face. Just then he heard the first woman who had accosted him speaking to her companion in a loud voice.

"Look," she said, "Red Bow is trying her best. Ah, my dear, do you think that you'll get a supper out of a holy Leyden ranter, or a skin off an eel for the asking?"

"Oh, he isn't such a selfish fish as he looks," answered Red Bow over her shoulder, while her eyes told Foy that it was his turn to play.

So he played to the best of his ability, with the result that ten minutes later any for whom the sight had interest might have observed, a yellow-haired young gallant and a black-haired young woman walking down the Broad Street with their arms affectionately disposed around each other's middles. Following them was a huge and lumbering serving man with a beard like fire, who, in a loyal effort to imitate the actions of his master, had hooked a great limb about the neck of Red Bow's stout little attendant, and held her thus headlock, which, if flattering, must have been uncomfortable. As Martin explained to the poor woman afterwards, it was no fault of his, since in order to reach her waist he must have carried her under his arm.

Foy and his companion chatted merrily enough, if in a somewhat jerky fashion, but Martin attempted no talk. Only as he proceeded he was heard to mutter between his teeth, "I am glad that Pastor Arentz can't see us now. He would never understand why we would treat women in this fashion in public."

Presently, at a hint from his lady, Foy turned down a side street, unobserved, as he thought, until he heard a mocking voice calling after them, "Goodnight, Red Bow, hope you will have a fine supper with your Leyden shopboy."

"Quick," whispered Red Bow, and they turned another corner, then another, and another. At this point they walked down narrow streets, ill-kept and unsavory, with sharp pitched roofs, gabled and overhanging so much that here and there they seemed almost to meet, leaving but a narrow ribbon of star-specked sky winding above their heads. Evidently it was a low quarter of the town and a malodorous quarter, for the canals, spanned by picturesque and high-arched bridges, were everywhere, and at this summer season the water in them was low, rotten, and almost stirless.

At length, Red Bow halted and knocked upon a small recessed door, which instantly was opened by a man who bore no light.

"Come in," he whispered, and all four of them passed into a dimly lit passage. "Quick, quick!" said the man, "I hear footsteps."

Foy heard them also echoing down the empty street, and as the door closed, it seemed to him that they stopped in the deep shadow of the houses. Then, holding each other by the hand, they crept along black passages and down stairs until at length they saw light shining through the crevices of an ill-fitting door. It opened mysteriously at their approach, and when they had all entered, shut behind them.

Foy uttered a sigh of relief, for he was weary of this long flight, and looked round him to discover that they were in a large windowless cellar, well furnished after a fashion by oak benches and a table set out with cold meats and flagons of wine. At the foot of this table stood a middle-aged man, prematurely gray, and with a face worn as though by constant care.

"Welcome, Foy van Goorl," said the man in a gentle voice. "Many years have passed since last we met; still I should have known you anywhere, though I think you would not have known me."

Foy looked at him and shook his head.

"I thought so," went on the man with a smile. "Well, I am Hendrik Brant, your cousin, once the burgemeester of The Hague and its richest citizen, but today a hunted rat who must receive his guests in secret cellars. Tell me now, did my daughter Elsa reach your good father's house in safety, and is she well?"

So Foy told him all that story.

"As I thought, as I thought," said Hendrik. "Ramiro knew of her journey and guessed that she might carry some letter. Oh!" he went on, shaking his fist in a kind of frenzy, and addressing the two women who had played the parts of Red Bow and her servant, "who among you is the traitor? Can it be that you, whom my bounty has fed, betray me? Nay, girls, do not weep, I know that it is not so, and yet, in this city, the very walls have ears, yes, even this deep vault gives up its secrets. Well, if only I can save my fortune from those wolves, what do I care? Then they may take my carcass and tear it. At least my daughter is safe for a while, and now I have but one desire left on earth—to rob them of my wealth also."

Then he turned to the girl decked out in the fancy clothes, who, now that the chase was over, sat upon a bench with her face hidden in her hand, and said, "Tell me your story, Gretchen," whereon she lifted her head and repeated all that happened.

"They press us hard," declared Brant, "but, friends, we will beat them yet. Eat now, and drink while you may."

So they sat down and ate and drank while Hendrick watched them, and the man who had led them to the vault listened outside the door.

When they had finished, Brant asked the two women, Red Bow and the other, to leave the cellar and send in the sentry. He entered, a hard-faced, grizzled man, and, taking a seat at the table, began to fill himself with food and wine.

"Hearken, my cousin Foy," said Brant forcefully, "this is the plan. A league away, near to the mouth of the great canal, lie certain boats, a score or more of them laden with trading goods and timber, in the charge of honest men who know nothing of their cargo, but who have orders to fire them if they should be boarded. Among these boats is one called the *Swallow*, small, but the swiftest on this coast, and handy in a sea. Her cargo is salt, and beneath it eight kegs of powder, and between the powder and the salt certain barrels which are filled with treasure. Now, presently, if you have the heart for it—and if you have not, say so, and I will go myself—this man here, Hans, under cover of darkness, will row you down to the boat *Swallow*. Then you must board her, and at the first break of dawn hoist her great sail and head out to sea, and away with her where the wind drives, tying the skiff behind. Likely enough, you will find foes waiting for you at the mouth of the canal, or elsewhere. Then I can give you only one counsel—get out with the *Swallow* if you can, and if you cannot, escape in the skiff or by swimming, but before you leave her, fire the fuses that are ready at the bow and the stern, and let the powder do its work and blow my wealth to the waters and the winds. Will you do it? Think, think well before you answer."

"Did we not come out from Leyden to be at your command, Cousin?" said Foy smiling. Then he added, "But why do you not accompany us on this adventure? You are in danger here, and even if we get clear with the treasure, what use is money without life?"

"To me none, anyway," answered Brant. "But you do not understand. I live in the midst of spies, I am watched day and night; although I came here disguised and secretly, it is probable that even my presence in this house is known. More, there is an order out that if I attempt to leave the town by land or water, I am to be seized, whereon my house will be searched instantly, and it will be found that my bullion is gone. Think, lad, how great is this wealth, and you will understand why the crows are hungry. It is talked of throughout the Netherlands, it has been reported to the King in Spain, and I learn that orders have come from him concerning its seizure. But there is another hand who would get hold of it first, Ramiro and his crew, and that is why I have been left safe so long, because the thieves strive one against the other and watch each other. Most of all, however, they watch me and everything that is mine. For though they do not believe that I would send the treasure away and stay behind, yet they are not sure."

"You think that they will pursue us then?" asked Foy.

"For certain. Messengers arrived from Leyden to announce your coming two hours before you set foot in the town, and it will be wonderful indeed if you leave it without a band of cut-throats at your heels. Be not deceived, lad, this business is no light one."

"You say the little boat sails fast, Master?" queried Martin.

"She sails fast, but perhaps others are as swift. Moreover, it may happen that you will find the mouth of the canal blocked by the guardship that was sent there a week ago with orders to search every craft that passes from stem to stern. Or—you may slip past her."

"My master and I are not afraid of a few blows," said Martin, "and we are ready to take our risks like brave men; still, Mynheer Brant, this seems to me a hazardous business, and one in which your money may well get itself lost. Now, I ask you, would it not be better to take this treasure out of the boat where you have hidden it, and bury it, and convey it away by land?"

Brant shook his head. "I have thought of that," he said, "as I have thought of everything, but it cannot now be done; also there is no time to make fresh plans."

"Why?" asked Foy.

"Because day and night men are watching the boats, which are known to belong to me, although they are registered in oth-er names, and only this evening an order was signed that they must be searched within an hour of dawn. My information is good, as it should be since I pay for it dearly."

"Then," said Foy, "there is nothing more to be said. We will try to get to the boat and try to get her away; and if we can get her away, we will try to hide the treasure; and if we can't we will try to blow her up as you direct and try to escape ourselves. Or—" and he shrugged his shoulders.

Martin said nothing, only he shook his great red head, nor did the silent pilot at the table speak at all.

Hendrik Brant looked at them, and his pale, careworn face began to work. "Have I the right?" he wondered to himself, and for an instant or two bent his head as though in prayer. When he lifted it again his mind seemed to be made up.

"Foy van Goorl," he said, "listen to me, and tell your father, my cousin and executor, what I say, since I have no time to write it; tell him word for word. You are wondering why I do not let this treasure take its chance without risking the lives of men to save it. It is because something in my heart pushes me to another path. It may be imagination, but I am a man standing on the edge of the grave, and as such I believe that the Almighty has given me an extra measure of discernment. I think that you will win through with the treasure, Foy, and that it will be the means of bringing some wicked ones to their doom. Yes, and more, much more, but what it is I cannot altogether see. Yet I am quite certain that thousands and tens of thousands of our folk will live to bless the gold of Hendrik Brant, and that is why I work so hard to save it from the Spaniards. Also that is why I ask you to risk your lives tonight; not for the wealth's sake, for wealth is dross, but for what the wealth will buy in days to come for my people's freedom."

He paused a while, then went on; "I think also, Cousin, that being, they tell me, unbethrothed, you will learn to love, and not in vain, that dear child of mine, whom I leave in your father's keeping and in yours. More, since time is short and we shall never meet again, I say to you plainly, that the thought is pleasing to me, young cousin Foy, for I have a good report of you and like your Christian character and zeal. Remember always, however dark may be your sky, that before he passed to glory Hendrik Brant had this vision concerning you and the daughter whom he loves, and whom you will learn to love as do all who know her. Remember also that priceless things are not lightly won, and do not woo her for her fortune, since, I tell you, this belongs not to her but to our people and our cause, and when the hour comes, for them it must be used."

Foy listened wondering, but he made no answer, for he knew not what to say. Yet now, on the edge of his first great adventure, these words were pleasing to him who had found already that Elsa's eyes were bright. Brant next turned towards Martin, but that worthy shook his red beard and stepped back a pace.

"Thank you kindly, Master," he said, "but I will do without the prophecies, which, good or ill, are things that fasten upon a man's mind. Once in my youth, an astrologer foretold that I should be drowned before I was twenty-five. I wasn't, but, my faith, the miles which I have walked round to bridges on account of that false prophet."

Brant smiled. "I have no special vision concerning you, good friend, except that I judge your arm will be always strong in battle; that you will love your masters well, and use your might to avenge the cause of God's slaughtered saints upon their murderers."

Martin nodded his head vigorously, and fumbled at the handle of the sword Silence, while Brant went on. "Friend, you have entered on a dangerous quarrel on behalf of me and mine, and if you live through it, you will have earned high pay."

Then he went to the table, and, taking writing materials, he wrote as follows: "To the Heer Dirk van Goorl and his heirs, the executors of my will, and the holders of my fortune, which is to be used as God shall show them. This is to certify that in payment of this night's work Martin, called the Red, the servant of the said Dirk van Goorl, or those heirs whom he may appoint, is entitled to a sum of five thousand florins, and I constitute such sum a first charge upon my estate, to whatever purpose they may put it in their discretion." This document he dated, signed, and caused the pilot Hans to sign also as a witness. Then he gave it to Martin, who thanked him by touching his forehead, remarking at the same time:

"After all, fighting is not a bad trade if you only stick to it long enough. Five thousand florins! I never thought to earn so much."

"You haven't got it yet," interrupted Foy. "And now, what are you going to do with that paper?"

Martin reflected. "Coat?" he said, "no, a man takes off his coat if it is hot, and it might be left behind. Boots? —no, that would wear it out, especially if it became wet. Jerkin? Sewn next to the skin, no, same reason. Ah! I have it," and, drawing out the great sword Silence, he took the point of his knife and began to turn a little silver screw in the hilt, one of many with which the handle of walrus ivory was fastened to its steel core. The screw came out, and he touched a spring, whereon one quarter of the ivory casing fell away, revealing a considerable hollow in the hilt, for, although Martin grasped it with one hand, the sword was made to be held by two.

"What is that hole for?" asked Foy.

"The executioner's drug," replied Martin, "which makes a man happy while he does his business with him, that is, if he can pay the fee. He offered his dose to me, I remember, before—" Here Martin stopped, and, having rolled up the parchment, hid it in the hollow.

"You might lose your sword," suggested Foy.

"Yes, Master, when I lose my life and exchange the hope of florins for a golden crown," replied Martin with a grin. "Until then, I do not intend to part with Silence."

Meanwhile Hendrik Brant had been whispering to the quiet man at the table, who now stood and said:

"Foster-brother, do not trouble about me; I am at peace with my decision and will trust to God's will. My wife is burnt, yet one of my girls out there is married to a man who knows how to protect them both. The dowries that I gave them are far away and safe. Do not trouble about me who have but one desire—to snatch the great treasure from the paw of the Spaniard that in a day to come it may bring doom upon the Spaniard." Then he relapsed into a silence, which spread over the whole company.

"It is time to be stirring," said Brant presently. "Hans, you will lead the way. I must bide here a while before I go abroad and show myself."

The pilot nodded. "Ready?" he asked, addressing Foy and Martin. Then he went to the door and whistled, whereon Red Bow with her pretended servant entered the vault. He spoke a word or two to them and kissed them each upon the brow. Next he went to Hendrik Brant, and throwing his arms about

him, embraced him with far more passion than he had shown towards his own daughters.

"Farewell, foster-brother," he said, "until we meet again here or hereafter—it matters little which. Have no fear, we will get the stuff through to England if need be, or send it to hell with some Spaniards to seek it there. Now, comrades, come on and stick close to me, and if any try to stop us, cut them down. When we reach the boat, you must take the oars and row while I steer her. The girls come with us to the canal, arm-in-arm with the two of you. If anything happens to me, either of them can steer you to the skiff called *Swallow*, but if naught happens, we will put them ashore at the next wharf. Come," and he led the way from the cellar.

At the threshold Foy turned to look at Hendrik Brant. He was standing by the table, the light shining full upon his pale face and grizzled head, about which it seemed to cast a halo. Indeed, at that moment, wrapped in his long, dark cloak, his lips moving in prayer, and his arms uplifted to bless them as they went, he might well have been, not a man, but some vision of a saint come back to earth. The door closed and Foy never saw him again, for ere long the Inquisition seized him and a while afterwards he died beneath their cruel hands. One of the charges against him was, that more than twenty years before, he had been seen by Black Meg reading the Bible at Leyden.

Now this scene, so strange and pathetic, ended at last, and the five of them were in the darkness of the street. Here, once more, Foy and Red Bow clung to each other, and once more the arm of Martin was about the neck of her who seemed to be the serving-maid, while ahead, as though he were paid to show the way, went the pilot. Soon footsteps were heard, for folk were after them. They turned once, they turned twice, they reached the bank of a canal, and Hans, followed by Red Bow and her sister, descended some steps and climbed into a boat which lay there ready. Next came Martin, and, last of all, Foy. As he set foot upon the first step, a figure shot out of the gloom towards him, a knife gleamed in the air and a blow took him between the shoulders that sent him tumbling headlong, for he was balanced upon the edge of the step.

But Martin had heard and seen the attacker. He swung round and struck out with the sword Silence. The assassin was far from him, still the tip of the long steel reached the outstretched murderous hand, and from it fell a broken knife, while he who held it sped on with a screech of pain. Martin darted back and seized the knife, then he leapt into the boat and pushed off. At the bottom of it lay Foy, who had fallen straight into the arms of Red Bow, dragging her down with him.

"Are you hurt, Master?" asked Martin.

"Not a bit," replied Foy, "but I am afraid the lady is. She took most of the blow."

"Mother's gifts are good gifts!" declared Martin as he pulled him, and the girl whose breath had been knocked out of her, up to a seat. "You ought to have an eight-inch hole through you, but that knife broke upon the shirt. Look here," and he threw the handle of the dagger on to his knees.

Foy examined it in the faint light, and there, still hooked above the guard, was a single severed finger, a long and skinny

finger, to which the point of the sword Silence had played surgeon, and on it a gold ring. "This may be useful," thought Foy, as
he slipped handle and finger into the pocket of his cloak.

Then they all took oars and rowed until they drew near a
wharf.

"Now, daughters, make ready," said Hans and the girls stood
up. As they touched the wharf, Red Bow bent down and kissed
Foy.

"The rest was in play, this is in earnest," she said, "Goodnight,
companion, and think of me sometimes. Godspeed."

"Goodnight, companion," answered Foy, pressing her hand.
Then she leapt ashore. They never met again.

"You know what to do, girls," said Hans. "Do it, and in three
days you should be safe in England, where, perhaps, I may meet
you, though do not count on that. Whatever happens, keep
honest, and remember me until we come together again, here
or hereafter, but, most of all, remember your mother and your
benefactor Hendrik Brant. Farewell."

"Farewell, Father," they answered with a sob, as the boat
drifted off down the dark canal, leaving the two of them alone
upon the wharf.

And now, having played their part in it, these two brave girls
are out of the story.

CHAPTER XIV
SWORD SILENCE
RECEIVES THE SECRET

For half an hour or more, they glided down the canal unmolested and in silence. The canal eventually ran into a broader waterway along which they slid towards the sea, keeping as much as possible under the shadow of one bank, for although the night was moonless a faint gray light lay upon the surface of the stream. At one point, Foy became aware that they were bumping against the sides of a long line of barges and river boats laden with timber and other goods. To one of these—it was the fourth—the pilot Hans made fast, tying their rowboat to her stern. Then he climbed to the deck, whispering to them to follow.

As they scrambled on board, two gray figures arose and Foy saw the flash of steel. Then Hans whistled like a bird, and dropping their swords, they came to him and fell into talk. A few moments later, Hans left them, and, returning to Foy and Martin, said:

"Listen, we must lie here a while, for the wind is against us, and it would be too dangerous for us to try to row or pole so big a boat down to the sea and across the bar in the darkness, for most likely we would run her upon a shoal. Before dawn it will turn, and, if I read the sky aright, blow hard off land."

"What have the sailors to say?" asked Foy.

"Only that for these four days they have been lying here forbidden to move, and that their craft are to be searched tomorrow by a party of soldiers, and the cargo taken out of them piecemeal."

"Well," said Foy, "I hope that by then what they seek will be far away. Now show us around this ship."

Then Hans took them down the hatchway, for the little vessel was decked, being in the shape of a small fishing boat. Then having lit a lantern, and moved below deck, he showed them the cargo. On the top were bags of salt. Dragging one or two of these aside, Hans uncovered the heads of five barrels, each of them marked with the initial "B" in white paint.

"That is what men will die for before tomorrow night," he said.

"The treasure?" asked Foy.

He nodded. "These five, none of the others." Then still lower down he pointed out other barrels, eight of them, filled with the best gunpowder, and showed them where the fuses ran to the little cabin, the cook's galley, the tiller and the prow. At any one of these stations, the appropriate fuse could be lit. After this, and such inspection of the ropes and sails as the light would allow, they sat in the cabin waiting for the wind to change while the two watchmen unmoored the vessel and made her sails ready for hoisting. An hour passed, and still the breeze blew from the sea, but in uncertain chopping gusts. Then it fell altogether.

"Pray God it comes soon," said Martin, "for the owner of that finger in your pocket will have laid the hounds on to our trail long ago, and, look! The east grows red."

The silent, hard-faced Hans leant forward and stared up the darkling water, his hand behind his ear.

"I hear them," he said with great emotion.

"Who?" asked Foy.

"The Spaniards and the wind—both," he answered. "Come, up with the mainsail and pole her out to midstream."

So the three of them took hold of the tackle and ran aft with it, while the rings and booms creaked and rattled as the great canvas climbed the mast. In a moment it was set, and after it the jib. Then, assisted by the two watchmen thrusting from another of the boats, they pushed the *Swallow* from her place in the line out into midstream. But all this made noise and took time, and now men appeared upon the bank, calling to know who dared to move the boats without permission. As no one gave them any answer, they fired a shot, and soon a beacon began to burn upon a neighboring mound.

"Bad business," said Hans, shrugging his shoulders. "Now we are in for trouble. They are warning the Government ship at the harbor mouth. Duck, Masters, duck. Here comes the wind," and he sprang to the tiller as the boom swung over, and the little vessel began to gather speed.

"Yes," said Martin, "and with it come the Spaniards."

Foy looked. Through the gray mist that was growing lighter every moment, for the dawn was breaking, he caught sight of a long boat with her canvas spread, which was sweeping round the bend of the stream towards them and not much more than a quarter of a mile away.

"They have had to pole down stream in the dark, and that is why they have been so long in coming," said Hans over his shoulder.

"Well, they are here now at any rate," answered Foy, "and plenty of them," he added, as a shout from a score of throats told them that they were discovered.

But now the *Swallow* had begun to fly, making the water hiss upon either side of her bows.

"How far is it to the sea?" asked Foy.

"About three miles," Hans called back from the tiller. "With this wind we should be there in fifteen minutes, Master." He added presently, "bid your man light the fire in the galley."

"What for," asked Foy, "to cook breakfast?"

The pilot shrugged his shoulders and stated, "Yes, if we live to eat it." But Foy saw that he was glancing at the fuse by his side, and understood.

Ten minutes passed, and they had swept round the last bend and were in the stretch of open water that ran down to the sea. By now the light was strong and in it they saw that the signal fire had not been lit in vain. At the mouth of the cutting, just where the bar began, the channel was narrowed in with earth to a width of not more than fifty paces, and on one bank of it stood a fort armed with short cannons. Out of the little harbor of this fort, a large open boat was being poled, and in it a dozen or more soldiers were hastily arming themselves.

"What now?" cried Martin. "They are going to stop the mouth of the channel."

The hard-featured Hans set his teeth and made no answer. He only looked backward at his pursuers and then onward at those who barred the way. One minute later, he called aloud, "Under hatches, both of you. They are going to fire from the fort," and he flung himself upon his back, steering with his uplifted arms.

Foy and Martin tumbled down the hatchway, for they could do no good on deck. Only Foy kept one eye above its level.

"Look out!" he said, and ducked.

As he spoke there was a puff of white smoke from the fort, followed by the scream of a shot, which passed ahead of them. Then came another puff of smoke, and a hole appeared in their brown sail. After this the fort did not fire again, for the gunners found no time to load their weapons, only some soldiers who were armed with hakebusses began to shoot as the boat swept past within a few yards of them. Heedless of their bullets, Hans the pilot rose to his feet again, for such work as was before him could not be done by a man lying on his back. By now, the large open boat from the fort was within two hundred yards of them, and, driven by the gathering gale, the *Swallow* rushed towards it with the speed of a dart. Foy and Martin crawled from the hatchway and lay down near the steersman under the shelter of the little bulwarks, watching the enemy's boat, which was in midstream just where the channel was narrowest, and on the hither side of the broken water of the bar.

"See" said Foy, "they are throwing out anchors fore and aft. Is there room to go past them?"

"No," answered Hans, "the water is too shallow under the bank, and they know it. Bring me a burning brand."

Foy crept forward, and returned with the fire.

"Now light the fuse, Master."

Foy opened his blue eyes and a cold shiver went down his back. Then he set his teeth and obeyed. Martin looked at Hans, muttering, "Good for a young one!"

Hans nodded and said, "Have no fear. Until that fuse burns to

the level of the deck we are safe. Now, mates, hold fast. I can't go
past that boat, so I am going through her. We may sink on the
other side, though I am sure that the fire will reach the powder
first. In that case, you can swim for it if you like, but I shall go
with the *Swallow.*"

"I will think about it when the time comes. Oh! Would to
God that I could push them," growled Martin, looking back at
the pursuing ship, which was not more than seven or eight hundred yards away.

Meanwhile, the officer in command of the boat, armed with
a musket, was shouting to them to pull down their sail and surrender; indeed, not until they were within fifty yards of him did
he seem to understand their desperate purpose. Then someone
in the boat called out "The devils are going to sink us!" And
there was a rush to bow and stern to get up the anchors. Only
the officer stood firm, screaming at them like a madman. It was
too late; a strong gust of wind caught the *Swallow,* causing her to
heel over and sweep down on the boat like a swooping falcon.

Hans stood and shifted the tiller ever so little, calculating all things with his eye. Foy watched the boat towards which they sprang like a thing alive, as Martin, lying at his side, watched the burning fuse.

Suddenly, when their prow was not more than twenty paces from him, the Spanish officer, ceased to shout, and lifting his weapon, fired. Martin, looking upwards with his left eye, thought that he saw Hans flinch, but the pilot made no sound. Only he did something to the tiller, putting all his strength on to it, and it seemed to the pair of them as though the *Swallow* was for an instant checked in her flight—certainly her prow appeared to lift itself from the water. Suddenly there was a sound of something snapping—a sound that could be heard in spite of the yell of terror from the soldiers in the boat. It was the bowsprit which had gone, leaving the jib flying loose like a great serpent.

Then came the crash. Foy shut his eyes for a moment, hanging on with both hands until the scraping and the trembling were finished. Now he opened them again, and the first thing he saw was the body of the Spanish officer hanging from the jagged stump of the bowsprit. He looked behind. The boat had nearly vanished, but in the water were to be seen the heads of three or four men swimming. As for themselves, they seemed to be clear and unhurt, except for the loss of their bowsprit; indeed, the little vessel was riding over the seas on the bar like any swan. Hans glanced at the fuse, which was smoldering away perilously near to the deck, whereon Martin stamped upon it, saying, "If we sink now it will be in deep water, so there is no need to blow up before we go down."

"Go and see if she leaks," said Hans.

They went and searched the forehold but could not find that the *Swallow* had taken any harm worth noting. Indeed, her massive oaken prow, with the weight of the gale-driven ship behind it, had crashed through the frail sides of the open Spanish boat like a knife through an egg.

"That was good steering," said Foy to Hans, when they returned, "and nothing seems to be amiss."

Hans nodded. "I hit him neatly," he muttered. "Look. He's gone." As he spoke the *Swallow* gave a sharp pitch, and the corpse of the Spaniard fell with a heavy splash into the sea.

"I am glad it has sunk," said Foy, "and now let's have some breakfast, for I am starving. Shall I bring you some, friend Hans?"

"No, Master, I want to sleep."

Something in the tone of the man's voice caused Foy to scrutinize his face. His lips were turning blue. He glanced at his hands. Although they still grasped the tiller tightly, these also were turning blue, as though with cold; moreover, blood was dripping on the deck.

"You are hit," he said. "Martin, Martin, Hans is hit!"

"Yes," replied the man, "he hit me and I hit him, and perhaps we shall both be meeting our Maker this day. No, don't trouble, it is through the body and mortal. Well, I expected nothing less, so I can't complain. Now, listen, while my strength holds. Can you lay a course for Harwich in England?"

Martin and Foy shook their heads. Like most Hollanders they were good sailormen, but they only knew their own coasts.

"Then you had best not try it," said Hans, "for there is a gale brewing, and you will be driven on the Goodwin Sands, or somewhere down that shore, and drowned and the treasure lost. Run up to the Haarlem Meer, comrades. You can hug the land with this small boat, while that big devil after you," and he nodded towards the pursuing vessel, which by now was crossing the bar, "must stand further out beyond the shoals." Then slip up through the narrow passage—the ruined farmstead marks it—and so into the meer. You know Mother Martha, the mad woman who is nicknamed the Mare? She will be watching at the mouth of it; she always is. Moreover, I warned her that we might pass her way, and if you hoist the white flag with a red cross—it lies in the locker—or, after nightfall, hang out four lamps upon your starboard side, she will come aboard to pilot you, for she knows this boat well. To her also you can tell your business without fear, for she will help you, and be secret as the dead. Then bury the treasure, or sink it, or blow it up, or do what you can, but, in the name of God, to whom I go, I charge you do not let it fall into the hands of Ramiro and his Spanish rats who are at your heels."

As Hans spoke, he sank down upon the deck. Foy ran to support him, but he pushed him aside with a feeble hand. "Let me be," he whispered. "I wish to pray. I have set you the course. Follow it to the end."

Then Martin took the tiller while Foy watched Hans. In ten minutes he was dead.

Now they were running northwards with a fierce wind abeam of them, and the larger Spanish ship behind, but standing further out to sea to avoid the banks. Half an hour later the wind, which was gathering to a gale, shifted several degrees to the north, so that they were enabled to sail against it under reefed canvas. Still they held on without accident, Foy attending to the sail and Martin steering.

The *Swallow* was a good sea boat, and if their progress was slow so was that of their pursuer, which dogged them continually, sometimes a mile away and sometimes less. At length, towards evening, they caught sight of a ruined house that marked the channel of the little passage, one of the outlets of the Haarlem Meer.

"The sea runs high upon the bar and it is ebb tide," said Foy.

"Even so we must try it, Master," answered Martin.

"Perhaps she will scrape through," and he put the *Swallow* about and ran for the mouth of the gut.

Here the waves were mountainous, and much water came aboard. Moreover, three times they bumped upon the bar, until at length, to their joy, they found themselves in the calm stream of the gut, and, by shifting the sail, were able to draw up it, though very slowly.

"At least we have pushed ahead of them," said Foy, "for they can never get across until the tide rises."

"We shall need it all," answered Martin. "Now let us hoist the white flag and eat while we may."

While they ate the sun sank, and the wind blew so that scarcely could they make a knot an hour, shift the sail as they might. Then, as there was no sign of Mother Martha, or any other pilot, they hung out the four lamps upon the starboard side, and, with a flapping sail, drifted on gradually, until finally they reached the mouth of the great meer, a vast confusing stretch of waters—deep in some places, shallow in others, and spotted everywhere with islets. Now the wind turned against them altogether, and, the darkness closing in, they were forced to drop anchor, fearing lest otherwise they should drift ashore. One comfort they had, however, as yet nothing could be seen of their pursuers.

Then, for the first time, their spirits failed them a little, as they stood together near the stern wondering what they should do. It was while they rested thus that, suddenly, a figure appeared before them as though it had risen from the deck of the ship. No sound of oars or footsteps had reached their ears, yet there, outlined against the dim sky, was the figure.

"I think that friend Hans has come to life again," said Martin with a slight quaver in his voice, for Martin was terribly afraid of ghosts.

"And I think that a Spaniard has found us," said Foy, drawing his knife.

Then a hoarse voice spoke, saying, "Who are you that signal for a pilot on my waters?"

"The question is—who are you?" answered Foy, "and be so good as to tell us quickly."

"I am the pilot," said the voice, "and this boat by the rig of her and her signals should be the *Swallow* of The Hague, but why must I crawl aboard of her across the corpse of a dead man?"

"Come into the cabin, pilot, and we will tell you," said Foy.

"Very well, Mynheer." So Foy led the way to the cabin, but Martin stopped behind awhile.

"We have found our guide, so what is the use of the lamps?" he said to himself as he extinguished them all, except one which he brought with him into the cabin. Foy was waiting for him by the door and they entered the place together. At the end of it, the light from the lamp showed them a strange figure clad in skins so shapeless and sack-like that it was impossible to say whether the form beneath were male or female. The figure was bareheaded, and about the brow locks of grizzled hair hung in tufts. The face, in which were set a pair of wandering gray eyes, was deep cut, tanned brown by exposure, scarred, and very ugly, with withered lips and projecting teeth.

"Good even to you, Dirk van Goorl's son, and to you, Red Martin. I am Mother Martha, she whom the Spaniards call the Mare and the Lake Witch."

"Little need to tell us that, Mother," said Foy, "although it is true that many years have gone by since I set eyes on you."

Martha smiled grimly as she answered, "Yes, many years. Well, what have you fat Leyden burghers to do with a poor old night-hag, except of course in times of trouble? Not that I blame you, for it is not well that you, or your parents either, should be known to traffic with such as I. Now, what is your business with me, for the signals show that you have business, and why does the corpse of Hendrik Brant's foster-brother lie there in the stern?"

"Because, to be plain, we have Hendrik Brant's treasure on board, Mother, and for the rest, look yonder." He pointed to what his eye had just caught sight of two or three miles away, a faint light, too low and too red for a star, that could only come from a lantern hung at the masthead of a ship.

Martha nodded. "Spaniards after you, poling through the narrow waterway against the wind. Come on, there is no time to lose. Bring your boat round, and we will tow the *Swallow* to where she will lie safe tonight."

Five minutes later they were all three of them rowing the oar boat in which they had escaped from The Hague towards some unknown point in the darkness, slowly dragging after them the little ship *Swallow*. As they went, Foy told Martha all the story of their mission and escape.

"I have heard of this treasure before," she said, "all the Netherlands has heard of Brant's hoard. Also dead Hans there let me know that perhaps it might come this way, for in such matters he thought that I could be trusted. She smiled grimly and added, "And now what would you do?"

"Fulfill our orders," said Foy. "Hide it if we can; if not, destroy it."

"Better the first than the last," interrupted Martin. "Hide the treasure, say I, and destroy the Spaniards, if Mother Martha here can think of a plan."

"We might sink the ship," suggested Foy.

"And leave her mast for a beacon," added Martin sarcastically.

"Or put the stuff into the boat and sink that," said Foy

"And never find it again in this great sea," objected Martin.

All this while Martha steered the boat as calmly as though it were daylight. They had left the open water, and were passing slowly in and out among islets, yet she never seemed to be doubtful or to hesitate. At last they felt the *Swallow* behind them take the mud gently, at which point Martha led the way aboard the main ship and threw out the anchor, saying that here was her berth for the night.

"Now," she said, "bring up this gold and lay it in the boat, for if you would save it, there is much to do before dawn."

So Foy and Martin went down while Martha, hanging over the hatchway, held the lighted lamp above them, since they dared not take it near the powder. Moving the bags of salt, soon they came to the five barrels of treasure marked "B." and, strong though they were, it was no easy task for the pair of them by the help of a pulley to sling them over the ship's side into the boat. At last it was done, and the place of the barrels having been filled with salt bags, they took two iron spades that were provided for such a task as this, and started, Martha steering as before. For an hour or more they rowed in and out among endless islands, at the dim shores of which Martha stared as they passed, until she finally motioned to them to ship their oars, and they touched ground.

Leaping from the boat, she made it fast and vanished among the reeds to survey the ground. Martha soon returned, saying that this was the spot. Then began the heavy labor of rolling the casks of treasure for thirty yards or more along otter paths that pierced the dense growth of reeds.

Now, having first carefully cut out reed sods in a place chosen by Martha, Foy and Martin set to their task of digging a great hole by the light of the stars. Hard indeed they toiled at it, yet had it not been for the softness of the marshy soil, they could not have finished while the night lasted, for the grave that would contain those barrels must be both wide and deep. After three feet of earth had been removed, they came to the level of the lake, and for the rest of the time worked in water, throwing up shovelfuls of mud. Still at last it was done, and the five barrels standing side by side in the water were covered up with soil and roughly planted over with the reed turf.

"Let us be going," said Martha. "There is no time to lose." So they straightened their backs and wiped the sweat from their brows.

"There is earth lying about, which may tell its story," said Martin.

"Yes," she replied, "if any see it within the next ten days, after which in this damp place the mosses will have hidden it."

"Well, we have done our best," said Foy, as he washed his mud-stained boots in the water, "and now the stuff must take its chance."

Then once more they entered the boat and rowed away somewhat wearily, Martha steering them. On they went and on, until Foy, tired out, nearly fell asleep at his oar. Suddenly Martha tapped him on the shoulder. He looked up and there, not two hundred yards away, its tapering mast showing dimly against the sky, was the vessel that had pursued them from The Hague, a single lantern burning on its stern. Martha looked and grunted; then she leaned forward and whispered to them imperiously.

"It is madness," gasped Martin.

"Do as I bid you," she hissed, and they let the boat drift with the wind until it came to a little island within thirty yards of the anchored vessel, an island with a willow tree growing upon its shore. "Hold to the twigs of the tree," she muttered, "and wait until I come again." Not knowing what else to do, they obeyed.

Then Martha rose and stood before them, a gaunt white figure armed with a gleaming knife. Next she put the knife to her mouth, and, nipping it between her teeth, slid into the water silently as a diving bird. A minute passed, not more, and they saw that something was climbing up the cable of the ship.

"What is she going to do?" whispered Foy.

"God in Heaven knows," answered Martin, "but if she does not come back, goodbye to Heer Brant's treasure, for she alone can find it again."

They waited, holding their breaths, until presently a curious choking sound floated to them, and the lantern on the ship vanished. Two minutes later, a hand with a knife in it appeared over the side of the boat, followed by a gray head. Martin put out his great arm and lifted, and, lo, the white form slid down between them like a big salmon turned out of a net.

"Put about and row," she gasped, and they obeyed while the Mare positioned herself in the boat.

"What have you done?" asked Foy.

"Something," she replied with a fierce chuckle. "I have stabbed the watchman, he thought I was a ghost, and was too frightened to call out. I have cut the cable, and I think that I have fired the ship. Ah! Do not look but row—row round the corner of the island."

They gave way, and as they turned the bank of reeds, they glanced behind them to see a tall tongue of fire shooting up the cordage of the ship, and to hear a babel of frightened and angry voices.

Ten minutes later they were on board the *Swallow*, and from her deck watched the fierce flare of the burning Spanish vessel nearly a mile away. Here they ate and drank, for they needed food badly.

"What shall we do now?" asked Foy when they had finished.

"Nothing at present," answered Martha, "but give me pen and paper."

They found them, and having shrouded the little window of the cabin, she sat at the table and very slowly but with much skill, drew a map of this portion of the Haarlem Meer. In that map were marked many islands according to their natural shapes, twenty of them perhaps, and upon one of these she set a cross.

"Take it and hide it," said Martha, when it was finished, "so that if I die you may know where to dig for Brant's gold. With this in your hand you cannot fail to find it, for I draw well. Remember that it lies thirty paces due south of the only spot where it is easy to land upon that island."

"What shall I do with this treasure map, which is worth so much?" said Foy helplessly, "for in truth, I fear to keep the thing."

"Give it to me, Master," said Martin. "The secret of the treasure may as well lie on my broad shoulders for a time." Then once more he unscrewed the handle of the sword Silence, and having folded up the paper and wrapped it round with a piece of linen, he thrust it away into the hollow hilt.

"Now that sword is worth more than some people might think," Martin said as he restored it to the scabbard, "but I hope that those who come to seek its secret may travel up its blade. Well, when shall we be moving?"

"Listen," said Martha. "Would you two men dare a great deed upon those Spaniards? Their ship is burnt, but there are a score or more of them, and they have two large boats. Starting at dawn they will see the mast of this vessel and attack it in the boats thinking to find the treasure. Well, if as they come aboard we can manage to fire the fuses—"

"There may be fewer Spaniards left to plague us," suggested Foy.

"And believing it to be blown up, no one will trouble about that money further," added Martin. "Oh! The plan is good, but dangerous. Come, let us talk it over."

The dawn broke in a flood of yellow light on the surface of the Haarlem Meer. At this early hour from the direction of the Spanish vessel, which was still smoldering, came a sound of beating oars. Now the three watchers in the *Swallow* saw two boatloads of armed men, one of them with a small sail set, swooping down towards them. When they were within a hundred yards, Martha muttered, "It is time," and Foy ran hither and thither with a candle firing the fuses; also to make sure he cast the candle among a few handfuls of oil-soaked shreds of canvas that lay ready at the bottom of the hatchway. Then with the others, without the Spaniards being able to see them, he slipped over the side of the little vessel into the shallow water that was clothed with tall reeds, and waded through it to the island.

Once on firm land, they ran a hundred yards or so until they reached a clump of swamp willows, and took shelter behind them. Indeed, Foy did more, for he climbed the trunk of one of the willows high enough to see over the reeds to the ship *Swallow* and the lake beyond. By this time the Spaniards were alongside the *Swallow*, for he could hear their captain hailing the figure who leaned over the ship's side. He commanded all on board to surrender under pain of being put to death. But from the man in the stern came no answer, which was scarcely strange, seeing that it was the dead pilot, Hans, to whom they talked in the misty dawn, whose body Martin had lashed thus to deceive them. So they fired at the pilot, who took no notice, and then began to clamber on board the ship. In moments, all the men were out of the first boat except two, the steersman and the captain, whom, from his dress and demeanor, Foy took to be the one-eyed Spaniard, Ramiro, although he was too far off to be sure. It was certain, however, that this man did not mean to board the *Swallow*, for he quickly put his boat about, and the wind catching the sail soon drew him clear of her.

"That fellow is cunning," said Foy to Martin and Martha below, "and I was a fool to light the tarred canvas, for he has seen the smoke drawing up the hatchway."

"And having had enough fire for one night, thinks that he will leave his mates to quench it," added Martin.

"The second boat is coming alongside," went on Foy, "and surely the mine should spring."

"Scarcely time yet," answered Martin, "the fuses were set for six minutes."

Then followed a silence in which the three of them watched and listened with beating hearts. In it they heard a voice call out that the steersman was dead, and the answering voice of the officer in the boat, whom Foy had been right in supposing to be Ramiro, warning them to beware of treachery. Now suddenly arose a shout of "A trap! A trap!" for they had found one of the lighted fuses.

"They are running for their boat," said Foy, "and the captain is sailing farther off. Heavens! How they scream."

As the words passed his lips a streak of flame shot into the skies. The island seemed to rock, a fierce rush of air struck Foy and shook him from the tree. Moments later came a dreadful, thunderous sound, and then the sky was darkened with fragments of wreck, limbs of men, a gray cloud of salt and torn shreds of sail and cargo, which fell here, there, and everywhere around and beyond them.

In five seconds it was over, and the three of them, shaken but unhurt, were clinging to each other on the ground. Then as the dark pall of smoke drifted southward, Foy scrambled up his tree again. But now there was little to be seen, for the *Swallow* had vanished utterly, and for many yards round where she lay the wreckage-strewn water was black as ink with the stirred mud. The Spaniards had gone also, nothing of them was left, save the two men and the boat that rode unhurt at a distance. Foy stared at them. The steersman was seated and wringing his hands, while the captain, on whose armor the rays of the rising sun now shone brightly, held to the mast like one stunned, and gazed at the place where, a minute before, had been a ship and a troop of living men. Presently he seemed to recover himself, for he issued an order, whereon the boat's head went about, and she began to glide away.

"Now we had best try to catch him," said Martha, who, by standing up, could see this also.

"Nay, let him be," answered Foy, "we have sent enough men to their account," and he shuddered.

"As you will, Master," grumbled Martin, "but I tell you it is not wise. That man is too clever to be allowed to live, else he would have accompanied the others on board and perished with them."

"Oh! I am sick," replied Foy. "The wind from that powder has shaken me. Settle it as you will with Mother Martha and leave me in peace."

So Martin turned to speak with Martha, but she was not

there.

Chuckling to herself in the madness of her hate and the glory of this great revenge, she had slipped away, knife in hand, to discover whether perchance any of the powder-blasted Spaniards still lived. Fortunately for them, they did not. The shock had killed them all, even those who at the first alarm had thrown themselves into the water. At length, Martin found her praying and giving thanks above a dead body, so shattered that no one could tell to what manner of man it had belonged, and led her away.

Although Martha was keen enough for the chase, by now it was too late, for, traveling before the strong wind, Ramiro and his boat had vanished.

CHAPTER XV
SEÑOR RAMIRO

If Foy van Goorl, could have seen what was passing in the mind of that fugitive in the boat, as Ramiro sailed swiftly away from the scene of death and ruin, bitterly indeed would he have cursed the folly and inexperience which led him to disregard the advice of Red Martin.

Let us look at this man as he goes gnawing his hand in rage and disappointment. There is something familiar about his face and bearing, still gallant enough in a fashion, yet the most observant would find it difficult to recognize in the Señor Ramiro the handsome and courtly Count Juan de Montalvo of over twenty years before. A long spell in the galleys changes the hardiest man, and as it turned out Montalvo, or Ramiro, to call him by his new name, had been forced to serve nearly his full time. He would have escaped earlier indeed, had he not been foolish enough to join in a mutiny, which was discovered and suppressed. It was in the course of this savage struggle for freedom that he lost his eye, knocked out with a belaying pin by an officer whom he had just stabbed. The innocent officer died and the rascal Ramiro recovered, but without his good looks.

To a person of gentle birth, however great a scoundrel he might be, the galleys, which represented penal servitude in the sixteenth century, were a very rough school. Indeed, for the most part, the man who went into them blameless became bad, and the man who went into them bad became worse, for, as the proverb says, those who have dwelt in hell always smell of brimstone. Who can imagine the awfulness of it—the chains, the arduous and continual labor, the whip of the quartemasters, the company of thieves, and all the dreadful squalid sameness?

Well, his strength and constitution, coupled with a sort of

grim philosophy, brought him through, and at length Ramiro found himself a free man, middle-aged indeed, but intelligent and still strong, the world once more before him. Yet what a world! His wife, believing him dead, or perhaps wishing to believe it, had remarried and gone with her husband to New Spain, taking his children with her. In regard to his friends, those of them that lived turned their backs upon him. But, although he had been an unsuccessful man, for with him wickedness had not prospered, he still had great energy and cunning.

The Count Montalvo was a penniless outlaw, a byword and a scorn, and so it was decided that the Count Montalvo must die. When the opportunity for a mock funeral could be arranged, Montalvo staged a public burial in the church of his native village. Strangely enough, however, about the same time the Señor Ramiro appeared in another part of Spain, where with success he practiced as a notary and man of affairs. Some years went by in this manner, until at length, having realized a considerable sum of money by the help of an ingenious fraud, he quickly determined to sail for the Netherlands.

In those dreadful days, in order to further the ends of religious persecution and of legalized theft, informers were rewarded with a portion of the goods of heretics. Ramiro's idea—a clever one in its way—was to organize this informing business, and, by interesting a number of confederates who practically were shareholders in the venture, to sweep into his net more fortunes, or shares of fortunes, than a single individual, however industrious, could hope to secure. As he had expected, soon he found plenty of worthy companions, and the company was floated. For a while, with the help of local agencies and spies, such as Black Meg and the Butcher, with whom, forgetting past injuries, he had secretly renewed his acquaintance, it did very well, the dividends being large and regular. In such times, handsome sums were obtained without risk, out of the properties of unfortunates who were brought to the stake. Still more was secured by a splendid system of blackmail extracted from those who wished to avoid execution, and who, when they had been sucked dry, could either be burnt or let go, as might prove more convenient.

Also there were other ways of making money by an intelligent method of robbery, by contracts to collect fines and taxes and so forth. Thus things went well, and after many years of suffering and poverty, the Señor Ramiro, that experienced man of affairs, began to grow rich, until, indeed, driven forward by a natural but unwise ambition, a fault inherent to daring minds, he entered upon a dangerous path.

The wealth of Hendrik Brant, the goldsmith, was a matter of common report, and glorious would be the fortune of him who could secure it. Ramiro began working on a plan to win this prize. Indeed, there was no particular reason why he should not do so, since Brant was undoubtedly a heretic, and, therefore, legitimate game for any honorable servant of the Church and King. Yet there were lions in the path, two large and formidable lions, or rather a lion and the ghost of a lion, for one was material and the other spiritual. The material lion was that the Government, or in other words, the powerful monarch Philip, desired the goldsmith's fortune for himself and was thus likely to be irritated by an interloper. The spiritual lion was that Brant was connected with Lysbeth van Goorl, once known as Lysbeth de Montalvo, a lady who had brought her reputed husband great misfortune. Quite often during dreary hours of reflection beneath tropic suns, for which the profession of galley-slave gave great leisure, the Señor Ramiro remembered that very energetic curse that his former wife had bestowed upon him, a curse in which she prayed that through her he might live in heavy labor, that through her and hers he might be haunted by fears and misfortunes, and at the last die in misery. Looking back upon the past, it would certainly seem that there had been virtue in this curse, for already through Lysbeth and his dealings with her, he had suffered degradation and severe toil, from nearly fourteen years of daily occupation in the galleys.

Well, he was clear of them, and thenceforward, the curse having exhausted itself for the time being, he had prospered—at any rate to a moderate extent. But if once more he began to interfere with Lysbeth van Goorl and her relatives, might it not reassert its power? That was one question. Was it worthwhile to take this risk on the chance of securing Brant's fortune? That was another. Brant, it was true, was only a cousin of Lysbeth's husband, but when once you meddled with a member of the family, it was impossible to know how soon other members would become mixed up in the affair.

The end may be guessed. The treasure was at hand and enormous, whereas the wrath of a Heavenly or an earthly king seemed far away. So greed, outstripping caution and superstitious fear, won the race, and Ramiro threw himself into the adventure with a resource and energy which in their way were as amazing as they were damnable.

Now, as always, he was a man who hated violence for its own sake. It was no wish of his that the worthy Heer Brant should be unnecessarily burnt or tortured. Therefore through his intermediaries, as Brant had narrated in his letter, he approached him with a proposal that, under the circumstances, was liberal enough—that Brant should hand over two thirds of his fortune to him and his confederates, on condition that he was assisted to escape with the remaining third. To his disgust, however, this obstinate Dutchman refused to buy his safety at the price of a single stiver. Indeed, he answered with rude energy that now as always he was in the hands of God, and if it pleased God that his life should be sacrificed and his great wealth divided amongst thieves, well, it must be so, but he, at least, would be no party to the arrangement.

In the whole course of the affair, Ramiro had made but one crucial mistake, and that sprang from what can only be called the weakness of his nature. Needless to say, it was that he had winked at the escape of Brant's daughter, Elsa. It may have been superstition that prompted him, or it may have been pity, or perhaps it was a certain oath of mercy that he had taken in an hour of need; at any rate, he was content that the girl should not share the doom that overshadowed her father. He did not think it at all likely that she would take with her any documents of importance, and the treasure, of course, she could not take; still, to provide against accidents, he arranged for her to be searched upon the road.

As we know this search was a failure, and when on the morrow Black Meg arrived to make report and to warn him that Dirk van Goorl's son and his great serving man, whose strength was known throughout the Netherlands, were on their road to The Hague, he was sure that after all the girl had carried with her some paper or message.

By this time the location of Brant's treasure had been practically solved. It was believed to lie in the string of vessels, although it was not known that one of these was laden with powder as well as gold. The plan of the Government agents was to search the vessels as they passed out to sea and seize the treasure as contraband, which would save much legal trouble, since under the law or the edicts wealth might not be shipped abroad by heretics. The plan of Ramiro and his friends was to facilitate the escape of the treasure to the open sea, where they proposed to swoop down upon it and convey it to more peaceful shores.

When Foy and his party started down the canal in the boat, Ramiro knew that his opportunity had come, and at once unmoored the big ship and followed. The attempted stabbing of Foy was not done by his orders, as he wished the party to go unmolested and to be kept in sight. That was a piece of private malice on the part of Black Meg, for it was she who was dressed as a man. On various occasions in Leyden, Foy had made remarks upon Meg's character, which she resented, and about her personal appearance, which she resented much more, and this was an attempt to pay off old scores that in the end cost her a finger, a good knife, and a gold ring which had associations connected with her youth.

At first everything had gone well. By one of the most daring and masterly maneuvers that Ramiro had ever seen in his long and varied experience upon the seas, the little *Swallow*, with her crew of three men, had run the gauntlet of the fort, which was warned and waiting for her; had sunk and sailed through the big Government boat and her crew of lubberly soldiers, many of whom, he was glad to reflect, were drowned; had crushed the officer, against whom he had a personal grudge, like an eggshell, and won through to the open sea. There he thought he was sure of her, for he took it for granted that she would run for the Norfolk coast, and knew that in the gale of wind his larger and well-manned vessel could pull her down. But then the same misfortune that always dogged him, when he began to interfere with the affairs of Lysbeth and her relatives, declared itself.

Instead of attempting to cross the North Sea, the little *Swallow* hugged the coast, where, for various nautical reasons connected with the wind, the water, and the build of their respective ships, she had the best of him. Next he lost her in the narrow water-way, and after that we know what happened. There was no disguising it; it was a most dreadful fiasco. To have one's vessel boarded, the expensive vessel in which so large a proportion of the gains of his honorable company had been invested, not only boarded, but fired, and the watchman stabbed by a single devil of unknown origin was bad enough. And then the end of it!

To have found the gold-laden ship, to have been tricked into attacking her, and—and—oh, he could scarcely bear to think of it! There was but one consolation. Although too late to save the others, even through the mist, he had seen that wisp of smoke rising from the hold; yes, he, the experienced, had smelt a rat and had kept his distance with the result that he was still alive.

But the others! Those gallant comrades in adventure, where were they? Well, to be frank, he did not greatly care. There was another question of higher importance. Where was the treasure? Now that his brain had cleared after the shock and turmoil, it was evident to him that Foy van Goorl, Red Martin, and the white devil who had boarded his ship, would not have destroyed so much wealth if they could help it, and still less would they have destroyed themselves. Therefore, to pursue the matter to a logical conclusion, it seemed probable that they had spent the night in sinking or burying the money, and preparing the pretty trap into which he had walked. So the secret was in their hands and, as they were still alive, very possibly means could be found to induce them to reveal its hiding place. There was still hope; indeed, now that he came to weigh things, they were not so bad.

To begin with, almost all the shareholders in the affair had perished by the stern decree of Providence, and he was the natural heir of their interests. In other words, the treasure, if it could be recovered, was henceforth his property. Further, when they came to hear the story, the Government would set down Brant's fortune as hopelessly lost, so that the galling competition from which he had suffered so much was at an end.

Under these circumstances, what was to be done? Very soon, as he sailed away over the lake in the sweet air of the morning, the Señor Ramiro found an answer to the question.

The treasure had left The Hague, so he must leave The Hague. The secret of its disposal was at Leyden, henceforth he must live at Leyden. Why not? He knew Leyden well. It was a pleasant place, but, of course, he might be recognized there; though, after so long, this was scarcely probable, for was not the Count de Montalvo notoriously dead and buried? Time and accident had changed him; moreover, he could bring art to the assistance of nature. In Leyden, too, he had confederates like Black Meg for one; also he had funds, for was he not the treasurer of the company that this very morning had achieved such remarkable and unsought-for opportunity?

There was only one thing against the scheme. In Leyden lived Lysbeth van Goorl and her husband, and with them a certain young man whose parentage he could guess. More, her son Foy knew the hiding place of Brant's hoard, and from him or his servant Martin that secret must be won. So once again he was destined to match himself against Lysbeth the wronged, the dreaded, the victorious Lysbeth, whose voice of denunciation still rang in his ear, whose eyes of fire still scorched his soul, the woman whom he feared above everything on earth. He had fought her once for money, and, although he won the money, it had done him little good, for in the end she had outwitted him. Now, if he went to Leyden, he must fight her again for money, and what would be the issue of that war? Was it worthwhile to take the risk? Would not history repeat itself? If he hurt her, would she not crush him? But the treasure, that mighty treasure, which could give him so much, and, above all, could restore to him the rank and station he had forfeited, and which he coveted more than anything in life. For, low as he had fallen, Montalvo could not forget that he had been born a gentleman.

He would take his chance; he would go to Leyden. Had he weighed the matter in the gloom of night, or even in a dull and stormy hour, perhaps—nay probably—he would have decided otherwise. But this morning the sun shone brightly, the wind made a merry music in the reeds; on the rippling surface of the lake the marsh-birds sang, and from the shore came a cheerful lowing of cattle. In such surroundings, his fears and superstitions vanished. He fancied that he was master of himself, and he was confident that all depended merely upon his own cleverness. Behind him lay the buried gold; before him rose the towers of Leyden, where he could find its key. Why then was he still haunted by this legend of a God of vengeance, in which priests and others affected to believe? Now that he came to think of it, what rubbish was this business of conscience, for as any agent of the Inquisition knew well, the vengeance always fell upon those who trusted in this same God; a hundred torture dens, a thousand smoking fires bore witness to the fact that divine justice sleeps. And if there was a God, why, recognizing his personal merits, only this morning He had selected him out of many to live on and be the inheritor of the wealth of Hendrik Brant. Yes, he would go to Leyden and fight the battle out.

At the entry of the narrow waterway, Señor Ramiro looked for a place to land his boat. At first he had thought of killing his companion, so that he might remain the sole survivor of the catastrophe, but on reflection he abandoned this idea, as the man was a faithful creature of his own who might be useful. So he told him to return to The Hague to tell the story of the destruction of the ship *Swallow* with the treasure, her attackers and her crew, whoever they might have been. He was to add, moreover, that so far as he knew the Captain Ramiro had perished also, as he, the steersman, was left alone in charge of the boat when the vessel blew up. Then he was to come to Leyden, bringing with him certain goods and papers belonging to him,

Ramiro.

This plan seemed to have advantages. No one would continue to hunt for the treasure. No one except himself, and perhaps Black Meg, would know that Foy van Goorl and Martin had been on board the *Swallow* and escaped; indeed, as yet, he was not quite sure of it himself. For the rest he could either lie hidden, or if it proved desirable, announce that he still lived. Even if his messenger should prove faithless and tell the truth, it would not greatly matter, seeing that he knew nothing that could be of service to anybody.

And so the steersman sailed away, while Ramiro, filled with memories, reflections, and hopes, walked quietly through the Morsch Poort into the good city of Leyden.

That evening, but not until dark had fallen, two other travelers entered Leyden, namely, Foy and Martin. Passing unobserved through the quiet streets, they reached the side door of the house in the Bree Straat. It was opened by a serving woman, who told Foy that his mother was in Adrian's room, also that Adrian was very much better. So forward, followed more slowly by Martin, went Foy, running upstairs three steps at a time, for he had a great story to tell!

The interior of the room, as he entered it, made an attractive picture that even in his hurry caught Foy's eye and fixed itself so firmly upon his mind that he never forgot its details. To begin with, the place was beautifully furnished, for his brother had a really good taste in tapestry, pictures, and other such adornments. Adrian himself lay upon a richly carved oak bed, pale from loss of blood, but otherwise little the worse. Seated by the side of the bed, looking wonderfully sweet in the lamplight that cast shadows from the curling hair about her brows on to the delicate face beneath, was Elsa Brant. She had been reading to Adrian from a book of Spanish chivalry such as his romantic soul loved, and he, resting on his elbow in the snowy bed, was contemplating her beauty with his languishing black eyes. Yet, although he only saw her for a moment before she heard his entry and looked up, it was obvious to Foy that Elsa remained quite unconscious of the handsome Adrian's admiration, indeed, that her mind wandered far away from the magnificent adventures and highly colored love scenes of which she was reading in her sweet, low voice. Nor was he mistaken, for, in fact, the poor child was thinking of her father.

At the further end of the room, talking together earnestly in the deep and curtained window-place, stood his mother and his father. Clearly they were as much preoccupied as the younger couple, and it was not difficult for Foy to guess that fears for his own safety upon his perilous errand were what concerned them most, and behind them other unnumbered fears. For the dwellers in the Netherlands in those days must walk from year to year through a valley of shadows so grim that our imagination can scarcely picture them.

"Sixty hours and he is not back," Lysbeth was saying.

"Martin said we were not to trouble ourselves before they had been gone for a hundred," answered Dirk consolingly.

Just then Foy, surveying them from the shadowed doorway, stepped forward, saying in his jovial voice:

"Sixty hours to the very minute."

Lysbeth uttered a little scream of joy and ran forward. Elsa let the book fall on to the floor and rose to do the same, then remembered and stood still, while Dirk remained where he was until the women had done their greetings, betraying his delight only by a quick rubbing of his hands. Adrian alone did not look particularly pleased—not, however, because he retained any special grudge against his brother for his share in the fracas of a few nights before, since, when once his furious gusts of temper had passed, he was able to put things into a better light. Indeed he was glad that Foy had come back safe from his dangerous adventure, only he wished that he would not blunder into the bedroom and interrupt his delightful occupation of listening, while the beautiful Elsa read him romance and poetry.

Since Foy was gone upon his mission, Adrian had been treated with the consideration that he felt to be his due. Even his stepfather had taken an opportunity to mumble some words of regret for what had happened, and to express a hope that noth-

ing more would be said about the matter, while his mother was sympathetic and Elsa most charming and attentive. Now, as he knew well, all this would be changed. Foy, the exuberant, unrefined, plain-spoken, nerve-shaking Foy, would become the center of attraction, and overwhelm them with long stories of very dull exploits, while Martin, that brutal bull of a man who was only fit to draw a cart, would stand behind and play the part of chorus, saying "Ja" and "Neen" at proper intervals. Well, he supposed that he must put up with it, but oh, what a weariness it was.

A minute later, and Foy was wringing him by the hand, saying in his loud voice, "How are you, old fellow? You look as well as possible, what are you lying in this bed for and being fed with gruel by the women?"

"For the love of Heaven, Foy," interrupted Adrian, "stop crushing my fingers and shaking me as though I were a rat. You mean it kindly, I know, but—" and Adrian dropped back upon the pillow, coughed and looked hectic and interesting.

Then both the women fell upon Foy, upbraiding him for his roughness, begging him to remember that if he were not careful he might kill his brother, whose arteries were understood to be in a most precarious condition. The poor man covered his ears with his hands and waited until he saw their lips stop moving.

"I apologize," he said. "I won't touch him, I won't speak loud near him. Adrian, do you hear?"

"Who could help it?" moaned the prostrate Adrian.

"Cousin Foy," interrupted Elsa, clasping her hands and looking up into his face with her big brown eyes, "forgive me, but I can wait no longer. Tell me, did you see or hear anything of my father yonder at The Hague?"

"Yes, Cousin, I saw him," answered Foy soberly.

"And how was he—oh, and all the rest of them?"

"He was well enough," said the young man painfully.

"And free and in no danger?

"And free, but I cannot say in no danger. We are all of us in danger nowadays, Cousin," replied Foy in the same quiet voice.

"Oh! Thank God for that," said Elsa.

"Perhaps I missed something during our visit with Heer Brant," mentioned Martin, who had entered the room and was standing behind Foy looking like a giant at a show. Elsa had turned her face away, so Foy struck backwards with all his force, hitting Martin in the pit of the stomach with the point of his elbow. Martin doubled himself up, recoiled a step and took the hint.

"Well, Son, what news?" said Dirk, speaking for the first time.

"News!" answered Foy, escaping joyfully from this treacherous ground. "Oh! Lots of it. Look here," and plunging his hands into his pockets he produced first the half of the broken dagger and secondly a long skinny finger of unwholesome hue with a gold ring on it.

"Bah!" said Adrian. "Take that horrid thing away."

"Oh! I beg your pardon," answered Foy, shuffling the finger back into his pocket, "you don't mind the dagger, do you? No?

Well, then, Mother, that mail shirt of yours is the best that was ever made; this knife broke on it like a carrot, though, by the way, it's uncommonly sticky wear when you haven't changed it for three days, and I shall be glad enough to get it off."

"Evidently Foy has a story to tell," said Adrian wearily, "and the sooner he rids his mind of it the sooner he will be able to wash. I suggest, Foy, that you should begin at the beginning."

So Foy began at the beginning, and his tale proved sufficiently moving to interest even the soul-worn Adrian. Some portions of it he softened down, and some of it he suppressed for the sake of Elsa—not very successfully, indeed, for Foy was no diplomat, and her quick imagination filled the gaps. Another part—that which concerned her future and his own—of necessity he omitted altogether. He told them very briefly, however, of the flight from The Hague, of the sinking of the Government boat, of the run through the gale to the Haarlem Meer with the dead pilot on board and the Spanish ship behind, and of the secret midnight burying of the treasure.

"Where did you bury it?" asked Adrian.

"I have not the slightest idea," said Foy. "I believe there are about three hundred islets in that part of the Meer, and all I know is that we dug a hole in one of them and stuck it in. However," he went on in a burst of confidence, "we made a map of the place, that is—" Here he broke off with a howl of pain, for an accident had happened.

While this narrative was proceeding, Martin, who was standing by him saying "Ja" and "Neen" at intervals, as Adrian foresaw he would, he had unbuckled the great sword Silence, and in an abstracted manner was amusing himself by throwing it towards the ceiling hilt downwards, and as it fell catching it in his hand. Now, most unaccountably, he looked the other way and missed his catch, with the result that the handle of the heavy weapon fell exactly upon Foy's left foot and then clattered to the ground.

"You awkward beast!" roared Foy, "you have crushed my toes," and he hopped towards a chair upon one leg.

"Your pardon, Master," said Martin. "I know it was careless;

my mother always told me that I was careless, but so was my father before me."

Adrian, overcome by the fearful crash, closed his eyes and sighed.

"Look," said Lysbeth in a fury, "he is fainting; I knew that would be the end of all your noise. If you are not careful, we shall have him breaking another blood vessel. Go out of the room, all of you. You can finish telling the story downstairs," and she forcefully drove them before her as one would treat a rented donkey.

"Martin," said Foy on the stairs, where they found themselves together for a minute, for at the first signs of the storm Dirk had preceded them, "why did you drop that accursed great sword of yours upon my foot?"

"Master," countered Martin imperturbably, "why did you hit me in the pit of the stomach with your elbow?"

"To keep your tongue quiet," responded Foy.

"And what is the name of my sword? Silence. Well, then, I dropped the sword Silence for the same reason. I hope it hasn't hurt you much, but if it did I can't help it."

Foy wheeled round. "What do you mean, Martin?"

"I mean," answered the great man with energy, "that you have no right to tell what became of that paper which Mother Martha gave us."

"Why not? I have faith in my brother."

"Very likely, Master, but that isn't the point. We carry a great secret, and this secret is a trust, a dangerous trust; it would be wrong to lay its burden upon the shoulders of other folk. What people don't know they can't tell, Master."

Foy still stared at him, half in question, half in anger, but Martin made no further reply in words. Only he went through certain curious motions, motions as of a man winding slowly and laboriously at something like a geared wheel. Foy's lips turned pale.

"The rack?" he whispered.

Martin nodded and answered beneath his breath, "They may all of them be on it yet. You let the man in the boat escape, and that man was the Spanish spy, Ramiro; I am sure of it. If they don't know they can't tell, and though we know we shan't tell; we shall die first, Master."

Now Foy trembled and leaned against the wall. "What would betray us?" he asked.

"Who knows, Master? A woman's torment, a man's—" and he put a strange meaning into his voice, "—a man's jealousy, or pride, or vengeance. Oh, bridle your tongue and trust no one, no, not your father or mother, or sweetheart—" and again that strange meaning came into Martin's voice, "or brother."

"Or you?" queried Foy looking up.

"I am not absolutely sure. Yes, I think you may trust me, though there is no knowing how the rack might change a man's mind. The fact still remains, however, that I already know the secret."

"If all this be so," said Foy, with a flash of sudden passion, "I have said too much already."

"A great deal too much, Master. If I could have managed it I would have dropped the sword Silence on your toe long before. But I couldn't, for the Heer Adrian was watching me, and I had to wait until he closed his eyes, which he did to hear the better without seeming to listen."

"You are unjust to Adrian, Martin, as you always have been, and I am angry with you. Say, what is to be done now?"

"Now, Master," replied Martin soberly, "to save the lives of those in this house, or perhaps our own lives some day, you must tell a lie. You must take up your tale where you left it off, and say that we made a map of the hiding place, but that I, being a fool—managed to drop it while we were lighting the fuses, so that it was blown away with the ship. I will tell the same story."

"Am I to say this to my father and mother?" questioned Foy.

"Certainly, and they will quite understand why you say it. As Pastor Arentz once taught us, in extreme cases involving the protection of life, God's servants may deceive to preserve life, as in the case of the wise men who deceived Herod. Besides, your mother was getting uneasy already, and that was why she drove us from the room. You will tell them that the treasure is buried but that the secret of its hiding place was lost."

"Even so, Martin, it is not lost; Mother Martha knows it, and they all will guess that she does know it."

"Why, Master, as it happened you were in such a hurry to get on with your story that I think you forgot to mention that she was present at the burying of the barrels. Her name was coming when I dropped the sword upon your foot."

"But she boarded and fired the Spanish ship, so the man Ramiro and his companion would probably have seen her."

"I think, Master, that the only person who saw her was he whose gizzard was slit, and he will tell no tales. Probably they think it was you or I who did that deed. But if she was seen, or if they know that she has the secret, then let them get it from Mother Martha. Oh! Mares can gallop, and ducks can dive, and snakes can hide in the grass. When they can catch the wind and make it give up its secrets, when they can charm from sword Silence the tale of the blood which it has drunk throughout the generations, when they can call back the dead saints from heaven and stretch them anew within the torture-pit, then and not before, they will win knowledge of the treasure's hiding place from the lips of the Mare of Haarlem Meer. Oh! Master, fear not for her, the grave is not so safe."

"Why did you not caution me before, Martin?" asked Foy.

"Because, Master," answered Martin stolidly, "I did not think that you would be such a fool. But I forgot that you are young— yes, I forgot that you are young and good, too good for the days we live in. It is my fault. On my head be it."

CHAPTER XVI
THE MASTER

In the sitting room, speaking more slowly and with greater caution, Foy continued the story of their adventures. When he came to the tale of how the ship *Swallow* was blown up with all the Spanish soldiers, Elsa clasped her hands, saying, "Horrible! Horrible! Think of the poor creatures hurled into eternity."

"And think of the business they were on," broke in Dirk grimly, adding, "May God forgive me who cannot feel grieved to hear of the death of Spanish cutthroats. It was well managed, Foy, excellently well managed. But go on."

"I think that is about all," said Foy shortly, "except that two of the Spaniards got away in a boat, one of whom is believed to be the head spy and captain, Ramiro."

"But, son, up in Adrian's chamber just now you said something about having made a map of the hiding place of the gold. Where is it for it should be put in safety?"

"Yes, I know I did," answered Foy, "but didn't I tell you?" he went on awkwardly. "Martin managed to drop the thing in the cabin of the *Swallow* while we were lighting the fuses, so it was blown up with the ship, and there is now no record of where the stuff was buried."

"Come, come, son," said Dirk. "Martha, who knows every island on the great lake, must remember the spot."

"Oh, no, she doesn't," answered Foy. "The truth is that she didn't come with us when we buried the barrels. She stopped to watch the Spanish ship, and just told us to land on the first island we came to and dig a hole, which we did, making a map of the place before we left, the same that Martin dropped."

All this clumsy falsehood Foy uttered with a wooden face and in a voice that would not have convinced a three-year-old child.

"Martin," asked Dirk, suspiciously, "is this true?"

"Absolutely true, Master," replied Martin. "It is wonderful how well he remembers."

"Son," said Dirk, turning white with suppressed anger, "you have always been a good lad, and now you have shown yourself a brave one, but I pray God that I may not be forced to add that you are false-tongued. Do you not see that this looks black? The treasure which you have hidden is the greatest in all the Netherlands. Will not folk say that you have forgotten its secret until it suits you to remember?"

Foy took a step forward, his face crimson with indignation, but the heavy hand of Martin fell upon his shoulder and dragged him back as though he were but a little child.

"I think, Master Foy," he said, fixing his eyes upon Lysbeth, "that your lady mother wishes to say something."

"You are right, Martin; I do. Do you not think, Husband, that in these days of ours, a man might have other reasons for hiding the truth than a desire to enrich himself by theft?"

"What do you mean, Wife?" asked Dirk. "Foy here says that he has buried this great hoard with Martin, but that he and Martin do not know where they buried it, and have lost the map they made. Whatever may be the exact wording of the will, that hoard belongs to my cousin here, subject to certain trusts that have not yet arisen, and may never arise, and I am her guardian while Hendrik Brant lives and his executor when he dies. Therefore, legally, it belongs to me also. By what right, then, do my son and my servant hide the truth from me, if, indeed, they are hiding the truth? Say what you have to say straight out, for I am a plain man and cannot read riddles."

"Then I will say it, Husband, though it is but my guess, for I have had no words with Foy or Martin, and if I am wrong they can correct me. I know their faces, and I think with you that they are not speaking all the truth. I think that they do not wish us to know it—not that they may keep the secret of this treasure for themselves, but because such a secret might well open those who know of it to torture and the stake. Is it not so, my son?"

"Mother," answered Foy, almost in a whisper, "it is so. The paper is not lost, but do not seek to learn its hiding place, for there are wolves who would tear your bodies limb from limb to get the knowledge out of you. Yes, even Elsa's, even Elsa's. If the trial must come, let it fall on me and Martin, who are fitter to bear it. Oh! Father, surely you know that, whatever we may be, neither of us are thieves."

Dirk advanced to his son, and kissed him on the forehead.

"My son," he said, "pardon me, and you, Red Martin, pardon me also. I spoke in my haste. I spoke as a fool, who, at my age should have known better. In light of all this, I tell you that I wish that this cursed treasure, these cases of priceless gems and these kegs of hoarded gold, had been shivered to the winds of heaven with the timbers of the ship *Swallow*. For, mark you, Ramiro has escaped, and with him another man, and they will know well that having the night to hide it, you did not destroy those jewels with the ship. They will track you down, these Spanish sleuth-hounds, filled with the lust of blood and gold, and it will be well if the lives of every one of us do not pay the price of the secret of the burying place of the wealth of Hendrik Brant."

He ceased, pale and trembling, and a silence fell upon the room and all in it, a sad and heavy silence, for in his voice they caught the note of prophecy. Martin broke it.

"It may be so, Master," he said, "but, your pardon, you should have thought of that before you undertook this duty. There was no call upon you to send the Heer Foy and myself to The Hague to bring away this trash, but you did it as would any other honest man. Well, now it is done and we must take our chance, but I say this—if you are wise, my masters, yes, and you ladies also, before you leave this room you will swear upon the Bible, every one of you, never to whisper the word 'treasure,' never to think of it except to believe that it is gone—lost beneath the waters of the Haarlemer Meer. Never to whisper it, no, Mistress, not even to the Heer Adrian, your son who lies sick upstairs."

"You have learned wisdom somewhere in recent years, Martin, since you stopped drinking and fighting," said Dirk dryly, "and for my part, before God I swear it."

"And so do I." "And I." "And I." "And I," echoed the others, Martin, who spoke last, adding, "Yes, I swear that I will never speak of it; no, not even to my young master Adrian, who lies sick upstairs."

Adrian made a good, though not a very quick recovery. He had lost a great deal of blood, but the vessel closed without further complications, so that it remained only to renew his strength by rest and ample food. For ten days or so after the return of Foy and Martin, he was kept in bed and nursed by the women of the house. Elsa's share in this treatment was to read to him from the Spanish romances he admired. Very soon, however, he found that he admired Elsa herself even more than the romances, and would ask her to shut the book that he might talk to her. So long as his conversation was about himself, his dreams, plans and ambitions, she fell into it readily enough, but when he began to turn it upon herself, and to lace it with compliment and amorous innuendo, then she withdrew and fled.

Handsome as he might be, Adrian had no attraction for Elsa. About him there was something too exaggerated for her taste; moreover he was Spanish, Spanish in his beauty, and Spanish in the form of his mind. Deep down in her heart also lay a second reason for this repugnance; the man reminded her of another man who for months had been a nightmare to her soul, the Hague spy, Ramiro. This Ramiro she had observed closely. Though she had not seen him very often, his terrible reputation was familiar to her. She knew also, for her father had told her as much, that it was he who was drawing the nets about him at The Hague, and who plotted day and night to rob him of his wealth.

At first sight, there was no great resemblance between the pair. How could there be indeed between a man on the wrong side of middle age, one-eyed, grizzled, battered, and bearing about with him an atmosphere of iniquity, and a young gentleman, handsome, distinguished, and wayward, but assuredly no criminal? Yet the likeness existed. She had seen it first when Adrian was pointing out to her how, were he a general, he would dispose his forces for the capture of Leyden, and from that moment her nature rose against him. Also it came out in other ways, in little tricks of voice and strangeness of manner that Elsa caught at unexpected moments, perhaps, as she told herself, because she had trained her mind to seek these similarities. Yet all the while she knew that the similarity was ridiculous, for what could these two men have in common with each other?

In those days, however, Elsa did not think much of Adrian, or of anybody except her beloved father, whose only child she was, and whom she adored with all the passion of her heart. She knew the terrible danger in which he stood, and guessed that she had been sent away that she should not share his perils. Now she had but one desire and one prayer—that he might escape in safety, and that she might return to him again. Once only, a message came from him sent through a woman whom she had never seen, the wife of a fisherman, who delivered it by word of mouth. This was the message:

Give my love and blessing to my daughter Elsa, and tell her that so far I am unharmed. To Foy van Goorl say, I have heard the news. Well done, thou good and faithful servant! Let him remember what I told him, and be sure that he will not strive in vain, and that he shall not lack for his reward here or hereafter.

That was all. Tidings reached them also that the destruction of so many men by the blowing up of the *Swallow*, and by her sinking of the Government boat as she escaped, had caused much excitement and fury among the Spaniards. But, as those who had been blown up were volunteers, and as the boat was sunk while the *Swallow* was flying from them, nothing had been done in the matter. Indeed, nothing could be done, for it was not known who manned the *Swallow*, and, as Ramiro had foreseen, her crew were supposed to have been destroyed with her in the Haarlemer Meer.

Then, after a while, came other news that filled Elsa's heart with a wild hope, for it was reported that Hendrik Brant had disappeared, and was believed to have escaped from The Hague. Nothing more was heard of him, however, which is scarcely strange, for the doomed man had gone down the path of rich heretics into the silent vaults of the Inquisition. The net had closed at last, and through the net fell the sword.

But if Elsa thought seldom of Adrian, except in gusts of spasmodic dislike, Adrian thought of Elsa, and little besides. So earnestly did he lash his romantic temperament, and so deeply did her beauty and charm appeal to him, that very soon he was truly in love with her. Nor did the fact that, as he believed, she was, potentially, the greatest heiress in the Netherlands, cool Adrian's amorous devotion. What could suit him better in his condition, than to marry this rich and lovely lady?

So Adrian made up his mind that he would marry her, for, in his vanity, it never occurred to him that she might object. Indeed, the only thought that gave him trouble was the difficulty of reducing her wealth into possession. Foy and Martin had buried it somewhere in the Haarlemer Meer. But they said, for this he had ascertained by repeated inquiries, although the information was given grudgingly enough, that the map of the hiding place had been destroyed in the explosion on the *Swallow.* Adrian did not believe this story for a moment. He was convinced that they were keeping the truth from him, and as the prospective master of that treasure, he resented this reluctance bitterly. Still, it had to be overcome, and as soon as he was engaged to Elsa, he intended to speak very clearly upon this point. Meanwhile, the first thing was to find a suitable opportunity to make his declaration in clear terms, after which he would be prepared to deal with Foy and Martin.

Towards evening it was Elsa's custom to walk abroad. As at that hour Foy left the foundry, naturally Foy accompanied her in these walks, Martin following at a little distance in case he should be needed. Soon those excursions became delightful to both of them. To Elsa, especially, it was pleasant to escape from the hot house into the cool evening air, and still more pleasant to exchange the labored tendernesses and highly colored compliments of Adrian for the cheerful honesty of Foy's conversation.

Foy admired his cousin as much as did his half-brother, but his attitude towards her was very different. He never said sweet things; he never gazed up into her eyes and sighed; although once or twice, perhaps by accident, he did squeeze her hand. His demeanor towards her was that of a friend and relative, and the subject of their talk for the most part was the possibility of her father's deliverance from the dangers which surrounded him, and other matters of the sort.

The time came at last when Adrian was allowed to leave his room, and as it happened, it fell to Elsa's lot to attend him on this first journey downstairs. In a Dutch home of the period and of the class of the Van Goorl's, all the women-folk of whatever degree were expected to take a share in the household work. At present, Elsa's share was to care for Adrian, who showed so much temper at every attempt made to replace her by any other woman, that, in respect of the doctor's instructions, Lysbeth did not dare to cross his whim.

It was with no small delight, therefore, that Elsa hailed the prospect of release, for the young man with his grandiose bearing and amorous sighs wearied her almost beyond endurance. Adrian was not equally pleased; indeed, he had feigned symptoms that caused him to remain in bed an extra week, merely in order that he might keep her near him. But now the inevitable hour had come, and Adrian felt that it was incumbent upon him to lift the veil and let Elsa see some of the secret of his soul. He had prepared for the event; indeed, the tedium of his confinement had been much relieved by the composition of lofty and heart-stirring addresses, in which he, the noble cavalier, laid his precious self and fortune at the feet of this undistinguished, but rich and attractive maid.

Yet now when the moment was with him, and when Elsa gave him her hand to lead him from the room, behold all these beautiful imaginings had vanished, and his knees shook with no phony weakness. Somehow Elsa did not look as a girl ought to look who was about to be proposed to; she was too cold and dignified, too utterly unconscious of anything unusual. It was disconcerting, but it must be done.

By a superb effort, Adrian recovered himself and opened with one of the fine speeches, not the best by any means, but the only specimen he could remember.

"Without," he began, "the free air waits to be pressed by my cramped wings, but although my heart bounds wild as that of any haggard hawk, I tell you, fairest Elsa, that in yonder gilded cage," and he pointed to the bed, "I—"

"Heaven above us! Heer Adrian," broke in Elsa in alarm. "Are you—are you—getting giddy?"

"She does not understand. Poor child, how could she?" he murmured in a stage aside. Then he started again. "Yes, most adorable, best beloved, I am giddy, giddy with gratitude to those fair hands, giddy with worship of those lovely eyes—"

Now Elsa, unable to contain her merriment any longer, burst out laughing, but seeing that her adorer's face was beginning to look as it did in the dining room before he broke the blood vessel, she checked herself, and said, "Oh! Heer Adrian, don't waste all this fine poetry upon me. I am too stupid to understand it."

"Poetry!" he exclaimed, becoming suddenly natural, "it isn't poetry."

"Then what is it?" she asked not realizing she should have bitten her tongue.

"It is—it is—love!" and he sank upon his knees before her, where, she could not but notice, he looked very handsome in the subdued light of the room, with his upturned face blanched by sickness, and his glowing eyes. "Elsa, I love you and no other, and unless you return that love, my heart will break and I shall die."

Now, under ordinary circumstances, Elsa would have been quite competent to deal with the situation, but the fear of over-agitating Adrian complicated it greatly. About the reality of his feelings at the moment, at any rate, it seemed impossible to be mistaken, for the man was shaking like a leaf. Still, she must make an end of these advances.

"Rise, Heer Adrian," she said gently, holding out her hand to help him to his feet.

He obeyed, and glancing at her face, saw that it was very calm and cold as winter ice.

"Listen, Heer Adrian," she said. "You mean this kindly, and doubtless many a maid would be flattered by your words, but I

must tell you that I am in no mood for your advances."

"Because of another man?" he queried, and suddenly becoming theatrical again, added; "Speak on, let me hear the worst. I will not quail."

"There is no need to," replied Elsa in the same quiet voice, "because there is no other man. I have never yet thought of marriage. I have no wish that way, and if I had, I should forget it now when from hour to hour I do not know where my dear father may be, or what fate awaits him. He is my only lover, Heer Adrian," and as Elsa spoke her soft brown eyes filled with tears.

"Ah!" said Adrian, "would that I might fly to save him from all dangers, as I rescued you, lady, from the bandits of the wood."

"I would you might," she replied, smiling sadly at the double meaning of the words, "but, hark, your mother is calling us. I know, Heer Adrian," she added gently, "that you will understand and respect my dreadful anxiety, and will not trouble me again with poetry and love-talk, for if you do I shall be—angry."

"Lady," he answered, "your wishes are my law, and until these clouds have rolled from the blue heaven of your life, I will be as silent as the stars. And, by the way," he added rather nervously, "perhaps you will be silent also—about our talk, I mean, as we do not want that buffoon, Foy, thrusting his street-boy fun at us."

Elsa bowed her head. She was inclined to resent the "we" and other things in this speech, but, above all, she did not wish to prolong this foolish and tiresome interview, so, without more words, she took her admirer by the hand and guided him down the stairs.

It was but three days after this ridiculous scene, on a certain afternoon, when Adrian had been out for the second time, that the evil tidings came. Dirk had heard them in the town, and returned home well-nigh weeping. Elsa saw his face and knew at once.

"Oh! Is he dead?" she gasped.

He nodded, for he dared not trust himself to speak.

"How? Where?"

"In the Poort prison at The Hague," said Dirk simply.

"How do you know?" questioned Elsa.

"I have seen a man who helped to bury him."

She looked up as though to ask for further details, but Dirk turned away pleading, "He is dead, he is dead, let us speak no more until our grief has passed."

Then she understood, nor did she ever seek to know any more. Whatever he had suffered, at least now he was with the God he worshipped, and with the wife he lost. Only the poor orphan, comforted by Lysbeth, crept from the chamber, and for a week was seen no more. When she appeared again, she seemed to be herself in all things, only she never smiled and was very indifferent to what took place around her. Thus she remained for many days.

Although this solemnness on Elsa's part was understood and received with sympathy and more by the rest of the household, Adrian soon began to find it irksome and even ridiculous. So colossal was this young man's vanity that he was unable to understand how a girl could be so wrapped up in the memories of a murdered father, that no place was left in her mind for the tendernesses of a present adorer. After all, this father, what was he? A middle-aged and, doubtless, quite uninteresting burgher, who could lay claim to but one distinction, that of great wealth, most of which had been amassed by his ancestors.

Now a rich man alive has points of interest, but a rich man dead is only interesting to his heirs. Also, this Brant was one of these narrow-minded, fanatical, Protestant fellows who were so wearisome to men of intellect and refinement. True, he, Adrian, was himself of the Reformed community, for circumstances had driven him into the herd, but oh, he found them a dreary set. Their strict doctrines regarding man's depravity, and of his utter dependence upon God to obtain personal redemption, as well as their insistence to ground all of their decisions in the Bible, did not appeal to him; moreover, they generally ended at the stake. Now about the pomp and circumstance of the Mother Church there was something attractive. Of course, as a matter of prudence he attended its ceremonials from time to time and found them comfortable and satisfying. Comfortable also were the dogmas of forgiveness to be obtained by an act of penitential confession, and the sense of a great supporting force whose whole weight was at the disposal of the humblest believer.

In short, there was nothing extraordinary about the excellent departed Hendrik, nothing that could justify the young woman in wrapping herself up in grief for him to the entire exclusion of a person who was ready, at the first opportunity, to wrap himself up in her.

After long brooding, assisted by a close study of the romances of the period, Adrian convinced himself that in all this there was something unnatural, that the girl must be under a species of spell, which in her own interest ought to be broken. But how? That was the question. Try as he would, he could do nothing. Therefore, like others in a difficulty, he determined to seek the assistance of an expert, namely, Black Meg, who, among her other occupations, for a certain fee payable in advance, was ready to give advice as a specialist in affairs of the heart.

In consequence to his perceived need, Adrian went to Black Meg secretly and by night, for he loved mystery, and in truth it was hardly safe that he should visit her by the light of day. Seated in a shadowed chamber, he poured out his artless tale to the pythoness, of course concealing all names. He might have spared himself this trouble, as he was an old client of Meg's, a fact that no disguise could keep from her. Before he opened his lips she knew perfectly what was the name of his new love and indeed all the circumstances connected with the pair of them.

The opportunistic woman listened patiently, and when he had done, shook her head, saying that the case was too hard for her. She proposed, however, to consult a Master more learned than herself, who, by great good fortune, was at that moment in Leyden, frequenting her house in fact, and begged that Adrian would return at the same hour on the morrow.

Now, as it turned out, oddly enough Black Meg had been commissioned by the so-called Master to bring about a meeting between himself and this very young man.

Adrian returned accordingly, and was informed that the Master, after consulting the stars and other sources of divination, had become so deeply interested in the affair that, for pure love of the thing and not for any temporal purpose of gain, he was in attendance to advise in person. Adrian was overjoyed, and prayed that he might be introduced. Presently a noble-looking form entered the room, wrapped in a long cloak. Adrian bowed, and the form, after contemplating him earnestly—very earnestly, if he had known the truth—acknowledged the salute with dignity. Adrian cleared his throat and began to speak, whereon the sage stopped him.

"Explanations are needless, young man," he said, in a measured and melodious voice, "for my studies of the matter have already informed me of more than you can tell. Let me see. Your name is Adrian van Goorl—no, called Van Goorl. The lady you desire to win is Elsa Brant, the daughter of Hendrik Brant, a heretic and well-known goldsmith, who was recently executed at The Hague. She is a girl of much beauty, but one unnaturally insensible to the influence of love, and who does not at present recognize your worth. There are, also, unless I am mistaken, other important circumstances connected with the case.

"This lady is a great heiress, but her fortune is at present missing. It is, I have reason to believe, hidden in the Haarlemer Meer. She is surrounded with influences that are opposed to you, all of which, however, can be overcome if you will place yourself unreservedly in my hands, for, young man, I accept no half-confidences, nor do I ask for any fee. When the fortune is recovered and the maiden is your happy wife, then we will talk of payment for services rendered, and not before."

"Wonderful, wonderful!" gasped Adrian. "Most learned Señor, every word you say is true."

"Yes, friend Adrian, and I have not told you all the truth. For instance—but, no, this is not the time to speak. The question is, do you accept my terms?"

"What terms, Señor?"

"The customary terms, without which no wonder can be worked—faith, absolute faith."

Adrian hesitated a little. Absolute faith seemed a large present to give a complete stranger at a first interview.

"I read your thought and I respect it," went on the sage, who, to tell the truth, was afraid he had ventured a little too far. "There is no hurry. These affairs cannot be concluded in a day."

Adrian admitted that they could not, but intimated that he would be glad of a little practical and immediate assistance. The sage buried his face in his hands and thought.

"The first thing to do," he said presently, "is to induce a favorable disposition of the maiden's mind towards yourself, and this, I think, can best be brought about—though the method is one which I do not often use—by means of a love potion carefully compounded to suit the circumstances of the case. If you will come here tomorrow at dusk, the lady of this house—a worthy woman, though rough of speech and no true sage—will hand it to you."

"It isn't poisonous?" suggested Adrian doubtfully.

"Fool, do I deal in poisons? It will poison the girl's heart in your favor, that is all."

"And how is it to be administered?" asked Adrian.

"In the water she drinks, and afterwards you must speak to

her again as soon as possible. Now that is settled," he went on airily, "so, young friend, goodbye."

"Are you sure that there is no fee?" hesitated Adrian.

"No, indeed," answered the sage, "at any rate, until all is accomplished. Ah!" and he sighed, "did you but know what a delight it is to a weary and world-worn traveler to help forward the bright ambitions of youth, to assist the pure and soaring soul to find the mate destined to it by heaven—ehem!—you wouldn't talk of fees. Besides, I will be frank. From the moment that I entered this room and saw you, I recognized in you a kindred nature, one that under my guidance is capable of great things, of things greater than I care to tell. Ah, what a vision do I see! You, the husband of the beautiful Elsa and master of her great wealth, and I at your side guiding you with my wisdom and experience—then what might not be achieved? Dreams, doubtless dreams, though how often have my dreams been prophetic! Still, forget them, and at least, young man, we will be friends," and he stretched out his hand.

"With all my heart," answered Adrian, taking those cool, agile-looking fingers. "For years I have sought someone on whom I could rely, someone who would understand me as I feel you do."

"Yes, yes," sighed the sage, "I do indeed understand you."

"To think," he said to himself, after the door had closed behind the delighted and flattered Adrian, "to think that I can be the father of such a fool as that. Well, it bears out my theories about cross-breeding, and, after all, in this case a good-looking, gullible fool will be much more useful to me than a young man of sense. Let me see; the price of the office is paid and I shall have my appointment duly sealed as the new Governor of the Gravensteen no later than next week, so I may as well begin to collect evidence against my worthy successor, Dirk van Goorl, his adventurous son Foy, and that red-headed ruffian, Martin. Once I have them in the Gravensteen, I will squeeze the secret of old Brant's money out of one of the three of them. The women wouldn't know, they wouldn't have told the women, besides I don't want to meddle with them, indeed nothing would persuade me to that"—and he shivered as though at some wretched recollection. "But there must be evidence. There is such a noise about these executions and questionings that they won't allow any more of them in Leyden without decent evidence; even General Alvarez and the Blood Council are getting a bit frightened. Well, who can furnish better testimony than that donkey, my worthy son, Adrian? Probably, however, he has a conscience somewhere, so it may be as well not to let him know that, when he thinks himself engaged in conversation, he is really in the witness box. Let me see, we must take the old fellow, Dirk, on the ground of heresy, and the youngster and the serving man on a charge of murdering the king's soldiers and assisting the escape of heretics with their goods. Murder sounds bad, and, especially in the case of a young man, excites less public sympathy than common heresy."

Then he went to the door, calling, "Meg, hostess of mine, Meg."

He might have saved himself the trouble, however, since, on opening it suddenly, that lady fell almost into his arms.

"What!" he said, "listening, oh my, and all for nothing. But then, ladies will be curious."

Then he escorted her into the room and thought to himself, "I must be more careful. Thank the stars that I didn't talk aloud just now." Ramiro breathed a sigh of relief as he proceeded to make certain arrangements.

CHAPTER XVII
BETROTHED

At nightfall on the following day, Adrian returned as appointed and was admitted into the same room, where he found Black Meg, who greeted him openly by name and handed to him a tiny vial containing a fluid clear as water. This, however, was not very strange, seeing that it was water and nothing else.

"Will it really work upon her heart?" asked Adrian, eyeing the stuff.

"Aye," answered the hag, "that's a wondrous medicine, and those who drink it go crazed with love for the giver. It is formulated according to the Master's own recipe, from very costly tasteless herbs that grow only in the deserts of Arabia."

Adrian understood and fumbled in his pocket. Meg stretched out her hand to receive the honorarium. It was a long, skinny hand, with long, skinny fingers, but there was this peculiarity about it, that one of these fingers happened to be missing. She saw his eyes fixed upon the gap, and rushed into an explanation.

"I have met with an accident," Meg explained. "In cutting up a pig the chopper caught this finger and severed it."

"Did you wear a ring on it?" asked Adrian.

"Yes," she replied, with somber fury.

"How very strange!" exclaimed Adrian.

"Why?" responded the seasoned liar.

"Because I have seen a finger, a woman's long finger with a gold ring on it, that might have come off your hand. I suppose the pork-butcher picked it up for a keepsake."

"Maybe, Heer Adrian, but where is it now?" asked Meg.

"Oh! It is, or was, in a bottle of spirits tied by a thread to the cork."

Meg's evil face contorted itself. "Get me that bottle," she said hoarsely. "Look you, Heer Adrian, I am doing much for you, do this for me."

"What do you want it for?" inquired Adrian, suspiciously.

"To give it a Christian burial," she replied sourly. "It is not fitting or lucky that a person's finger should stand about in a bottle like a pickle. Get it, I say, get it—I ask no question where—or, young man, you will have little help in your love affairs from me."

"Do you wish the dagger hilt also?" he asked mischievously.

She looked at him out of the corners of her black eyes. This Adrian knew too much.

"I want the finger and the ring on it which I lost in chopping up the pig," insisted the irate women.

"Perhaps, Mother, you would like the pig, too. Are you not making a mistake? Weren't you trying to cut his throat, and didn't he bite off the finger?"

"If I want the pig, I'll search his stye. You bring that bottle, or—"

She did not finish her sentence, for the door opened, and through it came the one-eyed sage.

"Quarrelling," he said in a tone of reproof. "What about? Let me guess," and he passed his hand over his shadowed brow. "Ah! I see, there is a finger in it, a finger of fate? No, not that," and, moved by a fresh inspiration, he grasped Meg's hand, and added, "Now I have it. Bring it back, friend Adrian, bring it back. A dead finger is most unlucky to all, save its owner. As a favor to me."

"Very well," said Adrian.

"My gifts grow," mused the master. "I have a vision of this honest hand and of a great sword—but, there, it is not worth while, too small a matter. Leave us, Mother. It shall be returned, my word on it. Yes, gold ring and all. And now, young friend, let us talk. You have the potion? Well, I can promise you that it is a good one, it would almost bring Galatea from her marble. Pygmalion must have known that secret. But tell me something of your life, your daily thoughts and daily deeds, for when I give my friendship I love to live in the life of my friends."

Thus encouraged, Adrian told him a great deal, so much, indeed, that the Señor Ramiro, nodding in the shadow of his hood, began to wonder whether the spy behind the cupboard door, expert as he was, could possibly make his pen keep pace with these outpourings. Oh, it was a dreary task, but he kept to it, and by putting in a sentence here and there artfully turned the conversation to matters of faith.

"No need to fence with me," he said presently. "I know how you have been brought up, how through no fault of your own you have wandered out of the warm bosom of the true Church to sit at the clay feet of an impostor. You doubt it? Well, let me look again, let me look. Yes, only last week you were seated in a whitewashed room overhanging the market-place. I see it all— an ugly little man with a harsh voice is preaching, preaching what I think blasphemy. Baskets—baskets? What have baskets to do with him?"

"I believe he used to make them," interrupted Adrian, taking the bait.

"That may be it, or perhaps he will be buried in one. At any rate, he is strangely mixed up with baskets. Well, there are others with you, a middle-aged, heavy-faced man, is he not Dirk van Goorl, your stepfather? And, wait—a young fellow with rather a pleasant face, also a relation. I see his name, but I can't spell it. F-F-o-i, faith in the French tongue, odd name for a heretic."

"F-o-y—Foy," interrupted Adrian again.

"Indeed! Strange that I should have mistaken the last letter but in the spirit sight and hearing can be cloudy. I also see that there is a great man with a red beard."

"No, Master, you're wrong," said Adrian with emphasis. "Martin was not there; he stopped behind to watch the house."

"Are you sure?" asked the seer doubtfully. "I look and I seem to see him," insisted the Master as he stared blankly at the wall.

"So you might see him often enough, but not at last week's meeting."

It is needless to follow the conversation further. The seer, by aid of a ball of crystal that he produced from the folds of his cloak, described his spirit visions, and the pupil corrected them from his intimate knowledge of the facts, until the Señor Ramiro and his confederates in the cupboard had enough evidence, as evidence was understood in those days, to burn Dirk, Foy, and Martin three times over, and, if it should suit him, Adrian also. Then, for that night, they parted.

The next evening, Adrian was back again with the finger in the bottle, which Meg grabbed as a pike snatches at a frog, and further fascinating conversation ensued. Indeed, Adrian found this well of mystic lore tempered with shrewd advice upon love affairs and other worldly matters, and with flattery of his own person and gifts, singularly attractive.

Several times did he return, for as it happened Elsa had been unwell and kept to her room, so that he discovered no opportunity of administering the magic potion that was to cause her heart to burn with love for him.

At length, when even the patient Ramiro was almost worn out by the young gentleman's lengthy visits, circumstances changed. Elsa appeared one day at dinner, and with great adroitness Adrian, quite unseen of anyone, managed to empty the potion into her goblet of water, which, as he rejoiced to see, she drank to the last drop.

But no opportunity such as he sought ensued, for Elsa, overcome, doubtless, by an unwonted rush of emotion, retired to battle against it in her own chamber. Since it was impossible to follow and propose to her there, Adrian, possessing his soul in such patience as he could command, sat in the sitting-room to await her return, for he knew that it was not her habit to go out until five o'clock. As it happened, however, Elsa had other arrangements for this afternoon, since she had promised to accompany Lysbeth upon several visits to the wives of neighbors. She also agreed to meet her cousin Foy at the factory and walk with him in the meadows beyond the town.

So while Adrian, lost in dreams, waited in the sitting room, Elsa and Lysbeth left the house by the side door.

They had made three of their visits when their path chanced to lead them past the old town prison which was called the Gravensteen. This place formed one of the gateways of the city, for it was built in the walls and opened on to the moat, water surrounding it on all sides. In front of its massive door, guarded by two soldiers, a small crowd had gathered on the drawbridge and in the street beyond, apparently in expectation of somebody or something. Lysbeth looked at the three-storied frowning building and shuddered, for it was here that heretics were given their mock trial, and here, too, many of them were tortured to death after the dreadful fashion of the day.

"Hasten," she said to Elsa, as she pushed through the crowd, "for doubtless some horror passes here."

"Have no fear," answered an elderly and good-natured woman who overheard her, "we are only waiting to hear the new governor of the prison read his deed of appointment."

As she spoke, the doors were thrown open and a man—he was a well-known executioner named Baptiste—came out carrying a sword in one hand and a bunch of keys on a salver in the other. After him followed the governor, gallantly dressed and escorted by a company of soldiers and the officials of the prison. Drawing a scroll from beneath his cloak he began to read it rapidly and in an almost inaudible voice.

It was his commission as governor of the prison, signed by General Álvarez himself, and set out in full his powers, which were considerable, and his responsibilities, which were small. Other matters were mentioned with the exception of the sum of money that he had paid for the office, which given certain conditions, was as a matter of fact, sold to the highest bidder. As may be guessed, this post of governor of a jail in one of the large Netherland cities was lucrative enough to those who did not object to such a fashion of growing rich. So lucrative was it, indeed, that the salary supposed to attach to the office was never paid; at least its occupant was expected to help himself to it out of heretical pockets.

As he finished reading through the paper, the new governor looked up, to see, perhaps, what impression he had produced upon his audience. Now Elsa saw his face for the first time and gripped Lysbeth's arm.

"It is Ramiro," she whispered, "Ramiro the spy, the man who

dogged my father at The Hague."

As well might she have spoken to a statue. Indeed, Lysbeth immediately seemed to be smitten into stone, for there she stood staring with a blank expression at the face of the man opposite to her. Well might she stare, for she also knew him. Across the gulf of years, one-eyed, bearded, withered, scarred as he was by suffering and evil thoughts, she knew him, for there before her stood one whom she deemed dead, the wretch whom she had believed to be her husband Juan de Montalvo. Some magnetism drew his gaze to her; out of all the faces of that crowd, it was hers that leapt to his eye. He trembled and grew white; he turned away, and swiftly was gone back into the hell of the Gravensteen. Like a demon he had come out of it to survey the human world beyond, and search for victims there; like a demon he went back into his own place. So at least it seemed to Lysbeth.

"Come, come," she urged and, drawing the girl with her, passed out of the crowd.

Elsa began to talk in a strained voice that from time to time broke into a sob.

"That is the man," she said. "He hounded down my father. It was his wealth he wanted, but my father swore that he would die before he should win it, and he is dead—dead in the Inquisition, and that man is his murderer."

Lysbeth made no answer, in part because she had no answer to give. A few minutes later, they halted at a shabby and humble home. Then she spoke for the first time in cold and constrained accents.

"I am going in here to visit the Vrouw Jansen. You have heard of her, the wife of him whom they burned. She sent to me to say that she is sick, I know not of what, but it may be smallpox. I have heard of four cases of it in the city, go, Cousin, it is wisest that you should not enter here. Give me the basket with the food and drink. Look, yonder is the factory, quite close at hand, and there you will find Foy. Oh, never mind Ramiro. What is done is done. Go and walk with Foy, and for awhile forget Ramiro."

At the door of the factory Elsa found Foy awaiting her, and they walked together through one of the gates of the city into the pleasant meadows that lay beyond. At first, they did not speak much, for each of them was occupied with thoughts that pressed their tongues to silence. When they were clear of the town, however, Elsa could contain herself no more; indeed, the anguish awakened in her mind by the sight of Ramiro working upon nerves already over strung had made her half-hysterical. She began to speak; the words broke from her like water from a dam that has been breached. She told Foy that she had seen the man, and more—much more. Elsa spoke of the misery which she had suffered, all the love for the father who was lost to her.

At last Elsa ceased speaking, and, standing still there upon the river bank, she wrung her hands and wept. Until now Foy had said nothing, for his good spirits and cheerful readiness seemed to have forsaken him. Even now he said nothing. All he did was to put his arms around this sweet maid and draw her to him, and kiss her upon her brow. She did not resist; it never seemed to occur to her to show resentment; indeed, she let her head sink upon his shoulder like the head of a little child, and there sobbed herself to silence. At last, she lifted her face and asked very simply:

"What do you want with me, Foy van Goorl?"

"What?" he repeated. "Why, I want to be your husband."

"Is this a time for marrying and giving in marriage?" she asked again, but almost as though she was speaking to herself.

"I don't know that it is," he replied, "but it seems the best thing to do, and in such days two are better than one."

She drew away and looked at him, shaking her head sadly.

"My father," she began—

"Yes," he interrupted brightening, "thank you for mentioning him, that reminds me. He wished this, so I hope now that he is gone you will take the same view."

"It is rather late to talk about that, isn't it, Foy?" she stammered, looking at his shoulder and smoothing her ruffled hair with her small white hand. "But what do you mean?"

So word for word, as nearly as he could remember it, he told her all that Hendrik Brant had said to him in the cellar at The Hague before they had entered upon the desperate adventure of their flight to the Haarlemer Meer. "He wished it, you see," he ended.

"My thought was always his thought, and—Foy—I wish it also," stated Elsa tenderly.

"Priceless things are not lightly won," said he, quoting Brant's words as though by some afterthought.

"There he must have been talking of the treasure, Foy," she answered, her face lightening to a smile.

"Aye, of the treasure, sweet, the treasure of your dear heart."

"Oh! My heart is but a poor thing, Foy. I have always believed that love is the greatest treasure God can give."

"Amen, Elsa, yet the best of coin may crack with rough usage."

"Mine will wear until death, Foy."

"I ask no more, Elsa. When I am dead, the love that we shared together shall be treasured even where there is no marrying or giving in marriage."

"How much time would we have to love or be loved in our time of peril and calamity?" questioned Elsa.

"Enough," he broke in impatiently. "Why do you talk of such things, as if any mortal can know the unknowable?"

"Because, because, we are not married yet, and—my heart has been so tossed about that it strains to know God's will. Perfect love and perfect peace cannot be bought with a few sweet words and kisses. They must be earned in trial and tribulation."

"Of which I have no doubt we shall find plenty," Foy replied cheerfully. "Meanwhile, the kisses make a good road to travel on."

After this Elsa did not argue any more.

A few minutes later, they turned and walked homeward through the quiet evening twilight, hand clasped in hand, and were happy in their way. It was not a very demonstrative way, for the Dutch have never been excitable, or at least they do not show their excitement. Moreover, the conditions of this betrothal were peculiar. It was as though their hands had been joined from a deathbed, the deathbed of Hendrik Brant, the martyr of The Hague, whose new-shed blood cried out to Heaven for vengeance. This sense pressing on both of them did not tend towards rapturous outbursts of youthful passion, and even if they could have shaken it off, there remained another sense—that of dangers ahead of them in which they would need the Almighty's favor.

"Two are better than one," Foy had said, and for her own reasons she had not wished to argue the point, still Elsa felt that to it there was another side. If two could comfort each other, could help each other, could love each other, could they not also suffer for each other? In short, by doubling their lives, did they not also double their anxieties, or if children should come, triple and quadruple them? This is true of all marriage, but how much more was it true in such days and in such a case as that of Foy and Elsa, both of them heretics, both of them rich, and, therefore, both liable at a moment's notice to be brought to prison or the stake? Knowing these things, and having but just seen the hated face of Ramiro, it is not surprising that, although she rejoiced as any woman must that the man to whom her soul turned had declared himself her lover, Elsa could only drink of this joyful cup with a chastened and a fearful spirit. Nor is it wonderful that even in the hour of his triumph, Foy's buoyant and hopeful nature was chilled by the shadow of her fears and the forebodings of his own heart.

When Lysbeth parted from Elsa that afternoon, she went straight to the chamber of the Vrouw Jansen. It was a poor place, for after the execution of her husband, his wretched widow had been robbed of all her property and now existed upon the charity of the Reformed community. Lysbeth found her in bed, an old woman nursing her, who said that she thought the patient was suffering from a fever. Lysbeth leaned over the bed and kissed the sick woman, but startled slightly when she saw that the glands of her neck were swollen into great lumps, while the face was flushed and the eyes so bloodshot as to be almost red. Still she knew her visitor, for she whispered, "What is the matter with me, Vrouw van Goorl? Is it the smallpox coming on? Tell me, friend, the doctor would not speak."

"I fear that it is worse. It is the plague," said Lysbeth, startled into candor.

The poor girl laughed hoarsely. "Oh! I hoped it," she said. "I am glad, I am glad, for now I shall die and go to join him. But I wish that I had caught it before," she rambled on to herself "for then I would have taken it to him in prison and they couldn't have treated him as they did." Suddenly she seemed to come to herself, for she added, "Go away, Vrouw van Goorl, go quickly or you may catch my sickness."

"If so, I am afraid that the mischief is done, for I have kissed you," answered Lysbeth. "But I do not fear such things, though perhaps if I caught it, this would save me many a trouble. Still, there are others to think of, and I will go." So, having knelt down to pray awhile by the patient, and given the old nurse the basket of soup and food, Lysbeth went.

The next morning she heard that the Vrouw Jansen was dead, the disease that struck her being of the most fatal sort.

Lysbeth knew that she had run a great risk, for there is no disease more infectious than the plague. She determined, therefore, that as soon as she reached home she would burn her dress and other articles of clothing and purify herself with the fumes of herbs. Then she dismissed the matter from her mind, which was already filled with another thought, a dominant, soul-possessing thought.

Oh God, Montalvo had returned to Leyden! Out of the blackness of the past, out of the gloom of the galleys, had arisen this evil genius. Lysbeth was a brave woman, one who had passed through many dangers, but her whole heart turned sick with terror at the sight of this man, and sick it must remain until she, or he, were dead. She could well guess what he had come to seek. It was that cursed treasure of Hendrik Brant's that had drawn him. She knew from Elsa that, for a year at least, the man Ramiro had been plotting to steal this money at The Hague. He had failed there, failed with overwhelming and shameful loss through the bravery and resource of her son Foy and their servant, Red Martin. Now he had discovered their identity; he was aware that they held the secret of the hiding place of that accursed hoard, they and no others, and he had established himself in Leyden to wring it out of them. It was clear, clear as the setting orb of the red sun before her. She knew the man, had she not lived with him? This man was now the new governor of the Gravensteen. Doubtless he had purchased that post for his own dark purposes, and to be near them.

Sick and half blind with the intensity of her dread, Lysbeth staggered home. She must tell Dirk, that was her one thought; but no, she had been in contact with the plague, first she must purify herself. So she went to her room, and although it was summer, lit a great fire on the hearth, and in it burned her garments. Then she bathed and fumigated her hair and body over a brazier of strong herbs, such as in those days of frequent and virulent sickness housewives kept at hand, after which she dressed herself afresh and went to seek her husband. She found him at a desk in his private room reading some paper, which at her approach he shuffled into a drawer.

"What is that, Dirk?" she asked with sudden suspicion.

He pretended not to hear, and she repeated the query.

"Well, Wife, if you wish to know," he answered in his blunt fashion, "it is my will."

"Why are you reading your will?" she asked again, beginning to tremble, for her nerves were afire, and this simple incident struck her as something awful and ominous.

"For no particular reason, Wife," he replied quietly, "only we all must die, early or late. There is no escape from that, and in these times it is more often early than late, so it is as well to be sure that everything is in order for those who come after us. Now, since we are on the subject, which I have never cared to speak about, listen to me."

"What about, Husband?"

"Why, about my will. Listen Wife, Hendrik Brant and his treasure have taught me a lesson. I am not a man of his substance, or a tenth of it, but in some countries I should be called rich, for I have worked hard and God has prospered me. Well, of late I have been investing where I could, also the bulk of my savings is in cash. But the cash is not here, not in this country at all. You know my correspondents, Munt and Brown, of Norwich, in England, to whom we ship our goods for the English market. They are honest folk, and Munt owes me everything, almost to his life. Well, they have the money, it has reached them safely, thanks be to God, and with it a counterpart of this my will duly attested, and here is their letter of acknowledgment stating that they have laid it out carefully at interest upon mortgage on great estates in Norfolk where it lies to my order, or that of my heirs, and that a duplicate acknowledgment has been filed in their English registries in case this should go astray. Little remains here except this house and the factory, and even on those I have raised money. Meanwhile the business is left to live on, and beyond it the rents that will come from England, so that whether I be living or dead you need fear no want. But what is the matter with you, Lysbeth? You look strange."

"Oh! Husband, Husband," she gasped, "Juan de Montalvo is here again. He has appeared as the new governor of the jail. I saw him this afternoon, I cannot be mistaken, although he has lost an eye and is much changed."

Dirk's jaw dropped and his face whitened. "Juan de Montalvo!" he said. "I heard that he was dead long ago."

"You are mistaken, Husband, a devil never dies. He is seeking Brant's treasure, and he knows that we have its secret. You can guess the rest. A while back, now that I think of it, I have heard that a strange Spaniard was lodging with Hague Simon, he whom they call the Butcher, and Black Meg, of whom we have cause to know. Doubtless it is he, and—Dirk, death overshadows us."

"Why should he know of Brant's treasure, Wife?"

"Because he is Ramiro, the man who hunted him down, the man who followed the ship *Swallow* to the Haarlemer Meer. Elsa was with me this afternoon, she recognized him." Dirk thought a while, resting his head upon his hand. Then he lifted it and said:

"I am very glad that I sent the money to Munt and Brown. Heaven gave me that thought. Well, Wife, what is your counsel now?"

"My counsel is that we should fly from Leyden—all of us, yes, this very night before worse happens."

He smiled. "That cannot be. There are no means of flight, and under the new laws we could not pass the gates. That trick has been played too often. Still, in a day or two, when I have had time to arrange, we might escape if you still wish to go."

"Tonight, tonight," she urged, "or some of us stay forever."

"I tell you, Wife, it is not possible. Am I a rat that I should be bolted from my hole thus by this ferret of a Montalvo? I am a man of peace and no longer young, but let him beware lest I stay here long enough to pass a sword through him."

"So be it, Husband," she replied, "but I think it is through my heart that the sword will pass," and she burst out weeping.

Supper that night was a somewhat melancholy meal. Dirk and Lysbeth sat at the ends of the table in silence. On one side of it were placed Foy and Elsa, who were also silent for a very different reason, while opposite to them was Adrian, who watched Elsa with an anxious and inquiring eye.

That the love potion worked he was certain, for she looked confused and a little flushed; also, as would be natural under the circumstances, she avoided his glance and made pretence to be interested in Foy, who seemed rather more stupid than usual. Well, as soon as he could find his chance all this would be cleared up, but meanwhile the general gloom and silence were affecting his nerves.

"What have you been doing this afternoon, Mother?" Adrian asked toward the end of the meal.

"I, Son?" she replied with a start, "I have been visiting the unhappy Vrouw Jansen, whom I found very sick."

"What is the matter with her, Mother?" inquired Arian.

Lysbeth's mind, which had wandered away, again returned to the subject at hand with an effort.

"The matter? Oh, she has the plague."

"The plague!" exclaimed Adrian, springing to his feet. "Do you mean to say you have been consorting with a woman who has the plague?"

"I fear so," she answered with a smile, "but do not be frightened, Adrian, I have burnt my clothes and fumigated myself."

Still Adrian was frightened. His recent experience of sickness had been ample; and, although he was no coward, he had a special dislike of infectious diseases, which at the time were many.

"It is horrible," he said, "horrible. I only hope that we—I mean you—may escape. The house is unbearably close. I am going to walk in the courtyard," and away he went, for the moment, at any rate, forgetting all about Elsa and the love potion.

Chapter XVIII
Foy Sees a Vision

Never since that day when, many years before, she had bought the safety of the man she loved by promising herself in marriage to his rival, had Lysbeth slept so ill as she did upon this night. Montalvo was alive. Montalvo was here, here to strike down and destroy those whom she loved, and triple armed with power, authority, and desire to do the deed. Well she knew that, when there was plunder to be won, he would not step aside or soften until it was in his hands. Yet there was reason to believe that if he could get the money, all of it, she was sure that he would leave them alone. Why should he not have it? Why should all their lives be menaced because of this trust that had been thrust upon them?

Unable to endure the torment of her doubts and fears, Lysbeth woke her husband, who was sleeping peacefully at her side, and told him what was passing in her mind.

"It is a true saying," answered Dirk with a smile, "that even the best of women are never quite honest when their families' interest pulls the other way. What, wife, would you have us buy our own peace with Brant's fortune, and thus break faith with a dear departed Christian brother and down God's judgment upon us?"

"The lives of men are more than gold, and Elsa would consent," she answered sullenly. "Already this treasure is stained with blood, the blood of Hendrik Brant himself, and of Hans the pilot."

"Yes, Wife, and since you mention it, with the blood of a good many Spaniards also, who tried to steal the stuff. There must have been several drowned at the mouth of the river, and quite twenty went up with the *Swallow,* so the loss has not been all on our side. Listen, Lysbeth, listen. It was my cousin, Hendrik Brant's belief that in the end this great fortune of his would do some service to our people or our country, for he wrote as much in his will and repeated it to Foy. I know not when or in what fashion this may come about; how can I know? But first will I die before I hand it over to the Spaniard. Moreover, I cannot, since its secret was never told to me."

"Foy and Martin have it," whispered Lysbeth with a nervous smile.

"Lysbeth," said Dirk sternly, "I charge you as you love me, do not work upon them to betray their trust. No, not even to save my life or your own—if we must die, let us die with honor. Do you promise?"

"I promise," she answered with dry lips, "but on this condition only, that you fly from Leyden with us all, tonight if possible."

"Good," answered Dirk, "a halfpenny for a herring. You have made your promise, and I'll give you mine. That's fair, although I am old to seek a new home in England. But it can't be tonight, Wife, for I must make arrangements. There is a ship sailing today, and we might catch her tomorrow at the river's mouth, after she has passed the officers, for her captain is a friend of mine. How will that do?"

"I had rather it had been tonight," said Lysbeth. "While we are in Leyden with that man we are not safe from one hour to the next."

"Wife, we are never safe. It is all in the hands of God, and, therefore, we should live like soldiers awaiting the hour to march, and rejoice exceedingly when it pleases our Captain to sound the call."

"I know," she answered, "but, oh! Dirk, it would be hard to part."

He turned his head aside for a moment, then said in a steady voice, "Yes, Wife, but it will be sweet to meet again and part no more, and it is this blessed hope that enables God's beloved to sleep peacefully."

While it was still early that morning, Dirk summoned Foy and Martin to his wife's chamber. Adrian for his own reasons he did not summon, making the excuse that he was still asleep, and it would be a pity to disturb him; nor Elsa, since as yet there was no necessity to trouble her. Then, briefly, for he was given to few words, he set out the gist of the matter, telling them that the man Ramiro whom they had beaten on the Haarlemer Meer was in Leyden, which Foy knew already, for Elsa had told him as much, and that he was none other than the Spaniard named the Count Juan de Montalvo, the villain who had deceived Lysbeth into a mock marriage by working on her fears, and who was the father of Adrian. All this time Lysbeth sat in a carved oak chair, listening with a stony face to the tale of her own shame and betrayal. She made no sign at all beyond a little twitching of her fingers, until Foy, guessing what she suffered in her heart, suddenly went to his mother and kissed her. Then she wept a few silent tears, and momentarily laid her hand upon his head as though in blessing, and, motioning him back to his place, became herself again—stern, unmoved, observant.

Next Dirk, taking up his tale, spoke of his wife's fears, and of her belief that there was a plot to wring out of them the secret of Hendrik Brant's treasure.

"Happily," he said, addressing Foy. "Neither your mother nor I, nor Adrian, nor Elsa, know that secret. You and Martin know it alone, you and perhaps one other who is far away and cannot be caught. We do not know it, and we do not wish to know it, and whatever happens to any of us, it is our earnest hope that neither of you will betray it, even if our lives, or your lives, need to be sacrificed. It is our firm conviction that we must keep our covenant with our departed brother at all costs. Is it not so, Wife?"

"It is so," answered Lysbeth hoarsely.

"Have no fear," said Foy. "We will die before we betray."

"We will try to die before we betray," grumbled Martin in his deep voice, "but flesh is frail and God knows."

"Oh! I have no doubt of you, honest man," said Dirk with a smile, "for you have no mother and father to think of in this matter."

"Then, Master, you may be disappointed," replied Martin, "for I repeat it—flesh is frail, and I always hated the look of a rack. However, I have a handsome legacy charged upon this treasure, and perhaps the thought of that would support me. Alive or dead, I should not like to think of my money being spent by any Spaniard."

While Martin spoke, the strangeness of the thing came home to Foy. Here were four of them, two of whom knew a secret and two who did not, while those who did not implored those who did to impart to them nothing of the knowledge which, if they had it, might serve to save them from a fearful doom. Then for the first time in his young and inexperienced life he understood how God might use trials and persecution to strengthen the faith of those who are committed to living by His Word, yea, even to enable his servants to defy the most hideous terrors of body and soul for the sake of honoring a trust. Indeed, that scene stamped itself upon his mind in such fashion that throughout his long existence, he never quite forgot it for a single day. His mother, clad in her frilled white cap and gray gown, seated cold-faced and resolute in the oaken chair. His father, standing by her with his hand resting upon her shoulder and addressing them in his quiet, honest voice. Martin standing also but a little to one side and behind, the light of the morning playing upon his great red beard, his round, pale eyes glittering as was their fashion when wrathful. Then there was Foy himself, leaning forward to listen, every nerve in his body strung tight with excitement, love, and fear.

Oh! He never forgot it, which is not strange, for so great was the strain upon him, so well did he know that this scene was but the prelude to terrible events, that for a moment, only for a moment, his steady reason was shaken and he saw a vision. Martin, the huge, patient, ox-like Martin, was changed into a red vengeance; he saw him, great sword aloft, he heard the roar of his battle cry, and before him men went down to death, and about him the floor seemed crimson with their blood. His father and his mother, too—no longer dwelling with the saints below—see the glory that shone over them, and look, too, the dead Hendrik Brant was whispering in their ears. And he, Foy, he was beside Martin playing his part in those bloody fights as best he might, and playing it not in vain.

Then all passed, and a wave of peace rolled over him, a great sense of duty done, of honor satisfied, of reward attained. Lo, the play was finished, and its ultimate meaning clear, but before he could read and understand—it had gone.

He gasped and shook himself, gripping his hands together.

"What have you seen, Son?" asked Lysbeth watching his face.

"Strange things, Mother," Foy answered. "A vision of war for Martin and me, of glory for my father and you, and of eternal peace for us all."

"Whether it be dream or vision, my son, we will soon discover," she said. "Fight your fight and leave us to fight ours. 'Through much tribulation we must enter into the Kingdom of God,' where at last there is a rest remaining for us all. All things will work together for good. Your father was right and I was wrong. Now I have no more fear. I am satisfied."

None of them seemed to be amazed or to find these words strange or out of keeping with the situation. For them the hand of approaching doom had opened the gates of distance, and they knew that through these some light had broken on their souls, a faint flicker of dawn from beyond the clouds. They accepted it in thankfulness.

"I think that is all I have to say," said Dirk in his usual voice. "No, it is not all," and he told them of his plan for flight. They listened and agreed to it, yet to them it seemed a thing far off and unreal. None of them believed that this escape would ever be carried out. All of them believed that here in Leyden they would endure the fiery trial of their faith and win each of them its separate crown.

When everything was discussed, and each had learned the lesson of what he must do that day, Foy asked if Adrian was to be told of the scheme. To this his father answered hastily that the less it was spoken of the better, therefore he proposed to tell Adrian late that night only, when he could make up his mind whether he would accompany them or stay in Leyden.

"Then he shan't go out tonight, and will come with us as far as the ship only if I can manage it," whispered Martin beneath his breath, but aloud he said nothing. Somehow it did not seem to him to be worthwhile to make trouble about it, for he knew that if he did his mistress and Foy, who believed so heartily in Adrian, would be angry.

"Father and Mother," said Foy again, "while we are gathered here there is something I wish to say to you."

"What is it, Son?" asked Dirk.

"Yesterday I became betrothed to Elsa Brant, and we wish to ask your consent and blessing."

"That will be gladly given, Son, for I think this very good news. Bring her here, Foy," answered Dirk.

But, although in his hurry Foy did not notice it, his mother said nothing. She liked Elsa well indeed—who would not?—but oh, this brought them a step nearer to that accursed treasure, the treasure that from generation to generation had been hoarded up that it might be a doom to men. If Foy were betrothed to Elsa, it was his inheritance as well as hers, for those trusts of Hendrik Brant's will were to Lysbeth things unreal and visionary, and its curse would fall upon him as well as upon her. Moreover, it might be said that he was marrying her to win the wealth.

"This betrothal does not please you. Are you sad, Wife?" said Dirk, looking at her quickly.

"Yes, Husband, for now I think that we shall never get out of Leyden. I pray that Adrian may not hear of it, that is all."

"Why, what has he to do with the matter?"

"Only that he is madly in love with the girl. Have you not seen it? And you know his temper."

"Adrian, Adrian, always Adrian," answered Dirk impatiently. "Well, it is a very fitting match, for if she has a great fortune hidden somewhere in a swamp, which in fact she has not, since the bulk of it is bequeathed to me to be used for certain purposes; he has, or will have, moneys also—safe at interest in England. Hark! Here they come, so, Wife, put on a pleasant face. They will be discouraged if you do not smile."

As he spoke, Foy re-entered the room, leading Elsa by the hand, and she looked as sweet a maid as ever the sun shone on. So they told their story, and kneeling down before Dirk, received his blessing in the old fashion way, and very glad were they in later years to remember that it had been so received. Then they turned to Lysbeth, and she also lifted up her hand to bless them, but before it touched their heads, do what she would to check it, a cry forced its way to her lips, and she said:

"Dear children, doubtless you love each other well, but is this a time for marrying and giving in marriage?"

"My own words, my very words," exclaimed Elsa, springing to her feet and turning pale.

Foy looked upset. Then recovering himself and trying to smile, he said, "And I give them the same answer—that two are better than one. Moreover, this is a betrothal, not a marriage."

"Aye," muttered Martin behind, thinking aloud after his fashion, "betrothal is one thing and marriage another," but low as he spoke, Elsa overheard him.

"Your mother is upset," broke in Dirk, "and you can guess why, so do not disturb her more at present. Let us to our business, you and Martin to the factory to make arrangements there as I have told you, and I, after I have seen the captain, to whatever God shall call me to do. So, until we meet again, farewell, my son—and daughter," he added, smiling at Elsa.

They left the room, but as Martin was following them Lysbeth called him back.

"Go armed to the factory, Martin," she said, "and see that your young master wears that steel shirt beneath his jerkin."

Martin nodded and went out of the room.

Adrian woke up that morning in an ill mood. He had, it is true, administered his love potion with singular dexterity and success, but as yet he reaped no fruit from his labors, and was desperately afraid lest the effect of the magic draught might wear off. When he came downstairs, it was to find that Foy and Martin were already departed to the factory, and that his step-father had gone out, whither he knew not. This was so much to the good, for it left the coast clear. Still he was none the better off, since either his mother and Elsa had taken their breakfast upstairs, or they had dispensed with that meal. His mother he could spare, especially after her recent contact with a plague patient, but under the circumstances Elsa's absence was annoying. Moreover, suddenly the house had become uncomfortable, for every person in it seemed to be running about carrying articles hither and thither in a fashion so aimless that it struck him as little short of insane. Once or twice also he saw Elsa, but she too was carrying things and had no time for conversation.

Adrian soon wearied of the incessant activity and departed to the factory with the view of making up his books, which, to tell the truth, had been somewhat neglected of late, to find that here, too, the same confusion reigned. Instead of attending to his ordinary work, Martin was marching to and fro bearing choice pieces of brassware, which were being packed into crates, and he noticed, for Adrian was an observant young man, that he was not wearing his usual artisan's dress. Why, he wondered to himself, should Martin walk about a factory upon a summer's day clad in his armor of quilted bull's hide, and wearing his great sword Silence strapped round his middle? Why, too, should Foy have removed the books and be engaged in going through them with a clerk? Was he auditing them? If so, he wished him much success, since to bring them to a satisfactory balance had proved recently quite beyond his own powers. Not that there was anything wrong with the books, for he, Adrian, had kept them quite honestly according to his very imperfect standards, only things must have been left out, for balance they would not. Well, on the whole, he was glad, since a man filled with lover's hopes and fears was in no mood for mathematical exercises. Upon realizing that he would be of little use, he decided to hang around for a while, then return home to dinner.

The meal was late, an unusual occurrence, which annoyed him. Moreover, neither his mother nor his stepfather appeared at the table. At length, Elsa came in looking pale and worried, and they began to eat, or rather to go through the form of eating, since neither of them seemed to have any appetite. Nor, as the servant was continually in the room, and as Elsa took her place at one end of the long table while he was at the other, had he realized any of the usual advantages.

At last, the waiting-woman went away, and, after a few moments' pause, Elsa rose to follow. By this time Adrian was desperate. He would bear it no more; things must be brought to a head.

"Elsa," he said, in an irritated voice, "everything seems to be very uncomfortable today, there is so much disturbance in the house that one might imagine we were going to shut it up and leave Leyden."

Elsa looked at him out of the corners of her eyes. Probably by this time she had learnt the real cause of the disturbance.

"I am sorry, Heer Adrian," she said, "but your mother was not very well this afternoon."

"Indeed. I only hope she hasn't caught the plague from the Jansen woman. But that doesn't account for everybody running about with their hands full, like ants in a broken nest, especially as it is not the time of year when women turn all the furniture upside down and throw the curtains out of the windows in the pretence that they are cleaning them. However, we are quiet here for a while, so let us talk."

Elsa became suspicious. "Your mother wants me, Heer Adrian," she said, turning towards the door.

"Let her rest, Elsa, let her rest. There is no medicine like sleep for the sick."

Elsa pretended not to hear him, so, as she still headed for the door, by a movement too active to be dignified, he placed himself in front of it, adding, "I have said that I want to speak with you."

"And I have said that I am busy, Heer Adrian, so please let me pass."

Adrian remained immovable. "Not until I have spoken to you," he said.

Now, as escape was impossible, Elsa drew herself up and asked in a cold voice, "What is your pleasure? I pray you, be brief."

Adrian cleared his throat, reflecting that she was keeping the workings of the love potion under wonderful control. Indeed, to look at her, no one could have guessed that she had recently absorbed this magic Eastern medicine. However, something must be done; he had gone too far to draw back.

"Elsa," he said boldly, as he clasped his hands, and looked at the ceiling. "I love you and the time has come to say so."

"If I remember right, it came some time ago, Heer Adrian," she replied with sarcasm. "I thought that by now you had forgotten all about it."

"Forgotten!" he sighed, "forgotten! With you ever before my eyes, how can I forget?"

"I am sure I cannot say," she answered, "but I know that I wish to forget this folly."

"Folly! She calls it folly!" he mused aloud. "Oh, Heaven, folly is the name she gives to the life-long adoration of my bleeding heart!"

"You have known me exactly five weeks, Heer Adrian—"

"Which, sweet lady, makes me desire to know you for fifty years."

Elsa sighed, for she found the prospect dreary.

"Come," he went on with a gush, "forego this virgin coyness, you have done enough and more than enough for honor, now throw aside pretence, lay down your arms and yield. No hour, I swear, of this long fight will be so happy to you as that of your sweet surrender, for remember, dear one, that I, your conqueror, am in truth the conquered. I, abandoning—"

He got no further, for at this point the sorely tried Elsa lost control of herself, but not in the fashion which he hoped for and expected.

"Are you crazed, Heer Adrian," she asked, "that you should insist thus in pouring this high-flown nonsense into my ears when I have told you that it is unwelcome to me? I understand that you ask me for my love. Well, once for all I tell you that I have none to give."

This was a blow, since it was impossible for Adrian to put a favorable construction upon language so painfully straightforward. His self-conceit was pierced at last and collapsed like a pricked bladder.

"None to give!" he gasped, "none to give! You don't mean to tell me that you have given it to anybody else?"

"Yes, I do," she answered, for by now Elsa was thoroughly angry.

"Indeed," he replied loftily. "Let me see, last time it was your lamented father who occupied your heart. Perhaps now it is that excellent giant, Martin, or even—no, it is too absurd"—and he laughed in his jealous rage, "even the family buffoon, my worthy brother Foy."

"Yes," she replied quietly, "it is Foy."

"Foy! Foy! Hear her, ye gods! My successful rival, mine, is the yellow-headed, muddy-brained, unlettered Foy—and they say that women have souls! Of your courtesy, answer me one question. Tell me when did this strange and monstrous thing happen? When did you declare yourself vanquished by the surpassing charms of Foy?"

"Yesterday afternoon, if you want to know," she said in the same calm and deliberate voice.

Adrian heard, and an inspiration took him. He dashed his hand to his brow and thought a moment. Then he laughed loud and shrilly.

"I have it," he said. "It is the love charm which has worked perversely. Elsa, you are under a spell, poor woman. You do not know the truth. I gave you the potion in your drinking water, and Foy, the traitor Foy, has reaped its fruits. Dear girl, shake yourself free from this delusion, it is I whom you really love, not that base thief of hearts, my brother Foy."

"What did you say? You gave me a potion? You dare to doctor my drink with your heathen concoctions? Out of the way, sir! Stand off, and never venture to speak to me again. Well will it be for you if I do not tell your brother of your infamy."

What happened after this Adrian could never quite remember, but a vision remained of himself crouching to one side, and of a door flung back so violently that it threw him against the wall; a vision, too, of a lady sweeping past him with blazing eyes and lips set in scorn. That was all.

For a while he was crushed, quite crushed. The blow had gone home. Adrian was not only a fool, he was also the vainest of fools. That any young woman on whom he chose to smile should actually reject his advances was bad and unexpected; that she should do so in favor of another man was worse, but that the other man should be Foy—oh, this was horrendous! He was handsomer than Foy, no one would dream of denying it. He was cleverer and better read. Had he not mastered the contents of every known romance—high-souled works that Foy bluntly declared were rubbish and refused even to open? Was he not a poet? But remembering a certain sonnet, he did not follow this comparison. In short, how was it conceivable that a woman looking upon himself, a very type of the chivalry of Spain, silver-tongued, a champion, who in every previous adventure of the heart had been a conqueror, could still prefer that broad-faced, painfully commonplace, if worthy, young representative of the Dutch middle classes, Foy van Goorl?

It never occurred to Adrian to ask himself another question, namely, how it comes about that eight young women out of ten are endowed with an intelligence or instinct sufficiently keen to enable them to discriminate between an empty-headed shell of a man, intoxicated with the fumes of his own vanity, and an honest young fellow of stable character and sterling worth? Not that Adrian was altogether empty-headed, for in some ways he was clever; also beneath all this foam and froth, the Dutch strain inherited from his mother had given a certain ballast and determination to his nature. Thus, when his heart was thoroughly set upon a thing, he could be very dogged and patient. Without question, for the last few weeks it had been set upon Elsa Brant, who he did truly desire to win above any other woman.

For a little while he was prostrate, his heart seemed swept clean of all hope and feeling. Then his unrighteous temper, the sinful character flaw that, above every other, was his curse and bane, came alive and occupied him like the seven devils of Scripture, bringing in its train his reawakened vanity, hatred, jealousy, and other maddening passions. It could not be true, there must be an explanation, and, of course, the explanation was that Foy had been so fortunate, or so cunning as to make advances to Elsa soon after she had swallowed the love potion. Adrian, like most people in his day, was very superstitious and credulous. It never even occurred to him to doubt the almost universally accepted power and efficacy of this witch's medicine, though even now he understood what a fool he was when, in his first outburst of rage, he told Elsa that he had trusted to such means to win her affections, instead of letting his own virtues and graces do their natural work.

Well, the mischief was done, the poison was swallowed, but— most poisons have their antidotes. Why was he lingering here? He must consult his friend, the Master, and at once.

Ten minutes later, Adrian was at Black Meg's house.

CHAPTER XIX
THE FRAY IN THE
SHOT TOWER

The door was opened by Hague Simon, who lived with Black Meg. In answer to his visitor's anxious inquiries, the Butcher said, searching Adrian's face with his pig-like eyes, that he could not tell for certain whether Meg was or was not at home. He rather thought that she was consulting the spirits with the Master, but they might have passed out without his knowing it, "for they had great gifts—great gifts," and he wagged his fat head as he showed Adrian into the accustomed room.

It was an uncomfortable kind of chamber, which in some unexplained way always gave Adrian the impression that people, or presences, were stirring in it whom he could not see. Also in this place there happened odd and unaccountable noises; creakings, and sighings that seemed to proceed from the walls and ceiling. Of course, such things were to be expected in a house where sojourned one of the great magicians of the day. Still he was not altogether sorry when the door opened and Black Meg entered, although some might have preferred the society of almost any ghost.

"What is it, that you disturb me at such an hour?" she asked sharply.

"What is it? What isn't it?" Adrian replied, his rage rising at the thought of his injuries. "That cursed potion of yours has worked all wrong, that's what it is. Another man has got the benefit of it, don't you understand, you old hag? And, by Heaven! I believe he means to abduct her, yes, that's the meaning of all the packing and fuss, blind fool that I was not to guess it before. The Master—I will see the Master. He must give me an antidote, another medicine—"

"You certainly look as though you want it," interrupted Black Meg dryly. "Well, I doubt whether you can see him. It is not his hour for receiving visitors. Moreover, I don't think he's here, so I shall have to signal for him.

"I must see him. I will see him," shouted Adrian.

"I daresay," replied Black Meg, squinting significantly at his pocket.

Enraged as he was, Adrian took the hint.

"Woman, you seek gold," he said, quoting involuntarily from the last romance he had read, as he handed her a handful of small coins, which was all he had.

Meg took the silver with a sniff, on the principle that something is better than nothing, and departed gloomily. Then followed more mysterious noises; voices whispered, doors opened and shut, furniture creaked, after which came a period of exasperating and rather disagreeable silence. Adrian turned his face to the wall, for the only window in the room was so far above his head that he was unable to look out of it. Indeed, it was more of a skylight than a window. Thus he remained a while, gnawing at the ends of his moustache and cursing his fortune, until presently he felt a hand upon his shoulder.

"Who the devil is that?" he exclaimed, wheeling round to find himself face to face with the draped and majestic form of the Master.

"The devil! That is an ill word upon young lips, my friend," said the sage, shaking his head in reproof.

"I daresay," replied Adrian, "but what I mean is how did you get here? I never heard the door open."

"How did I get here? Well, now that you mention it, I wonder how I did. The door—what have I to do with doors?"

"I am sure I don't know," answered Adrian shortly, "but most people find them useful."

"Enough of such material talk," interrupted the sage with sternness. "Your spirit cried to mine, and I am here, let that suffice."

"I suppose that Black Meg fetched you," went on Adrian,

sticking to his point, for the potion fiasco had made him suspicious.

"Verily, friend Adrian, you can suppose what you will. And now, as I have little time to spare, be so good as to set out the matter. Nay, what need, I know all, for have I not been right in every case? You administered the potion to the maid and neglected my instructions to offer yourself to her at once. Another saw it and took advantage of the magic draught. While the spell was on her, he proposed and he was accepted—yes, your brother Foy. Oh, fool, careless fool, what else did you expect?"

"At any rate, I didn't expect that," replied Adrian in a fury. "And now, if you have all the power you pretend, tell me what I am to do."

Something glinted ominously beneath the hood, it was the sage's one eye.

"Young friend," he said, "your manner is brusque, yes, even rude. But I understand and I forgive. Come, we will take counsel together. Tell me what has happened."

Adrian told him with much emphasis, and the recital of his adventures seemed to move the Master deeply, at any rate he turned away, biding his face in his hands, while his back trembled with the intensity of his feelings.

"The matter is grave," he said solemnly, when at length the lovesick and angry son had finished. "There is but one thing to be done. Your treacherous rival—oh, what fraud and deceit are hidden beneath that homely countenance—has been well advised, by whom I know not, though I suspect one, a certain practitioner of the black arts named Arentz—"

"Arentz!" exclaimed Adrian.

"I see you know the man. Beware of him. He is, indeed, a wolf in sheep's clothing, who wraps his devilish incantations in a cloak of seditious doctrine. Well, I have thwarted him before, for can Darkness stand before Light? Now, attend and answer my questions clearly, slowly and truthfully. If the girl is to be saved to you, mark this, young friend, your cunning rival must be removed from Leyden for a while until the charm works out its power."

"You don't mean—" said Adrian, and stopped.

"No, no. I mean the man no harm. I mean only that he must take a journey, which he will do fast enough, when he learns that his witchcrafts and other crimes are known. Now answer, or make an end, for I have more business to attend to than the love problems of a headstrong youth. First: What you have told me of the attendances of Dirk van Goorl, your stepfather, and others of his household, namely, Red Martin and your half-brother Foy, at the tabernacle of your enemy, the wizard Arentz, is true, is it not?"

"Yes," answered Adrian, "but I do not see what that has to do with the matter."

"Silence!" thundered the Master. Then he paused a while, and Adrian seemed to hear certain strange squeakings proceeding from the walls. The sage remained lost in thought until the squeakings ceased. Again he spoke:

"What you have told me of the part played by the said Foy and the said Martin as to their sailing away with the treasure of the dead heretic, Hendrik Brant, and of the murders committed by them in the course of its hiding in the Haarlemer Meer, is true, is it not?"

"Of course it is," answered Adrian, "but—"

"Silence!" again thundered the sage, "or by my Lord Zoroaster, I throw up the case."

Adrian collapsed, and there was another pause.

"You believe," he went on again, "that the said Foy and the said Dirk van Goorl, together with the said Martin, are making preparations to abduct that innocent and unhappy maid, the heiress, Elsa Brant, for evil purposes of their own?"

"I never told you so," said Adrian, "but I think it is a fact. At least there is a lot of packing going on."

"You never told me so! Do you not understand that there is no need for you to tell me anything?" yelled the sage.

"Then, in the name of your Lord Zoroaster, why do you ask?" exclaimed the exasperated Adrian.

"That you will know very soon," he answered musing.

Once more Adrian heard the strange squeaking as of young

and hungry rats.

"I think that I will not take up more of your time," he said, growing thoroughly alarmed, for really the proceedings were a little odd, and he rose to go.

The Master made no answer, only, which was curious conduct for a sage, he began to whistle a tune.

"By your leave," said Adrian, for the magician's back was against the door. "I have business—"

"And so have I," replied the sage, and went on whistling.

Then suddenly the side of one of the walls seemed to fall out, and through the opening emerged a man wrapped in a priest's robe, and after him, Hague Simon, Black Meg, and another particularly evil-looking fellow.

"Got it all down?" asked the Master in an easy, everyday kind of voice.

The monk bowed, and producing several folios of manuscript, laid them on the table together with an ink-horn and a pen.

"Very well. And now, my young friend, be so good as to sign there, at the foot of the writing," directed Ramiro.

"Sign what?" gasped Adrian.

"Explain to him," said the Master. "He is quite right. A man should know what he puts his name to."

Then the monk spoke in a low, business-like voice.

"This is the information of Adrian, called Van Goorl, as taken down from his own lips, wherein, among other things, he deposes to certain crimes of heresy, murder of the king's subjects, an attempted escape from the king's dominions, committed by his stepfather, Dirk van Goorl, his half-brother, Foy van Goorl, and their servant, a Frisian known as Red Martin. Shall I read the papers? It will take some time."

"If the witness so desires," said the Master.

"What is that document for?" whispered Adrian in a hoarse voice.

"To persuade your treacherous rival, Foy van Goorl, that it will be desirable in the interests of his health that he should retire from Leyden for a while," sneered his late mentor, while the Butcher and Black Meg chuckled audibly. Only the monk

stood silent, like a black watching fate.

"I'll not sign!" shouted Adrian. "I have been tricked! There is treachery!" and he bent forward to spring for the door.

Ramiro made a sign, and in another instant the Butcher's fat hands were about Adrian's throat, and his thick thumbs were digging viciously at the victim's windpipe. Still Adrian kicked and struggled, whereon, at a second sign, the villainous-looking man drew a great knife, and, coming up to him, pricked him gently on the nose.

Then Ramiro spoke to him very suavely and quietly.

"Young friend," he said, "where is that faith in me you promised, and why, when I wish you to sign this quite harmless writing, do you so violently refuse?"

"Because I won't betray my stepfather and brother," gasped Adrian. "I know why you want my signature," and he looked at the man in a priest's robe.

"You won't betray them," sneered Ramiro. "Why, you young fool, you have already betrayed them fifty times over, and what is more, which you don't seem to remember, you have betrayed yourself. Now look here. If you choose to sign that paper, or if you don't choose, makes little difference to me, for, dear pupil, I would almost as soon have your evidence by word of mouth."

"I may be a fool," said Adrian, turning sullen. "Yes, I see now that I have been a fool to trust in you and your sham arts, but I am not fool enough to give evidence against my own people in any of your courts. What I have said I said never thinking that it would do them harm."

"Not caring whether it would do them harm you mean," corrected Ramiro, "as you had your own object to gain the young lady whom, by the way, you were quite ready to doctor with a love medicine."

"Because love blinded me," said Adrian loftily.

Ramiro put his hand upon his shoulder and shook him slightly as he answered:

"And has it not struck you, you vain puppy, that other things may blind you also—hot irons, for instance?"

"What do you mean?" gasped Adrian.

"I mean that the rack is a wonderful persuader. It makes the most silent talk and the most solemn sing. Now take your choice. Will you sign or will you go to the torture chamber?"

"What right have you to question me?" asked Adrian, striving to build up his tottering courage with bold words.

"Just this right—that I to whom you speak am the Captain and Governor of the Gravensteen in this town, an official who has considerable powers."

Adrian turned pale but said nothing.

"Our young friend has gone to sleep," remarked Ramiro, reflectively. "Here you, Simon, twist his arm a little. No, not the right arm; he may want that to sign with, which will be awkward if it is out of joint. The other arm if you please."

With an ugly grin the Butcher, taking his fingers from Adrian's throat, gripped his captive's left wrist, and very slowly and deliberately began to screw it round.

Adrian groaned.

"Painful, isn't it?" said Ramiro. "Well, I have no more time to waste, break his arm."

Then Adrian gave in, for he was not fitted to bear torture. His imagination was too lively.

"I will sign," he whispered, the perspiration pouring from his pale face.

"Are you quite sure you do it willingly?" queried his tormentor, adding, "another little half-turn, please, Simon; and you, Mistress Meg, if he begins to faint, just prick him in the thigh with your knife."

"Yes, yes," groaned Adrian.

"Very good. Now here is the pen. Sign."

So Adrian signed what amounted to a death warrant for his stepfather and his half-brother.

"I congratulate you for your discretion, pupil," remarked Ramiro, as he scattered sand on the writing and pocketed the paper. "Today you have learned a very useful lesson that life teaches to most of us, namely, that the inevitable must rule our little fancies. I think that by now the soldiers will have executed their task, so, as you have done what I wished, you can go, for I shall know where to find you if I want you. But, if you will take my advice, which I offer as that of one friend to another, you will hold your tongue about the events of this afternoon. Unless you speak of it, nobody need ever know that you have furnished certain useful information, for in the Gravensteen the names of witnesses are not mentioned to the accused. Otherwise, you may possibly come into trouble with your heretical friends and relatives. Good afternoon. Butcher, be so good as to open the door for this gentleman."

A minute later Adrian found himself in the street, towards which he had been helped by the kick of a heavy boot. His first impulse was to run, and he ran for half a mile or more without stopping, until at length he paused breathless in a deserted street, and, leaning against the wheel of an unharnessed wagon, tried to think. Think! How could he think? His mind was one mad whirl; rage, shame, disappointed passion, all boiled together like bones in a butcher's cauldron. He had been fooled, he had lost his love, and he had betrayed his kindred to the hell of the Inquisition. They would be tortured and burnt. Yes, even his mother and Elsa might be burned, since those devils respected neither age nor sex, and their blood would be upon his head. It was true that he had signed under compulsion, but who would believe that, for had they not taken down his talk word for word? For once Adrian saw himself in a true light. The cloaks of vanity and self-love were stripped from his soul, and he knew what others would think when they came to learn the story. He thought of suicide; there was water, here was steel, the deed would not be difficult. No, he could not. It was too horrible. Moreover, how dared he enter the other world so unprepared, so steeped in every sort of evil? What, then, could he do to save his character and those whom his folly had betrayed? He looked round him; there, not three hundred yards away, rose the tall chimney of the factory. Perhaps there was yet time. Perhaps he could still warn Foy and Martin of the fate which awaited them.

Acting on the impulse of the moment, Adrian started forward, running like a hare. As he approached the buildings, he saw that the workmen had left, for the big doors were shut. He raced round to the small entrance. It was open—he was through it, and figures were moving in the office. God be praised! The two men were Foy and Martin. To them he sped, a white-faced creature with gaping mouth and staring eyes, the very picture of terror and doom.

Martin and Foy saw him and shrank back. Could this be Adrian, they thought, or was it an evil vision?

"Fly!" he gasped. "Hide yourselves! The officers of the Inquisition are after you!" Then another thought struck him, and he stammered, "My father and mother. I must warn them!" And before they could speak he had turned and was gone, as he went crying, "Fly! Fly!"

Foy stood astonished until Martin struck him on the shoulder, and said roughly, "Come, let us get out of here. Either he is mad, or he knows something. Have you your sword and dagger? Quick, then."

They passed through the door, which Martin paused to lock, and into the courtyard. Foy reached the gate first, and looked through its open bars. Then very deliberately he shot the bolts and turned the great key.

"Are you brain-sick," asked Martin, "that you lock the gate on us?"

"I think not," replied Foy, as he came back to him. "It is too late to escape. Soldiers are marching down the street."

Martin ran and looked through the bars. It was true enough. There they came, fifty men or more, a whole company, heading straight for the factory, which it was thought might be garrisoned for defense.

"Now I can see no help but to fight for it," Martin said cheerfully, as he hid the keys in a nearby bucket.

"What can two men do against fifty?" asked Foy, lifting his steel-lined cap to scratch his head.

"The Almighty will have to show us, Master, for it was He who declared that one could chase a thousand. At least, as nothing but a cat can climb the walls, and the gateway is stopped, I think we may as well die fighting as in the torture-chamber of the Gravensteen, for that is where they mean to lodge us."

"I think so too," answered Foy, taking courage. "Now how can we hurt them most before they quiet us?"

Martin looked around him carefully. In the center of the courtyard stood a building not unlike a guard tower, or the shelter that is sometimes set up in the middle of a market beneath which merchants gather. In fact, it was a shot tower, where lead bullets of different sizes were cast and dropped through an opening in the floor into a shallow tank below to cool, for this was part of the trade of the foundry.

"That would be a good place to make our stand," he said, "and crossbows hang upon the walls."

Foy nodded, and they ran to the tower, but not without being seen, for as they set foot upon its stair, the officer in command of the soldiers called upon them to surrender in the name of the King. They made no answer, and as they passed through the doorway, a bullet from an arquebus struck its woodwork.

The shot tower stood upon oaken piles, and the chamber above, which was round, and about twenty feet in diameter, was reached by a broad ladder of fifteen steps, such as is often used in stables. This ladder ended in a little landing of about six feet square, and to the left of the landing opened the door of the chamber where the shot were cast. They went up into the place.

"What shall we do now?" asked Foy, "barricade the door?"

"I can see no use in that," answered Martin, "for then they would batter it down, or perhaps burn a way through it. No, let us take it off its hinges and lay it on blocks about eight inches high, so that they may catch their shins against it when they try to rush us."

"A good notion," said Foy, and they lifted off the narrow oaken door and propped it up on four molds of metal across the threshold, weighting it with other molds. Also they strewed the floor of the landing with three-pound shot, so that men in a hurry might step on them and fall. Foy also put one more idea into action. At the end of the chamber were the iron baths in which the lead was melted, and beneath them furnaces ready laid for the next days founding. These Foy set alight, pulling out the dampers to make them burn quickly, and so melt the lead bars that lay in the troughs.

"They may come underneath," he said, pointing to the trap through which the hot shot were dropped into the tank, "and then molten lead will be useful."

Martin smiled and nodded. Then he took down a crossbow from the walls, for in those days, when every dwelling and warehouse might have to be used as a place of defense, it was common to keep a good store of weapons hung somewhere ready to distribute. Red Martin examined the bow and then went to the narrow window which overlooked the gate.

"As I thought," he said. "They can't get in and don't like the look of the iron spikes, so they are fetching a smith to burst it open. We must wait."

Very soon Foy began to fidget, for this waiting to be butchered by an overwhelming force wore upon his nerves. He thought of Elsa and his parents, whom he would never see again. He thought of death and all the terrors and wonders that might lie beyond it; death whose depths he must so soon explore. He had looked to his crossbow, had tested the string and laid a good store of quarrels on the floor beside him; he had taken a pike from the walls and seen to its shaft and point; he had stirred the fires beneath the leaden bars until they roared in the sharp draught.

"Is there nothing more to do?" he asked.

"Yes," replied Martin "we would do well to say our prayers, for they may well be our last," and suiting his action to the word, the great man knelt down, an example which Foy followed.

"Do you speak," said Foy, "I can't think of anything proper for my mind is stirred up."

So Martin began a prayer which is perhaps worthy of record:

"O Lord," he said, "forgive me all my sins, which are too many to count, or at least I haven't the time to try, and especially for cutting off the head of the executioner with his own sword, although I had no death quarrel against him, and for killing a Spaniard in a boxing match. O Lord, I thank you very much because you have arranged for us to die fighting instead of being tortured and burnt in the prison, and I pray that we may be able to kill enough Spaniards first to make them remember us for years to come. O Lord, protect my dear master and mistress, and let the former learn that we have made an end of which he would approve. Sovereign Lord and merciful Savior, into thy hands I commit my spirit, and I ask you to bless Foy. That is all I have to say. Amen."

Then Foy did his own praying, and it was hearty enough, but we need scarcely stop to set down its substance.

Meanwhile the Spaniards had found a blacksmith, who was getting to work upon the gate, for they could see him through the open upper bars.

"Why don't you shoot?" asked Foy. "You might catch him with a bolt."

"Because he is a poor Dutchman whom they have pressed for the job, while they stand upon one side. We must wait until they break down the gate. Also we must fight well when the time comes, Master Foy, for, see, folk are watching us, and they will expect it," and he pointed upwards. Foy looked. The foundry courtyard was surrounded by tall gabled houses, and in these the windows and balconies were already crowded with spectators. Word had gone round that the Inquisition had sent soldiers to seize one of the young Van Goorls and Red Martin—that they were battering at the gates of the factory. Therefore the citizens, some of them their own workmen, gathered there, for they did not think that Red Martin and Foy van Goorl would be taken easily.

The hammering at the gate went on, but it was very stout and would not give.

"Martin," said Foy honestly, "I am frightened. I feel quite sick. I know that I shall be no good to you when the pinch comes."

"Now I am sure that you are a brave man," answered Martin with a short laugh, "for otherwise you would never have admitted that you feel afraid. Of course you feel afraid, and so do I. It is the waiting that does it. But when once the first blow has been struck, why, you will be as sturdy as an oak. Look you, Master. As soon as they begin to rush the ladder, do you get behind me, close behind, for I shall want all the room to sweep with my sword, and if we stand side by side we shall only hinder each other, while with a pike you can thrust past me, and be ready to deal with any who win through."

"You mean that you want to shelter me with your big carcass," answered Foy. "But you are captain here. At least, I will do my best," and putting his arms about the great man's middle, he hugged him affectionately.

"Look! Look!" cried Martin. "The gate is down. Now, first shot to you," and he stepped to one side.

As he spoke, the oaken doors burst open and the Spanish soldiers began to stream through them. Suddenly Foy's nerve returned to him and he grew steady. Lifting his crossbow he aimed and pulled the trigger. The string twanged, the quarrel rushed forth with a whistling sound, and the first soldier, pierced through breastplate and through breast, sprang into the air and fell forward. Foy stepped to one side to string his cock.

"Good shot," said Martin taking his place, while from the spectators in the windows went up a sudden shout. Martin fired and another man fell. Then Foy fired again and missed, but Martin's next bolt struck the last soldier through the arm and pinned him to the timber of the broken gate. After this they could shoot no more, for the Spaniards were beneath them.

"To the doorway," said Martin, "and remember what I told you. Away with the bows, cold steel must do the rest."

Now they stood by the open door, Martin, a helmet from the walls upon his head, tied beneath his chin with a piece of rope because it was too small for him, the great sword Silence lifted ready to strike, and Foy behind gripping the long pike with both bands. Below them from the gathered mob of soldiers came a confused clamor, then a voice called out an order and they heard footsteps on the stair.

"Look out! They are coming," said Martin, turning his head so that Foy caught sight of his face. It was transfigured, it was terrible. The great red beard seemed to bristle, the pale blue unshaded eyes rolled and glittered, they glittered like the blue steel of the sword Silence that wavered above them. In that dread instant of expectancy Foy remembered his vision of the morning. Lo, it was fulfilled, for before him stood Martin, the peaceful, patient giant, transformed into a red vengeance.

A man reached the head of the ladder, stepped upon one of the loose cannon-balls and fell with an oath and a crash. But behind him came others. Suddenly they turned the corner; suddenly they burst into view, three or four of them together. Gallantly they rushed on. The first of them caught his feet in the trap of the door and fell headlong across it. Of him Martin took no heed, but Foy did; for before ever the soldier could rise, he had driven his pike down between the man's shoulders, so that he died there upon the door. At the next Martin struck, and Foy saw this one suddenly grow small and double up. Another man followed so quickly that Martin could not lift the sword to meet him. But he pointed with it, and in the next instant was shaking the corpse off his blade.

After this Foy could keep no count. Martin slashed with the sword, and when he found a chance Foy thrust with the pike, until at length there were none to thrust at, for this was more than the Spaniards had bargained. Two of them lay dead in the doorway, and others had been dragged or had tumbled down the ladder, while from the onlookers at the windows without, as they caught sight of them being brought forth slain or sorely wounded, went up shout upon shout of joy.

"So far we have done very well," said Martin quietly, "but if they come up again, we must be cooler and not waste our strength so much. Had I not struck so hard, I might have killed another man."

But the Spaniards showed no sign of coming up any more; they had seen enough of that narrow way and of the red swordsman who awaited them in the doorway round the corner. Indeed it was a bad place for attackers, since they could not shoot with arquebuses or arrows, but must pass in to be slaughtered like sheep in the dim room beyond. So, being cautious men who loved their lives, they took a safer approach.

The tank beneath the shot-tower, when it was not in use, was closed with a stone cover, and around this they piled firewood and peats from a stack in the corner of the yard, and standing in the center out of the reach of arrows, set light to it. Martin lay down watching them through a crack in the floor. Then he signed to Foy, and whispered, and going to the iron baths, Foy drew from them two large buckets of molten lead, each as much as a man could carry. Again Martin looked through the crack, waiting until several of the burners were gathered beneath. Then, with a swift motion he lifted up the trap-door, and as those below stared upwards wondering, full into their faces came the buckets of molten lead. Down went two of them never to speak more, while others ran out shrieking and aflame, tearing at their hair and garments.

After this the Spaniards grew more wary, and built their fires round the oak piers until the flames grew up to the building, and the room above grew full of curling little wreaths of smoke.

"Now we must choose," said Martin, "whether we will be roasted like fowls in an oven, or go down and have our throats cut like pigs in the open."

"For my part, I mean to die in the air," coughed Foy.

"So say I, Master. Listen. We can't get down the stair, for they are watching for us there, so we must drop from the trap-door

and charge through the fire. Then, if God permits, back to back and fight it out."

Half a minute later, two men bearing naked swords in their hands might have been seen running through the barrier of flaming wood. Out they came safely enough, and there in an open space not far from the gateway, halted back to back, rubbing the smoke from their smarting eyes. On them, a few seconds later, like hounds on a wounded boar, dashed the mob of soldiers, while from every throat of the hundreds who were watching went up shrill cries of encouragement, grief, and fear. Men fell before them, but others rushed in. They were down, they were up again, once more they were down, and this time only one of them rose, the great man Martin. He staggered to his feet, shaking off the soldiers who tried to hold him, as a dog in the game-pit shakes off rats. He was up, he stood across the body of his companion, and once more that fearful sword was sweeping round, bringing death to all it touched. They drew back, but a soldier, seasoned in war, crept behind him and suddenly threw a cloak over his head. Then the end came, and slowly, very slowly, they overmatched his strength, and bore him down and bound him, while the watching mob groaned and wept with grief.

CHAPTER XX
IN THE GRAVENSTEEN

When Adrian left the factory, he ran on to the house in the Bree Straat.

"Oh! What has happened?" said his mother as he burst into the room where she and Elsa were at work.

"They are coming for him," he gasped. "The soldiers from the Gravensteen. Where is he? Let him escape quickly—my stepfather."

Lysbeth staggered and fell back into her chair.

"How do you know?" she asked.

At the question Adrian's head swam and his heart stood still. Yet his lips found a lie.

"I overheard it," he said. "The soldiers are attacking Foy and Martin in the factory, and I heard them say that they were coming here for him."

Elsa moaned aloud, then she turned on him like a tiger, asking, "If so, why did you not stay to help them?"

"Because," he answered with a touch of his old depravity, "my first duty was towards my mother and you."

"He is out of the house," broke in Lysbeth in a low voice that was dreadful to hear. "He is out of the house, I know not where. Go, Son, and search for him. Swift! Be swift."

So Adrian went forth, not sorry to escape the presence of these tormented women. Here and there he wandered to one haunt of Dirk's after another, but without success, until finally a noise of tumult drew him, and he ran towards the sound. He was soon around the corner, and this was what he saw.

Advancing down the wide street leading to the Gravensteen came a body of Spanish soldiers, and in the center of them were two figures whom it was easy for Adrian to recognize—Red

Martin and his brother Foy. Martin, although his bull-hide jerkin was cut and slashed and his helmet had gone, seemed to be little hurt, for he was still upright and proud, walking along with his arms lashed behind him, while a Spanish officer held the point of a sword, his own sword Silence, near his throat ready to drive it home should he attempt to escape. With Foy the case was different. At first Adrian thought that he was dead, for they were carrying him upon a ladder. Blood flowed from his head and legs, while his doublet seemed literally to be rent to pieces with sword-cuts and dagger-thrusts; and in truth had it not been for the shirt of mail which he wore beneath, he must have been slain several times over. But Foy was not dead, for as Adrian watched he saw his head turn upon the ladder and his hand rise up and fall again.

But this was not all, for behind appeared a cart drawn by a gray horse, and in it were the bodies of Spanish soldiers—how many Adrian could not tell, but there they lay with their harness still on them. After these again, in a long and melancholy procession, marched other Spanish soldiers, some of them sorely wounded, and, like Foy, carried upon doors or ladders, and others limping forward with the help of their comrades. No wonder that Martin walked proudly to his doom, since behind him came the rich harvest of the sword Silence. Also, there were other signs to see and hear, since about the cavalcade surged and roared a great mob of the citizens of Leyden.

"Bravo, Martin! Well fought, Foy van Goorl!" they shouted, "We are proud of you! We are proud of you!" Then from the back of the crowd someone cried, "Rescue them! Kill the Inquisition dogs! Tear the Spaniards to pieces!"

A stone flew through the air, then another and another, but at a word of command the soldiers faced about and the mob drew back, for they had no leader. So it went on until they were within a hundred yards of the Gravensteen.

"Don't let them be murdered," cried the voice. "A rescue! A rescue!" and with a roar the crowd fell upon the soldiers. It was too late, for the Spaniards, trained to arms, closed up and fought their way through, taking their prisoners with them.

But this cost them dear, for the wounded men, and those who supported them, were cut off. They were cut off, and they were struck down. In a minute they were dead, every one of them, and although they still held its fortresses and walls, from that hour the Spaniards lost their grip on Leyden, nor did they ever win it back again. From that hour to this, Leyden has been free. Such were the first fruits of the fight of Foy and Martin against fearful odds.

The great doors of oak and iron of the Gravensteen closed behind the prisoners, the locks were secured, and the bars fell home, while outside raved the furious crowd.

The place was not large nor very strong, merely a drawbridge across the narrow arm of a moat, a gateway with a walled courtyard beyond, and over it a three-storied house built in the common Dutch fashion, but with straight barred windows. To the right, under the shadow of the archway, which, space being limited, was used as an armory, hung the weapons. Beyond this archway lay the courtroom where prisoners were tried, and to the left a vaulted place with no window, not unlike a large cellar in appearance. This was the torture-chamber. As one moved deeper into the facility, they would come to the courtyard, and at the back of it rose the main prison. In this yard were waiting the new governor of the jail, Ramiro, and with him a little red-faced, pig-eyed man dressed in a rusty doublet. He was the Inquisitor of the district, especially empowered as delegate of the Blood Council, under various edicts and laws, to try and to butcher heretics.

The officer in command of the troops advanced to make his report.

"What is all that noise?" asked the Inquisitor in a frightened, squeaky voice. "Is this city also in rebellion?"

"And where are the rest of you?" said Ramiro, scanning the thin ranks.

"Sir," answered the officer saluting, "the rest of us are dead. Several were killed by this red rogue and his companion, and the mob have the others."

Then Ramiro began to curse and to swear, for he knew that

when this story reached headquarters, his credit with General Álvarez (Alva) and the Blood Council would be gone.

"Coward!" he yelled, shaking his fist in the face of the officer. "Coward to lose a score or more of men in taking two lousy heretics."

"Don't blame me, Sir," answered the man quickly, for the insult stirred his bile, "blame the mob and this red devil's steel, which went through us as though we were wet clay," and he handed him the sword Silence.

"It fits the man," muttered Montalvo, "for few men could wield such a blade. Go hang it in the gateway, it may be wanted in evidence," but to himself he thought, "Bad luck again, the luck that follows me whenever I pit myself against Lysbeth van Hout." Then he gave an order, and the two prisoners were taken away up some narrow stairs.

At the top of the first flight was a solid door through which they passed, to find themselves in a large and darksome place. Down the center of this place ran a passage. On either side of the passage, dimly lighted by high iron barred windows, were cages built with massive oaken bars, and measuring each of them eight or ten feet square. These dens were such as might have served for wild beasts, but were instead filled with human beings charged with offences against the doctrines of the Roman Catholic Church.

Into one of these dreadful holes they were thrust, Foy, wounded as he was, being thrown roughly upon a heap of dirty straw in the corner. Then, having bolted and locked the door of their den, the soldiers left them.

As soon as his eyes grew accustomed to the light, Martin stared around him. The conveniences of the dungeon were not many. Indeed, being built above the level of the ground, it struck the imagination as even more terrible than any subterranean vault devoted to the same dreadful purpose. By kind Providence, however, in one corner of it stood an earthenware basin and a large jug of water.

"I will take the risk of its being poisoned," thought Martin to himself, as lifting the jug he drank deep of it, for what between fighting, fire, and fury there seemed to be no moisture left in him. Then, his burning thirst satisfied at last, he went to where Foy lay unconscious and began to pour water, little by little, into his mouth, which, senseless as he was, he swallowed mechanically and then groaned a little. Next, as well as he could, Martin examined his comrade's wounds, to find that what had made him insensible was a cut upon the right side of the head, which, had it not been for his steel-lined cap, would certainly have killed him, but as it was, beyond the shock and bruise, seemed in no way serious.

His second injury was a deep wound in the left thigh, but being on the outside of the limb, although he bled much it had severed no artery. Other injuries he had also upon the forearms and legs, also beneath the chain shirt his body was bruised with the blows of swords and daggers, but none of these were dangerous.

Martin stripped him as carefully as he might and washed his wounds. Then he paused, for both of them were wearing garments of flannel, which is unsuitable for the dressing of wounds.

"You need linen," said a woman's voice, speaking from the next den. "Wait awhile and I will give you my smock."

"How can I take your garment, Lady, whoever you may be," answered Martin, "to bind about the limbs of a man, even if he is wounded?"

"Take it and welcome," answered the unknown figure in sweet, low tones. "I want it no more. They are going to execute me tonight."

"Execute you tonight?" repeated Martin.

"Yes," replied the voice, "in the courtroom or one of the cellars, I believe, as they dare not do it outside because of the people. By beheading—am I not fortunate? Only by beheading."

"Oh! God, we need You!" groaned Martin.

"Don't feel sorry for me," answered the voice, "I am very glad. There were three of us, my father, my sister, and I, and—you can guess—well, I wish to join them. Also it is better to die than to go through what I have suffered again. But here is the garment. I fear that it is stained about the neck, but it will serve if you tear it into strips," and a trembling, delicate hand, which held the linen, was thrust between the oaken bars.

Even in that light, however, Martin saw that the wrist was cut and swollen. He saw it, and because of that tender, merciful hand he registered an oath about priests and Spaniards. Also, he paused awhile wondering if all this was of any good, wondering if it would not be best to let Foy die sooner rather than later.

"What are you thinking about, Sir?" asked the lady on the other side of the bars.

"I am thinking," answered Martin, "that perhaps my young master here would be better dead, and that I am a fool to stop the bleeding."

"No, no," said the sweet voice, "do your utmost and leave the rest to God. It pleases God that I should die, for I believe that my work on earth is done. It may please Him that this young man shall live to be of service to his country and his faith. I say, bind up the wounds, good Sir."

"Perhaps you are right," answered Martin. "Who knows, there's a key to every lock, if only it can be found." Then he set to work upon Foy's wounds, binding them round with strips of the girl's garment dipped in water, and when he had done the best he could he clothed him again, even to the chain shirt.

"Are you not also hurt?" asked the voice presently.

"A little, nothing to speak of. A few cuts and bruises, that's all. This bull's hide turned their swords."

"Tell me whom you have been fighting," she said.

So, to pass away the time while Foy still lay senseless, Martin told her the story of the attack upon the shot tower, of how they had driven the Spaniards down the ladder, of how they had drenched them with molten lead, and of their last stand in the courtyard when they were forced from the burning building.

"Oh! What a fearful fight—two against so many," said the voice with a ring of admiration in it.

"Yes," answered Martin, "it was a good fight—the hottest that ever I was in. For myself I don't much care, for they've paid a price for my carcass. I didn't tell you, did I, that the mob set on them as they escorted us here and pulled four wounded men and those who carried them to bits? Oh, yes, they have paid a price, a very good price for a Frisian boor and a Leyden burgher."

"God pardon their souls," murmured the unknown girl.

"That's as He likes," said Martin, "and no affair of mine. I had only to do with their bodies and—" At this moment Foy groaned, sat up, and asked for something to drink.

Martin gave him water from the pitcher.

"Where am I?" he asked, and Red Martin told him.

"Martin, old fellow," said Foy in an uncertain voice, "we are in a very bad way, but as we have lived through this"—here his characteristic hopefulness asserted itself—"I believe, I believe that we shall live through the rest."

"Yes, young sir," echoed the thin, faint notes out of the darkness beyond the bars, "I believe, too, that you will live through the rest, and I am praying that it may be so."

"Who is that?" asked Foy drowsily.

"Another prisoner," answered Martin.

"A prisoner who will soon be free," asserted the voice again through the blackness, for by now night had fallen, and no light came from the hole above.

Then Foy fell into sleep or stupor, and there was silence for a long while, until they heard the bolts and bars of the door of the dungeon creaking, and the glint of a lantern appeared floating on the gloom. Several men tramped down the narrow gangway, and one of them, unlocking their cage, entered, filled the jug of water from a leather jack, and threw down some loaves of black bread and pieces of stockfish, as food is thrown to dogs. Having examined the pair of them he grunted and went away, little knowing how near he had been to death, for the heart of Martin was mad. But he let him go. Then the door of the next cell was opened, and a man said, "Come out. It is time."

"It is time and I am ready," answered the thin voice. "Goodbye, friends, God be with you."

"Goodbye, lady," answered Martin. "May you soon be with God." Then he added, by an afterthought, "What is your name? I should like to know."

"Mary," she replied, and began to sing a hymn, and so, still singing the hymn, she passed away to her death. They never saw her face, they never learned who she might be, this poor girl who was but one martyr among the countless victims of one of the most hideous tyrannies that the world has ever known—one of Alva's slaughtered sixty thousand.

The long night wore away in silence, broken only by the groans and prayers of prisoners in dens upon the same floor, or with the solemn rhythm of hymns sung by those above, until at length the light, creeping through the dungeon lattices told them that it was morning. At its first ray Martin awoke much refreshed, for even there his health and weariness had brought sleep to him. Foy also awoke, stiff and sore, but in his right mind and very hungry. Then Martin found the loaves and the stock-fish, and they filled themselves, washing down the meal with water, after which he dressed Foy's wounds, making a poultice for them out of the crumb of the bread, and doctored his own bruises as best he could.

It must have been ten o'clock or later when again the doors were opened, and men appeared who commanded that they should follow them.

"One of us can't walk," said Martin. "Still, perhaps we can manage," and, lifting Foy in his arms as though he had been a baby, he passed with the jailers out of the den, down the stair, and into the courtroom. Here, seated behind a table, they found Ramiro and the little, squeaky-voiced, red-faced Inquisitor.

"Heaven above us!" said the Inquisitor, "what a great hairy ruffian. It makes me feel nervous to be in the same place with him. I beg you, Governor Ramiro, instruct your soldiers to be watching and to stab him at the first movement."

"Have no fear, noble sir," answered Ramiro, "the villain is quite unarmed."

"I daresay, I daresay, but let us get on. Now what is the charge against these people? Ah! I see, heresy like the last upon the evidence of—oh, well never mind. Well, we will take that as proved, and, of course, it is enough. But what more? Ah! Here it is. Escaped from The Hague with the goods of a heretic, killed

sundry of his Majesty's lieges, blew up others on the Haarlemer
Meer, and yesterday, as we know for ourselves, committed a
whole series of murders in resisting lawful arrest. Prisoners, have
you anything to say?"

"Plenty," answered Foy.

"Then save your trouble and my time, since nothing can
excuse your godless, rebellious, and damnable behavior. Friend
Governor, into your hands I deliver them, and may God have
mercy on their souls. See, by the way, that you have a priest
at hand to hear their confession, if they will be absolved, just
for the sake of charity, but all the other details I leave to you.
Torment? Oh, of course if you think there is anything to be
gained by it, or that it will purify their souls. And now I will
be going on to Haarlem, for I tell you frankly, friend Governor,
that I don't think this town of Leyden safe for an honest officer
of the law. There are too many bad characters here, schismatics
and resisters of authority. What? The warrant not ready? Well,
I will sign it in blank so that you can fill it in. God forgive you,
heretics. May your souls find peace, which is more, I fear, than
your bodies will for the next few hours. Bah! Friend Governor,
I wish you had not made me assist at the execution of that girl
last night, especially as I understand she leaves no property
worth having. Her white face haunts my mind, I can't get rid of
the look of those great eyes. Oh, these heretics, to what sorrow
do they put us orthodox people! Farewell, friend Governor; yes,
I think I will go out by the back way, some of those turbulent
citizens might be waiting in front. Farewell, and temper justice
with mercy if you can," and he was gone.

Presently Ramiro, who had accompanied him to the gate,
returned. Seating himself on the further side of the table, he
drew his rapier and laid it before him. Then, having first commanded them to bring a chair in which Foy might sit, since he
could not stand because of his wounded leg, he told the guard to
fall back out of hearing, but to be ready should he need them.

"Not much dignity about that fellow," he said, addressing
Martin and Foy in a cheerful voice. "Quite different from the
kind of thing you expected, I daresay. No hooded Dominican

priests, no clerks taking notes, no solemnities, nothing but a little red-faced wretch, perspiring with terror lest the mob outside should catch him, as for my part I hope they may. Well, gentlemen, what can you expect, seeing that, to my knowledge, the man is a bankrupt tailor of Antwerp? However, it is the substance we have to deal with, not the shadow, and that's real enough, for his signature on a death warrant is as good as that of the Pope, or his gracious Majesty King Philip, or, for the matter of that, of General Álvarez himself. Therefore, you are dead men."

"As you would have been had I not been fool enough to neglect Martin's advice out in the Haarlemer Meer and let you escape," answered Foy.

"Precisely, my young friend, but you see my guardian angel was too much for you, and you did neglect that excellent counsel. But, as it happens, it is just about the Haarlemer Meer that I want to have a word with you."

Foy and Martin looked at each other, for now they understood exactly why they were there, and Ramiro, watching them out of the corners of his eyes, went on in a low voice:

"Let us drop this and come to business. You hid it, and you know where it is, and I am in need of a reserve for my old age. Now, I am not a cruel man. I wish to put no one to pain or death; moreover, I tell you frankly, I admire both of you very much. The escape with the treasure on board your boat *Swallow*, and the blowing up, were both exceedingly well managed, with but one mistake which you have pointed out," and he bowed and smiled. "The fight that you made yesterday was splendid, and I have entered the details of it in my own private diary because they ought not to be forgotten."

Now it was Foy's turn to bow, while even on Martin's grim and impassive countenance flickered a faint smile.

"Naturally," went on Ramiro, "I wish to save such men, I wish you to go hence quite free and unharmed," and he paused.

"How can we after we have been condemned to death?" asked Foy.

"Well, it does not seem difficult. My friend, the tailor—I mean the Inquisitor—who, for all his soft words, is a cruel man indeed, was in a hurry to be gone, and—he signed a blank warrant, always an incautious thing to do. Well, a judge can acquit as well as condemn, and this one is no exception. What is there to prevent me from filling this paper in with an order for your release?"

"And what is there to show us that you would release us after all?" asked Foy.

"Upon the honor of a gentleman," answered Ramiro laying his hand on his heart. "Tell me what I want to know, give me a week to make certain necessary arrangements, and as soon as I am back, you shall both of you be freed."

"Doubtless," said Foy, angrily, "upon such honor as gentlemen learn in the galleys, Señor Ramiro—I beg your pardon, Count Juan de Montalvo."

Ramiro's face grew crimson to his forehead.

"Sir," he said, "were I a different sort of man, for those words you should die in a fashion from which even the boldest might shrink. But you are young and inexperienced, so I will overlook them. Now this bargaining must come to a head. Which will you have, life and safety, or the chance—which under the circumstances is no chance at all—that one day, not you, of course, but somebody interested in it, may recover a hoard of money and jewels?"

Then Martin spoke for the first time, very slowly and respectfully.

"Worshipful Sir," he said, "we cannot tell you where the money is because we do not know. To be frank with you, nobody ever knew except myself. I took the stuff and sank it in the water in a narrow channel between two islands, and I made a little drawing of them on a piece of paper."

"Exactly, my good friend, and where is that piece of paper?"

"Alas! Sir, when I was lighting the fuses on board the *Swallow*, I let it fall in my haste, and it is—in exactly the same place as are all your worship's worthy comrades who were on board that ship. I believe, however, that if you will put yourself under my guidance I could show your Excellency the spot, and this, as I do not want to be killed, I should be most happy to do."

"Good, simple man," said Ramiro with a little laugh, "how charming is the prospect that you paint of a midnight row with you upon those lonely waters. The tarantula and the butterfly arm in arm! Mynheer van Goorl, what have you to say?"

"Only that the story told by Martin here is true. I do not know where the money is, as I was not present at its sinking, and the paper has been lost."

"Indeed? I am afraid, then, that it will be necessary for me to refresh your memory, but, first, I have one more argument, or rather two. Has it struck you that another life may hang upon your answer? As a rule men are loth to send their fathers to death."

Foy heard, and terrible as was the hint, yet it came to him as a relief, for he had feared lest he was about to say "your mother" or "Elsa Brant."

"That is my first argument, a good one, I think, but I have another which may appeal even more forcibly to a young man and prospective heir. The day before yesterday you became engaged to Elsa Brant—don't look surprised. People in my position have long ears, and you needn't be frightened, the young lady will not be brought here; she is too valuable."

"Be so good as to speak plainly," said Foy.

"With pleasure. You see this girl is the heiress, is she not? and whether or not I find out the facts from you, sooner or later, in this way or that, she will doubtless discover where her heritage is hidden. Well, that fortune a husband would have the advantage of sharing. I myself labor at present under no matrimonial engagements, and am in a position to obtain an introduction—ah! My friend, are you beginning to see that there are more ways of killing a dog than by hanging him?"

Weak and wounded as he was, Foy's heart sank in him at the words of this man, this devil who had betrayed his mother with a mock marriage, and who was the father of Adrian. The idea of making the heiress his wife was one worthy of his evil ingenuity, and why should he not put it into practice? Elsa, of course, would rebel, but Alva's officials in such days had means of overcoming any maidenly reluctance, or at least of forcing women to choose between death and degradation. Was it not common for them even to dissolve marriages in order to give heretics to new husbands who desired their wealth? There was no justice left in the land. Human beings were the chattels and slaves of their oppressors. Oh God! What was there to do, except to trust in God? Why should they be tortured, murdered, married against their wills, for the sake of a miserable pile of treasure? Why not tell the truth and let the fellow take the money? He had measured up his man, and believed that he could drive a bargain with him. Ramiro wanted money, not lives. He was no fanatic. Horrors gave him no pleasure; he cared nothing about his victims' souls. As he had betrayed his mother, Lysbeth, for gold, so he would be willing to let them all go for gold. Why not make the exchange?

Then distinct, formidable, overwhelming, the answer rose up in Foy's mind. Because he had sworn to his father that nothing that could be imagined should induce him to reveal this secret and betray this trust. And not only to his father, to Hendrik Brant also, who already had given his own life to keep his treasure out of the hands of the Spaniards, believing that in some unforeseen way it would help his own land and the cause of Christ. No, great as was the temptation, he must keep the letter of his bond and pay its dreadful price. So again Foy answered,

"It is useless to try to bribe me, for I do not know where the money is."

"Very well, Heer Foy van Goorl, now we have a plain issue before us, but I will still try to protect you against yourself—the warrant shall remain blank for a little while."

Then he called aloud, "Sergeant, ask the Professor Baptiste to be so good as to step this way."

CHAPTER XXI
HOW MARTIN TURNED COWARD

The sergeant left the room but soon returned, followed by the Professor, a tall slimy looking rogue, clad in rusty black, with broad, horny hands, and nails bitten down until they bled.

"Good morning to you, Professor," said Ramiro.

"Here are two subjects for your gentle art. You will begin upon the big one, and from time to time report progress, and be sure, if he becomes willing to reveal what I want to know never mind what it is, that is my affair, come to summon me at once."

"What methods does your Excellency wish employed?"

"Man, I leave that to you. Am I a master of your filthy trade? Any method, provided it is effective."

"I don't like the look of him," grumbled the Professor, gnawing at his short nails. "I have heard about this mad brute. He is capable of anything."

"Then you have a great deal in common, Heer Professor," quipped Ramiro. "If you must, take the whole guard with you. One naked wretch can't do much against eight armed men. And, listen; take the young gentleman also, and let him see what goes on; the experience may modify his views, but don't touch him without telling me. I have reports to write, and shall stop back later."

"I don't like the look of him," repeated the Professor. "I say that he makes me feel cold down the back—he has the evil eye; I'd rather begin with the young one."

"Begone and do what I tell you," said Ramiro, glaring at him fiercely. "Guard, attend upon the executioner Baptiste."

"Bring them along," grumbled the Professor.

"No need for violence, worthy sir," declared Martin. "Show the way and we follow," and stooping down he lifted Foy from his chair.

Then the procession started. First went Baptiste and four soldiers, next came Martin bearing Foy, and after them four more soldiers. They passed out of the courtroom into the passage beneath the archway. Martin, shuffling along slowly, glanced down it and saw that on the wall, among some other weapons, hung his own sword, Silence. The big doors were locked and barred, but at a smaller door by the side of them stood a sentry, whose office it was to let people in and out upon their lawful business. Making pretence to shift Foy in his arms, Martin scanned this doorway as narrowly as time would allow, and observed that it seemed to be secured by means of iron bolts at the top and the bottom, but that it was not locked, since the socket into which the tongue went was empty. Doubtless, while he was on guard there, the porter did not think it necessary to go to the effort of using the great key that hung at his girdle.

The sergeant in charge of the victims opened a low and massive door, which was almost exactly opposite to that of the courtroom, by shooting back a bolt and pushing it ajar. Evidently the place beyond at some time or other had been used as a prison, which accounted for the bolt on the outside. A few seconds later they were locked into the torture chamber of the Gravensteen, which was nothing more than a good-sized vault like that of a cellar, lit with lamps, and by a horrid little fire that flickered on the floor. The equipment in this place or torture may be imagined. Let us pass them over as unfit even for description, although these terrors, of which we scarcely like to speak today, were very familiar to the sight of Bible believing Christians of that period.

Martin sat Foy down upon some terrible contraption that roughly resembled a chair, and once more let his blue eyes wander about him. Amongst the various implements was one leaning against the wall, not very far from the door, which excited his particular interest. It was made for a dreadful purpose, but Martin reflected only that it seemed to be a stout bar of iron exactly suited to the breaking of an enemy's head.

"Come," sneered the Professor, "undress that big gentleman while I make ready his little bed."

So the soldiers stripped Martin, nor did they assault him with sneers and insults, for they remembered the man's deeds of yesterday, and admired his strength and endurance, and the huge, muscular frame beneath their hands.

"Now he is ready if you are," said the sergeant.

The Professor rubbed his hands. "Come on, my little man," he said.

Then Martin's nerve gave way, and he began to shiver and to shake.

"Oho!" laughed the Professor, "even in this stuffy place he is cold without his clothes. Well, we must warm him—we must warm him."

"Who would have thought that a big fellow, who can fight well, too, was such a coward at heart," said the sergeant of the guard to his companions. "After all, he will give no more play than a Rhine salmon."

Martin heard the words, and he was seized with such an intense access of fear that he burst into a sweat all over his body.

"I can't bear it," he said, covering his eyes—which, however, he did not shut but peaked through his fingers. "The rack was always my nightmare, and now I see why. I'll tell all I know."

"Oh! Martin, Martin," broke out Foy in a kind of wail, "I was doing my best to keep my own courage. I never dreamt that you would turn coward."

"Every well has a bottom, Master," whined Martin, "and mine is the rack. Forgive me, but I can't abide the sight of it."

Foy stared at him open-mouthed. Could he believe his ears? And if Martin was so horribly scared, why did his eye glint in that peculiar way between his fingers? He had seen this light in it before, no later indeed than the last afternoon just as the soldiers tried to rush the stair. He gave up the problem as insoluble, but from that moment he watched very carefully.

"Do you hear what this young lady says, Professor Baptiste?"

said the sergeant. "She says," (imitating Martin's whine) "that she'll tell all she knows."

"Then the great cur might have saved me this trouble. Stop here with him. I must go and inform the Governor; those are my orders. No, no, you needn't give him his clothes yet—that cloth is enough—one can never be sure."

Then he walked to the door and began to unlock it, striking Martin in the face with the back of his hand, and saying, "Take that, cur." At which point, as Foy observed, the cowed prisoner perspired more profusely than before, and shrank away towards the wall. God in Heaven! What had happened?

The door of the torture den was opened, and suddenly, uttering the words, "To me, Foy!" Martin made a movement more quick than he could follow. Something flew up and fell with a fearful thud upon the executioner in the doorway. The guard sprang forward, and a great bar of iron, hurled with awful force into their faces, swept two of them broken to the ground.

Another instant, and one arm was around Foy's middle, the next they were outside the door, Martin standing straddle-legged over the body of the dead Professor Baptiste.

They were outside the door, but it could not be shut, for now, on the other side of it six men were pushing with all their might. Martin dropped Foy. "Take his dagger and look out for the porter," he gasped as he hurled himself against the door.

In a second, Foy had drawn the weapon out of the belt of the dead man and wheeled round. The porter from the narrow doorway was running at them, sword in hand. Foy forgot that he was wounded—for the moment his leg seemed sound again. He doubled himself up and sprang at the man like a wild-cat, as one springs who has the rack behind him. There was no fight; yet in that thrust, the skill which Martin had taught him so patiently served him well, for the sword of the Spaniard passed over his head, whereas Foy's long dagger went through the porter's throat. A glance showed Foy that from him there was nothing more to fear, so he turned.

"Help if you can," groaned Martin, as well he might, for with his naked shoulder wedged against one of the cross pieces of the door, he was striving to press it so that the bolt could be shot into its socket.

Heavens! What a struggle that was. Martin's blue eyes seemed to be bulging from his head, his tongue lolled out, and the muscles of his body rose in great knots. Foy hopped to him and pushed as well as he was able. It was little that he could do standing upon one leg only, for now the sinews of the other had given way again. Still that little made the difference, for let the soldiers on the further side strive as they might, slowly, very slowly, the thick door quivered to its frame. Martin glanced at the bolt, for he could not speak, and with his left hand Foy slowly worked it forward. It was stiff with disuse, it caught upon the edge of the socket.

"Closer," he gasped.

Martin made an effort so fierce that it was hideous to behold, for beneath the pressure, the blood trickled from his nostrils, but the door went in the sixteenth of an inch and the rusty bolt creaked home into its stone notch.

Martin stepped back and, for a moment, stood swaying like a man about to fall. Then, recovering himself, he leapt at the sword Silence, which hung upon the wall, and passed its thong over his right wrist. Next he turned towards the door of the courtroom.

"Where are you going?" asked Foy.

"To bid him farewell," hissed Martin.

"You're mad," said Foy. "Let's fly while we can. That door may give—they are shouting."

"Perhaps you are right," answered Martin doubtfully. "Come. Onto my back with you."

A few seconds later, the two soldiers on guard outside the Gravensteen were amazed to see a huge, red-bearded man—naked except for a loin-cloth, and waving a great bare sword—rush straight at them with a roar. They never waited his onset; they were terrified and thought that he was a devil. This way and that they sprang, and the man with his burden passed between them over the little drawbridge down the street of the city, heading for the Morsch poort.

Finding their wits, again the guards started in pursuit, but a voice from among the passers-by cried out:

"It is Martin, Red Martin, and Foy van Goorl, who escape from the Gravensteen," and instantly a stone flew towards the soldiers.

Then, remembering the fate of their comrades the day before, those men shuffled back to the friendly shelter of the prison gate.

When at length Ramiro, growing weary of waiting, came out from an inner chamber beyond the courtroom, where he had been writing, he found the Professor and the porter dead in the passage, and the guards locked in his own torture chamber. The panic-stricken sentries declared that they had seen nothing at all of prisoners clothed or naked.

For a while he believed them, and diligent was the hunt from the clocktower of the Gravensteen down to the lowest stone of its cellars, yes, and even in the waters of the moat. But when the Governor found out the truth, it went very badly for those soldiers, and still worse with the guard from whom Martin had escaped in the torture room like an eel out of the hand of a fish-wife. For by this time, Ramiro's temper was roused, and he began to think that it was foolish for him to have returned to Leyden.

But he still had a card to play. In a certain room in the Gravensteen sat another victim. Compared to the dreadful dens where Foy and Martin had been confined, this was quite a pleasant chamber upon the first floor, being reserved, indeed, for political prisoners of rank, or officers captured upon the field who were held to ransom. Thus it had a real window, secured, however, by a double set of iron bars, which overlooked the little inner courtyard and the kitchen. Also, it was furnished after a fashion, and was more or less clean. This prisoner was none other than Dirk van Goorl, who had been neatly captured as he returned towards his house after making certain arrangements for the flight of his family, and was hurried away to the prison. On that morning, Dirk also had been put upon his trial before the squeaky-voiced and agitated ex-tailor. He also had been condemned to death, the method of his end, as in the case of Foy and Martin, being left in the hands of the Governor. Then they led him back to his room, and shut the bolts upon him there.

Some hours later a man entered his cell, to the door of which he was escorted by soldiers, bringing him food and drink. He was one of the cooks and, as it turned out, a talkative fellow.

"What passes in the prison, friend?" asked Dirk looking up, "that I see people running to and fro across the courtyard, and hear trampling and shouts in the passages? Is the Prince of Orange coming, perchance, to set all of us poor prisoners free?" and he smiled sadly.

"Umph!" grunted the man, "we have prisoners here who set themselves free without waiting for any Prince of Orange. Magicians they must be—magicians and nothing less."

Dirk's interest was excited. Putting his hand into his pocket he drew out a gold piece, which he gave to the man.

"Friend," he said, "you cook my food, do you not, and look

after me? Well, I have a few of these about me, and if you prove kind, they may as well find their way into your pocket as into the pocket of someone else. Do you understand?"

The man nodded, took the money, and thanked him.

"Now," went on Dirk, "while you clean the room, tell me about this escape, for small things amuse those who hear no tidings."

"Well, Mynheer," answered the man, "this is the tale of it so far as I can gather. Yesterday they captured two fellows, heretics, I suppose, who made a good fight and did them much damage in a warehouse. I don't know their names, for I am a stranger to this town, but I saw them brought in; a young fellow, who seemed to be wounded in the leg and neck, and a great red-bearded giant of a man. They were put upon their trial this morning, and afterwards sent across, the two of them together, with eight men to guard them, to call upon the Professor—you understand?"

Dirk nodded, for this Professor was well known in Leyden. "And then?" he asked.

"And then? Why, Mother in Heaven! They came out, that's all—the big man stripped and carrying the other on his back. Yes, they killed the Professor with the branding iron, and out they came—like ripe peas from a pod."

"Impossible!" said Dirk.

"Very well, perhaps you know better than I do. Perhaps it is impossible also that they should have pushed the door closed, and let all those Spanish cocks inside do what they might, and bolted them in; perhaps it is impossible that they should have slain the porter and got clean away through the outside guards, the big one still carrying the other upon his back. Perhaps all these things are impossible, but they're true nevertheless, and if you don't believe me, after they get away from the whipping-post, just ask the bridge guard, why they ran so fast when they saw that great, blue-eyed fellow come at them, roaring like a lion, with his big sword flashing above his head. Oh, there's an ugly scandal brewing, I can tell you, and in one way or another, we shall all pay the price of it, from the Governor down. Indeed, some backs are paying for it now."

"But, friend, were they not arrested outside the prison?"

"Taken? Who was to take them when the rascally mob made them an escort five hundred strong as they went down the street? No, they are far away from Leyden now, you may swear to that. I must be going, but if there is anything you'd like while you're here just tell me, and as you are so generous I'll try and see that you get what you want."

As the bolts were shut home behind the man, Dirk clasped his hands and almost laughed aloud with joy. So Martin was free and Foy was free, and until they could be taken again, the secret of the treasure remained safe. Montalvo would never have it, of that he was sure. And as for his own fate? Well, he cared little about it, especially as the Inquisitor had decreed that, being a man of so much importance, he was not to be put to the "question." This order, however, was prompted, not by mercy, but by discretion, since the fellow knew that, like other of the Dutch towns, Leyden was on the verge of open revolt. He feared lest, should it leak out that one of the wealthiest and most respected of its burghers was actually being tormented for his faith's sake, the populace might step over the boundary line.

When Adrian had seen the wounded Spanish soldiers and their bearers torn to pieces by the rabble, and had heard the great door of the Gravensteen close upon Foy and Martin, he turned to go home with his evil news. But for a long while, the mob would not go home, and had it not been that the draw-bridge over the moat in front of the prison was up, and that they had no means of crossing it, they probably would have attacked the building then and there. Presently, however, rain began to fall and they melted away, wondering, not too happily, whether, in that time of daily slaughter, the Duke of Alva would consider a few common soldiers worthwhile making a stir about.

Adrian entered the upper room to tell his tidings, since they must be told, and found it occupied by his mother alone. She was sitting straight upright in her chair, hands resting upon her knees, staring out of the window with a face like marble.

"I cannot find him," he began, "but Foy and Martin are taken after a great fight in which Foy was wounded. They are in the Gravensteen."

"I know all," interrupted Lysbeth in a cold, heavy voice. "My husband is taken also. Someone must have betrayed them. May God reward him! Leave me, Adrian."

Then Adrian turned and crept away to his own chamber, his heart so full of remorse and shame that at times he thought that it must burst. Weak as he was, wicked as he was, he had never intended this outcome. Now, oh Heaven, his brother Foy and the man who had been his benefactor, whom his mother loved more than her life, were through him given over to a death worse than the mind could conceive. Somehow, that night wore away, and of this we may be sure, that it did not go half as heavily with the victims in their dungeon as with the betrayer in his free comfort. More than once during its dark hours, indeed, Adrian was on the verge of a nervous breakdown. Better would it have been for him, perhaps, could he have kept his courage; at least he would have been spared much added shame and misery.

As soon as Adrian had left Lysbeth she rose, robed herself, and took her way to the house of her cousin, van de Werff, now a successful citizen of middle age and the burgemeester-elect of Leyden.

"You have heard the news?" she said.

"Alas! Cousin, I have," he answered, "and it is very terrible. Is it true that this treasure of Hendrik Brant's is at the bottom of it all?"

She nodded, and answered, "I believe so."

"Then could they not bargain for their lives by surrendering its secret?"

"Perhaps. That is, Foy and Martin might—Dirk does not know its whereabouts—he refused to know, but they have sworn that they will die first."

"Why, Cousin?"

"Because they promised as much to Hendrik Brant, who believed that if his gold could be kept from the Spaniards, it would do some mighty service for his country in time to come, and who has persuaded them all that this is so."

"Then God grant it may be true," said van de Werff with a sigh, "for otherwise it is sad to think that more lives should be sacrificed for the sake of a heap of money."

"I know it, Cousin, but I come to you to save those lives."

"How?" responded the burgermeester.

"How?" she answered fiercely. "Why, by raising the town; by attacking the Gravensteen and rescuing them; by driving the Spaniards out of Leyden—"

"And thereby bringing upon ourselves the fate of Mons. Would you see this place also given over to sack by the soldiers of Noircarmes and Don Frederic, Álvarez's son?"

"I care not what I see so long as I save my son and my husband," she answered desperately.

"There speaks the woman, not the patriot. It is better that three men should die than a whole city full."

"That is a strange argument to find in your mouth, Cousin, the argument of Caiaphas the Jew."

"Nay, Lysbeth, be not angry with me, for what can I do? The Spanish troops in Leyden are not many, it is true, but more have been sent for from Haarlem and elsewhere after the troubles of yesterday arising out of the capture of Foy and Martin, and in forty-eight hours at the longest they will be here. This town is not provisioned for a siege, its citizens are not trained to arms, and we have little powder stored. Moreover, the city council is divided. For the killing of the Spanish soldiers we may escape retaliation, but if we attack the Gravensteen, that is open rebellion, and we shall bring the army of Don Frederic down upon us."

"What matter, Cousin? It will come sooner or later."

"Then let it come later, when we are more prepared to beat it off. Oh, do not reproach me, for I tell you that I am working day and night to make ready for the hour of trial. I love your husband and your son, my heart bleeds for your sorrow and their doom, but at present I can do nothing, nothing. You must bear your burden, they must bear theirs, and I must bear mine. We must all wander through the night not knowing where we wander until God causes the dawn to break, the dawn of freedom and retribution."

Lysbeth made no answer, only she rose and stumbled from the house, while van de Werff sat down groaning bitterly and praying for help and light.

CHAPTER XXII
A MEETING AND A PARTING

Lysbeth did not sleep that night, for even if her misery would have let her sleep, she could not because of the physical fire that burnt in her veins, and the strange pangs of agony which pierced her head. At first she thought little of them, but when at last the cold light of the autumn morning dawned, she went to a mirror and examined herself, and there upon her neck she found a hard red swelling the size of a nut. Then Lysbeth knew that she had caught the plague from the Vrouw Jansen, and laughed aloud, a dreary little laugh, since if all she loved were to die, it seemed to her good that she should die also. Elsa was in bed prostrated with grief, and, shutting herself in her room, Lysbeth permitted none to come near her except one woman whom she knew had recovered from the plague in past years, but even to her she said nothing of her sickness.

About eleven o'clock in the morning this woman rushed into her chamber crying, "They have escaped! They have escaped!"

"Who?" gasped Lysbeth, springing from her chair.

"Your son Foy and Red Martin," and she told the tale of how the mighty man with the mighty sword, carrying the wounded Foy upon his back, burst his way roaring from the Gravensteen, and, protected by the people, had run through the town and out of the Morsch poort, heading for the Haarlemer Meer.

As she listened, Lysbeth's eyes flamed up with a fire of joy.

"Oh, good and faithful servant," she murmured, "you have saved my son, but, alas your master you could not save."

Another hour passed, and the woman appeared again bearing a letter.

"Who brought this?" she asked.

"A Spanish soldier, Mistress," said the servant.

Then she cut the silk and read it. It was unsigned, and stated:

> One in authority sends greetings to the Vrouw van
> Goorl. If the Vrouw van Goorl would save the life of the
> man who is dearest to her, she is advised to veil herself and
> follow the bearer of this letter. For her own safety she need
> have no fear; it is assured hereby.

Lysbeth thought awhile. This might be a trick; very probably
it was a trick to take her. Well, if so, what did it matter since she
would rather die with her husband than live on without him;
moreover, why should she turn aside from death, she in whose
veins the plague was burning? But there was another thing
worse than that. She could guess who had penned this letter; it
even seemed to her, after all these many years, that she recognized the writing, disguised though it was. Could she face him!
Well, why not—for Dirk's sake?

And if she refused and Dirk was murdered, would she not
reproach herself, if she lived to remember it, because she had left
a stone unturned?

"Give me my cloak and veil," she said to the woman, "and
now go tell the man that I am coming."

At the door she found the soldier, who saluted her, and said
respectfully, "Follow me, lady, but at a little distance."

So they started, and through side streets Lysbeth was led to
a back entrance of the Gravensteen, which opened and closed
behind her mysteriously, leaving her wondering whether she
would ever pass that gate again. Within, a man was waiting—she
did not even notice what kind of man—who also said, "Follow
me, lady," and led her through gloomy passages and various
doors into a little empty chamber furnished with a table and
two chairs. Moments later, the door opened and shut; then her
whole being shrank and sickened as though beneath the breath
of poison, for there before her, still the same, still handsome,
although marred by time and scars and evil, stood the man who
had been her husband, Juan de Montalvo. But whatever she felt,
Lysbeth showed nothing of it in her face, which remained white

and stern; moreover, even before she looked at him, she was aware that he feared her more than she feared him.

It was true, for from this woman's eyes went out a sword of terror that seemed to pierce Montalvo's heart. Back flew his mind to the scene of their betrothal, and the awful words that she had spoken then re-echoed in his ears. How strangely things had come round, for on that day, as on this, the stake at issue was the life of Dirk van Goorl. In the old times she had bought it, paying as its price herself, her fortune, and, worst of all to a woman, her lover's scorn. What would she be prepared to pay now? Well, fortunately, he need ask but little of her. And yet his own soul mistrusted these bargainings with Lysbeth van Hout for the life of Dirk van Goorl. The first had ended poorly with a sentence of fourteen years in the galleys, most of which he had served. How would the second end?

"It is most good of you, Vrouw van Goorl," he began, "to have responded so promptly to my invitation."

"Perhaps, Count de Montalvo," she replied, "you will do me the favor to set out your business in as few words as possible."

"Most certainly; that is my desire. Let me free your mind of apprehension. The past has mingled memories for both of us, some of them bitter, some, let me hope, sweet," and he laid his hand upon his heart and sighed. "But it is a dead past, so, dear lady, let us agree to bury it in a fitting silence."

Lysbeth made no answer, only her mouth grew a trifle more stern.

"Now, one word more, and I will come to the point. Let me congratulate you upon the gallant deeds of a gallant son. Of course his courage and dexterity, with that of the red giant, Martin, have told against myself, have, in short, lost me a trick in the game. But I am an old soldier, and I can assure you that the details of their fight yesterday at the factory, and of their marvelous escape from—from—well, painful surroundings this morning, have stirred my blood and made my heart beat fast."

"I have heard the tale. Do not trouble to repeat it," said Lysbeth. "It is only what I expected of them, but I am thankful that it has pleased God to let them live on, so that in due course they may mightily avenge a beloved father and master."

"Well," he went on, "a truce to compliments. They escaped and I am glad of it, whatever murders they may contemplate in the future. Yes, notwithstanding their great crimes and man-slayings in the past, I am glad that they escaped, although it was my duty to keep them while I could—and, if I should catch them, it will be my duty—but I needn't talk of that to you. Of course, however, you know there is one gentleman who was not quite so fortunate."

"My husband?"

"Yes, your worthy husband, who, happily for my reputation as captain of one of His Majesty's prisons, occupies an upstairs room."

"What of him?" asked Lysbeth.

"Dear lady, don't be over anxious. There is nothing as wearing as anxiety. I was coming to the matter." Then, with a sudden change of manner, he added, "It is needful, Lysbeth, that I should set out the situation."

"What situation do you mean?" inquired Lysbeth.

"Well, principally that of the treasure," responded the Captain.

"What treasure?"

"Oh, woman, do not waste time in trying to fool me. The treasure, the vast, the incalculable treasure of Hendrik Brant that Foy van Goorl and Martin, who have escaped"—and he ground his teeth together at the anguish of the thought—"disposed of somewhere in the Haarlemer Meer."

"Well, what about this treasure?"

"I want it, that is all," screamed Montalvo.

"Then you had best go to seek it," replied the victim of the plague.

"That is my intention, and I shall begin to search—in the heart of Dirk van Goorl," he added, slowly crushing the hand-kerchief he held with his long fingers, as though it were a living thing that could be choked to death.

Lysbeth never stirred, she had expected this. "You will find it a poor mine to dig in," she said, "for he knows nothing of the whereabouts of this money. Nobody knows anything of it now. Martin hid it, as I understand, and lost the paper, so it will lie there until the Haarlemer Meer is drained."

"Dear me! Do you know I have heard that story before; yes, from the excellent Martin himself—and, do you know, I don't quite believe it."

"I cannot help what you believe or do not believe. You may remember that it was always my habit to speak the truth."

"Quite so, but others may be less conscientious. See here," and drawing a paper from his doublet, he held it before her. It was nothing less than the death-warrant of Dirk van Goorl, signed by the Inquisitor.

Mechanically she read it and understood.

"You will observe," he went on, "that the method of the criminal's execution is left to the good wisdom of myself alone. Now might I trouble you so far as to look out of this little window? What do you see in front of you? A kitchen? Quite so; always a homely and pleasant sight in the eyes of an excellent housewife like yourself. Do you mind bending forward a little? What do you see up there? A small barred window? Well, let us suppose, for the sake of argument, that a hungry man, a man who grows hungrier and hungrier, sat behind that window watching the cooks at their work and seeing the meat carried into this kitchen, to come out an hour or two later as hot, steaming, savory joints, while he wasted, wasted, wasted, and starved, starved, starved. Don't you think, my dear lady, that this would be a very unpleasant experience for that man?"

"Are you a devil?" gasped Lysbeth, springing back.

"I have never regarded myself as such, but if you seek a definition, I should say that I am a hard-working, resilient, and somewhat unfortunate gentleman who has been driven to rough methods in order to secure a comfortable old age. I can assure you that I do not wish to starve anybody; I wish only to find Hendrik Brant's treasure, and if your worthy husband won't tell me where it is—why, I must make him, that is all. In six or eight days, under my treatment, I am convinced that he will become quite fluent on the subject, for there is nothing that should cause a fat burgher, accustomed to good living, to open his heart more than a total lack of the food that he can see and smell."

Then Lysbeth's pride broke down, and in the abandonment of her despair, flinging herself upon her knees before this monster, she begged for her husband's life, begged, in the name of God, yes, and even in the name of Montalvo's son, Adrian. So low had her misery brought her that she pleaded with the man by the son of shame whom she had borne to him.

He asked her to rise. "So you want to save your husband's life," he said. "I give you my word that if only he will tell me what I desire to know, I will save it. Yes, although the risk is great, I will even manage his escape, and I shall ask you to go upstairs soon to explain my amiable intentions to him." Then he thought a moment and added, "But you mentioned one Adrian. Pray do you mean the gentleman whose signature appears here?" He handed her another document, saying, "Read it quietly, there is no hurry. The good Dirk is not starving yet; I am informed, indeed, that he has just had an excellent breakfast—not his last by many thousands, let us hope."

Lysbeth took the sheets and glanced at them. Then her intelligence awoke, and she read on fiercely until her eye came to the well-known signature at the foot of the last page. She cast the pages down with a cry, as though a serpent had sprung from its pages and bitten her.

"I fear that you are pained," said Montalvo sympathetically, "and no wonder, for myself I have gone through such disillusionments, and know how they wound a generous nature. That's why I showed you this document, because I also am generous and wish to warn you against this young gentleman, who, I understand, you allege is my son. You see the person who would betray his brother might even go a step further and betray his mother, so, if you take my advice, you will keep an eye upon the young man. Also I am bound to remind you that it is more or less your own fault. It is a most unlucky thing to curse a child before it is born—you remember the incident? That curse has come home to roost with a vengeance. What a warning against giving way to the passion of the moment!"

Lysbeth heeded him no longer; she was thinking as she had never thought before. At that moment, as though by an inspiration, there floated into her mind the words of the dead Vrouw Jansen. "The plague, I wish that I had caught it before, for then I would have taken it to him in prison, and they couldn't have treated him as they did." Dirk was in prison, and Dirk was to be starved to death, for, whatever Montalvo might think, he did not know the secret, and, therefore, could not tell it. She had the plague on her; she knew its symptoms well, and its poison was burning in her every vein, although she still could think and speak and walk.

Well, why not? It would be no crime. Indeed, if it was a crime, she cared little. It would be better that he should die of the plague in five days, or perhaps in two, if it worked quickly, as it often did with the full-blooded, than that he should linger on starving for twelve or more, and perhaps be tormented besides.

Swiftly, very swiftly, Lysbeth came to her dreadful decision. Then she spoke in a hoarse voice.

"What do you wish me to do?"

"I wish you to reason with your husband, and to persuade him to cease from his obstinacy, and to surrender to me the secret of the hiding place of Brant's hoard. In that event, so soon as I have proved the truth of what he tells me, I undertake that he shall be set at liberty unharmed, and that, meanwhile, he shall be well treated."

"And if I will not, or he will not, or cannot?" inquired Lysbeth.

Then I have told you the alternative, and to show you that I am not joking, I will now write and sign the order. Then, if you decline this mission, or if it is fruitless, I will hand it to the officer before your eyes, and within the next ten days or so let you know the results, or witness them if you wish."

"I will go," she said, "but I must see him alone."

"Well it is unusual," he answered, "but provided you satisfy me that you carry no weapon, I do not know that I need object."

So, when Montalvo had written his order and scattered dust

on it from the sand-box, for he was a man of neat and methodical habits, he himself with every possible courtesy conducted Lysbeth to her husband's cell. Having ushered her into it, with a cheerful "Friend van Goorl, I bring you a visitor," he locked the door upon them, and patiently waited outside.

It is, perhaps, a matter of poor taste to reveal exactly what was said by this couple during their intimate moments together. Whether Lysbeth told her husband of her dread yet sacred purpose, or did not tell him; whether he ever learned of the treason of Adrian, or did not learn it; what were their parting words and their parting prayers, all these things we need not address. Let us be content to know that the joy of the Lord was the strength that upheld them during those dreary hours and that the power of God's love did not fail to sustain their spirits.

Growing impatient at length, Montalvo unlocked the prison door and opened it, to discover Lysbeth and her husband kneeling side by side in the center of the room, like the figures on some ancient marble monument. They heard him and rose. Then Dirk folded his wife in his arms in a long, last embrace, and, loosing her, held one hand above her head in blessing. He then pointed to the door with his other hand.

So infinitely pathetic was this silent show of farewell, for no word passed between them while he was present, that not only his barbed comments, but the questions that he meant to ask, died upon the lips of Montalvo. Try as he might, he could not speak to them in their dignified company.

"Come," he said, and Lysbeth walked out.

At the door she turned to look, and there, in the center of the room, still stood her husband, tears streaming from his eyes, down a face radiant with an angelic smile, and his right hand lifted towards the heavens. And so she left him.

Presently Montalvo and Lysbeth were together again in the little room.

"I fear," he said, "from what I saw just now, that your mission has failed."

"It has failed," she answered in such a voice as might be expected from the lips of a corpse. "He does not know the secret you seek, and, therefore, he cannot tell it."

"I am sorry that I cannot believe you," said Montalvo, "so"— and he stretched his hand towards a bell upon the table.

"Stop," she said. "For your own sake stop. Man, will you really commit this awful, this useless crime? Think of the reckoning that must be paid here and hereafter; think of me, the woman you dishonored standing before the Judgment Seat of God, and bearing witness against your naked, shivering soul. Think of him, the good and harmless man whom you are about to cruelly butcher, crying in the ear of Christ, 'Look upon Juan de Montalvo, my pitiless murderer—'"

"Silence!" shouted Montalvo, shrinking back against the wall as though to avoid a sword thrust. "Silence, you ill-omened witch, with your talk of God and judgment. It is too late, I tell you, it is too late! My hands are too red with blood, my heart is too black with sin, upon the tablets of my mind is written too long a record. What more can this one crime matter? You simply don't understand, I must have money—money to buy my pleasures, money to make my last years happy and my deathbed soft. I have suffered enough, I have toiled enough, and I will win wealth and peace, who am now once more a beggar. Yes, had you twenty husbands, I would crush the life out of all of them, inch by inch, to win the gold that I desire."

As he spoke and the passions in him broke through their crust of cunning and reserve, his face changed. Now Lysbeth, watching for some sign of pity, knew that hope was dead, for his countenance was as it had been on that day twenty-six years ago when she sat at his side while the great race was run. There was the same starting eyeball, the same shining fangs appeared between the curled lips, and above them the moustachio, now grown gray, touched the high cheekbones. The fit passed, and Montalvo sank down gasping, while even in her woe and agony Lysbeth shuddered at this naked vision of a Satan-haunted soul.

"I have one more thing to ask," she said. "Since my husband must die, let me die with him. Will you refuse this also, and cause the cup of your crimes to flow over, and the last angel of God's mercy to flee away?"

"Yes," he answered. "You, woman with the evil eye, do you suppose that I wish you here to bring all the ills you prate of upon my head? I say that I am afraid of you. Why, for your sake, once, years ago, I made a vow to the Blessed Virgin that, whatever I worked on men, I would never again lift a hand against a woman. To that oath I look to help me at the last, for I have kept it sacredly, and am keeping it now, else by this time both you and the girl, Elsa, might have been stretched upon the rack. No, Lysbeth, get you gone, and take your curses with you," and he snatched and rang the bell.

A soldier entered the room, saluted, and asked his commands.

"Take this order," he said, "to the officer in charge of the heretic, Dirk van Goorl. It details the method of his execution. Let it be strictly adhered to, and a report made to me each morning of the condition of the prisoner. Now, show this lady from the prison."

The man saluted again and went out of the door. After him followed Lysbeth. She spoke no more, but as she passed she looked at Montalvo, and he knew well that though she might be gone, yet her curse remained behind.

The plague was on her, the plague was on her, her head and bones were racked with pain, and the swords of sorrow pierced her poor heart. But Lysbeth's mind was still clear, and her limbs still supported her. She reached her home and walked upstairs to the sitting room, commanding the servant to find the Heer Adrian and bid him join her there.

In the room was Elsa, who ran to her crying, "Is it true? Is it true?"

"It is true, Daughter, that Foy and Martin have escaped—"

"Oh! God is good!" wept the girl.

"And that my husband is a prisoner and condemned to death," added Lysbeth.

"Ah!" gasped Elsa, "I am selfish."

"It is natural that a woman should think first of the man she loves. No, do not come near me; I fear that I am stricken with the plague."

"I am not afraid of that," answered Elsa. "Did I never tell you? As a child I had it in The Hague."

"That, at least, is good news among much ill; but be silent, here comes Adrian, to whom I wish to speak. Nay, you need not leave us. It is best that you should learn the truth."

Moments later Adrian entered, and Elsa, watching everything, noticed that he looked sadly changed and ill.

"You sent for me, Mother," he began, with some attempt at his old pompous air. Then he caught sight of her face and was silent.

"I have been to the Gravensteen, Adrian," she said, "and I have news to tell you. As you may have heard, your brother Foy and our servant Martin have escaped, I know not wither. They escaped out of the very jaws of worse than death, out of the torture chamber, indeed, by killing that wretch who was known as the Professor, and the warden of the gate, Martin carrying Foy, who is wounded, upon his back."

"I am indeed rejoiced," cried Adrian excitedly.

"Hypocrite, be silent," hissed his mother, and he knew that the worst had overtaken him.

"My husband, your stepfather, has not escaped. He is in the prison still, for there I have just bidden him farewell, and the sentence upon him is that he shall be starved to death in a cell overlooking the kitchen."

"Oh! Oh!" cried Elsa, and Adrian groaned.

"It was my good, or my evil, fortune," went on Lysbeth, in a voice of ice, "to see the written evidence upon which my husband, your brother Foy, and Martin were condemned to death, on the grounds of heresy, rebellion, and the killing of the king's servants. At the foot of it, duly witnessed, stands the signature of—Adrian van Goorl."

Elsa's jaw fell. She stared at the traitor like one paralyzed, while Adrian, seizing the back of a chair, rested upon it, and rocked his body to and fro.

"Have you anything to say?" asked Lysbeth.

There was still one chance for the wretched man, had he been more dishonest than he was. He might have denied all knowledge of the signature. But to do this never occurred to him. Instead, he plunged into a wandering, scarcely intelligible, explanation, for even in his dreadful plight his vanity would not permit him to tell all the truth before Elsa. Moreover, in that fearful silence, soon he became utterly bewildered, until at length he hardly knew what he was saying, and in the end came to a full stop.

"I understand you to admit that you signed this paper in the house of Hague Simon, and in the presence of a man called Ramiro, he who is Governor of the prison, and who showed it to me," said Lysbeth, lifting her head which had sunk upon her breast.

"Yes, Mother, I signed something, but—"

"I wish to hear no more," interrupted Lysbeth. "Whether your motive was jealousy, or greed, or wickedness of heart, or fear, you signed that which, had you been a man, you would have allowed yourself to be torn to pieces with redhot pincers before you put a pen to it. Moreover, you gave your evidence fully and freely, for I have read it, and noted how you supported it with the severed finger of the woman Meg, which you stole from Foy's room. You are the murderer of your benefactor and of your mother's heart, and the would-be murderer of your brother and of Martin Roos."

Lysbeth paused for a few moments, and then added, "I do not curse you, I call down no ill upon you. Adrian, I give you over into the hands of God to deal with as He sees fit. Here is money," and, going to her desk, she took from it a heavy purse of gold that had been prepared for their flight and thrust it into the pocket of his doublet, wiping her fingers upon her kerchief after she had touched him. "Go hence and never let me see your face again. You were born of my body, you are my flesh and blood, but for this world and the next I renounce you, Adrian. Traitor and covenant breaker, I know you not. Murderer, get you gone."

Adrian fell upon the ground; he groveled before his mother trying to kiss the hem of her dress, while Elsa sobbed aloud hysterically. But Lysbeth spurned him in the face with her foot, saying, "Get you gone before I call up such servants as are left to me to thrust you into the street."

Then Adrian rose and with great gasps of agony, like some sore-wounded thing, crept from that awful and majestic presence of outraged motherhood. He crept down the stairs and away into the city.

When he had gone, Lysbeth took pen and paper and wrote in large letters these words:

Notice to all the good citizens of Leyden. Adrian, called van Goorl, upon whose written evidence his stepfather, Dirk van Goorl, his half-brother, Foy van Goorl, and the serving man, Martin Roos, have been condemned to death in the Gravensteen by torment, starvation, water, fire, and sword, is known here no longer. Lysbeth van Goorl.

Then she called a servant and gave orders that this paper

should be nailed upon the front door of the house where every passer-by might read it.

"It is done," she said. "Cease weeping, Elsa, and lead me to my bed, whence I pray God that I may never rise again."

Two days went by, and a fugitive rode into the city, a worn and wounded man, with horror stamped upon his face.

"What news?" cried the people in the market-place, recognizing him.

"Mechlin! Mechlin!" he gasped. "I come from Mechlin."

"What of Mechlin and its citizens?" asked Pieter van de Werff, stepping forward.

"Don Frederic has taken it. The Spaniards have butchered them; everyone, old and young, men, women, and children. They are all butchered. I escaped, but for two leagues and more I heard the sound of the death-wail of Mechlin. Give me to drink." They gave him drink, and by slow degrees, in broken sentences, he told the tale of one of the most awful crimes that has ever been committed by cruel men against innocent human beings in the name of Christ. It is written large in history; we need not repeat it here, except to say that it was one of the most outrageous acts of infamy in the bloody years of the Spanish Inquisition.

Then, when they knew the truth, a roar of wrath went up from the multitude of men of that great city, and a cry of vengeance for their slaughtered kin. They took arms, each what he had, the burgher his sword, the fisherman his fish-spear, the boor his ox-goad or his pick; leaders sprang up to command them, and there arose a shout of "To the gates! To the Gravensteen! Free the prisoners!"

They surged round the hateful place, thousands of them.

The drawbridge was up, but they bridged the moat. Some shots were fired at them, then the defense ceased. They battered in the massive doors, and, when these fell, rushed to the dens and loosed those who remained alive within them.

But they found no Spaniards, for by now Ramiro and his garrison had vanished away, whither they knew not. A voice cried,

"Dirk van Goorl, seek for Dirk van Goorl," soon they came to the chamber overlooking the courtyard, shouting, "Van Goorl, we are here!"

They broke in the door, and there they found him, lying upon his crude bed, his hands clasped, his face upturned, and already dead. His swift death was due to the fact that his captors left him unfed and unattended while his body was being attacked by the plague.

Book Three
THE HARVESTING

CHAPTER XXIII
FATHER AND SON

When Adrian left his mother's house in the Bree Straat, he wandered away in a state of confusion. He was so miserable that he could form no plans as to what he was to do or where he should go. Eventually he found himself at the foot of that great mound in Leyden, which is still known as the Burg, a strange place with a circular wall upon the top of it, said to have been constructed by the Romans. Up this mound he climbed, and throwing himself upon the grass under an oak that grew in one of the little recesses of those ancient walls, he buried his face in his hands and tried to think.

Think! How could he think? Whenever he shut his eyes there arose before them a vision of his mother's face, a face so fearful in its awesome and unnatural calm that vaguely he wondered how he, the outcast son, could have seen it and still been alive. Why did he live? Why was he not dead, he who had a sword at his side? Was it because of his innocence? He was not guilty of this dreadful crime. He had never intended to hand over Dirk van Goorl and Foy and Martin to the Inquisition. He had only talked about them to a man whom he believed to be a professor of judicial astrology, and who said that he could develop potions that would bend the wills of women. Could he help it if this fellow was really an officer of the Blood Council? Of course not. But, oh, why had he talked so much? Oh! Why had he signed that paper. Why did he not let them kill him first? He had signed, and explain as he would, he could never look an honest man in the face again, and less still a woman, if she knew the truth. So he was not still alive because he was innocent, since for all the good that this very doubtful innocence of his was likely to be even to his own conscience, he might as well have been guilty.

No, he lived on because before he died he had a hate to satisfy, a revenge to work. He would kill this dog, Ramiro, who had tricked him with his crystal gazing and his talk of friendship, who had frightened him with the threat of death until he became like some poor girl and for fear signed away his honor. He who prided himself upon his noble Spanish blood, the blood of warriors—this treacherous dog, who, having used him, had not hesitated to betray his shame to her from whom most of all it should have been hidden, and, for aught he knew, to the others also. Yes, if ever he met him—his own brother—Foy would spit upon him in the street; Foy, who was so open and honest, who could not understand into what degradation a man's nerves may drag him. And Martin, who had always mistrusted and despised him, why, if he found the chance, he would tear him limb from limb as a lion tears a lamb. And, worse still, Dirk van Goorl, the man who had befriended him, who raised him up although he was no son of his, but the child of some rival, would now sit there in his prison cell until he looked like a living skeleton. He would sit there by the window, watching the dishes of savory food pass in and out beneath him, and between the pangs of his long-drawn, hideous agony, put up his prayer to God to pay back to him, Adrian, all the woe that he had caused.

Oh! It was too much. Under the crushing weight of his suffering, his senses left him, and he stayed senseless for several minutes. When Adrian came to himself again, he felt cold, for already the autumn temperature had begun to fall, and there was a feel in the clear still air as of approaching frost. Also he was hungry (Dirk van Goorl, too, must be growing hungry now, he remembered) for he had eaten nothing since yesterday. He would go into the town, get food, and then make up his mind what he should do.

Accordingly, descending from the Burg, Adrian went to the best inn in Leyden, and, seated himself at a table under the trees that grew in a terrace outside. He beckoned the waiter to bring him food and drink. Unconsciously, for he was thinking of other things, in speaking to him, Adrian had assumed the haughty, Spanish hidalgo manner that was customary with him when addressing his inferiors. Even then he noticed, with the indignation of one who dwells upon his dignity, that this server did not bow, but merely called his order to someone in the house, and, turning his back upon him, began to speak to a man who was loitering near. Soon Adrian became aware that he was the subject of that conversation, for the two of them looked at him out of the corners of their eyes, and jerked their thumbs towards him.

Moreover, first one, then two, then quite a number of people stopped and joined in the conversation, which appeared to interest them very much. Boys came also, a dozen or more of them, and women of the fishwife status, and all of these looked at him out of the corners of their eyes, and from time to time jerked their thumbs towards him. Adrian began to feel uneasy and angered, but, drawing down his cap, and folding his arms upon his breast, he took no notice. Presently the server thrust his meal and drink before him with such clattering clumsiness that some of the drink splashed over upon the table.

"Be more careful, and wipe that up," said Adrian.

"Wipe it yourself," answered the man, rudely turning upon his heel.

Now Adrian was minded to be gone, but he was hungry and thirsty, so first, thought he, he would satisfy himself. Accordingly he lifted the tankard and took a long pull at it, when suddenly something struck the bottom of the vessel, jerking fluid over his face and doublet. He set it down with an oath and, laying his hand upon his sword hilt, asked who had done this. But the mob, which by now numbered fifty or sixty, and was gathered about him in a triple circle, made no answer. They stood there staring sullenly, and in the fading light their faces seemed dangerous and hostile.

He was frightened. What could they mean? Yes, he was frightened, but he determined to brave it out, and lifted the cover from his meat when something passed over his shoulder and fell into the dish, something stinking and abominable—to be particular, a dead cat. This was too much. Adrian sprang to his feet, and asked who dared thus to foul his food. The crowd did not jeer, did not even mock; it seemed too much in earnest for talk, but a voice at the back called out:

"Take it to Dirk van Goorl. He'll be willing to eat it soon."

Now Adrian understood. All these people knew of his infamy. The whole of Leyden knew that tale. His lips turned dry, and the sweat broke out upon his body. What should he do? Brave it out? He sat down, and the fierce ring of silent faces drew a pace or two nearer. He tried to bid the man to bring more meat, but the words stuck in his throat. Now the mob saw his fear, and believed this was a confirmation of his guilt, and decided to pass sentence on him in their hearts. At least, they who had been so quiet broke out into yells and hoots.

"Traitor! Spanish spy! Murderer!" they screamed. "Who gave evidence against our Dirk? Who sold his brother to the rack?"

Then came another shriller note. "Kill him." "Hang him up by the heels and stone him." " Twist off his tongue!" Out shot a hand, a long, skinny, female hand, and a harsh voice cried, "Give us a keepsake, my pretty boy!" Then there was a sharp wrench at his head, and he knew that from it a lock of hair was missing.

This was too much. He ought to have stopped there and let them kill him if they would, but a terror of these human wolves entered his soul and mastered him. To be trodden beneath those mire-stained feet, to be rent by those filthy hands, to be swung up living by the ankles to some pole and then carved piece-meal—he could not bear it. He drew his sword and turned to fly.

"Stop him," yelled the mob, whereon he lunged at them wildly, running a small boy through the arm.

The sight of the blood and the screech of the wounded lad settled the question, and those who were foremost came at him with a spring. But Adrian was swifter than they, and before a hand could be laid upon him, amidst a shower of stones and filth, he was speeding down the street. After him came the mob, and then began one of the finest manhunts that was ever known in Leyden.

From one street to another, round this turn and round that,

sped the quarry, and after him, a swiftly growing pack, came the hounds. Some women drew a washing-line across the street to trip him. Adrian jumped it like a deer. Four men got ahead and tried to cut him off. He dodged them. Down the Bree Straat he went, and on his mother's door he saw a paper and guessed what was written there. They were gaining, they were gaining, for always fresh ones took the place of those who grew weary. There was but one chance for him now. Near by ran the Rhine, and here it was wide and unbridged. Perhaps they would not follow him through the water. In he went, having no choice, and swam for his life. They threw stones and bits of wood at him, and called for bows but, happily for him, by now the night was falling fast, so that soon he vanished from their sight, and heard them crying to each other that he was drowned.

But Adrian was not drowned, for at that moment he was dragging himself painfully through the deep, greasy mud of the opposing bank and hiding among the old boats and lumber which were piled there, until his breath came to him again. But he could not stay long, for even if he had not been afraid that they would come and find him, it was too cold. So he crept away into the darkness.

Half an hour later, as Hague Simon and his consort Meg were seated at their evening meal, a knock came at the door, causing them to drop their knives and to look at each other suspiciously.

"Who can it be?" marveled Meg.

Simon shook his fat head. "I have no appointment," he murmured, "and I don't like strange visitors. There's a nasty spirit abroad in the town, a very nasty spirit."

"Go and see," said Meg.

"Go and see yourself, you—" and he added an epithet calculated to anger the meekest woman.

She answered it with an oath and a metal plate, which struck him in the face, but before the quarrel could go further again came the sound of raps, this time louder and more hurried. Then Black Meg went to open the door, while Simon took a knife and hid himself behind a curtain. After some whispering, Meg bade the visitor enter, and ushered him into the room, that same fateful room where the evidence was signed. Now he was in the light, and she saw him.

"Oh, come here," she gasped. "Simon, come and look at our little grandee." So Simon came, whereon the pair of them, clapping their hands to their ribs, burst into screams of laughter.

"It's the Don! Mother of Heaven! It is the Don," gurgled Simon.

Well might they laugh, they who had known Adrian in his pride and rich attire, for before them, crouching against the wall, was a miserable, bareheaded object, his hair stained with mud and rotten eggs, blood running from his temple where a stone had caught him, his garments a mass of filth and dripping water, one boot gone and his stockings torn to tatters. For a while the fugitive bore it, then suddenly, without a word, he drew the sword that still remained to him and rushed at the bestial looking Simon, who skipped away round the table.

"Stop laughing," he said, "or I will put this through you. I am a desperate man."

"You look it," said Simon, but he laughed no more, for the joke had become risky. "What do you want, Heer Adrian?"

"I want food and lodging for so long as I please to stop here. Don't be afraid, I have money to pay you."

"I am thinking that you are a dangerous guest," broke in Meg.

"I am," replied Adrian. "But I tell you that I shall be more dangerous outside. I was not the only one concerned in that matter of the evidence, and if they get me they will have you too. You understand?"

Meg nodded. She understood perfectly. For those of her trade, Leyden was becoming a risky habitation.

"We will accommodate you with our best, Mynheer," she said. "Come upstairs to the Master's room and put on some of his clothes. They will fit you well; you have much the same figure."

Adrian's breath caught in his throat.

"Is he here?" he asked.

"No, but he keeps his room," said Meg.

"Is he coming back? asked Adrian.

"I suppose so, sometime, as he keeps his room. Do you want to see him?"

"Very much, but you needn't mention it; my business can wait until we meet. Get my clothes washed and dried as quickly as you can, will you? I don't like wearing other men's garments."

A quarter of an hour later, Adrian, cleaned and clothed, different indeed to look on from the torn and hunted fugitive, re-entered the sittingroom. As he came clad in Ramiro's suit, Meg nudged her husband and whispered, "Like, ain't they?"

"Like as two devils in hell," Simon answered critically, then added, "Your food is ready; come Mynheer, and eat."

So Adrian ate and drank heartily enough, for the meat and drink were good, and he needed them. Also it encouraged him in a dull way to find that there was something left in which he could take pleasure, even if it were but eating and drinking. When he had finished, he told his story—or so much of it as he wished to tell—and afterwards went to bed wondering whether his hosts would murder him in his sleep for the purse of gold he carried, half hoping that they might indeed, and slept for twelve hours without stirring.

All that day and until the evening of the next, Adrian sat in the home of his hired friends recovering his strength and brooding over his fearful fall. Black Meg brought in news of what passed without; thus he learned that his mother had sickened with the plague, and that the sentence of starvation was being carried out upon the body of her husband, Dirk van Goorl. He learned also the details of the escape of Foy and Martin, which were the talk of all the city. In the eyes of the common people they had become heroes, and some local poet had made a song about them, which men were singing in the streets. Two verses of that song were devoted to him, Adrian. Indeed Black Meg repeated them to him word for word with a suppressed but malignant joy. Yes, this was what had happened; his brother had become a popular hero and he, Adrian, who in every way was so infinitely that brother's superior, an object of popular ridicule. And of all this the man, Ramiro, was the cause.

Well, he was waiting for Ramiro. That was why he risked his life by staying in Leyden. Sooner or later Ramiro would be bound to visit this haunt of his, and when he did, Adrian was determined to be ready to run him through. Of course in the struggle that must come, the man Ramiro, who doubtless was a skillful swordsman, might get the upper hand. It might be his, Adrian's throat, that was between the point and the ground. Well, it scarcely mattered—he did not care. At any rate, for this once he would play the man, and then let the devil take his own, himself, Ramiro, or both of them.

On the afternoon of the second day, Adrian heard shouting in the streets, and Hague Simon came in and told him that a man had arrived with bad news from Mechlin. What it was he could not say, he was going to find out. A couple of hours went by and there was more shouting, this time of a determined and ordered

nature. Then Black Meg appeared and informed him that the
news from Mechlin was that everyone in that unhappy town
had been massacred by the Spaniards; that further the people of
Leyden had risen and were marching to attack the Gravensteen.
Out she hurried again, for when the waters were stormy then
Black Meg must go fishing.

Another hour went by, and once more the street door was
opened with a key, to be carefully shut when the visitor had
entered.

Simon or Meg, thought Adrian, but as he could not be sure he
took the precaution of hiding himself behind the curtain. The
door of the room opened, and not Meg or Simon, but Ramiro
entered. So his opportunity had come!

The Master seemed disturbed. He sat down upon a chair
and wiped his brow with a silk handkerchief. Then aloud, and
shaking his fist in the air, he uttered a most comprehensive
curse upon everybody and everything, but especially upon the
citizens of Leyden. After this once more he lapsed into silence,
sitting, with his one eye fixed upon the floor, while he twisted
his waxed mustache with his hand.

Now was Adrian's chance. He had only to step out from behind
the curtain and run him through before he could rise from his
seat. The plan had great charms, and doubtless he might have
put it into execution had not Adrian's prideful instincts stayed
his hand. If he killed Ramiro thus, he would never know why
he had been killed, and above all things Adrian desired that he
should know. He wanted not only to avenge his wrongs, but to
let his adversary learn who was the better man. Also, to do him
justice, he preferred a fair fight to a secret stab delivered from
behind, for gentlemen fought, but assassins stabbed.

Still, as there were no witnesses, he might have been willing to waive this point, if only he could make sure that Ramiro
should learn the truth before he died. He thought of springing
out and wounding him, and then, after he had explained matters, finishing him off at his leisure. But how could he be sure
of his sword thrust, which might do too much or too little? No,
come what would, the matter must be concluded in the proper

fashion.

Choosing his opportunity, Adrian stepped from behind the hanging and placed himself between Ramiro and the door, the bolt of which he shut adroitly that no one might interrupt their interview. At the sound, Ramiro startled and looked up. In an instant he grasped the situation, and though his bronzed face paled, for he knew that his danger was great, rose to it, as might have been expected from a gentleman of his long and varied experience.

"The Heer Adrian called van Goorl, as I live!" he said. "My friend and pupil, I am glad to see you. But, if I might ask, although the times are rough, why in this narrow room do you wave about a naked rapier in that dangerous fashion?"

"Villain," answered Adrian, "you know why; you have betrayed me and mine, and I am dishonored, and now I am going to kill you in payment."

"I see," said Ramiro, "the van Goorl affair again. I can never be clear of it for even half an hour. Well, before you begin, it may interest you to know that your worthy stepfather, after two days of fasting, is by now, I suppose, free, for the rabble have stormed the Gravensteen. Truth, however, compels me to add that he is suffering badly from the plague, which your excellent mother, with a resource that does her credit, managed to communicate to him, thinking this end less disagreeable on the whole than that which the law had appointed."

Thus spoke Ramiro, slowly and with purpose, for all the while he was so maneuvering that the light from the lattice fell full upon his antagonist, leaving himself in the shadow, a position that experience taught him would prove an advantage in an emergency.

Adrian made no answer, but lifted his sword.

"One moment, young gentleman," went on Ramiro, drawing his own weapon and putting himself on guard. "Are you in earnest? Do you really wish to fight?"

"Yes," answered Adrian.

"What a fool you must be," mused Ramiro. "Why at your age should you seek to be rid of life, seeing that you have no more chance against me than a rat in a corner against a terrier dog? Look!" and suddenly he lunged most viciously straight at his heart. But Adrian was watching and parried the thrust.

"Ah!" continued Ramiro, "I knew you would do that, otherwise I should not have let fly, for all the angels know I do not wish to hurt you." But to himself he added, "The lad is more dangerous than I thought—my life hangs on it. The old fault, friend, too high, too high."

Then Adrian came at him like a tiger, and for the next thirty seconds nothing was heard in the room but the raspings of steel and the hard breathing of the two men.

At first, Adrian had somewhat the better of it, for his assault was fierce, and he forced the older and cooler man to be satisfied with guarding himself. He did more indeed, for quickly thrusting over Ramiro's guard, he wounded him slightly in the left arm. The sting of his hurt seemed to stir Ramiro's blood. He changed his tactics and began to attack in turn. Now, moreover, his skill and seasoned strength came to his aid; slowly but surely Adrian was driven back before him until his retreat in the narrow confines of the room became continuous. Suddenly, half from exhaustion and half because of a stumble, he reeled right across it, to the further wall. With a guttural sound of triumph, Ramiro sprang after him to make an end of him while his guard was down, caught his foot on a small stool which had been overset in the struggle, and fell prone to the ground.

This was Adrian's chance. In an instant, he was on him and had the point of his rapier at his throat. But he did not stab at once, not from any compunction, but because he wished his enemy to feel a little before he died, for, Adrian could be vindictive and bloodthirsty enough when his hate was roused. Rapidly Ramiro considered the position. In a physical sense he was helpless, for Adrian had one foot upon his breast, the other upon, his sword-arm, and the steel at his throat. Therefore, if time were given him, he must trust to his wit.

"Make ready, you are about to die," said Adrian.

"I think not," replied the prostrate Ramiro.

"Why not?" asked Adrian, astonished.

"If you will be so kind as to move that sword-point a little, it is pricking me. Thank you. Now I will tell you why. Because it is not usual for a son to stick his father as though he were a farmyard pig."

"Son? Father?" said Adrian. "Do you mean—?"

"Yes, I do mean that we have the happiness of filling those sacred relationships to each other."

"You lie," said Adrian.

"Let me stand up, and give me my sword, young sir, and you shall pay for that. Never yet did a man tell the Count Juan de Montalvo that he lied, and live."

"Prove it," said Adrian.

"In this position, to which misfortune, not skill, has reduced me, I can prove nothing. But if you doubt it, ask your mother, or your hosts, or consult the registers of the Groote Kerke, and see whether on a date, which I will give you, Juan de Montalvo was, or was not, married to Lysbeth van Hout, of which marriage was born one Adrian. Man, I will prove it to you. Had I not been your father, would you have been saved from the Inquisition with others, and should I not within the last five minutes have run you through twice over? For though you fought well, your swordsmanship is no match for mine."

"Even if you are my father, why should I not kill you, who have forced me to your will by threats of death, you who wronged and shamed me. It is because of you that I have been hunted through the streets like a mad dog, and made an out-cast!" And Adrian looked so fierce, and brought down his sword so close, that hope sank very low in Ramiro's heart.

"There are reasons that might occur to the religious," he said, "but I will give you one that will appeal to your self-interest. If you kill me, the curse that follows the parent will follow you to your last hour—of the beyond I say nothing."

"It would need to be a heavy one," answered Adrian, "if it was worse than that of which I know." But there was hesitation in his voice, for Ramiro, the skilful player upon human hearts, had struck the right string, and Adrian's superstitious nature answered to the note.

"Son," went on Ramiro, "be wise and hold your hand before
you do that for which all hell itself would cry shame upon you.
You think that I have been your enemy, but it is not so. All this
while, I have striven to work you good, but how can I talk lying
thus like a calf before its butcher? Take the swords, both of them,
and let me sit up, and I will tell you all my plans for the advantage of us both. Or if you wish it, thrust on and make an end. I
will not plead for my life with you. It is not worthy of an hidalgo
of Spain. Moreover, what is life to me who have known so many
sorrows that I should seek to cling to it? Oh! God, who seest all,
receive my soul, and I pray Thee pardon this youth his horrible
crime, for he is mad and foolish, and will live to sorrow for the
deed."

Since it was no further use to him, Ramiro had let the sword
fall from his hand.

Drawing it towards him with the point of his own weapon,
Adrian stooped and picked it up.

"Rise," he said, lifting his foot, "I can kill you afterwards, if
I wish."

Could he have looked into the heart of his new-found parent—as stiff and aching he staggered to his feet—the execution
would not have been long delayed.

"Oh, my young friend, you have given me a nasty fright,"
thought Ramiro to himself, "but it is over now, and if I don't pay
you in kind before I have finished with you, my sweet boy, your
name is not Adrian."

Ramiro rose, dusted his garments, seated himself deliberately,
and began to talk with great earnestness. It will be sufficient to
summarize his arguments. First of all, with the most convincing sincerity, he explained that when he had made use of him,
Adrian, he had no idea that he was his son. Of course, this was
a statement that will not bear a moment's examination, but
Ramiro's object was to gain time, and Adrian let it pass. Then he
explained that it was only after his mother had, not by his wish,
but accidentally, seen the written evidence upon which her husband was convicted, that he found out that Adrian van Goorl
was her child and his own. However, as he hurried to point out,

all these things were now ancient history that had no bearing on the present. Owing to the turbulent violence of the mob, which had just driven him from his post and fortress, he, Ramiro, was in temporary difficulties, and owing to other circumstances, he, Adrian, was, so far as his own party and people were concerned, an absolutely dishonored person. In this state of affairs, he had a suggestion to make. Let them join forces. Let the natural relationship that existed between them, and which had been so nearly severed by a sword thrust that both must have regretted, become real and tender. He, the father, had rank, although it suited him to sink it; he had wide experience, friends, intelligence, and the prospect of enormous wealth, which, of course, he could not expect to enjoy forever. On the other side, he, the son, had youth, great beauty of person, agreeable and distinguished manners, a high heart, the education of a young man of the world, and ambition and powers of mind that would carry him far. Also for the immediate future an object to gain, the affection of a lady whom all acknowledged to be as good as she was charming, and as charming as she was personally attractive.

"She hates me," broke in Adrian.

"Ah!" laughed Ramiro, "there speaks the voice of small experience. Fickle youth, so easily exalted and so easily depressed! Joyous, chequered youth! How many happy marriages have I known that began with such hate as this? Well, there it is, you must take my word for it. If you want to marry Elsa Brant, I can manage it for you, and if not, why, you can leave it alone."

Adrian reflected, then as his mind had a practical side, he put a question. "You spoke of the prospect of enormous wealth. What is it?"

"I will tell you, I will tell you," whispered his parent, looking around him cautiously, "It is the vast hoard of Hendrik Brant which, I intend to recover; indeed, my search for it has been at the root of all this trouble. And now, Son, you can see how open I have been with you, for if you marry Elsa that money will legally be your property, and I can only claim whatever it may please you to give me. Well, as to that question, in the spirit of the glorious motto of our race, 'Trust to God and me,' shall leave it to your sense of honor, which, whatever its troubles, has never yet failed the house of Montalvo. What does it matter to me who is the legal owner of the stuff, so long as it remains in the family?"

"Of course not," replied Adrian, loftily, "especially as I am not mercenary."

"Yes, well," went on Ramiro, "we have talked for a long while, and if I continue to live, there are affairs to which I ought to attend. You have heard all I have to say, and you have the swords in your hand, and, of course, I am only your prisoner on parole. So now, my Son, be so good as to settle this matter without further delay. Only, if you make up your mind to use the steel, allow me to show you where to thrust, as I do not wish to undergo any unnecessary discomfort."

Moments later, Adrian directed his father to stand up. In a casual manner, Ramiro rose and he stood before him and bowed in a very courtly and dignified fashion.

Adrian looked at him and hesitated. "I don't trust you," he said. "You have tricked me once and I daresay that you will trick me again. Also I don't think much of people who masquerade under false names and lay such traps as you laid to get my evidence against the rest of them. But I am in a bad place and without friends. I want to marry Elsa and recover my position in the world; also, as you know well, I can't cut the throat of my own father in cold blood," and he threw down one of the swords.

"Your decision is just such as I should have expected from my knowledge of your noble nature, son Adrian," remarked Ramiro as he picked up his weapon and restored it to the scabbard." But now, before we enter upon this perfect accord, I have two little stipulations to make on my side."

"What are they?" asked Adrian.

"First, that our friendship should be complete, such as ought to exist between a loving father and son, a friendship without reservations. Secondly, and this is a condition that I feel you may find more difficult. It is my earnest desire that we become united in our faith. Although fortune has led me into stony paths, and I fear some doubtful companions, there was always one thing which I have striven to cherish and keep pure, and that in turn has rewarded me for my devotion in many a dangerous hour, my religious belief. Now I am Catholic, and I could wish that my son should be Catholic also. These horrible errors, believe me, are as dangerous to the soul as just now they happen to be fatal to the body. May I hope that you, who were brought up but not born in heresy, will consent to receive instruction in the right faith?"

"Certainly you may," answered Adrian, almost with enthusiasm. "I have had enough of dreary meeting halls, endless Bible readings, psalm-singing, and the daily risk of being burned; indeed, from the time when I could think for myself I always wished to be a Catholic."

"Your words make me a happy man," answered Ramiro. "Allow me to unbolt the door, I hear our hosts. Worthy Simon and Vrouw, I make you parties to a solemn and joyful celebration. This young man is my son, and in token of my fatherly love, which he has been pleased to desire, I now take him in my arms and embrace him before you," and he suited the action to the word.

But Black Meg, watching his face in astonishment from over Adrian's shoulder, saw its one bright eye suddenly become eclipsed. Could it be that the noble Master had winked?

Chapter XXIV
Martha Preaches a Sermon and Tells a Secret

Two days after his reconciliation with his father, Adrian was admitted into membership in the Roman Catholic Church. His preparation had been short; indeed, it consisted of three interviews with a priest who was brought to the house at night. The good man found in his pupil so excellent a disposition and a mind so open to his teaching that, acting on a hint given him by Ramiro, who, for reasons of his own not altogether connected with religion, was really anxious to see his son a member of the true and Catholic Church, he declared it unnecessary to prolong the period of probation. Therefore, on the third day, as the dusk of evening was closing, for in the present state of public feeling they dared not go out while it was light, Adrian was taken to the baptistery of the Groote Kerke. Here he made confession of his sins to a certain priest known as Father Dominic, a simple ceremony, for although the list of them that he had prepared was long, its hearing proved short. Thus all his offences against his family, such as his betrayal of his stepfather, were waived aside by the priest as matters of no account; indeed, crimes of this nature, he discovered, to the sacerdotal eye wore the face of virtue. Other misdoings also, such as a young man might have upon his mind, were not thought weighty. What really was considered important proved to be the earnestness of his recantation of heretical errors, and when once his confessor was satisfied upon that point, the penitent soul was relieved by absolution full and free.

After this came the service of his baptism, which, because Ramiro wished it for a certain secret reason, was carried out with as much formal publicity as the circumstances would allow. Indeed, several priests assisted at the rite, Adrian's sponsors being his father and the estimable Hague Simon, who was paid a gold piece for his pains. While the sacrament was still in progress, a memorable incident occurred. From its commencement, the trampling and voices of a mob had been heard in the open space in front of the church, and now they began to hammer on the great doors and to cast stones at the painted windows, breaking the beautiful and ancient glass. At this moment, a beadle hurried into the baptistery, and whispered something in the ear of the priest which caused that ecclesiastic to turn pale and to conclude the service in a somewhat hasty fashion.

"What is it?" asked Ramiro.

"Alas! My son," said the priest, "these heretic dogs saw you, or our new-found brother—I know not which—enter this holy place, and a great mob of them have surrounded it, ravening for our blood."

"Then we had best be gone," said Ramiro.

"Señor, it is impossible," broke in the priest's assistant. "They watch every door. Hark!" and as he spoke there came the sound of battering on the oaken portals.

"Can your reverences make any suggestion?" asked Ramiro, "for we are in grave danger."

"Let us pray," said one of them in a trembling voice.

"By all means, but I should prefer to do so as I go. Fool, is there any hiding place in this church, or must we stop here to have our throats cut?" questioned Ramiro.

Then the priest, with white lips and knocking knees, whispered, "Follow me, all of you. Let us blow out the lights."

So the candles were extinguished, and in the darkness they grasped each other's hands and were led by the verger to an uncertain location. Across the wide spaces of the empty church they crawled, its echoing silence contrasting strangely with the muffled roar of angry voices without and the dull sound of battering on the doors. One of their number, the fat Abbé Dominic, became separated from them in the gloom, and wandered away down an arm of the vast transept, from where they could hear him calling to them. The priest called back, but Ramiro fiercely told him to be silent, adding:

"Are we all to be snared for the sake of one priest?" So they went on, until eventually in that great place his shouts grew fainter, and were lost in the roar of the multitude without.

"Here is the spot," declared the priest, after feeling the flooring with his hands, and by a dim ray of moonlight, which just then pierced the windows of the Church, Adrian saw that there was a hole in the pavement before him.

"Descend, there are steps," said their guide. "I will shut the stone," and one by one they passed down six or seven narrow steps into some dark place.

"Where are we?" asked Adrian, after he had pulled the stone close and joined them.

"In the family vault of the noble Count van Valkenburg, who was buried three days ago. Fortunately the masons have not yet come to cement down the stone. If your Excellencies find it too stuffy, you can get air by standing upon the coffin of the noble Count."

Adrian did find it close, and took the hint, to discover that in a line with his head was some ornate stonework, pierced with small apertures, the front doubtless of the marble tomb in the church above, for through them he could see the pale moon rays wavering on the pavement of the church. As he looked the priest at his side whispered, "Hark! The doors are down. Aid us, St. Pancras!" and falling upon his knees he began to pray very earnestly.

Yielding at last to the blows of the battering beam, the great portals had flown open with a crash, and now through them poured the mob. On they came with a rush and a roar, like that of the sea breaking through a dyke, carrying in their hands torches, lanterns hung on poles, axes, swords and staves, until at length they reached the screen of wonderful carved oak, on the top of which, rising to a height of sixty feet above the floor of the church, stood the great Rood, with the images of the Virgin and St. John on either side. Here, in just a matter of moments, the vastness and the silence of the place that they had known, every one, from childhood, with its echoing aisles, the moonlit windows, its consecrated lamps twinkling here and there like fisher lights upon the darkling waters, seemed to have a calming effect upon the crowd. Their passions seemed to flicker down and their wrath rested.

"They are not here, let us be going," said a voice.

"They are here," answered another voice, a woman's voice with a note of vengeance in it. "I tracked them to the doors, the Spanish murderer Ramiro, the spy Hague Simon, the traitor Adrian, called van Goorl, and the priests, the priests, the priests who butcher us."

"Let God deal with them," said the first voice, which to Adrian sounded familiar. "We have done enough and must not bring shame upon our cause by destroying property needlessly. Let us go home in peace for the murderers of Dirk van Goorl have escaped."

The crowd quickly responded, "The pastor is right. Obey Pastor Arentz." The more orderly of the multitude turned to depart, when suddenly, from the far end of the transept, arose a cry.

"Here's one of them. Catch him! Catch him!" A minute more and into the circle of the torchlight rushed the Abbé Dominic, his eyes bulging from his head with terror, his torn robe flapping on the ground. Exhausted and bewildered, he sat himself down, and groping the pedestal of an image began to cry for mercy, until a dozen fierce hands dragged him to his feet again.

"Let him go," said the voice of Pastor Arentz. "We fight against tyranny and murder, not against ministers. We do not have the Scriptural authority to return evil for evil. In the name of justice, I exhort you to stop this action and go to your homes."

"Hear me first," she answered who had spoken before, and men turned to see standing above them in the immense pulpit of the church, a fierce-eyed woman, gray-haired, skinny-armed, long-faced like a horse, and behind her two other women, each of whom held a torch in her right hand.

"It is the Mare," roared the multitude. "It is Martha of the Meer. Preach on, Martha. What's your text?"

"Whoso sheddeth man's blood by man shall his blood be shed," she answered in a ringing, solemn voice. Instantly, a deep silence fell upon the place.

"You call me the Mare," she went on. "Do you know how I got that name? They gave it me after they had shrivelled up my lips and marred the beauty of my face with irons. And do you know what they made me do? They made me carry my husband to the stake upon my back because they said that a horse must be ridden. And do you know who said this? *That priest who stands before you.*"

As the words left her lips, a yell of rage beat against the roof. Martha held up her thin hand, and again there was silence.

"He said it—the holy Father Dominic. Let him deny it if he can. What? He does not know me? Perchance not, for time and grief and madness and hot pincers have changed the face of Vrouw Martha van Muyden, who was called the Lily of Brussels. Ah, look at him now. He remembers the Lily of Brussels. He remembers her husband and her son also, for he burned them. O God, judge between us. O people, deal with that devil as God shall teach you."

"Who are the others? He who is called Ramiro, the Governor of the Gravensteen, the man who years ago would have thrust me beneath the ice to drown had not the Vrouw van Goorl bought my life; he who set her husband, Dirk van Goorl, the man you loved, to starve to death sniffing the steam of kitchens. O people, deal with that devil as God shall teach you."

"And the third, the half-Spaniard, the traitor Adrian called van Goorl, he who has come here tonight to be baptised anew into the bosom of the Holy Church; he who signed the evidence upon which Dirk was murdered." Once again, the roar of hate and rage went up and beat along the roof. O people, do with that devil also as God shall teach you."

"And the fourth, Hague Simon the spy, the man whose hands for years have smoked with innocent blood; Simon the Butcher—Simon the false witness."

"Enough, enough!" roared the crowd that remained. "A rope, a rope! Up with him to the arm of the Rood."

"My friends," cried Arentz "let the man go. 'Vengeance is mine, saith the Lord, and I will repay.'"

"Yes, but we will give him something on account," shouted a voice in bitter blasphemy. "Well climbed, Jan, well climbed," and they looked up to see, sixty feet above their heads, seated upon the arm of the lofty Rood, a man with a candle bound upon his brow and a coil of rope upon his back.

"He'll fall," said one.

"Pish!" answered another. "It is steeplejack Jan. He can hang on a wall like a fly."

"Look out for the ends of the rope," cried the thin voice above, and down they came.

"Spare me," screamed the wretched priest, as his executioners caught hold of him.

"Yes, yes, as you spared the Heer Jansen. A few months ago."

"It was to save his soul," groaned Dominic.

"Quite so, and now we are going to save yours; your own

medicine, father, your own medicine."

"Spare me, and I will tell you where the others are," said the priest.

"Well, where are they?" asked the self appointed ringleader, pushing his companions away.

"Hidden in the church, hidden in the church," responded the desperate priest.

"We knew that, you traitorous dog. Now is the time for your soul saving. Your rope awaits you, so move from this platform and run away with it. A horse should be ridden, father—your own saying—and an angel must learn to fly."

Thus ended the life of the infamous Dominic at the hands of avenging men. Without a doubt, this lawless and vengeful mob was fierce and bloody-minded, for the reader must not suppose that all the wickedness of those days lies on the heads of the Inquisition and the Spaniards. The adherents of the Protestant faith did evil things also, things that sound dreadful in our ears. In looking at this period, however, it must be stressed that the unrighteous acts of the Protestants compared to those of their oppressors, were as single trees compared to a forest full; also that they who worked them had been maddened by their sufferings. If our fathers, husbands and brothers had been burned at the stake, or murdered under the name of Jesus in the dens of the Inquisition, and if our wives and daughters had been shamed, if our houses had been burned, our goods taken, and our liberties trampled upon, then, my reader, is it not possible that we might have been cruel when our hour came? God alone knows if we would do any better managing our passions under similar circumstances.

Far aloft in the gloom there, swinging from the arm of the Cross, whose teachings his life had mocked, like some mutinous sailor at the yard of the vessel he had striven to betray, the priest hung dead, but his life did not appease the fury of the triumphant mob.

"The others," they cried, "find the others," and with torches and lanterns they hunted round the enormous church. They ascended the belfry, they rummaged the chapels, they explored the crypt; then, baffled, drew together in a countless crowd in the nave, shouting, gesticulating, suggesting.

"Get dogs," cried a voice. "Dogs will smell them out." And dogs were brought, which yapped and ran to and fro, but, confused by the multitude, and not knowing what to seek, found nothing. Then someone threw an image from a niche, and moments later, with a cry of "Down with the idols," the work of destruction began.

Fanatics sprang at the screens and the altars. All the carved work thereof they broke down with hatchet and hammer, they tore the hangings from the shrines, they found the sacred cups, and filling them with sacramental wine, drank with gusts of robust laughter. In the center of the church they built a bonfire and fed it with pictures, carvings, and oaken benches, so that it blazed and roared furiously. Moving on—for this mob did not come to steal but to work vengeance—they threw utensils of gold and silver, the priceless jeweled offerings of generations, and danced around its flames in triumph while from every side came the crash of falling statues and the tinkling of shattered glass.

The light of that furnace shone through the lattice stonework of the tomb, and in its lurid and ominous glare, Adrian beheld the faces of those who refuged with him. What a picture it was; the niches filled with crumbling boxes, and the white gleam of human bones that here and there had fallen from them. The bright furnishings and velvet pall of the coffin of the newcomer on which he stood—and then those faces. The priests, still crouched in corners, rolling on the ground, their white lips muttering who knows what; Hague Simon hugging a coffin in a niche, as a drowning man hugs a plank, and, standing in the midst of them, calm, sardonic and watchful, a drawn rapier in his hand, his father Ramiro.

"We are lost," moaned a priest, losing control of himself. "We are lost. They will kill us as they have killed the holy Abbé."

"We are not lost," hissed Ramiro, "we are quite safe, but, friend, if you open that cursed mouth of yours again it shall be for the last time," and he lifted his sword, saying, "Silence. He who speaks, dies."

How long did it last? Was it one hour, or two or three? None of them knew, but eventually the image-breaking was done, and it came to an end. The interior of the church, with all its wealth and adornments, was utterly destroyed, but the flames did not reach the roof, and the walls could not catch fire.

By degrees, the lawless mob wearied; there seemed to be nothing more to break, and the smoke choked them. Two or three at a time they left the ravaged place, and once more it became solemn and empty; a symbol of peace conquering tumult, of the patience and purpose of God triumphant over the passions and ravings of man. Little curls of smoke went up from the smoldering fire; now and again a fragment of shattered stonework fell with an echoing crash, as the cold wind of the coming winter sighed through the gaping windows. The deed was done. The revenge of a tortured multitude had set its seal upon the ancient building, and once more quiet brooded upon the place, and the shafts of the sweet moonlight pierced its desecrated solitude.

One by one, the fugitives crept from the shelter of the tomb, crept across the transepts to the little door of the baptistery, and with much peeping and precaution, out into the night, to vanish this way and that, hugging their hearts as though to feel whether they still beat safely in their bosoms.

As he passed the Rood, Adrian looked up, and there above the broken carvings and the shattered statue of the Virgin, hung the calm face of the Savior crowned with thorns. There, too, not far from it, looking small and somewhat piteous at that great height, and revolving slowly in the stiff breeze caused by the broken windows, hung another face, the horrid face of the Abbé Dominic, lately the envied, prosperous dignitary who not four hours before had baptized him into the bosom of the Catholic Church. It terrified Adrian; no ghost could have frightened him more, but he set his teeth and staggered on, guided by the light gleaming faintly from the sword of Ramiro—to whatever haven that sword should lead him.

Before dawn broke, Ramiro had led Adrian out of Leyden.

It was after ten o'clock that night when a woman, wrapped in a rough frieze coat, knocked at the door of the house in the Bree Straat and asked for the Vrouw van Goorl.

"My mistress lies between life and death with the plague," answered the servant. "Get you gone from this house, whoever you are."

"I do not fear the plague," said the visitor. "Is the Jufvrouw Elsa Brant still up? Then tell her that Martha, called the Mare, would speak with her."

"She can see none at such an hour," answered the servant.

"Tell her I come from Foy van Goorl."

"Enter," said the servant wondering, and shut the door behind her.

A minute later Elsa, pale-faced, worn, but still beautiful, rushed into the waiting room, gasping, "What news? Does he live? Is he well?"

"He lives, lady, but he is not well, for the wound in his thigh has festered, and he cannot walk, or even stand. Nay, have no fear, time and clean dressing will heal him, and he lies in a safe place."

In the rapture of her relief, Elsa seized the woman's hand and would have kissed it.

"Touch it not, it is bloodstained," said Martha, drawing her hand away.

"Blood? Whose blood is on it?" asked Elsa, shrinking back.

"Whose blood?" answered Martha with a hollow laugh. "Why that of many a Spanish man. Why do you think that the Mare gallops at night? Ask it of the Spaniards who travel by the Haarlemer Meer. Aye, and now Red Martin is with me and we run together, taking our tithe where we can gather it. Too many of our people forget that we are at war with Spain and with Rome."

"Oh! Tell me no more," said Elsa. "From day to day it is ever the same tale, a tale of death. Nay, I know your wrongs have driven you mad, but that a woman should slay—"

"A woman! I am no woman. My womanhood died with my husband and my son. Girl, I tell you that I am no woman; I am a Sword of God appointed to a special mission in this war. And so to the end I kill, and kill, and kill until the hour when I am killed. Go, look in the church yonder, and see who hangs to the high arm of the Rood—the tyrant Dominic. Well, I sent him there tonight. Ramiro and Adrian called van Goorl, and Simon the spy should have joined him there, only I could not find them because their hour has not come. But the idols are down and the paintings burnt, and the gold, silver, and jewels are cast upon the dung-heap. Swept and garnished is the temple, made clean and fit for the Lord to dwell in."

"Made clean with the blood of murdered priests, and fit by the smoke of unlawful destruction?" broke in Elsa. "Oh, Woman, how can you do such wicked things and not be afraid?"

"Afraid?" she answered. "Have I not told you that we are at war with those that are at war with us? Those who have passed through hell have no more fear. Death I seek, and when judgment comes I will say to the Lord: What have I done that the Voice that speaks to me at night did not tell me to do? Look down, the blood of my husband and my son still smokes upon the ground. Hearken, Lord God, it cries to Thee for vengeance!" and as she spoke she lifted her blackened hands and shook them. Then she went on for a moment before Elsa began to speak.

"Tell me more of Foy and Martin," said Elsa, who was frightened and bewildered.

At her words, a change seemed to come over this woman, at once an object of pity and of terror, for the scream went out of her voice and she answered quietly:

"They reached me safe enough five days ago, Red Martin carrying Foy upon his back. From afar I saw him, and knew him by his size and beard. And oh, when I heard his tale I laughed as I have not laughed since I was young."

"Tell it to me," said Elsa.

And she told it while the girl listened with clasped hands.

"Oh, it was brave, brave," she murmured. "Red Martin overpowering five men at the door while Foy, weak and wounded, slayed the warder. Was there ever such a story?"

"Men are brave and desperate with the torture pit behind

them," answered Martha grimly, "but they did well, and now they are safe with me where no Spaniard can find them unless they hunt in great companies after the ice forms and the reeds are dead."

"Would that I could be there also," said Elsa, "but I tend his mother who is very sick, so sick that I do not know whether she will live or die."

"Nay, you are best here among your people," answered Martha. "And now that the Spaniards are driven out, here Foy shall return also so soon as it is safe for him to travel. But as yet he cannot stir, and Red Martin stays to watch him. Before long, however, he must move, for I have tidings that the Spaniards are about to besiege Haarlem with a great army, and then the Meer will be no longer safe for us, and I shall leave it to fight with the Haarlem folk."

"And Foy and Martin will return?" asked Elsa.

"I think so, if they are not stopped."

"Stopped?" and she put her hand upon her heart.

"The times are rough, Jufvrouw Elsa. Who that breathes the air one morning can know what breath will pass his nostrils at the nightfall? The times are rough, and Death is king of them. The hoard of Hendrik Brant is not forgotten, nor those who have its key. Ramiro slipped through my hands tonight, and doubtless by now is far away from Leyden seeking the treasure."

"The treasure! Oh, that thrice accursed treasure!" broke in Elsa, shivering as though beneath an icy wind. "Would that we were rid of it."

"That you cannot do until it is appointed, for is this not the heritage your father died to save? Listen. Do you know, lady, where it lies hid?" and she dropped her voice to a whisper.

Elsa shook her head, saying,"I neither know nor wish to know."

"Still it is best that you should be told, for we three who have the secret may be killed, every one of us—no, not the place, but where to seek a clue to the place."

Elsa looked at her questioningly, and Martha, leaning forward, whispered in her ear, "It lies in the hilt of the sword

Silence. If Red Martin should be taken or killed, seek out his sword and open the hilt. Do you understand?"

Elsa nodded and answered. "But if aught happens to Martin the sword may be lost."

Martha shrugged her shoulders. "Then the treasure will be lost also, that is if I am gone. It is as God wills. But at least in name you are the heirness, and you should know where to find its secret, which may serve you or your country in good stead in time to come. I give you no paper, I tell you only where to seek a paper, and now I must be gone to reach the borders of the Meer by daybreak. Have you any message for your love, lady?"

"I would write a word, if you can wait. They will bring you food."

"Good. Write on and I will eat. Love for the young and meat for the old, and for both let God be thanked."

CHAPTER XXV
THE RED MILL

A week had gone by since Adrian and his companions had left Leyden for a remote setting called the Red Mill. After a week's experience in that delectable dwelling and its neighborhood, Adrian began to grow weary of the place. Nine or ten Dutch miles to the northwest of Haarlem is a place called Velsen, situated on the borders of the sand dunes, to the south of a great drainage dyke. Velsen was little more than a deserted village. In fact, all of the land in this region was deserted, for some years before a Spanish force had passed through it, burning, slaying, laying waste, so that few were left to tend the windmills and repair the dyke. Holland is a country won from swamps and seas, and if the water is not pumped out of it, and the ditches are not cleaned, very quickly it relapses into marsh; indeed, it is a blessing when the ocean, bursting through the feeble barriers reared by the industry of man, does not turn it into vast lagoons of salt water.

Once the Red Mill had been a pumping station, which, when the huge sails of the windmill worked, delivered the water from the fertile meadows into the great dyke, whence it ran through floodgates to the North Sea. Now, although the embankment of this dyke still held, the meadows had gone back into swamps. Rising out of these—for it was situated upon a low mound of earth—raised, doubtless, as a point of refuge by marsh-dwellers who lived and died long ago, towered the wreck of a narrow-waisted windmill, built of brick below and wood above. This windmill cast a very lonesome and commanding appearance in its gaunt solitude. There were no houses near it, and no cattle grazed around its base. It was a dead thing in a dead landscape. To the left, but separated from it by a wide and slimy dyke, stretched an arid area of sand dunes, clothed with sparse grass, which grew like bristles upon the back of a wild hog. Beyond these dunes, the ocean roared and moaned as the wind and weather stirred its depths. In front, not fifty paces away, ran the big dyke like a raised road, secured by embankments, and discharging day by day its millions of gallons of water into the sea. But these embankments were weakening now, and here and there could be seen a spot that looked as though a small crack had already developed, for a pile of brown earth had been heaped up in these areas leaving them still standing, and as yet sufficient for their purpose. To the right again and behind, were more marshes, broken only in the distance by the towers of Haarlem and the spires of village churches.

Such was the refuge to which Ramiro and his son Adrian had been led by Hague Simon and Black Meg, after they escaped with their lives from Leyden upon the night of the image-breaking in the church. On the journey to Red Mill, Adrian asked no questions as to their destination. He was too broken in heart and too shaken in body to be curious; life in those days had become for him a confusing blackness out of which appeared vengeful, red-handed figures, that echoed dismal, despairing voices calling him to doom.

They came to the place and found its great basement and the floors above, or some of them, furnished after a fashion. The mill had been inhabited recently, as Adrian gathered, by smugglers or thieves with whom Meg and Simon were in alliance, or by some such outcast evildoers who knew that here the arm of the law could not reach them. Though, indeed, while the Duke of Alva ruled in the Netherlands there was little law to be feared except by those who were rich or who dared to worship God in a manner unapproved by Rome.

"Why have we come here—father," Adrian was about to ask, but the word stuck in his throat.

Ramiro shrugged his shoulders and looked round him with his one critical eye.

"Because our guides and friends, the worthy Simon and his wife, assure me that in this spot alone our throats are for the present safe. And by St. Pancras, after what we saw in the church yonder I am inclined to agree with them. He looked a poor thing up under the roof there, the holy Father Dominic, hanging there like a black spider from the end of his cord. My backbone aches when I think of him."

"And how long are we to stop here?" asked Adrian.

"Until Don Frederic has taken Haarlem and these fat Hollanders, or those who are left of them, lick our boots for mercy." Then he ground his teeth, and added, "Son, do you play cards? Good, well let us have a game. Here are dice; it will serve to turn our thoughts. Now then, a hundred guilders on it."

So they played and Adrian won, whereon, to his amazement, his father paid him the money.

"What is the use of that?" asked Adrian.

"Gentlemen should always pay their debts at cards."

"And if they cannot?" inquired the son.

"Then they must keep score of the amount and discharge it when they are able. Look you, young man, everything else you may forget, but what you lose over the dice is a debt of honor. There lives no man who can say that I cheated him out of a guilder at cards, though I fear some others have my name standing in their books."

When they rose from their game that night, Adrian had won between three and four hundred florins. The next day, his winnings amounted to a thousand florins, for which his father gave him a carefully executed note. During the third sitting the game changed, or perhaps skill began to tell, and he lost two thousand florins. These he paid up by returning his father's note, his own winnings, and all the balance of the purse of gold that his mother had given to him when he was driven from the house, so that now he was practically penniless.

The rest of the history may be guessed. At every game the stakes were increased, for since Adrian could not pay, it was a matter of indifference to him how much he wagered. Moreover, he found a kind of mild excitement in playing at the handling of such great sums of money. By the end of a week, he had lost a queen's dowry. As they rose from the table that night his father filled in the usual form, requested him to be so good as to sign it, and bid a sour-faced woman who had arrived at the mill—Adrian knew not when—to put her name as witness.

"What is the use of this farce?" asked Adrian. "Brant's treasure would scarcely pay that bill."

His father pricked his ears.

"Indeed? I lay it at as much again. What is the use? Who knows. One day you might become rich, for, as the great Emperor said, 'Fortune is a woman who reserves her favors for the young,' and then, doubtless, being the man of honor that you are, you would wish to pay your old gambling debts."

"Oh, yes, I would pay if I could," answered Adrian with a yawn. "But it seems hardly worth while talking about, does it?" and he sauntered out of the place into the open air.

His father rose, and, standing by the great peat fire, watched him depart thoughtfully.

"Let me take stock of the position," he said to himself. "The dear child hasn't a farthing left; therefore, although he is getting bored, he can't run away. Moreover, he owes me more money than I ever saw; therefore, if he should chance to become the husband of the Jufvrouw Brant, and the legal owner of her parent's wealth, whatever disagreements may ensue between him and me, I shall have earned my share of it in a clean and gentlemanly fashion. If, on the other hand, it should become necessary for me to marry the young lady, which God forbid, at least no harm is done, and he will have had the advantage of some valuable lessons from the most accomplished card player in Spain.

"And now what we need to enliven this detestable place is the presence of Beauty herself. Our worthy friends should be back soon, bringing their sheaves with them, let us hope, for otherwise matters will be complicated. Let me see, have I thought of everything, for in such affairs one oversight can be fatal. Adrian is a Catholic, therefore, can contract a legal marriage under the Proclamations—it was lucky I remembered that point of law, though it nearly cost us all our lives—and the priest, I can summon him to his place, a discreet man, who won't hear if the lady says no, yet one who is established beyond question with the power and virtue of his holy office. No, I have nothing to reproach myself with in the way of preparation, nothing at all. I have sown the seed well and truly. It remains only for Providence to give the increase. Well, it is time that you met with a little success and settled down, for you have worked hard, Juan, my friend, and you are getting old—yes, Juan, you are getting old. Bah! What a hole and what weather!" concluded Montalvo as he positioned himself by the fireside to doze away his boredom.

When Adrian shut the door behind him, the late November day was drawing to its close, and between the rifts in the sullen snow clouds, now and again, a beam from the setting sun struck upon the tall, skeleton-like sails of the mill, through which the wind rushed with a screaming noise. Adrian had intended to walk on the marsh, but finding it too sodden, he crossed the western dyke by means of a board laid from bank to bank, and struck into the sand dunes beyond. In the summer, when the air was still and flowers bloomed and larks sang, these dunes were fantastic and almost unnatural in appearance, with their deep, wind-scooped hollows of pallid sand, their sharp angles, miniature cliffs, and their crests crowned with coarse grasses. But now, beneath the dull pall of the winter sky, no spot in the world could have been more lonesome or more desolate. Only the voices of creation remained in all their majesty, the dreary screams and moan of the rushing wind, and above it, now low and now voluminous as the gale veered, the deep and constant roar of the ocean.

Adrian reached the highest crest of the ridge, and the sea suddenly became visible, a vast, slate-colored expanse, twisted here and there into heaps, hollowed here and there into valleys, and broken everywhere with angry lines and areas of white. Some might have found a kind of consolation in this sight, for the actions and moods of the sea in its greatness command a mastery of our senses and stun or hush to silence the petty turmoil of our souls. This, at least, is so with those who have the capacity to meditate on the glory of God's creation, and pray for the grace to appreciate it.

In Adrian's case, however, the strangeness of the sand hills, the grandeur of the seascape with the bitter wind that blew, and the solitude that brooded over all served only to exasperate nerves that already were strained almost to breaking.

Why had his father brought him to this hideous swamp bordered by a sailless sea? To save their lives from the fury of the mob? This he understood, but there was more in it than that, some plot that he did not understand, and which the ruffian, Hague Simon, along with his companion, had gone away to execute. Meanwhile, he must sit here day after day playing cards with the wretch Ramiro, whom, for no fault of his own, God had chosen out to be his parent. By the way, why was the man so fond of playing cards? And what was the meaning of all that nonsense about promissory notes? Yes, here he must sit, and for company he had the sense of his unalterable shame, the memory of his mother's face as she spurned and rejected him, the vision of the woman whom he loved and had lost, and the ghost of Dirk van Goorl.

He shivered as he thought of it. His hair lifted and his lip twitched involuntarily, for to Adrian's racked nerves and distorted vision this ghost of the good man whom he had betrayed was no child of fantasy. He had woken in the night and seen it standing at his bedside, plague-defiled and hunger-wasted, and because of it he dreaded to sleep alone, especially in that creaking, rat-haunted mill, whose every board seemed charged with some tale of death and blood. Heavens! At this very moment he thought he could hear that dead voice calling down the gale. No, it must be the sea birds calling. Perhaps they are calling him to go home? Home, that place home—with not even a priest near to confess to and be comforted!

Thanks be to the saints! The wind had dropped a little, but now in place of it came the snow, dense, whirling, white; so dense indeed that he could scarcely see his path. What an end that would be, to be frozen to death in the snow on these sand hills while the spirit of Dirk van Goorl sat near and watched him die with those hollow, hungry eyes. The sweat came upon Adrian's forehead at the thought, and he broke into a run, heading for the bank of the great dyke that pierced the dunes half a mile or so away, the bank that must, he knew, lead him to the mill. He reached it and trudged along what had been the tow-path, though now it was overgrown with weeds and rushes. It was not a pleasant journey, for the twilight had closed in with speed, and the thick flakes, which seemed to leap into his face and sting him, turned it into a darkness mottled with faint white. Still he stumbled forward with bent head and close-wrapped cloak until he judged that he must be near to the mill, and halted staring through the gloom.

Just then the snow ceased for a while and light crept back to the cold face of the earth, showing Adrian that he had done well to halt. In front of where he stood, within a few paces of his feet, he noted that the lower part of the bank had slipped away, washed from the stone core with which it was faced by a slow and neglected flow of water. Had he walked on, he would have fallen his own height or more into a slough of mud, from where he might or might not have been able to extricate himself. As it was, however, by such light as remained, he could crawl upon the outside of the stonework that was still held in place with old struts of timber that, until they had been compromised by the slow and constant leakage, had been buried and supported in the vanished earthwork. It was not a pleasant bridge, how-ever, for to the right lay the mud-bottomed gulf, and to the left, almost level with his feet, were the black and peaty waters of the rain-fed dyke pouring onwards to the sea.

"Next flood this will go," thought Adrian to himself, "and then the marsh will become a meer, which will be bad for whomever happens to be living in the Red Mill." He was on firm ground again now, and there, looming tall and spectral against the gloom, not five hundred yards away, rose the gaunt sails of the mill. To reach it he walked on six score paces or more to the little landing way, whence a raised path ran to the building. As he drew near to it, he was astonished to hear the rattle of oars working in rowlocks and a man's voice say, "Steady, here is the place, praise the Saints! Now, then, out passengers and let us be gone."

Adrian, whom events had made timid, drew beneath the shadow of the bank and watched, while from the dim outline of the boat arose three figures, or rather two figures arose, dragging the third between them.

"Hold her," said a voice that seemed familiar, "while I give these men their hire," and there followed a noise of clinking coin, mingled with some oaths and grumbling about the weather and the distance, which were abated with more coin. Then again the oars rattled and the boat was pushed off, whereon a sweet voice cried in agonized tones, "Sirs, you who have wives and daughters, will you leave me in the hands of these wretches? In the name of God take pity upon my helplessness."

"It is a shame, and she so fair a maid," grumbled another thick and raucous voice, but the steersman cried, "Mind your business, Marsh Jan. We have done our job and got our pay, so leave the gentry to settle their own love affairs. Goodnight to you, passengers. Give way, give way," and the boat swung round and vanished into the gloom.

For a moment, Adrian's heart stood still; then he sprang forward to see before him Hague Simon, the Butcher, Black Meg his wife, and between them a bundle wrapped in shawls.

"What is this?" he asked.

"You ought to know, Heer Adrian," answered Black Meg with a chuckle, "seeing that this charming piece of goods has been brought all the way from Leyden, regardless of expense, for your special benefit."

The bundle lifted its head, and the faint light shone upon the white and terrified face of Elsa Brant.

"May God reward you for this evil deed, Adrian, called van Goorl," said the pitiful voice.

"This deed! What deed?" he stammered in answer. "I know nothing of it, Elsa Brant."

"You know nothing of it? Yet it was done in your name, and you are here to receive me, who was kidnapped as I walked outside Leyden to be dragged hither with force by these monsters. Oh, have you no heart and no fear of judgment that you can speak thus?"

"Free her!" roared Adrian, rushing at the Butcher while noting a knife gleaming in his hand and another in that of Black Meg.

"Stop your nonsense, Master Adrian, and stand back. If you have anything to say, say it to your father, the Count. Come, let us pass, for we are cold and weary," and taking Elsa by the elbows they brushed past him, nor, indeed, even had he not been too bewildered to interfere, could Adrian have stopped them, for he was unarmed. Besides, what would be the use, seeing that the boat had gone and that they were alone on a winter's night in the wind-swept wilderness, with no refuge for miles save such as the mill house could afford. So Adrian bent his head, for the snow had begun to fall again, and, sick at heart, followed them along the path. Now he finally understood why they had come to the Red Mill.

Simon opened the door and entered, but Elsa hung back at its ominous threshold. She even tried to struggle a little, poor girl, whereon the ruffian in front jerked her towards him with an oath, so that she caught her foot and fell upon her face. This was too much for Adrian. Springing forward, he struck the Butcher full in the mouth with his fist. The next moment, they were rolling over each other upon the floor, struggling fiercely for the knife which Simon held.

During all her life, Elsa never forgot that scene. Behind her the howling blackness of the night and the open door, through which flake by flake the snow leapt into the light. In front the large round room, fashioned from the basement of the mill, lit only by the great fire of turfs and a single horn lantern, hung from the ceiling, which was ribbed with beams of black and massive oak. And there, in that forbidding place, which rocked and quivered as the gale caught the tall arms of the mill above, seated by the hearth in a rude chair of wood and sleeping, was Ramiro, the Spanish sleuth-hound. It was this servant of Satan who had hunted down her father, he whom above every other she held in horror and in hate; and the two, Adrian and the spy, at death-grips on the floor, between them the sheen of a naked knife.

Ramiro awoke at the noise, and there was fear on his face as though some ill dream lingered in his brain. In an instant he saw and understood.

"I will run the man through who strikes another blow," he said, in a cold clear voice as he drew his sword. "Stand up, you fools, and tell me what this means."

"It means that this brute beast just now threw Elsa Brant upon her face," gasped Adrian as he rose, "and I punished him."

"It is a lie," hissed the other. "I pulled the girl on, that is all, and so would you have done, if you had been cursed with such a wildcat for twenty-four hours. Why, when we took her she was more trouble to hold than any man."

"Oh! I understand," interrupted Ramiro, who had recovered his composure. "A little maidenly reluctance, that is all, my worthy Simon, and as for this young gentleman, a little lover-like anxiety—doubtless in bygone years you have felt the same," and he glanced mockingly at Black Meg. "So do not be too ready to take offence, good Simon. Youth will be youth."

"And youth will get a knife between its ribs if it is not careful," grumbled Hague Simon, as he spat out a piece of broken tooth.

"Why am I brought here, Señor," broke in Elsa, "in defiance of laws and justice?"

"Laws! I did not know that there were any left in the Netherlands. Justice! Well, all is fair in love and war, as any lady will admit. And the reason why—I think you must ask Adrian, he knows more about it than I do."

"He says that he knows nothing, Señor," responded Elsa.

"Does he, the rogue? Does he indeed? Well, it would be rude to contradict him, wouldn't it, so I for one unreservedly accept his statement that he knows nothing, and I advise you to do the same. No, no, my boy, do not trouble to explain, we all quite understand. Now, my good dame," he went on addressing the serving-woman who had entered the place, "take this young lady to the best room you have above. And, listen, both of you, she is to be treated with all kindness, do you hear, for if any harm comes to her, either at your hands or her own, by Heaven, you shall pay for it to the last drop of your blood. Now, no excuses and no mistakes."

The two women, Meg and the other, nodded and motioned to Elsa to accompany them. She considered a moment, looking first at Ramiro and next at Adrian. Then her head dropped upon her breast, and turning without a word she followed them up the creaking oaken stair that rose from a niche near the wall of the inglenook.

"Father," said Adrian when the massive door had closed behind her and they were left alone. "Father, for I suppose that I must call you so."

"There is not the slightest necessity," broke in Ramiro. "Facts, my dear son, need not always be paraded in the cold light of day, fortunately. But, proceed."

"What does all this mean?" questioned Adrian.

"I wish I could tell you. It appears to mean, however, that without any effort upon your part, for you seem to me a young man singularly devoid of resource, your love affairs are prospering beyond expectation."

"I have had nothing to do with the business. I wash my hands of it."

"That is as well. Some sensitive people might think they need a deal of washing. You young fool," he went on, dropping his mocking manner, "listen to me. You are in love with this pink and white piece of goods, and I have brought her here for you to marry."

"And I refuse to marry her against her will," insisted the son.

"As to that you can please yourself. But somebody has got to marry her—you, or I."

"You—you!" gasped Adrian.

"Quite so. The adventure is not one, to be frank, that attracts me. At my age, memories are sufficient. But material interests must be attended to, so if you decline—well, I am still eligible and hearty. Do you see the point?"

"No, what is it?" asked Adrian in a frustrated manner.

"It is a sound title to the inheritance of the departed Hendrik Brant. That wealth we might, it is true, obtain by artifice or by arms, but how much better that it should come into the family in a regular fashion, thereby ousting the claim of the Crown. Things in this country are disturbed at present, but they will not always be disturbed, for in the end somebody must give way and order will prevail. Then questions might be asked, for persons in possession of great riches are always the mark of envy. But if the heiress is married to a good Catholic and loyal subject of the king, who can challenge the rights sanctified by the laws of God and man? Think it over, my dear Adrian, think it over. Stepmother or wife—you can take your choice."

With impotent rage, with turmoil of heart and torment of conscience, Adrian did think it over. All that night he thought, tossing on his rat-haunted bed, while without the snow whirled and the wind beat. If he did not marry Elsa, his father would, and there could be no doubt as to which of these alternatives would be best and happiest for her. Elsa married to that wicked, cynical, devil-possessed, battered, fortune-hunting adventurer with a nameless past! This must be prevented at any cost. With his father, her lot must be a hell. With himself, after a period of storm and doubt perhaps, it could scarcely be other than happy, for was he not young, handsome, sympathetic, and—devoted? Ah, there was the real point. He loved this lady with all the earnestness of which his nature was capable, and the thought of her passing into the possession of another man gave him the acutest anguish. That the man should be Foy, his half-brother, was bad enough. That it should be Ramiro, his father, was unthinkable.

At breakfast the following morning, when Elsa did not appear, the pair met.

"You look pale, Adrian," said his father presently, "I fear that this wild weather kept you awake last night, as it did me, although at your age I have slept through the roar of a battle. Well, have you thought over our conversation? I do not wish to trouble you with these incessant family matters, but time presses, and it is necessary to decide."

Adrian looked out of the lattice at the snow, which fell and fell without pause. Then he turned and said:

"Yes. Of the two, it is best that she should marry me, though I think that such a crime will bring its own reward."

"Wise young man," answered his father. "Under all your cloakings of vagary, I observe that you have a foundation of common sense, just as the giddiest weathercock is bedded on a stone. As for the reward, considered properly, it seems to be one upon which I can heartily congratulate you."

"Enough of your folly," said Adrian, angrily. "You forget that there are two parties to such a contract; her consent must be gained, and I will not ask it."

"No? Then I will. A few arguments occur to me. Now look here, friend, we have struck a bargain, and you will be so good as to keep it or to take the consequences. Never mind what those may be. I will bring this lady to the altar—or, rather, to that table—and you will marry her, after which you can settle matters just exactly as you please. Live with her as your wife, or take your bow and walk away, which, I care nothing about so long as you are married. Now I am weary of all this talk, so be so good as to leave me in peace on the subject."

Adrian looked at him, opened his lips to speak, then changed his mind and marched out of the house into the blinding snow.

"Thank heaven he is gone at last!" reflected his father, and called for Hague Simon, with whom he held a long and careful interview.

"You understand?" he ended.

"I understand," answered Simon, with a sigh. "I am to find this priest, who should be waiting at the place you name, and to bring him here by nightfall tomorrow. That is a rough job for a Christian man in such weather as this."

"The pay, friend Simon, remember the pay."

"Oh, yes, it all sounds well enough, but I should like something on account."

"You shall have it—is not such a laborer worthy of his hire?" replied his employer with enthusiasm. He then produced from his pocket the purse that Lysbeth had given Adrian, with a smile of peculiar satisfaction, for really the thing had a comic side. He counted a handsome sum into the hand of this accomplished spy and reprobate.

Simon looked at the money, concluded, after some reflection, that it would scarcely do to hold out for more at present, pouched it, and having wrapped himself in a thick frieze coat, opened the door and vanished into the falling snow.

CHAPTER XXVI
THE BRIDEGROOM AND
THE BRIDE

The day passed, and through every hour of it the snow fell incessantly. Night came, and it was still falling in large, soft flakes that floated to the earth as gently as thistledown, for now there was no wind. Adrian met his father at meals only; the rest of the day he preferred to spend out of doors in the snow or hanging about the old sheds at the back of the mill, rather than endure the society of this terrible man; this man of mocking words and iron purpose, who was forcing him into the commission of a great crime.

It was at breakfast, on the following morning, that Ramiro inquired of Black Meg whether the Jufvrouw Brant had sufficiently recovered from the fatigues of her journey to honor them with her presence. The woman replied that she absolutely refused to leave her room, or even to speak more than was necessary.

"Then," said Ramiro, "as it is important that I should have a few words with her, be so good as to tell the young lady, with my homage, that I will do myself the honor of waiting on her in the course of the forenoon."

Meg departed on her errand, and Adrian looked up suspiciously.

"Calm yourself, young friend," said his father, "although the interview will be private, you have really no cause for jealousy. At present, remember, I am but the second string in the bow case, the understudy who has learnt the part, a humble position, but one that may prove useful."

Adrian winced at each of the cutting and snide comments

provided by his father. But he did not reply, for by now he had learned that he was no match for his father's bitter wit.

Elsa received the message, as she received everything else, in silence.

Three days before, as after a fearful illness during which on several occasions she was at the very doors of death, Lysbeth van Goorl had been declared out of danger, Elsa, her nurse, ventured to leave her for a few hours. That evening the town seemed to stifle her, and feeling that she needed the air of the country, she passed the Morsch poort and walked a little way along the banks of the canal, never noticing that her footsteps were dogged. When it began to grow dusk, she halted and stood a while gazing towards the Haarlemer Meer, letting her heart go out to the lover who, as she thought and hoped, within a day or two would be at her side.

As she strolled along something was thrown over her head, and for a while all was black. She awoke to find herself lying in a boat, and watching her, two wretches, whom she recognized as those who had assailed her when first she came to Leyden from The Hague.

"Why have you kidnapped me, and where am I going?" she asked.

"Because we are paid to do it, and you are going to Adrian van Goorl," was the answer.

Then she understood and was silent.

Thus they brought her to this lonesome, gloomy place, where sure enough Adrian was waiting for her, waiting with a lie upon his lips. Now, doubtless, the end was at hand. She, who loved his brother with all her heart and soul, was to be given forcibly in marriage to a man whom she despised and loathed, the vain, furious-tempered traitor, who, for revenge, jealousy, or greed, she knew not which, had not hesitated to send his benefactor, and mother's husband, to perish in the fires of the Inquisition.

What was she to do? Escape seemed out of the question, imprisoned as she was on the third story of a lofty mill standing in a lonely, snow-shrouded wilderness, cut off from the sight of every friendly face, and spied on hour after hour by two fierce-eyed women. Escape would indeed be difficult, for she had no weapon, and day and night the women kept guard over her, one standing sentinel, while the other slept. Moreover, she had no mind to die in a failed escape, being young and healthy, with a love to live for, and from her childhood up she had been taught that she had the duty to preserve her life whenever possible. No, she would trust in God, and overwhelming though it was, fight her way through this trouble as best she might. The helpless find friends sometimes. Therefore, that her strength might be preserved, Elsa rested and ate the food they brought to her, refusing to leave the room or to speak more than she was obliged.

On the second morning of her imprisonment, Ramiro's message reached her, to which, as usual, she made no answer. In due course also Ramiro himself arrived, and stood bowing in the doorway.

"Have I your permission to enter, Jufvrouw?" he asked. Then Elsa, knowing that the moment of trial had come, braced herself for the encounter.

"You are master here," she answered, in a voice cold as the falling snow without. "Why then do you mock me?"

He motioned to the women to leave the room, and when they had gone, replied:

"I have little thought of such a thing, lady. The matter in hand is too serious for smart sayings," and with another bow he sat himself down on a chair near the hearth, where a fire was burning. Elsa soon stood up and moved across the room, for upon her feet she felt stronger.

"Will you be so good as to set out this matter, Señor Ramiro? Am I brought here to be tried for heresy?" questioned Elsa.

"Yes, indeed. For heresy against the god of love, and the sentence of the Court is that you must atone for your sin, not at the stake, but at the altar."

"I do not understand," responded Elsa as she slowly paced the room.

"Then I will explain. My son Adrian, a worthy young man on the whole—you know that he is my son, do you not—has had the misfortune, or I should say the good fortune to fall earnestly in love with you, whereas you have the bad taste—or, perhaps, the good taste—to give your affections elsewhere. Under the circumstances, Adrian, being a youth of spirit and resource, has fallen back upon primitive methods in order to bring his suit to a successful conclusion. He is here, you are here, and this evening I understand that the priest will be here. I need not dwell upon the obvious issue. Indeed, it is a private matter upon which I have no right to intrude, except, of course, as a relative and a well-wisher."

Elsa made an impatient movement with her hand, as though to brush aside all this web of words.

"Why do you take so much trouble to force an unhappy girl into a hateful marriage?" she asked. "How can such a thing work toward your advantage?"

"Ah!" answered Ramiro briskly, "I perceive I have before me a woman of business, one who has that rarest of gifts, common sense. I will be frank. Your esteemed father died possessed of a very large fortune, which today is your property as his sole issue and heiress. Under the marriage laws, which I myself think unjust, that fortune will pass into the power of any husband whom you choose to take. Therefore, as soon as you are made his wife, it will pass to Adrian. I am Adrian's father, and, as it happens, he is financially indebted to me to a considerable amount, so that, in the upshot, as he himself has pointed out more than once, this alliance will provide for both of us. But business details are wearisome, so I need not enlarge."

"The fortune you speak of, Señor Ramiro, is lost."

"It is lost, but I have reason to hope that it will be found," remarked the one-eyed schemer.

"You mean that this is purely a matter of money?" she asked.

"So far as I am concerned, purely. For Adrian's feelings I cannot speak, since who knows the mystery of another's heart?"

"Then, if the money were forthcoming, or a clue to it, there need be no marriage?"

"So far as I am concerned, none at all," responded Ramiro.

"And if the money is not forthcoming, and I refuse to marry

the Heer Adrian, or he to marry me, what then?"

"That is a riddle, but I think I see an answer at any rate to half of it. Then the marriage would still take place, but with another bridegroom."

"Another bridegroom! Who?" asked Elsa.

"Your humble and devoted adorer," said the Spaniard, with a slight smile and a bow.

Elsa shuddered and recoiled a step.

"Ah!" he said, "I should not have bowed, you saw my white hairs—to the young a hateful sight."

Elsa's indignation rose, and she answered, "It is not your white hair that I shrink from, Señor, which in some would be a crown of honor, but—"

"In my case suggests to you other reflections. Be gentle and spare me them. In a world of rough actions, what need to emphasize them with rough words?" commented Ramiro.

For a few minutes there was silence, which Ramiro, glancing out of the lattice, broke by remarking that "the snowfall was extraordinarily heavy for the time of year." Then followed another silence.

"I understood you just now, dear lady, to make some sort of suggestion that might lead to an arrangement satisfactory to both of us. The exact locality of this wealth is at present obscure, you mentioned some clue. Are you in a position to furnish such a clue?"

"If I am in a position, what then?"

"Then, perhaps, after a few days visit to an interesting, but little explored part of Holland, you might return to your friends as you left them—in short, as a single woman."

A struggle shook Elsa, and do what she would, some trace of it appeared in her face.

"Will you swear to that?" she whispered.

"Most certainly, on my honor," said Ramiro.

"Do you swear before God that if you have this clue you will not force me into a marriage with the Heer Adrian, or with yourself—that you will let me go, unharmed?"

"I swear it—before God," said Adrian's father with an earnest tone of voice.

"Knowing that God will be revenged upon you if you break the oath, you still swear?" repeated Elsa nervously.

"I still swear. Why these needless repetitions?"

"Then—then," and she leaned towards him, speaking in a hoarse whisper, "believing that you, even you, will not dare to be false to such an oath, for you, even you, must fear death, a miserable death, and vengeance, eternal vengeance I give you the clue. It lies in the hilt of the sword Silence."

"The sword Silence? What sword is that?" inquired Ramiro.

"The great sword of Red Martin."

Stirred out of his self-control, Ramiro struck his hand upon his knee.

"And to think," he said, "that for over twelve hours I had it hanging on the wall of the Gravensteen. Well, I fear that I must ask you to be more explicit. Where is this sword?"

"Wherever Red Martin is, that is all I know. I can tell you no more. The plan of the hiding place is there."

"Or was there. Well, I believe you, but to win a secret from the hilt of the sword of the man who broke his way out of the torture-chamber of the Gravensteen, is a labor that would have been not unworthy of Hercules. First, Red Martin must be found, then his sword must be taken, which, I think, will cost men their lives. Dear lady, I am obliged for your information, but I fear that the marriage must still go through."

"You swore, you swore," she gasped, "you swore before God!"

"Quite so, and I shall leave the Power you mentioned to manage the matter. Doubtless He can attend to His own affairs—I must attend to mine. I hope that about seven o'clock this evening will suit you, by which time the priest and a bridegroom will be ready."

Then Elsa broke down.

"Devil!" she cried in the torment of her despair. "To save my honor I have betrayed my father's trust. I have betrayed the secret for which Martin was ready to die by torment, and given him over to be hunted like a wild beast. Oh! God forgive me, and

God help me!"

"Doubtless, dear young lady, He will do the first, for your temptations were really considerable. I, who have more experience, outwitted you, that was all. Possibly, also, He may do the second, though many have uttered that cry unheard. For my own sake, I trust that He was sleeping when you uttered yours. But it is your affair and His; I leave it to be arranged between you. Until this evening, Jufvrouw," and he bowed himself and left the room.

But Elsa, shamed and broken-hearted, threw herself upon the bed and wept.

At midday she arose, hearing upon the stair the step of the woman who brought her food, and to hide her tearstained face went to the barred lattice and looked out. The scene was dismal indeed, for the wind had veered suddenly, the snow had ceased, and in place of it rain was falling with a steady persistence. When the woman had gone, Elsa washed her face, and although her appetite turned from it, ate of the food, knowing how necessary it was that she should keep her strength.

Another hour passed, and there came a knock on the door. Elsa shuddered, for she thought that Ramiro had returned to torment her. Indeed it was almost a relief when, instead of him, appeared his son. One glance at Adrian's nervous, shaken face, yes, and even the sound of his uncertain step brought hope to her heart. Her woman's instinct told her that now she had no longer to do with the merciless and terrible Ramiro, to whose eyes she was but a pretty pawn in a game that he must win, but with a young man who loved her. She could only hope that her influence over the pliable Adrian would give her some real advantage in her efforts to secure his aid.

"Your pleasure?" said Elsa.

In the old days, Adrian would have answered with some magnificent compliment, or far-fetched simile lifted from the pages of romancers. In truth he had thought of several such accolades while, like a half-starved dog seeking a home, he wandered round and round the mill-house in the snow. But he was now far beyond all rhetoric or gallantries.

"My father wished," he began humbly—"I mean that I have come to speak to you about our marriage."

All of a sudden Elsa's delicate features seemed to turn to ice, while, to his fancy at any rate, her brown eyes became fire.

"Marriage," she said in a strange voice. "Oh! What a coward you must be to speak that word. Call what is proposed by any foul title you will, but at least leave the holy name of marriage undefiled."

"It is not my fault," he answered soberly, but shrinking beneath her words. "You know, Elsa, that I wished to wed you honorably enough."

"Yes," she broke in, "and because I would not listen, because you do not please me, and you could not win me as a man wins a maid, you laid a trap and kidnapped me, thinking to get by brute force that which my heart withheld. Oh, in all the Netherlands lives there another pathetic creature like Adrian called van Goorl, the base-born son of Ramiro the galley slave?"

"I have told you that it is false," he replied furiously. "I had nothing to do with your capture. I knew nothing of it until I saw you here."

Elsa laughed a very bitter laugh. "Spare your breath," she said, "for if you swore it before the face of an angel, I would not believe you. Remember that you are the man who betrayed your brother and your benefactor, and then guess, if you can, what worth I put upon your words."

In the bitterness of his heart, Adrian groaned aloud; and from that groan Elsa, listening eagerly, gathered some kind of hope.

"Surely," she went on, with a changed and softened manner, "surely you will not do this wickedness. The blood of Dirk van Goorl lies on your head. Will you add mine to his? For be sure of this, I swear it by my Maker, that before I am indeed a wife to you I shall be dead, or perhaps you will be dead, or both of us. Do you understand?"

"I understand, but—"

"But what? Where is the use of this wickedness? For your soul's sake, refuse to have anything to do with such a sin," she pleaded.

"But if so, my father will marry you," exclaimed Adrian.

It was a random arrow, but it went home, for very soon Elsa's strength and eloquence seemed to leave her. She ran to him with her hands clasped, and then flung herself upon her knees.

"Oh! Help me to escape," she moaned, "and I will bless you all my life."

"It is impossible," he answered. "Escape from this guarded place, through those leagues of melting snow? I tell you that it is impossible."

"Then," and her eyes grew wild, "Kill him and free me. He is a devil, he is your evil genius. It would be a righteous deed. Kill him and free me."

"I should like to," answered Adrian. "I nearly did once, but for my soul's sake, I can't put a sword through my own father. It is the most horrible of crimes. When I confessed—"

"Then," she broke in, "if this farce, this infamy must be gone through, swear at least that you will treat it as such, that you will respect me."

"It is a hard thing to ask of a husband who loves you more than any woman in the world," he answered turning aside his head.

"Remember," she went on, with another flash of defiant spirit, "that if you do not, you will soon love me better than any woman out of the world, or perhaps we shall both settle what lies between us before the Judgment Seat of God. Will you swear?"

He hesitated.

Oh, she reflected, what if he should answer—"Rather than this I hand you over to Ramiro?" What if he should think of that argument? Happily for her, at the moment he did not.

"Swear," she implored, "swear," clinging with her hands to the lappet of his coat and lifting to him her white and piteous face.

"I make it an offering in expiation of my sins," he groaned, "you shall go free of me."

Elsa uttered a sigh of relief. She put no faith whatever in Adrian's promises, but at the worst it would give her time.

"I thought that I should not appeal in vain—" remarked Elsa, before she was rudely interrupted.

"To so amusing and passionate a donkey," said Ramiro's mocking voice speaking from the gloom of the doorway, which now Elsa observed for the first time had swung open silently.

"My dear son and daughter-in-law, how can I thank you sufficiently for the entertainment with which you have enlivened one of the most dreary afternoons I can remember. Don't look dangerous, my boy. Recall what you have just told this young lady, that the crime of removing a parent is one which, though agreeable, is not lightly to be indulged. Then, as to your future arrangements, how touching! The soul of a Diana, I declare, and the self-sacrifice of a—no, I fear that the heroes of antiquity can furnish no suitable example. And now, adieu, I go to welcome the gentleman that both of you so eagerly expect."

He went, and a minute later without speaking, for the situation seemed beyond words, Adrian crept down the stairs after him, more miserable and crushed than when he had crept up them half an hour before.

Another two hours went by. Elsa was in her apartment with Black Meg for company, who watched her as a cat watches a mouse in a trap. Adrian had taken refuge in the place where he slept above. It was a dreary chamber that once had held stones and other machinery for the mill. This miserable place was now the home of spiders and half-starved rats, where a lean black cat hunted continually. Across its leaky ceiling ran great beams with interlacing ends, among which sharp drafts whistled with an endless and exasperating sound.

In the round living-chamber below Ramiro was alone. No lamp had been lit, but the glow from the great turf fire played upon his face as he sat there, watching, waiting, and scheming in the chair of black oak. Presently a noise from without caught his quick ear, and calling to the serving woman to light the lamp, he went to the door, opened it, and saw a lantern floating towards him through the thick steam of falling rain. Another minute and the bearer of the lantern, Hague Simon, arrived, followed by two other men.

"Here he is," said Simon, nodding at the figure behind him, a short round figure wrapped in a thick frieze cloak, from which water ran. "The other is the head boatman."

"Good," said Ramiro. "Tell him and his companions to wait in the shed without, where liquor will be sent to them. They may be wanted later on."

Then followed talk and oaths, and at length the man retreated grumbling.

"Enter, Father Thomas," said Ramiro. "You have had a wet journey, I fear. Enter and give us your blessing."

Before he answered the priest threw off his dripping, hooded cape of Frisian cloth, revealing a coarse, wicked face, red and puffy-eyed from intemperance.

"My blessing?" he said in a raucous voice. "Here it is, Señor Ramiro, or whatever you call yourself now. Curse you all for bringing out a holy priest upon one of your devil's errands in weather that is only fit for a bald-headed coot to travel through. There is going to be a flood; already the water is running over the banks of the dam, and it gathers every moment as the snow melts. I tell you there is going to be such a flood as we have not seen for years."

"The more reason, Father, for getting through this little business quickly. But first you will wish for something to drink."

Father Thomas nodded, and Ramiro filling a small mug with brandy, gave it to him. He gulped it down.

"Another?" he asked. "Don't be afraid. A chosen vessel should also be a seasoned vessel; at any rate, the one is. Ah, that's better now then, what's the exact job?"

Ramiro took him aside and they talked together for a while.

"Very good," said the priest at length. "I will take the risk and do it, for where heretics are concerned, such things are not too closely inquired into nowadays. But first down with the money. No paper or promises, if you please."

"Ah! You churchmen," said Ramiro, with a faint smile, "in things spiritual or temporal how much have we poor laity to learn from you!" With a sigh he produced the required sum, then paused and added, "Now, with your leave we will see the papers first. You have them with you?"

"Here they are," answered the priest, drawing some documents from his pocket. "But they haven't been married yet; the rule is, marry first, then certify. Until the ceremony is actually performed, anything might happen, you know."

"Quite so, Father. Anything might happen, either before or after; but still, with your leave, I think that in this case we may as well certify first; you might want to be getting away, and it will save so much trouble later. Will you be so kind as to write your certificate?"

Father Thomas hesitated, while Ramiro gently clinked the gold coins in his hand and murmured, "I should be sorry to think, Father, that you had taken such a rough journey for nothing."

"What trick are you at now?" growled the priest, "Well, after all it is a mere form. Give me the names."

Ramiro gave them to Father Thomas and he scrawled them down, adding some words and his own signature, then said, "There you are, that will hold good against anyone except the Pope."

"A mere form," repeated Ramiro, "of course. But the world attaches so much importance to forms, so I think that we will have this one witnessed—No, not by myself, who am an interested party, by someone independent," and, calling Hague Simon and the waiting-woman, he directed them to set their names at the foot of the documents.

"Papers signed in advance, fees paid in advance!" he went on, handing over the money, "and now, just one more glass to drink the health of the bride and bridegroom, also in advance. You will not refuse, nor you, worthy Simon, nor you, most excellent Abigail. Ah! I thought not, the night is cold."

"And the brandy strong," muttered the priest thickly, as this third dose of raw spirit took effect upon him. "Now get on with the business, for I want to be out of this hole before the flood comes."

"Quite so. Friends, will you be so good as to summon my

son and the lady? The lady first, I think, and all three of you might go to escort her. Brides sometimes consider it right to fain a slight reluctance—you understand? On second thought, you need not trouble the Señor Adrian. I have a few words of pre-nuptial advice to offer, so I will go to him."

A minute later father and son stood face to face. Adrian leaped up; he shook his fist, he raved and stormed at the cold, impassive man before him.

"You fool, you contemptible fool," said Ramiro when he had done. "Heavens! To think that such a creature should have sprung from me, a human donkey only fit to bear the blows and burdens of others, to fill the field with empty brayings, and wear himself out by kicking at the air. Oh, don't twist up your face at me, for I am your master as well as your father, however much you may hate me. You are mine, body and soul, don't you under-stand; a bond-slave, nothing more. You lost the only chance you ever had in the game when you got me down at Leyden. You dare not draw a sword on me again for your soul's sake, dear Adrian, for your soul's sake. And if you dared, I would run you through. Now, are you coming?"

"No," answered Adrian.

"Think a minute. If you don't marry her I shall, and before she is half an hour older; also—" and he bent forward and whis-pered into his son's ear.

"Oh! You devil, you devil!" Adrian gasped; then he moved towards the door.

"What? Changed your mind, have you, Mr. Weathercock? Well, it is the prerogative of all feminine natures—but, your doublet is awry, and allow me to suggest that you should brush your hair. There, that's better; now, come, on. No, you go first, if you please, I'd rather have you in front of me."

When they reached the room below, the bride was already there. Gripped on either side by Black Meg and the other wom-an, white as death and trembling, but still defiant, stood Elsa.

"Let's get through with this," growled the half-drunken, ruf-fian priest. "I take the willingness of the parties for granted."

"I am not willing," cried Elsa. "I have been brought here by

force. I call everyone present to witness that whatever is done is against my will. I appeal to God to help me."

The priest turned upon Ramiro. "How am I to marry them in the face of this?" he asked. "If only she were silent, it might be done—"

"The difficulty has occurred to me," answered Ramiro. He made a sign, at which point Simon seized Elsa's wrists, and Black Meg, slipping behind her, deftly fastened a handkerchief over her mouth in such fashion that she was gagged, but could still breathe through the nostrils.

Elsa struggled a little, then was quiet, and turned her piteous eyes on Adrian, who stepped forward and opened his lips.

"You remember the alternative," said his father in a low voice, and he stopped.

"I suppose," broke in Father Thomas, "that we may at any rate reckon upon the consent, or at least upon the silence of the Heer bridegroom."

"You may reckon on his silence, Father Thomas," replied

Ramiro.

Then the ceremony began. They dragged Elsa to the table. Three times she flung herself to the ground, and each time they lifted her to her feet, but eventually, weary of the weight of her body, they permitted her to rest upon her knees, where she remained as though in prayer, gagged like some victim on the scaffold. It was a strange and brutal scene, and every detail of it burned itself into Adrian's mind. The round, rude room, with its glowing turf fire and its rough oaken furniture, half in light and half in dense shadow. The lamp rays that chanced to fall on the pathetic kneeling bride, with a white cloth across her tortured face; the red-chopped, hanging-lipped hedge priest reading from a book, his back almost turned so he might not see her attitude and struggles. Also, the horrible women; the flat-faced villain, Simon, grinning by the hearth; Ramiro, cynical, mocking, triumphant, and yet somewhat anxious, his one bright eye fixed in mingled contempt and amusement upon him, Adrian. There was something else also that caught and oppressed his sense, a sound that at the time Adrian thought he heard in his head alone, a soft, heavy sound with a moan in it, not unlike that of the wind, which grew gradually to a dull roar.

It was over. A ring had been forced onto Elsa's unwilling hand and, until the thing was undone by some competent and authorized Court, she was in name the wife of Adrian. The handkerchief was unbound, her hands were loosed. Physically, Elsa was free again, but, in that day and land of outrage, tied, as the poor girl knew well, by a chain more terrible than any that hemp or steel could fashion.

"Congratulations! Señora," muttered Father Thomas, eyeing her nervously. "I fear you felt a little faint during the service, but a sacrament—"

"Cease your mockings, you false priest," cried Elsa. "Oh, let the swift vengeance of God fall upon every one of you, and first of all upon you, false priest."

Drawing the ring from her finger, as she spoke she cast it down upon the oaken table, whence it sprang up to drop again and rattle itself to silence. Then with one tragic motion of despair, Elsa turned and fled back to her chamber.

The red face of Father Thomas went white, and his yellow teeth chattered. "A virgin's curse," he muttered, "and in her wedding hour. It is deadly, deadly!" and he crossed himself. "Misfortune always follows, and it is sometimes death—yes, by St. Thomas, death. And you, you brought me here to do this wickedness, you dog, you galley slave!"

"Father," broke in Ramiro, "you know I have warned you against it before at The Hague. Sooner or later it always breaks up the nerves," and he nodded towards the flagon of spirits. "Bread and water, Father, bread and water for forty days, that is what I prescribe." And as he spoke the door was burst open, and two men rushed in, their eyes wide, their very beards bristling with terror.

"Come forth!" they cried.

"What has happened?" screamed the priest.

"The great dyke has burst—hark, hark, hark! The floods are upon you, the mill will soon be swept away."

God in Heaven, it was true! Now through the open doorway they heard the roar of waters, whose note Adrian had caught before, yes, and in the gloom appeared their foaming crest as they rushed through the great and ever-widening breach in the lofty dyke down upon the flooded lowland.

Father Thomas bounded through the door yelling, "The boat, the boat!" For a moment Ramiro thought, considering the situation, then he said:

"Fetch the Jufvrouw. No, not you, Adrian, she would die rather than come with you. You, Simon, and you, Meg. Swift, obey."

They departed on their errand.

"Men," went on Ramiro, "take this gentleman and lead him to the boat. Hold him if he tries to escape. I will follow with the lady. Go, you fool, go, there is not a second to be lost," and Adrian, hanging back and protesting, was dragged away by the boatmen.

Now Ramiro was alone, and though, as he had said, there was little time to spare, again for a few moments he thought deeply. His face flushed and went pale, then entered into it a great resolve. "I don't like doing it, for it is against my vow, but the chance is good. She is safely married, and at best she would be very troublesome hereafter, and might bring us to justice or the galleys since others seek her wealth," he muttered with a shiver, adding, "as for the spies, we are well rid of them and their evidence." Then, with swift resolution, stepping to the door at the foot of the stairs, Ramiro shut it and closed the great iron bolt!

He ran from the mill. The raised path was already three feet deep in water; he could scarcely make his way along it. Ah, there lay the boat. Now he was in it, and now they were flying before the crest of a huge wave. The dam of the cutting had given way altogether, and fed from sea and land at once, by snow, by rain, and by the inrush of the high tide, its waters were pouring in a measureless volume over the doomed marshes.

"Where is Elsa?" screamed Adrian.

"I don't know. I couldn't find her," answered Ramiro. "Row, row for your lives! We can take her off in the morning, and the priest too, if he comes back."

On the following morning, the cold winter sun rose over the watery waste, calm enough now, for the floods were out, in places ten to fifteen feet deep. Through the mists that brooded on the face of them Ramiro and his crew groped their way back to where the Red Mill should be. It was gone!

There stood the brick walls of the bottom story rising above the flood level, but the wooden upper part had snapped before the first great wave when the bank gave way, and afterwards was swept away by the rushing current, swept away with those within.

"What is that?" said one of the boatmen, pointing to a dark object which floated among the tangled debris of weeds and woodwork collected against the base of the Mill.

They rowed to the thing. It was the body of Father Thomas, who must have missed his footing as he ran along the pathway, and fallen into deep water.

"Well!" said Ramiro, "'a virgin's curse.' Observe, friends, how the merest coincidences may give rise to superstition. Allow me," and, holding the dead man by one hand, he felt in his pockets with the other, until, with a smile of satisfaction, he found the purse containing the gold which he had paid him on the previous evening.

"Oh! Elsa, Elsa," moaned Adrian.

"Comfort yourself, my son," said Ramiro as the boat put about, leaving the dead Father Thomas bobbing up and down in the ripple. "You have indeed lost a wife whose temper gave you little prospect of happiness, but at least I have your marriage papers duly signed and witnessed, and—you are her heir."

He did not add that he in turn was Adrian's. But Adrian thought of it and, even in the midst of his shame and misery, wondered with a shiver how long he who was Ramiro's next of kin was likely to adorn this world.

Until he had something that was worth inheriting, perhaps.

CHAPTER XXVII
WHAT ELSA SAW IN THE MOONLIGHT

It will be remembered that some weeks before Elsa's forced marriage in the Red Mill, Foy, on their escape from the Gravensteen, had been carried upon the naked back of Martin to the shelter of Mother Martha's lair in the Haarlemer Meer. Here he lay sick many days, for the sword cut in his thigh festered so badly that, at one time, his life was threatened by gangrene. But, in the end, his own strength and healthy constitution, helped with Martha's herbal remedies, cured him. So soon as he was strong again, accompanied by Martin, he traveled into Leyden, which now was safe enough for him to visit, since the Spaniards were driven from the town.

How his young heart swelled as, still limping a little and somewhat pale from recent illness, he approached the well-known house on the Bree Straat, the home that sheltered his mother and his love. Soon he would see them again, for the news had been brought to him that Lysbeth was out of danger and Elsa must still be nursing her.

Lysbeth he found indeed, turned into an old woman by grief and prolonged sickness, but Elsa he did not find. She had vanished. On the previous night, she had gone out for a walk and returned no more. What had become of her, none could say. All the town talked of it, and his mother was half-crazed with anxiety and concern.

From one location to another they went inquiring, seeking, tracking, but no trace of Elsa could they discover. She had been seen to pass the Morsch poort; then she disappeared. For a while, Foy was profoundly depressed and unstable. As time passed, however, he regained his hopeful attitude and began to think clearly. Drawing from his pocket the letter that Martha had brought to him on the night of the church burning, he reread it in the hope of finding a clue, since it was just possible that for private reasons Elsa might have set out on some journey of her own. It was a very sweet letter, telling him of her deep joy and gratitude at his escape; of the events that had happened in the town; of the death of his father in the Gravensteen, and ending thus:

> Dear Foy, my betrothed, I cannot come to you because of your mother's sickness, for I am sure that it would be your wish, as it is my desire and duty, that I should stay to nurse her. Soon, however, I hope that you will be able to come to her and me. Yet, in these dreadful times, who can tell what may happen? Therefore, Foy, whatever happens, I am sure you will remember that in life or in death I am yours alone. While or wherever I have sense or memory, I will be true; through life, through death; through whatever may lie beyond our deaths, I will be true as woman may be to man. So, dear Foy, for this present, fare you well until we meet again in the days to come, or after all earthly days are done with for you and me. My love be with you, the blessing of God be with you, and when you lie down at night and when you wake at morn, think of me and put up a prayer for me as your true lover Elsa does for you. Martha waits. Most loved, most dear, most desired, fare you well.

Here was no hint of any journey, so if such had been taken it must be without Elsa's own consent.

"Martin, what do you make of it?" asked Foy, staring at him with anxious, hollow eyes.

"Ramiro—Adrian—stolen away—" answered Martin.

"Why do you say that?" questioned Foy as he rubbed his leg.

"Hague Simon was seen hanging about outside the town yesterday, and there was a strange boat upon the river. Last night the Jufvrouw went through the Morsch poort. The rest you can guess."

"Why would they take her?" asked Foy hoarsely.

"Who can tell?" said Martin shrugging his mighty shoulders.

"Yet I see two reasons. Hendrik Brant's wealth is supposed to be hers, when it can be found. Therefore, being a thief, Ramiro would want her. Adrian is in love with her; therefore, being a man, of course he would want her. These seem enough, the pair being what they are."

"When I find them, I will kill them both," said Foy, grinding his teeth.

"Of course, so will I, but first we have got to find them—and her, which is the same thing."

"How, Martin, how?"

"I don't know."

"Can't you think, man?" pleaded Foy.

"I am trying to, Master. It's you who don't think. You talk too much. Be silent a while."

"Well," asked Foy thirty seconds later, "have you finished thinking?"

"No, master, it's no use, there is nothing to think about. We must leave this place and go back to Martha. If anyone can track her out, she can. Here we can learn no more."

So they returned to the Haarlemer Meer and told Martha their sad tale.

"Bide here a day or two and be patient," she said. "I will go out and search."

"Never," answered Foy, "we will come with you."

"If you choose, but it will make matters more difficult. Martin, get ready the big boat."

Three nights had gone by, and it was an hour or more past noon on the fourth day, the day of Elsa's forced marriage.

The snow had ceased falling and the rain had come instead—rain, pitiless, bitter and continual. Hidden in a nook at the north end of the Haarlemer Meer and almost buried beneath bundles of reeds, partly as a protection from the weather and partly to escape the eyes of Spaniards, of whom companies were gathering from every direction to besiege Haarlem, lay the big boat. In it were Red Martin and Foy van Goorl. Mother Martha was not there for she had gone alone to an inn at a distance, to gather information if she could. To hundreds of the boers in these parts she was a known and trusted friend, although many of them might not choose to recognize her openly, and from among them, she hoped to gather tidings of Elsa's whereabouts.

For two weary nights and days the Mare had been employed thus, but as yet without a shadow of success. Foy and Martin sat in the boat staring at each other gloomily; indeed, Foy's face was piteous to behold.

"What are you thinking of, Master?" asked Martin presently.

"I am thinking," he answered, "that even if we find her now it will be too late. Whatever was to be done, murder or marriage, will be done."

"Time to trouble about that when we have found her," said Martin, for he knew not what else to say, and added, "listen, I hear footsteps."

Foy drew apart two of the bundles of reeds and looked out into the driving rain.

"All is well," he said, "it is Martha and a man."

Martin let his hand fall from the hilt of the sword Silence, for in those days hand and sword must be near together. Another minute and Martha and her companion were in the boat.

"Who is this man?" asked Foy.

"He is a friend of mine named Marsh Jan."

"Have you news?" asked Martin.

"Yes, at least Marsh Jan has," declared Martha.

"Speak, and be swift," said Foy, turning on the man fiercely.

"Am I safe from vengeance?" asked Marsh Jan, who was a good fellow that had drifted into evil company.

"Have I not said so," answered Martha, "and does the Mare break her word?"

Then Marsh Jan told his tale: How he was one of the party that three nights before had rowed Elsa, or at least a young woman who answered to her description, to the Red Mill, not far from Velzen, and how she was in the immediate charge of a man and a woman who could be no other than Hague Simon and Black Meg. Also he told of her piteous appeal to the boatmen in the names of their wives and daughters; and at the telling of it, Foy wept with fear and rage, and even Martha gnashed her teeth. Only Martin cast off the boat and began to put her out into deep water.

"Is that all?" asked Foy.

"That is all, Mynheer, I know nothing more, but I can describe to you where the place is."

"You can show us, you mean," said Foy.

The man immediately became filled with excuses. The weather was bad, there would be a flood, his wife was ill and expected him, and so forth. Then he tried to get out of the boat, at which point, catching hold of him suddenly, Martin threw him into the stern, saying, "You could travel to this mill, once taking with you a girl whom you knew to be kidnapped, now you can travel there again to get her out. Sit still and steer straight, or I will make you food for fishes."

Then Marsh Jan professed himself quite willing to sail to the Red Mill, which he said they ought to reach by nightfall.

All that afternoon they sailed and rowed, until, in growing darkness, before the mill was in sight, the great flood came down upon them and drove them in many directions. This type of flooding had not been seen in those districts for a dozen years. But Marsh Jan knew his bearings well; he had the instinct of locality that is bred in those whose forefathers for generations have won a living from the seas, and through it all he held upon a straight course.

Once Foy thought that he heard a voice calling for help in the darkness, but it was not repeated and they went forward. At last, the sky cleared and the moon shone out upon such a waste of waters as Noah might have beheld from the ark. Only there were things floating in them that Noah would scarcely have seen; hayricks, dead and drowning cattle, household furniture, and once even a coffin washed from some graveyard, while beyond stretched the dreary outline of the sand dunes.

"The mill should be near," said Marsh Jan, "let us put about." So they turned, rowing with weary arms, for the wind had fallen.

At this point in the story, some readers may be curious as to what happened to Elsa after the storm hit the windmill. Let us go back a little. Elsa, on escaping from the scene of her mock marriage, fled to her room and bolted its door. A few seconds later she heard hands hammering at it, and the voices of Hague Simon and Black Meg calling to her to open. She took no note, and the hammering ceased. It was then, for the first time, she became aware of a dreadful, roaring noise—a noise of many waters. Time passed as it passes in a nightmare, until suddenly, above the dull roar, came sharp sounds as of wood cracking and splitting, and Elsa felt that the whole fabric of the mill had tilted. Beneath the pressure of the flood it had given way where it was weakest, at its narrow waist, and now its red cap hung over like a wind-laid tree.

Terror took hold of Elsa, and running to the door she opened it, hoping to escape down the stairs. Behold! Water was creeping up them, she could see it by the lantern in her hand—her retreat was cut off. But there were other stairs leading to the top storey of the mill that now lay at a steep angle, and along these she climbed, since the water was pouring through her doorway and there was nowhere else to go. In the very roof of the place was a manhole with a rotten hatch. She passed through this, to find herself upon the top of the mill just where one of the great naked arms of the sails projected from it. Her lantern was blown out by now, but she clung to the arm, and became aware that the wooden cap of the structure, still anchored to its brick foundation, lay upon its side rocking to and fro like a boat upon an angry sea. The water was near her; that she knew by its heaving and rush, although she could not see it, but as yet it did not even wet her feet.

The hours went by slowly. How many, she never learned, until eventually the clouds cleared; the moon became visible, and by its light she saw an awful scene. Everywhere around was water; it lapped within a yard, and it was rising still. Now Elsa saw that in the great beam which she clasped were placed short spokes for the use of those who set the sails above. Up these she climbed as best she might, until she was able to pass her body between two

of the vanes and support her hips upon the flat surface of one
of them, as a person does who leans out of a window. From her
position, there was something amazing to see. Quite near to her,
but separated by fifteen or twenty feet of yellow frothing water,
a little portion of the swelling shape of the mill stood clear of
the flood. To this foam-lapped island clung two human beings—
Hague Simon and Black Meg. They saw her also and screamed
for help, but she had none to give.

Surely it was a dream—nothing so awful could happen outside of a dream.

The structure of the mill continued to tilt more and more;
the space to which the two vile creatures hung grew less and
less. There was no longer room for both of them. They began
to quarrel, to curse and shout at each other, their fierce, bestial
faces not an inch apart as they crouched there on hands and
knees. The water rose a little, they were kneeling in it now, and
the man proceeded to thrust his bald head at the woman, almost
thrusting her from her perch. But she was strong and active, so
she struggled back again with an eel-like wriggle and climbed
upon his back, weighing him down. He strove to shake her off
but could not, for on that heaving, rolling surface he dared not
loose his grip, so he turned his flat and horrid face, and, seizing
her leg between his teeth, bit and chomped at it. In her pain and
rage, Meg screeched aloud, then suddenly she drew a knife from
her bosom and stabbed downwards several times in the moonlight.

Elsa shut her eyes. When she opened them again, the woman
was alone upon the little patch of red boarding, her body spread
out over it like that of a dead frog. So she lay a while until suddenly the cap of the Red Mill dipped slowly like a lady who
makes a Court curtsey, and she vanished. It rose again and Meg
was still there, moaning in her terror and water running from
her dress. Then again it dipped, this time more deeply, and when
the patch of rusty boarding slowly reappeared, it was empty. No,
not quite, for clinging to it, yowling and spitting, was the half-
wild black cat which Elsa had seen wandering around the mill.
But of Black Meg there was no trace.

It was dreadfully cold up there hanging to the sail-bar, for now that the rain had finished, it began to freeze. Indeed, had it not been that Elsa was dressed in her warm winter gown with fur upon it, and dry from her head to her feet, she might have fallen off and perished in the water. As it was, her body gradually became numb and her senses faded as hours, and even days passed on. She seemed to know that all this matter of her forced marriage, of the flood, and of the end of Simon and Meg, was nothing but an evil nightmare from which she would soon awake to find herself snug and warm in her own bed in the Bree Straat. Of course it must be a nightmare, for look, there, on the bare patch of boarding beneath, the hideous struggle repeated itself. There lay Hague Simon gnawing at his wife's foot, only his fat, white face was gone, and in place of it he wore the head of a cat, for she, the watcher, could see its glowing eyes fixed upon her. And Meg, look how her lean limbs gripped him round the body. Listen to the thudding noise as the great knife fell between his shoulders.

Just then, she awoke once again and, through the shadows, wondered how much time had passed and whether the nightmare was over. Oh! She must fall, but first she would scream for help—surely the dead themselves could hear that cry. Perhaps it would be better to have remained silent for it might bring Ramiro back. Better to join the dead. What? Did I hear Meg's voice? My, how it has changed! The next thing she knew, she thought she heard the thudding sound of oars not of knife thrusts. This would be Ramiro's boat coming to seize her. Of him and Adrian, she could bear no more; she would throw herself into the water and trust to God. Voices, more voices, as Elsa struggled to regain a clear mind.

Elsa suddenly became aware that light was shining around her, also that somebody was kissing her upon the face and lips. A horrible fear struck her that it might be Adrian, and she opened her eyes ever so little to look. No, no, how very strange, it was not Adrian, it was Foy! Well, doubtless this must be all part of her vision, and in a dream or out of it Foy had a perfect right to kiss her if he chose, she saw no reason to interfere. Now she

seemed to hear a familiar voice, that of Red Martin, asking someone how long it would take them to make Haarlem with this
wind, to which another voice answered, "About three-quarters
of an hour."

It was very odd, and why did he say Haarlem and not Leyden?
Next the second voice, which also seemed familiar, said, "Look
out, Foy, she's coming to herself."

Then someone poured water down her throat, whereupon,
unable to bear this bewilderment any longer, Elsa sat up and
opened her eyes wide, to see before her Foy, and none other than
Foy in the flesh.

She gasped and began to sink back again with joy and weakness, whereon he cast his arms around her and drew her to his
breast. Then she remembered everything.

"Oh! Foy, Foy," she cried, "You must not kiss me."

"Why not?" he asked.

"Because—because I am married." stammered Elsa.

All of a sudden his happy face became ghastly. "Married!" he
cried. "To whom?"

"To your brother, Adrian," she answered timidly.

He stared at her in amazement, then asked slowly. "Did you run away from Leyden to marry him?"

"How dare you ask such a question?" replied Elsa with a flash of spirit.

"Perhaps, then, you would explain?" requested Foy.

"What is there to explain? I thought that you knew. They dragged me away, just before the flood burst, I was gagged and married by force."

"Oh! Adrian, my friend," groaned Foy, "wait until I catch you, my friend Adrian."

"To be just," explained Elsa, "I don't think Adrian wanted to marry me much, but he had to choose between marrying me himself or seeing his father Ramiro marry me."

"So he sacrificed himself—the good, kind-hearted man," interrupted Foy, grinding his teeth.

"Yes," said Elsa.

"And where is your unselfish—oh! I can't say the word."

"I don't know. I suppose that he and Ramiro escaped in the boat, or perhaps he was drowned."

"In which case, you are a widow sooner than you could have expected," said Foy more cheerfully, edging himself towards her.

But Elsa moved a farther away and Foy saw with a sinking heart that, however distasteful it might be to her, clearly she attached some weight to this marriage.

"I do not know," she answered, "how can I tell? I suppose that we shall hear sometime, and then, if he is still alive, I must set to work to get free of him. But, until then, Foy," she added, warningly, "I suppose that I am his wife in law, although I will never speak to him again. Where are we going?"

"To Haarlem. The Spaniards are closing in upon the city, and we dare not try to break through their lines. Those are Spanish boats behind us. But eat and drink a little, Elsa, then tell us your story."

"One question first, Foy. How did you find me?"

"We heard a woman scream twice, once far away and once

near at hand, and rowing to the sound, saw someone hanging to the arm of an overturned windmill only three or four feet above the water. Of course we knew that you had been taken to the mill; that man there told us. Do you remember him? But at first we could not find it in the darkness and the flood."

Then, after she had swallowed something, Elsa told her story, while the three of them clustered round her forward of the sail, and Marsh Jan managed the helm. When she had finished it, Martin whispered to Foy, and as though by a common impulse, all four of them knelt down upon the boards in the bottom of the boat and returned thanks to the Almighty that this maiden, quite unharmed, had been delivered out of such manifold and terrible dangers. When they had finished their service of thanksgiving, which was as simple as it was solemn and heartfelt, they rose, and now Elsa did not forbid that Foy should hold her hand.

"Say, Sweetheart," he asked, "is it true that you think anything of this forced marriage?"

"Hear me before you answer," broke in Martha. "It is no marriage at all, for none can be wed without the consent of their own will, and you gave no such consent."

"It is no marriage," echoed Martin, "and if it be, and I live, then the sword shall cut its knot."

"It is no marriage," said Foy, "for although we have not stood together before the altar, yet our hearts are wed, so how can you be made the wife of another man?"

"Dearest," replied Elsa, when they had all spoken, "I too am sure that it is no marriage, yet a priest spoke the marriage words over me, and a ring was thrust upon my hand, so, to the law, if there be any law left in the Netherlands, I am perhaps in some sort a wife. Therefore, before I can become wife to you these facts must be made public, and I must appeal to the law to free me, lest in days to come others should be troubled."

"And if the law cannot or will not, Elsa, what then?" inquired Foy.

"Then, dear, our consciences being clean, we will appeal to the higher law of God and live together at common law. But first we must wait a while. Are you satisfied now, Foy?"

"No," answered Foy sulkily, "for it is monstrous that such devil's work should keep us apart even for an hour. Yet in this, as in all, I will respect you, dear."

"Marrying and giving in marriage!" broke in Martha in a shrill voice. "Talk no more of such things, for there is other work before us. Look yonder, girl, what do you see?" and she pointed to the dry land. "The hosts of the Amalekites marching in their thousands to slaughter us and our brethren, the children of the Lord. Look behind you, what do you see? The ships of the tyrant sailing up to encompass the city of the children of the Lord. It is the day of death and desolation, the day of deliverance I pray, and ere the sun sets red upon it, many a thousand must pass through the gates of doom, we, perhaps, among them. Then up with the flag of freedom; out with the steel of truth, gird on the buckler of righteousness, and snatch the shield of hope. Fight, fight for the liberty of the land that bore you, for the memory of Christ, the King who died for you, for the faith to which you were covenanted. It is time to fight, fight, and when the fray is done, then, and not before, should we think of peace and love.

"Nay, children, look not so fearful, for I, the mad warrior, tell you, by the Grace of God, that you have nought to fear. Who preserved you in the torture den, Foy van Goorl? What hand was it that held your life and honor safe when you sojourned among devils in the Red Mill yonder and kept your head above the waters of the flood, Elsa Brant? You know well, and I, Martha, tell you that this same hand shall hold you safe until the end. Yes, I know it, I know it. Thousands shall fall upon your right hand and tens of thousands upon your left, but you shall live through the hunger. The arrows of the pestilence shall pass you by, the sword of the wicked shall not harm you. For me it is otherwise, at length my doom draws near and I am well content. But for you two Foy and Elsa, I believe there will be many years of earthly joy."

Thus spoke Martha, and it seemed to those who watched her that her wild, disfigured face shone with a light of inspiration. At the least they took comfort from her words, and for a while were no more afraid.

Yet they had great trials to face. By a strange twist of Providence, they had been delivered from great dangers only to fall into dangers greater still, for as it happened, on this tenth of December, 1572, they sailed straight into the path of the thousands of Spanish soldiers that had been drawn like a net round the doomed city of Haarlem. There was no escape for them; nothing that had not wings could pass those lines of ships and soldiers. Their only refuge was the city, and in that city they must stay until the struggle, one of the most fearful of all that hideous war, was ended. But at least they had this comfort, they would face the war together, and with them were two who loved them, Martha, the "Spanish Scourge," and Red Martin, the free Frisian, the mighty man of war whom God had appointed to them as a shield of defense.

So they smiled on each other, these two lovers of long ago, and sailed bravely on to the closing gates of Haarlem.

Chapter XXVIII
Atonement

Seven months had gone by, seven of the most dreadful months that the people of Haarlem had ever endured. For all this space of time, through the frosts and snows and fogs of winter, through the icy winds of spring, and now deep into the heart of summer, the city of Haarlem had been closely beleaguered by an army of thirty thousand Spaniards. Most of the besiegers were veteran troops under the command of Don Frederic, the son of Alva. Against this disciplined host were opposed the little garrison of four thousand Hollanders and Germans aided by a few Scottish and English soldiers, together with a population of about twenty thousand old men, women and children. From day to day, from week to week, from month to month, the struggle was waged between these unequal forces, marked on either side by the most heroic efforts and by cruelties that would strike our age as monstrous. For in those times, the captive prisoner of war could expect no mercy and would often end up dying slowly within eyeshot of his friends.

There were battles without number, hundreds of men perished almost daily in mass assaults. Among the besieging armies alone, over twelve thousand lost their lives, so that the neighborhood of Haarlem became one vast graveyard, and the fish in the lake were poisoned by the dead. Assault, sortie, ambuscade, artifice of war; combats to the death upon the ice between skate-shod soldiers; desperate sea fights, attempts to storm; the explosion of mines and counter-mines that brought death to hundreds—all these became the familiar incidents of daily life.

Then there were other horrors. Cold from insufficient fuel, pestilences of various sorts such as always attend a siege, and, worst of all for the beleaguered, hunger. Week by week as the summer aged, the food grew less and less, until at length there was nothing. The weeds that grew in the street, the refuse of tanneries, the last ounce of lard, the mice and the cats, all had been devoured. On the lofty steeple of St. Bavon, for days and days, had floated a black flag to tell the Prince of Orange in Leyden that below it was despair as dark as the night. The last attempt at rescue had been made. Batenburg had been defeated and Blain, together with the Seigneurs of Clotingen and Carloo, and five or six hundred men. Now, from the earthly perspective there was no more hope.

Desperate measures were suggested: That the women, children, aged and sick should be left in the city, while the able-bodied men cut a way through the battalions of their besiegers. On these non-combatants it was hoped that the Spaniard would have mercy—as though the Spaniard could have mercy, he who afterwards dragged the wounded and the ailing to the door of the hospital and there slaughtered them in cold blood. Aye! Here and elsewhere, they did other things too dreadful to write down. Says the old chronicler, "But this being understood by the women, they assembled all together, making the most pitiful cries and lamentations that could be heard, the which would have moved a heart of flint, so as it was not possible to abandon them."

Next, another plan was formed: that all the women and helpless should be set in the center of a square of the fighting men, to march out and give battle to the foe until everyone was slain. Then the Spaniards hearing this and growing afraid of what these desperate men might do, resorted to guile and craftiness. If they would surrender, the citizens of Haarlem were told, and pay two hundred and forty thousand florins, no punishment should be inflicted. So, having neither food nor hope, they finally surrendered, they who had fought until their garrison of four thousand was reduced to eighteen hundred men.

It was past noon on the fatal twelfth of July. The gates were open, the Spaniards, those who were left alive of them, Don Frederic at their head, with drums beating, banners flying,

and swords sharpened for murder, marched into the city of Haarlem. In a deep niche between two great brick piers of the cathedral were gathered four people whom we know. War and famine had left them all alive, yet they had borne their share of both. In every enterprise, however desperate, Foy and Martin had marched, or stood, or watched side by side, and well did the Spaniards know the weight of the great sword Silence and the red-headed giant who wielded it. Mother Martha, too, had not been idle. Throughout the siege she had served as the lieutenant of the widow Hasselaer, who with a band of three hundred women fought day and night alongside of their husbands and brothers. Even Elsa, who although she was too delicate and by nature timid and unfitted to go out to battle, had done her part, for she labored at the digging of mines and the building of walls until her soft hands were rough and scarred.

How changed they were. Foy, whose face had been so youthful, looked now like a man on the wrong side of middle age. The huge Martin might have been a great skeleton on which hung clothes, or rather rags and a rent bull's hide, with his blue eyes shining in deep pits beneath the massive, projecting skull. Elsa too had become quite small, like a child. Her sweet face was no longer pretty, only pitiful, and all the roundness of her figure had vanished—she might have been an emaciated boy. Of the four of them Martha the Mare, who was dressed like a man, showed the least change. Indeed, except that now her hair was snowy, that her features were rather more horse-like, that the yellow, lipless teeth projected even further, and the thin nervous hands had become almost like those of an Egyptian mummy, she was much as she always had been.

Martin leaned upon the great sword and groaned. "Curses on them, the cowards," he muttered. "Why did they not let us go out and die fighting? Fools, mad fools, who would trust to the mercy of the Spaniard."

"Oh! Foy," said Elsa, throwing her thin arms about his neck, "you will not let them take me, will you?"

"Certainly not," he answered in a harsh, unnatural voice, "but oh! God, if Thou will, have pity upon her. Oh! God have pity."

"Blaspheme not, doubt not my words" broke in the shrill voice of Martha. "Has it not been as I told you last winter in the boat? Have you not been protected, and shall you not be protected to the end? Only blaspheme not, doubt not!"

The niche in which they were standing was out of sight of the great square and those who thronged it, but as Martha spoke, a band of the victorious Spaniards, seven or eight of them, came round the corner and caught sight of the party in the nook.

"There's a girl," said the sergeant in command of them, "who isn't bad looking. Pull her out, men."

Some fellows stepped forward to do his bidding. Now Foy went mad and he flew straight at the throat of the brute who had spoken, and next instant his sword protruded from the sergeant's neck. Then after him with a kind of low cry, came Martin, plying the great blade Silence, and Martha after him with her long knife. It was all over in a minute, but before it was done there were five men down—three dead and two severely wounded.

"A tithe and an offering!" yelled Martha as, bounding forward, she bent over the wounded men, and their comrades fled round the corner of the cathedral.

There was a minute's pause. The bright summer sunlight shone upon the faces and armor of the dead Spaniards. It also shown upon the naked sword of Foy, who stood over Elsa crouched to the ground in a corner of the niche with her face hidden in her hands. Then there came the sound of marching men, and a company of Spaniards appeared before them, and at their head Ramiro and Adrian, called van Goorl.

"There they are, Captain," said a soldier, one of those who had fled. "Shall we shoot them?"

Ramiro looked, carelessly enough at first, then again a long, scrutinizing look. So he had caught them at last! Months ago he had learned that Elsa had been rescued from the Red Mill by Foy and Martin, and now, after much seeking, the birds were in his net.

"No," he said, "I think not. Such desperate characters must be reserved for separate trial."

"Where can they be kept, Captain?" asked the frustrated sergeant.

"I observed, friend, that the house that my son and I have taken as our quarters has excellent cellars. They can be imprisoned there for the present—that is, except the young lady, whom the Señor Adrian will look after. As it happens, she is his wife."

At this the soldiers laughed openly.

"I repeat—his wife, for whom he has been searching these many months," shouted Ramiro, "and, therefore, to be respected. Do you understand, men?"

Apparently they did understand, at least no one made any answer. Their captain, as they had found, was not a man who loved argument.

"Now, then, you fellows," went on Ramiro, "give up your arms."

Martin thought a while. Evidently he was wondering whether it would not be best to rush at them and die fighting. At that moment, as he said afterwards indeed, the old saying came into his mind, "A game is not lost until it is won," and remembering that dead men can never have another chance of winning games, he gave up the sword.

"Hand that to me," said Ramiro. "It is a curious weapon to which I have taken a fancy."

So the sword Silence was handed to him, and he slung it over his shoulder. Foy looked at the kneeling Elsa, and he looked at his sword. Then an idea struck him, and he looked at the face of Adrian, his brother, whom he had last seen when Adrian ran to warn him and Martin at the factory, for though he knew that he was fighting with his father among the Spaniards, during the siege they had never met. Even then, in that dire extremity, with a sudden flash of thought he wondered how Adrian, being the villain that he was, had taken the trouble to come and warn them yonder in Leyden, thereby giving them time to make a very good defense in the shot tower.

Foy looked up at his brother. Adrian was dressed in the uniform of a Spanish officer, with a breastplate over his quilted doublet, and a steel cap, from the front of which rose a frayed and weather-worn plume of feathers. The face had changed; there was none of the old pomposity about those handsome features. It looked worn and cowed, like that of an animal that has been trained to do tricks by hunger and the use of the whip. Yet, through all the shame and degradation, Foy seemed to catch the glint of some kind of light, a light of hopeful yearning shining behind that piteous mask, as the sun sometimes shines through a dark cloud. Could it be that Adrian was not quite the villain after all? That he was, in fact, the Adrian that he, Foy, had always believed him to be, vain, silly, passionate, exaggerated, born to be a tool and think himself the master, but beneath everything, well-meaning? Who could say? At the worst, too, was it not better that Elsa should become the wife of Adrian than that her life should cease there and then.

These things passed through his brain as the lightning passes through the sky. In an instant, his mind was made up, and Foy flung down his sword at the feet of a soldier. As he did so his eyes met the eyes of Adrian, and to his imagination they seemed to be full of thanks and promise.

They took them all. With jabs and blows, the soldiers hauled them away through the tumult and the agony of the fallen town and its doomed defenders. Out of the rich sunlight, they led them into a house that still stood not greatly harmed by the cannon shot, but a little way from the shattered Ravelin (half-moon fortification) and the gate, which had been the scene of such fearful conflict. Here Foy and Elsa were parted. She struggled to his arms, from which they tore her and dragged her away up the stairs. Martin, Martha, and Foy were thrust into a dark cellar, locked in, and left.

A while later, the door of the cellar was unbarred and some hand—they could not see whose—passed through it water and food, good food such as they had not tasted for months. They were given meat and bread and dried herring, more than they could possibly eat.

"Perhaps it is poisoned," said Foy, smelling at it hungrily.

"What need to take the trouble to poison us?" answered Martin. "Let us eat and drink, while we yet have life."

So, like starving animals, they devoured the food with thankfulness to God and then they slept, yes, in the midst of all their misery and doubts they slept.

It seemed but a few minutes later—in fact it was eight hours—when the door opened again and there entered Adrian carrying a lantern in his hand.

"Foy, Martin," he said, "get up and follow me if you would save your lives."

Instantly, they were wide awake.

"Follow you—*you?*" stammered Foy in a choked voice.

"Yes," Adrian answered quietly. "Of course, you may not escape, but if you stay here what chance have you? Ramiro, my father, will be back shortly and then—"

"It is madness to trust ourselves to you," interrupted Martin, and Adrian seemed to wince at the contempt in his voice.

"I knew that you would think that," he answered humbly, "but what else is to be done? I can pass you out of the city, I have made a boat ready for you to escape in, all at the risk of my own life. What more can I do? Why do you hesitate?"

"Because we do not believe you," said Foy. "Besides, there is Elsa. I will not go without Elsa."

"I have thought of that," answered Adrian. "Elsa is here. Come, Elsa, show yourself."

Then from the stairs Elsa crept into the cellar, a new Elsa, for she too, had been fed, and in her eyes there shone a light of hope. A wild jealousy filled Foy's heart. Why did she look thus? But she, she ran to him, she flung her arms about his neck and kissed him, and Adrian did nothing, he only turned his head aside.

"Foy," she gasped, "he has repented. He will be true to his word this time. Come quickly, there is a chance for us; come before that devil returns. Now he is at a council of the officers settling with Don Frederic who are to be killed, but soon he will be back, and then—"

So they hesitated no more, but went forward at the brisk pace.

They passed out of the house, none stopping them, for the guard had gone to sleep. At the gate by the ruined Ravelin there stood a sentry, but the man was careless, or drunken, or bribed, who knows? At least, Adrian gave him a password, and, nodding his head, he let them by. A few minutes later they were at the Meer side, and there among some reeds lay the boat.

"Enter and be gone," said Adrian.

They scrambled into the boat and took the oars, while Martha began to push off.

"Adrian," said Elsa, "what is to become of you?"

"Why do you trouble about that?" he asked with a bitter laugh. "I go back to my death, my blood is the price of your freedom. Well, I owe it to you."

"Oh, no," she cried, "come with us."

"Yes," echoed Foy, although again that bitter pang of jealousy gripped his heart, "come with us—brother."

"Do you really mean it?" Adrian asked, hesitating. "Think, I might betray you."

"If so, young man, why did you not do it before?" growled

Martin, and stretching out his great, bony arm he gripped him by the collar and dragged him into the boat.

Then they rowed away.

"Where are we going?" asked Martin.

"To Leyden, I suppose," said Foy, "if we can get there, which, without a sail or weapons, seems unlikely."

"I have put some arms in the boat," interrupted Adrian, "the best I could get." And from a locker he drew out a common heavy axe, a couple of Spanish swords, a knife, a smaller axe, a crossbow and some bolts.

"Not so bad," said Martin, rowing with his left hand as he handled the big axe with his right, "but I wish that I had my sword Silence, which that accursed Ramiro took from me and hung about his neck. I wonder why he troubled himself with the thing? It is too long for a man of his inches."

"I don't know," said Adrian, "but, when last I saw him, he was working at its hilt with a chisel, which seemed strange. He always wanted that sword. During the siege he offered a large reward to any soldier who could kill you and bring it to him."

"Working at the hilt with a chisel?" gasped Martin. "By Heaven, I had forgotten! The map, the map! Some wicked villain must have told him that the treasure map was there—that is why he wanted the sword."

"Who could have told him?" asked Foy. "It was only known to you and me and Martha, and we are not of the sort to tell. What? Give away the secret of Hendrik Brant's treasure that he could die for and we were sworn to keep, to save our miserable lives? Shame upon the thought!"

Martha heard and looked at Elsa, a questioning look beneath which the poor girl turned a fiery red, though as it happened in that light none could see her blush. Still, she must speak lest the suspicion should lie on others.

"I ought to have told you before," she said in a low voice, "but I forgot—I mean that I have always been so dreadfully ashamed. It was I who betrayed the secret of the sword Silence."

"You? How did you know it?" asked Foy.

"Mother Martha told me on the night of the church burning

after you escaped from Leyden."

Martin grunted. "One woman to trust another, and at her age too. What a fool!"

"Fool yourself, you thick-headed Frisian," broke in Martha angrily, "where did you learn to teach your betters wisdom? I told the Jufvrouw because I knew that we might all of us be swept away, and I thought it well that then she should know where to look for a key to the treasure."

"A woman's kind of reason," answered Martin rashly "and a bad one at that, for if we had been finished off, she must have found it difficult to get hold of the sword. But all this is done with. The point is why did the Jufvrouw tell Ramiro?"

"Because I am a coward," answered Elsa with a sob. "You know, Foy, I always was a coward, and I never shall be anything else. I told him to save myself."

"From what?" hesitated Foy.

"From being married," responded Elsa.

Adrian winced noticeably, and Foy, seeing it, could not resist pushing the point.

"From being married? But I understood—doubtless Adrian will explain the thing," he added grimly, "—that you were forced through some ceremony."

"Yes," answered Elsa feebly, "I—I—was. I tried to buy myself off by telling Ramiro the secret, which will show you all how mad I was with terror at the thought of this hateful marriage"— here a groan burst from the lips of Adrian, and something like a chuckle from those of Red Martin. "Oh! I am so sorry," went on Elsa in confusion. "I am sure that I did not wish to hurt Adrian's feelings, especially after he has been so good to us."

"Never mind Adrian's feelings and his goodness. Go on with the story," interrupted Foy.

"There isn't much more to tell. Ramiro swore before God that if I gave him the clue he would let me go, and then—then, well, then, after I had fallen into the pit and disgraced myself, he said that it was not sufficient, and that the marriage must still take place."

At this both Foy and Martin laughed outright. Yes, even there they laughed.

"Why, you silly child," said Foy, "what else did you expect him to say?"

"Oh! Martin, do you forgive me?" said Elsa. "Immediately after I had done it, I knew how shameful it was, and that he would try to hunt you down, and that is why I have been afraid to tell you ever since. But I pray you believe me. I only spoke because, between shame and fear, I did not know right from wrong. Do you forgive me?"

"Lady," answered the Frisian, smiling in his slow fashion, "if I had been there unknown to Ramiro, and you had offered him this head of mine on a dish as a bribe, not only would I have forgiven you but I would have said that you did right. You are a maid, and you had to protect yourself from a very dreadful thing. Who can blame you?"

"I can," said Martha. "Ramiro might have torn me to pieces with red-hot pincers before I told him."

"Yes," said Martin, who felt that he had a debt to pay, "Ramiro might, but I doubt whether he would have gone to that trouble to persuade you to take a husband. No, don't be angry. 'Frisian thick of head, Frisian free of speech,' goes the saying."

Not being able to think of any appropriate rejoinder, Martha turned again upon Elsa.

"Your father died for that treasure," she said, "and Dirk van Goorl died for it, and your lover and his servingman there went to the torture den for it, and I—well, I have done a thing or two. But you, girl, why, at the first pinch, you betray the secret. But, as Martin says, I was fool enough to tell you."

"Oh! You are hard," said Elsa, beginning to weep under Martha's bitter reproaches, "but you forget that at least none of you were asked to marry—oh! I mustn't say that. I mean to become the wife of one man. ..." Then her eyes fell upon Foy and an inspiration seized her; here, at least, was one of whom she could make a friend, "... when you happen to be very much in love with another."

"Of course not," said Foy, "there is no need for you to explain."

"I think there is a great deal to explain," went on Martha, "for you cannot fool me with pretty words. But I turn my attention to Foy van Goorl, and ask; what is to be done? We have striven hard to save that treasure, all of us. Is it to be lost at the last?"

"Aye," echoed Martin, growing very serious, "is it to be lost at the last? Remember what the worshipful Hendrik Brant said to us yonder on that night at The Hague; that he believed that in a day to come, thousands and tens of thousands of our people would bless the gold he entrusted to us."

"I remember it all," answered Foy, "and other things too. His will, for instance," and he thought of his father and of those hours that Martin and he had spent in the Gravensteen. Then he looked up at Martha and said briefly, "Mother, though they call you mad, you are the wisest among us; what is your counsel?"

She pondered a while and answered, "This is certain, that as soon as Ramiro finds that we have escaped, having the key to it, he will take boat and sail to the place where the barrels are buried, knowing well that otherwise we shall be off with them. Yes, I tell you that by dawn, or within an hour of it, he will be there," and she stopped.

"You mean," said Foy, "that we ought to be there before him."

Martha nodded and answered, "If we can, but I think that at best there must be a fight for it."

"Yes," said Martin, "a fight. Well, I should like another fight with Ramiro. That fork-tongued adder has got my sword, and I want to get it back again."

"Oh," broke in Elsa, "is there to be more fighting? I hoped that at last we were safe, and going straight to Leyden, where the Prince is. I hate this bloodshed. I tell you, Foy, it frightens me to death; I believe that I shall die of it."

"You hear what she says?" asked Foy.

"We hear," answered Martha. "Take no heed of her, the child has suffered much, she is weak and squeamish. Now, although I believe that my death lies before me, my counsel is still to go on and fear not."

"But I do take heed," said Foy. "Not for all the treasures in the world shall Elsa be put in danger again if she does not wish it; she shall decide, and she alone."

"How good you are to me," she murmured, then she mused a moment. "Foy," she said, "will you promise something to me?"

"After your experience with Ramiro's oaths, I wonder that you ask," he answered, trying to be cheerful.

"Will you promise," she went on, taking no note, "that if I say yes and we go, not to Leyden, but to seek the treasure, and live through it, that you will take me away from this land of blood-shed and murder and torments, to some country where folk may live at peace? It is much to ask, but oh! Foy, will you promise?"

"Yes, I promise," said Foy, for he, too, was weary of this daily terror. Who would not have been, especially those who had lived through the siege of Haarlem?

Foy was steering, but now Martha slipped aft and took the tiller from his hand. For a moment, she studied the stars that grew clearer in the light of the sinking moon, then shifted the helm a point or two to port and sat still.

"I am hungry again," said Martin presently. "I feel as though I could eat for a week without stopping."

Adrian looked up from over his oar, at which he was laboring dejectedly, and said, "There is food and drink in the locker. I hid them there. Perhaps Elsa could serve them to those who wish to eat."

So Elsa, who was doing nothing, found the food and handed it out to the rowers, who ate and drank as best they might with a thankful heart, but without ceasing from their task. To men who have starved for months, the taste of wholesome provender and sound meat is a delight that cannot be written in words.

When at length they had filled themselves, Adrian spoke.

"If it is your good will, brother," he said, addressing Foy, "as we do not know what lies in front, nor how long any of us have to live, I, who am an outcast and a scorn among you, wish to tell you a story."

"Speak on," said Foy.

So Adrian began from the beginning, and told them his tale. He told them how, at first, he had been lead astray by superstitions, vanity, and love; how his foolish confidences had been written down by spies; how he had been startled and terrified into signing them with the results of which they knew. Then he told them how he was hunted like a mad dog through the streets of Leyden after his mother had turned him from her door; how he took refuge in the den of Hague Simon, and there had fought with Ramiro and been conquered by the man's crafty words and his own horror of shedding a father's blood. He told them of his admission into the Roman faith, of the dreadful scene in the church when Martha had denounced him, of their flight to the Red Mill. He told them of the kidnapping of Elsa, and how he had been quite innocent of it, although he loved her dearly; of how, at last, he was driven into marrying her, meaning her no harm, to save her from the grip of Ramiro, while knowing at heart that it was no marriage. He then told of how, when the flood burst upon them, he had been hustled from the mill where, since she could no longer be of service to him and might work him injury, as he discovered afterwards, Ramiro had left Elsa to her fate. Lastly, in a broken voice, he told them of his life during the long siege, which was as the life of a damned spirit, and of how, when death thinned the ranks of the Spaniards, he had been made an officer among them, and by the special malice of Ramiro forced to conduct the executions and murders of such Hollanders as they took.

Then, at last, his chance had come. Ramiro, thinking that now he could never turn against him, had given him Elsa, and left him with her while he went about his duties and to secure a share of the plunder, meaning to deal with his prisoners on the morrow. So he, Adrian, a man in authority, had provided the boat and freed them. That was all he had to say, except to renounce any claim upon her who was called his wife, and to beg their forgiveness for his sins.

Foy listened to the end. Then, dropping his oar for a moment, he put his arm around Adrian's shoulder and hugged him, saying in his old cheery voice:

"I was right after all. You know, Adrian, I always stood up for you, notwithstanding your temper and unusual habits. No, I never would believe that you were a villain, but neither could I ever have believed that you would become an honorable man."

To this outspoken estimate of his character, so fallen and crushed was he, his brother had not the spirit to reply. He could merely tug at his oar and groan, while the tears of shame and repentance ran down his pale and handsome face.

"Never mind, old fellow," said Foy consolingly. "It all went wrong, thanks to you, and thanks to you I believe that it will all come right again. So we will forgive now and forget the rest."

Poor Adrian glanced up at Foy and at Elsa sitting on the thwart of the boat by his side.

"Yes, brother," he answered, "for you and Elsa it may come right, but not for me in this world, for I—I have sold myself to the devil and—got no pay."

After that for, a while, no one spoke. All felt that the situation was too tragic for speech; even the follies and indeed the wickedness of Adrian were covered up and blotted out in the tragedy of his utter failure, yes, and redeemed by the depth of his sincere repentance.

The gray light of the summer morning began to grow on the surface of the great inland sea. Far behind them, they beheld the sun's rays breaking upon the gilt crown set above the tower of St. Bavon's Church, soaring over the lost city of Haarlem and the doomed patriots who lay there presently to meet their death at the murderer's sword. They looked and shuddered. Had it not been for Adrian, they would be prisoners now, and what that meant they knew. If they had been in any doubt, what they saw in the water must have enlightened them, for here and there upon the misty surface of the lake, or stranded in its shallows, were the half-burnt out hulls of ships, the remains of the conquered fleet of William the Silent; a poor record of the last desperate effort to relieve the starving city. Now and again, too, something limp and soft would cumber their oars, the corpse of a drowned or slaughtered man.

After several minutes, they passed out of these dismal remains of lost men, and Elsa could look about her without shuddering.

Now they were in fleet water, and in among the islands whereon the lush summer growth of weeds and the beautiful marsh flowers grew as greenly and bloomed as bright as though no Spaniard had trampled their roots under foot during all those winter months of siege and death. These islets, scores and hundreds of them, appeared on every side, but between them all Martha steered an unerring path. As the sun rose she stood up in the boat, shading her eyes with her hand to shut out its level rays. For almost a minute, she stared intently ahead of the boat.

"There is the place," she said, pointing to a little bulrush-clad isle, from which a kind of natural causeway, not more than six feet wide, projected like a tongue among muddy shallows.

Martin rose too. Then he looked back behind him and said, "I see the cap of a sail upon the skyline. It is Ramiro."

"Without doubt," answered Martha calmly. "Well, we have barely half an hour to get our work done. Pull, the oars, pull, we will go round the island and beach her in the sand on the further side. They will be less likely to see us there, and I know a place where we can push off in a hurry."

Chapter XXIX
Adrian Comes Home Again

They landed on the island, wading to it through the mud, which at this spot had a gravelly bottom. All of them except Elsa, who remained in the boat to keep watch. Following otter-paths through the thick rushes they came to the center of the islet, some thirty yards away. Here, at a spot that Martha ascertained by a few hurried pacings, grew a dense tuft of reeds. In the midst of these reeds was a duck's nest with the young having just hatched.

"Beneath this nest lay the treasure, if some party has not been here before us. At any rate, the place has not been disturbed lately," said Foy. Then, in spite of his frantic haste, he lifted the little fledglings—for he loved all things that had life, and did not wish to see them hurt—and deposited them where they might be found again by the mother.

"Nothing to dig with," muttered Martin, "not even a stone." Martha, in response to this complaint, made her way to a willow bush that grew near, and with the smaller of the two axes, which she held in her hand, cut down the thickest of its stems and ran back with them. Through the assistance of these sharpened stakes, and with their axes, they began to dig furiously, until finally the point of Foy's implement struck upon the head of a barrel.

"The stuff is still here. Keep to it, friends," he said, and they worked on with a will until three of the five barrels were almost free from the mud.

"Best make these secure," said Martin. "Help me, Master," and between them, one by one, they rolled them to the water's edge, and with great effort, Elsa aiding them, lifted them into the boat. As they approached with the third cask they found her staring white-faced over the tops of the feathery reeds.

"What is it, sweet?" asked Foy.

"The sail, the following sail," she answered.

They rested the barrel of gold upon the gunwale and looked back across the little island. Yes, there it came, sure enough, a tall, white sail not eight hundred yards away and bearing down straight upon the place. Martin rolled the barrel into position.

"I hoped that they would not find it," he said, "but Martha draws maps well, too well."

"What is to be done?" asked Elsa.

"I don't know," he answered, and as he spoke Martha ran up, for she also had seen the boat. "You see," he went on, "if we try to escape they will catch us, for oars can't race a sail."

"Oh!" said Elsa, "must we be taken after all?"

"I hope not, girl," said Martha, "but it is as God wills. Listen, Martin," and she whispered in his ear.

"Good," he said, "if it can be done, but you must watch for your opportunity. Come, now, there is no time to lose. And you, lady, come also, for you can help to roll the last two barrels."

Then they ran back to the hole, from where Foy and Adrian, with great toil, had just dragged the last of the barrels. For they, too, had seen the sail, and knew that time was short.

"Heer Adrian," said Martin, "you have the crossbow and the bolts, and you used to be the best shot of all three of us. Will you help me to hold the causeway?"

Now Adrian knew that Martin said this, not because he was a good shot with the crossbow, but because he did not trust him, and wished to have him close to his hand, but he answered, "With all my heart, as well as I am able."

"Very good," said Martin. "Now let the rest of you get those two casks into the boat, leaving the Jufvrouw hidden in the reeds to watch it, while you, Foy and Martha, come back to help us. Lady, if they sail round the island, call and let us know."

So Martin and Adrian went down to the end of the little gravelly shore and crouched among the tall meadow grasses while the others, working furiously, rolled the two barrels to the water's edge and shipped them, throwing rushes over them that they might not catch the eye of the Spaniards.

The sailing-boat drew on. In the stern of it sat Ramiro, an open paper, which he was studying, upon his knee, and still slung about his body the great sword Silence.

"Before I am half an hour older," reflected Martin, for even now he did not like to trust his thoughts to Adrian, "either I will have that sword back again, or I shall be a dead man. But the odds are great, eleven of them, all tough fellows, and we but three men and two women."

Just then Ramiro's voice reached them across the stillness of the water.

"Down with the sail," he cried cheerily, "for without a doubt that is the place—there are the six islets in a line, there in front the other island shaped like a herring, and there the little promontory marked 'landing place.' How well this artist draws to be sure!"

The rest of his remarks were lost in the creaking of the blocks as the sail came down.

"Shallow water ahead, Señor," said a man who was working with the anchor.

"Good," answered Ramiro, "throw out the little anchor, we will wade ashore."

As he spoke, the Spanish soldier with the boat-hook suddenly pitched head first into the water, a quarrel from Adrian's cross-bow through his heart.

"Ah!" said Ramiro, "so they are here before us. Well, there can't be many of them. Now then, prepare to land."

Another quarrel whistled through the air and stuck in the mast, doing no harm. After this no more bolts came, for in his eagerness Adrian had broken the mechanism of the bow by overwinding it, so that it became useless. They leaped into the water, Ramiro with them, and charged for the land, when out of nowhere, almost at the tip of the little promontory, from among the reeds rose the gigantic shape of Red Martin, clad in his tattered jerkin and bearing in his hand a heavy axe, while behind him appeared Foy and Adrian.

"Why by the Saints!" cried Ramiro, "there's my weather-cock son again, fighting against us this time. Well, weather-cock this is your last veer." Then he began to wade towards the promontory. "Charge," he cried, but not a man would advance within reach of that axe. They stood here and there in the water looking at it doubtfully, for although they were brave enough, there was none of them that were unaware of the strength and deeds of the red Frisian giant, and half-starved as he was, they feared to meet him face to face. Moreover, he had a position on higher ground, of that there could be no doubt.

"Can I help you to land, friends?" said Martin, mocking them. "No, it is no use looking right or left, the mud there is very deep."

"An arquebus, shoot him with an arquebus!" shouted the men in front. But there was no such weapon in the boat, for the Spaniards, who had left in a hurry, and without expecting to meet Red Martin, had nothing but their swords and knives.

Ramiro considered a moment, for he saw that to attempt to storm this little landing-place would cost many lives, even if it were possible. Then he gave an order, "Back aboard." The men obeyed with speed. "Out oars and up anchor!" he cried.

"He is clever," said Foy. He knows that our boat must be somewhere, and he is going to hunt for it."

Martin nodded, and for the first time looked afraid. Then, as soon as Ramiro had begun to row round the islet, leaving Martha to watch so he did not return and rush the landing stage, they crossed through the reeds to the other side and climbed into their boat. Scarcely were they there, when Ramiro and his men appeared, and a shout announced that they were discovered.

On crept the Spaniards as near as they dared, that is to within a dozen fathoms of them, and anchored, for they were afraid to run their own heavy sailing cutter upon the mud lest they might be unable to get her off again. Also, for evident reasons, being without firearms and knowing the character of the defenders, they feared to make a direct attack. The position was curious and threatened to be prolonged. At last, Ramiro stood and addressed them across the water.

"Gentlemen and lady of the enemy," he said, "for I think that I see my little captive of the Red Mill among you, let us take counsel together. We have both of us made this expedition for a purpose, have we not—namely, to secure certain filthy lucre, which, after all, would be of slight value to dead men? Now, as you, or some of you know, I am a man opposed to violence. I wish to hurry the end of none, nor even to inflict suffering, if it can be avoided. But there is money in the question, and I have already gone through a great deal of inconvenience and anxiety. To be brief, that money I must have, while you, on the other hand are doubtless anxious to escape hence with your lives. So I make you an offer. Let one of our party come under safe conduct on board your boat and search it, just to see if anything lies beneath those rushes, for instance. Then, if it is found empty, we will withdraw to a distance and let you go, or the same if full, that is, upon its contents being unladen into the mud."

"Are those all your terms?" asked Foy.

"Not quite all, worthy Heer van Goorl. Among you I observe a young gentleman whom doubtless you have managed to carry off against his will, to wit, my beloved son, Adrian. In his own interests, for he will scarcely be a welcome guest in Leyden, I ask that, before you depart, you should place this noble cavalier ashore in a position where we can see him. Now, what is your answer?"

"That your terms will be acceptable, if and when hell freezes over," replied Martin crudely, while Foy added:

"What other answer do you expect from folk who have escaped out of your clutches in Haarlem?"

As he said the words, at a nod from Martin, Martha, who by now had crept into the water, under cover of the surrounding reeds, let go of the stern of the boat and vanished under the waves.

"Plain words from plain, uncultivated people, not unnaturally irritated by the course of political events with which, although Fortune has mixed me up in them, I have nothing whatever to do," answered Ramiro. "But once more I beg you to consider. It is probable that you have no food upon your boat, whereas we have plenty. Also, in due course, darkness will fall, which must give us a certain advantage; moreover, I have reason to hope for assistance. Therefore, in a waiting game like this the cards are with me, and as I think your poor prisoner, Adrian, will tell you, I know how to play a hand at cards."

About eight yards from the sailboat, in a thick patch of water-lilies, just at this moment an otter rose to take air, an old otter, for it was gray-headed. One of the Spaniards in the boat caught sight of the ring it made, and picking up a stone from the ballast threw it at the creature idly. The otter vanished.

"We have been seeking each other a long while, but have never come to blows yet, although, being a brave man, I know you would wish it," said Red Martin modestly. "Señor Ramiro, will you do me the honor to overlook my humble birth and come ashore with me for a few minutes, man against man. The odds would be in your favor, for you have armor and I have nothing but a worn bull's hide, also you have my good sword Silence and I only a woodman's axe. Still I will risk it, and, what is more, trusting to your good faith, we are willing to wager the treasure of Hendrik Brant upon the issue."

So soon as they understood this challenge, a roar of laughter went up from the Spaniards in the boat, in which Ramiro himself joined heartily. The idea of anyone voluntarily entering upon a single combat with the terrible Frisian giant, who for months had been a name of fear among the thousands that beleaguered Haarlem, struck them as really ludicrous.

It was not long, however, before they ceased laughing, and one and all stared with a strange anxiety at the bottom of their boat, much as terrier dogs stare at the earth beneath which they hear invisible vermin on the move. Then a great shouting arose among them, and they looked eagerly over the gunwales; yes, and began to stab at the water with their swords. But all the while, through the tumult and voices came a steady, regular sound as of a person knocking heavily on the opposite side of a thick door.

"Mother of Heaven!" screamed someone in the sailboat, "we

are scuttled!" And they began to tear at the false bottom of their boat, while others stabbed still more furiously at the surface of the Meer.

Now, rising one by one to the surface of that quiet water, could be seen bubbles, and the line of them ran from the sailboat towards the rowing boat. Moments later, within six feet of it, axe in hand, rose the strange and dreadful figure of a skeleton-like woman covered with mud and green weeds, and bleeding from great wounds in the back and sides.

There she stood, shaking an axe at the terror-stricken Spaniards, and screaming in short gasps, "Paid back! Paid back, Ramiro! Now sink and drown, you dog, or come, visit Red Martin on the shore."

"Well done, Martha," roared Martin, as he dragged her dying into the boat. While he spoke, lo, the sailboat cutter began to fill and sink.

"There is but one chance for it," cried Ramiro, "overboard and at them. It is not deep," and springing into the water, which reached to his neck, he began to wade towards the shore.

"Push off," cried Foy, as they pushed and pulled. But the gold was heavy, and their boat had settled far into the mud. Do what they might, she would not stir. Then uttering some strange Frisian oath, Martin sprang over her stern, and putting out all his mighty strength thrust at it to loose her. Still she would not move. The Spaniards came up, now the water reached only to their thighs, and their bright swords flashed in the sunlight.

"Cut them down!" yelled Ramiro. "At them for your lives' sake."

The boat trembled, but she would not stir.

"Too heavy in the bows," screamed Martha, and struggling to her feet, with one wild scream she launched herself straight at the throat of the nearest Spaniard. She gripped him with her long arms, and down they went together.

Once they rose, then fell again, and through a spray of mud might be seen struggling upon the bottom of the Meer until eventually they lay still, both of them.

The lightened boat lifted and, in answer to Martin's mighty

efforts, glided forward through the clinging mud. Again he thrust, and she was clear.

"Climb in, Martin, climb in," shouted Foy as he stabbed at a Spaniard.

"By heaven! No!" roared Ramiro splashing towards him with the face of a devil.

For a second, Martin stood still. Then he bent, and the sword thrust fell harmless upon his leather jerkin. In the next moment his great arms shot out; he seized Ramiro by the thighs and lifted, and there was seen the sight of a man thrown into the air as though he were a ball tossed by a child at play. Ramiro fell headlong upon the casks of treasure in the skiff prow and lay still.

Martin sprang forward and gripped the tiller with his outstretched hand as it glided away from him.

"Row, Master, row," he cried, and Foy rowed madly until they were clear of the last Spaniard, clear by ten yards. Even Elsa snatched a rollock, and with it struck a soldier on the hand who tried to stop them, forcing him to loose his grip—a deed of valor she boasted of with pride all her life through. Then they dragged Martin into the boat.

"Now, you Spanish dogs," the great man roared back at them as he shook the water from his flaming hair and beard, "go dig for Brant's treasure and live on ducks' eggs here until Don Frederic sends to fetch you."

The island had melted away into a mist of other islands. No living thing was to be seen save the wild creatures and birds of the great lake, and no sound was to be heard except their calling and the voices of the wind and water. They were alone, alone and safe, and there at a distance towards the skyline rose the church towers of Leyden, for which they headed.

"Jufvrouw," said Martin presently, "there is another bottle of water in that locker, and we should be glad of a pull at it."

Elsa, who was steering the boat, stood and found the drink and a horn mug, which she filled and handed first to Foy.

"Here's a health," said Foy as he drank, "to the memory of Mother Martha, who saved us all. Well, she died as she would have wished to die, taking a Spaniard for company, and her story will live on."

"Amen," said Martin. Then a thought struck him, and, leaving his oars for a minute, for he rowed two as against Foy's and Adrian's one, he went forward to where Ramiro lay stricken senseless on the kegs of gold and jewels in the bows, and took from him the great sword Silence. But he strapped the Spaniard's legs together with his belt.

"That crack on the head keeps him quiet enough," he said in explanation, "but he might come to and give trouble, or try to swim for it, since such cats have many lives. Ah! Señor Ramiro, I told you I would have my sword back before I was half an hour older, or go to the throne of God." Then he touched the spring in the hilt and examined the cavity. "Why," he said, "here's my legacy left in it, safe and sound. No wonder my good angel made me yearn to get that sword again."

"No wonder," echoed Foy, "especially as you got Ramiro with it," and he glanced at Adrian, who was laboring at the bow oar, looking, now that the excitement of the fight had gone by, most downcast and wretched. Well he might, seeing the welcome that, as he feared, awaited him in Leyden.

For a while they rowed on in silence. All that they had gone through during the last twenty-four hours, and the seven preceding months of war and privation, had broken their nerve. Even now, although they had escaped the danger and won back the buried gold, capturing the arch-villain who had brought them so much death and misery, they still could not be at ease. Where so many had died, where the risks had been so fearful, it seemed almost incredible that they four should be living and hale, though weary, with a prospect of continuing to live for many years.

That the girl whom he loved so dearly, and whom he had so nearly lost, should be sitting before him safe and sound, ready to become his wife whenever he might wish it, seemed to Foy also a thing too good to be true. Too good to be true was it, moreover, that his brother, the wayward, passionate, Adrian, should have been dragged before it was too late, out of the net of the fowler, have repented of his sins and follies, and, at the risk of his own life, shown that he was a new creature in Christ. For Foy had always loved his brother, and knowing him better than any others knew him, had found it hard to believe that however black things might look against him, he would remain a villain.

Thus he thought, and Elsa too had her thoughts, which may be guessed. They were silent all of them, until all of a sudden, Elsa seated in the stern-sheets, saw Adrian suddenly let fall his oar, throw his arms wide, and pitch forward against the back of Martin. Yes, and in place of where he had sat appeared the dreadful countenance of Ramiro, stamped with a grin of hideous hate such as Satan might wear when souls escape him at the last. Ramiro recovered and sat up, for to his feet he could not rise because of the sword strap around his legs. He had a thin bloody knife in his hand.

"*Habet!*" he said with a short laugh, "*habes*, Weathercock!" and he turned the knife against himself.

But Martin was on him, and in five more seconds the murderer lay trussed like a fowl in the bottom of the boat.

"Shall I kill him?" said Martin to Foy, who with Elsa was bending over Adrian.

"No," answered Foy grimly, "let him take his trial in Leyden. Oh! What accursed fools were we not to search him!"

Ramiro's face turned a shade more ghastly.

"It is your hour," he said in a hoarse voice, "you have won, thanks to that dog of a son of mine, who, I trust, may linger long before he dies, as die he must. Ah, well, this is what comes of breaking my oath to the Virgin and again lifting my hand against a woman." He looked at Elsa and shuddered, then went on: "It is your hour, make an end of me at once. I do not wish to appear thus before those boors."

"Gag him," said Foy to Martin, "lest our ears be poisoned," and Martin obeyed with good will. Then he flung him down, and there the man lay, his back supported by the kegs of treasure he had worked so hard and sinned so deeply to win, making, as he knew well, his last journey prior to his death and to whatever may lie beyond that solemn gate.

They were passing the island that, many years ago, had formed the turning post of the great sleigh race in which his passenger had been the fair Leyden heiress, Lysbeth van Hout. Ramiro could see her now as she was that day; he could see also how that race, which he just failed to win, had been for him an harbinger of disaster.

Like his son Adrian, Ramiro was superstitious, and his intellect, his reading—which in youth had been considerable—his observation of men and women, all led him to the conclusion that death is a wall with many doors in it. He was convinced that, on this side of the wall, we may not linger or sleep but must pass each of us through his appointed portal straight to the domain prepared for us. If so, what would be his lot, and who would be waiting to greet him yonder? Oh, terrors may attend the wicked after death, but in the case of some, these terrors do not wait until death; they leap toward him whom it is decreed must die, forcing attention with their eager, craving hands, with their obscure and ominous voices.

Before he passed the gates of Leyden, in those few short hours, Ramiro, to Elsa's eyes, had aged by twenty years.

Their little boat was heavy laden, the wind was against them, and they had a dying man and a prisoner aboard. So it came about that the day was closing before the soldiers challenged them from the watergate, asking who they were and where they were going. Foy stood up and said:

"We are Foy van Goorl, Red Martin, Elsa Brant, a wounded man and a prisoner, escaped from Haarlem, and we go to the house of Lysbeth van Goorl in the Bree Straat."

Then they let them through the watergate, and there were many gathered on the further side who thanked God for their deliverance and begged tidings of them.

"Come to the house in the Bree Straat and we will tell you from the balcony," answered Foy.

So they rowed from one canal to another until at last they came to the private boathouse of the van Goorls and entered it, and there by the small door into the house.

Lysbeth van Goorl, recovered from her illness now, but aged and grown stern with suffering, sat in an armchair in the great parlor of her home in the Bree Straat, the room where as a girl she had confronted Montalvo; where not a year ago, she had driven his son, the traitor Adrian, from her presence. At her side was a table on which stood a silver bell and two brass holders with candles ready to be lighted. She rang the bell and a woman-servant entered, the same who, with Elsa, had nursed her in the plague.

"What is that murmuring in the street?" Lysbeth asked. "I hear the sound of many voices. Is there more news from Haarlem?"

"Alas, yes," answered the woman. "A fugitive says that the executioners there are weary, so now they tie the poor prisoners back to back and throw them into the Meer to drown."

A groan burst from Lysbeth's lips. "Foy, my son, is there," she lamented, "and Elsa Brant his betrothed wife, and Martin his servant, and many another friend. Oh! God, how long, how long?" and her head sank upon her bosom.

Soon she raised it again and said, "Light the candles, woman, this place grows dark, and in its gloom I see the ghosts of all my dead."

They flamed up—two stars of light in the great room.

"Whose feet are those upon the stairs?" asked Lysbeth curiously, "the feet of men who bear burdens. Open the large doors, woman, and let those enter which it pleases God to send us."

So the doors were flung wide, and through them came people carrying a wounded man, then following him Foy and Elsa, and, lastly, towering above them all, Red Martin, who thrust before him another man. Lysbeth rose from her chair to look.

"Do I dream?" she said, "or, son Foy, has the Angel of the Lord delivered you out of the hell of Haarlem?"

"We are here, Mother," he answered.

"And whom," she said, pointing to the figure covered with a cloak, "do you bring with you?"

"Adrian, Mother, who is dying."

"Then, Foy, take him hence. Alive, dying, or dead, I have

done with—"

Here her eyes fell upon Red Martin and the man he held, "Martin the Frisian," she muttered, "but who—"

Martin heard, and in place of an answer lifted up his prisoner so that the fading light from the balcony windows fell full upon his face.

"What!" she cried, "Juan de Montalvo as well as his son Adrian, and in this room—?" Then she checked herself and added, "Foy, tell me your story."

In a few words and quickly he told it, or as much as she need to know to understand. His last words were, "Mother, be merciful to Adrian. From the first he meant no ill. He saved all our lives, and he lies dying by that man's dagger."

"Lift him up," she said.

So they lifted him up, and Adrian, who, since the knife pierced him had uttered no word, spoke for the first and last time, whispering hoarsely, "Mother, take back your words and forgive me before I die."

Now the sorrow-frozen heart of Lysbeth melted, and she bent over him and said, speaking so that all might hear:

"Welcome to your home again, Adrian. You who once were led astray, have done bravely, and I am proud to call you son. Though you once strayed from the faith in which you were bred, the living God has called you back to the fold. Therefore, here and hereafter may God bless you and reward you, beloved Adrian!" Then she bent and kissed his dying lips. Foy and Elsa kissed him also in farewell before they carried him, smiling happily to himself, to the chamber, his own chamber, where within some few hours death found him.

Adrian had been borne away, and for a little while there was silence. Then, none commanding him, but as though an instinct pushed him forward, Red Martin began to move up the length of the long room, half dragging, half-carrying his captive Ramiro. It was as if some automaton had suddenly been put in motion, some machine of gigantic strength that nothing could stop. The man in his grip set his heels in the floor and hung back, but Martin scarcely seemed to heed his resistance. On he came, and the victim with him, until they stood together before the oaken chair and the stern-faced, white-haired woman who sat in it, her cold countenance lit by the light of the two candles. She looked and shuddered. Then she spoke, asking, "Why do you bring this man to me, Martin?"

"For judgment, Lysbeth van Goorl," he answered.

"Who made me a judge over him?" she asked.

"My master, Dirk van Goorl, your son, Adrian, and Hendrik Brant. Their blood makes you judge of his blood."

"I will have none of it," Lysbeth said passionately, "let the people judge him." As she spoke, from the crowd in the street below there swelled a sudden clamor.

"Good," said Martin, "the people shall judge," and he began to turn towards the window, when suddenly, by a desperate effort, Ramiro wrenched his doublet from his hand, and flung himself at Lysbeth's feet and groveled there.

"What do you seek?" she asked, drawing back her dress so that he should not touch it.

"Mercy," he gasped.

"Mercy! Look, Son and Daughter, this man asks for mercy who for many a year has given none. Well, Juan de Montalvo, take your prayer to God and to the people. I am done with you."

"Mercy, mercy!" he cried again.

"Eight months ago," she said, "I uttered that prayer to you, begging of you in the Name of Christ to spare the life of an innocent man, and what was your answer, Juan de Montalvo?"

"Once you were my wife," he pleaded. "Being a woman, does not that weigh with you?"

"Once he was my husband, being a man did that weigh with you? The last word is spoken. Take him, Martin, to those who deal with murderers."

Then that look came upon Montalvo which two or three times before Lysbeth had seen written on his face—once when the race was run and lost, and once when in later years she had petitioned for the life of her husband. Lo! It was no longer the face of a man, but such a countenance as might have been worn by a devil or a beast. The eyeball started, the grey moustachio curled upwards, the cheekbones grew, high and sharp.

"Night after night," he gasped, "you lay at my side, and I might have killed you, as I have killed that brat of yours—and I spared you, I spared you."

"God spared me, Juan de Montalvo, that He might bring us to this hour. Let Him spare you also if He will. I do not judge. He judges and the people," and Lysbeth rose from her chair.

"Stay!" he cried, gnashing his teeth.

"No, I stay not, I go to receive the last breath of him you have murdered, my son and yours."

He raised himself upon his knees, and for a moment their eyes met for the last time.

"Do you remember?" she said in a quiet voice, "many, years ago, in this very room, after you had bought me at the cost of Dirk's life, certain words I spoke to you? Now I do not think that it was I who spoke, Juan de Montalvo."

And she swept past him and through the wide doorway.

Red Martin stood upon the balcony gripping the man Ramiro. Beneath him the broad street was packed with people, hundreds and thousands of them, a dense mass seething in the shadows, save here and again where a torch, or a lantern flared showing their white faces, for the moon, which shone upon Martin and his captive, scarcely reached those down below. As gaunt, haggard, and long-haired, he stepped upon the balcony, they saw him and his burden, and there went up such a yell as shook the very roofs of Leyden. Martin held up his hand, and there was silence, deep silence, through which the breath of all that multitude rose in sighs, like the sighing of a little wind.

"Citizens of Leyden, my masters," the Frisian cried, in a great, deep voice that echoed down the street, "I have a word to say to you. This man here—do you know him?"

"Aye!" yelled the crowd in response.

"He is a Spaniard," went on Martin, "the Count Juan de Montalvo, who many years past forced one Lysbeth van Hout of this city into a false marriage, buying her at the price of the life of her betrothed husband, Dirk van Goorl, that he might win her fortune."

"We know it," they shouted.

"Afterwards he was sent to the galleys for his crimes. He came back and was made Governor of the Gravensteen by the bloody Alva, where he brought to death your brother and past burgemeester, Dirk van Goorl. Afterwards, he kidnapped the person of Elsa Brant, the daughter of Hendrik Brant, whom the Inquisition murdered at The Hague. We rescued her from him, my master, Foy van Goorl, and I. Afterwards, he served with the Spaniards as a captain of their forces in the siege of Haarlem, that same Haarlem that fell three days ago, and whose citizens they are murdering tonight, throwing them two by two to drown in the waters of the Meer."

"Kill him! Cast him down!" roared the mob. "Give him to us, Red Martin."

Again the Frisian lifted his hand and again there was silence; a sudden, terrible silence.

"This man had a son; my mistress, Lysbeth van Goorl, to her shame and sorrow, was the mother of him. That son, repenting, saved us from the sack of Haarlem, yea, through him the three of us, Foy van Goorl, Elsa Brant, and I, Martin Roos, their servant, are alive tonight. This man and his Spaniards overtook us on the lake, and there we conquered him with the help of Martha the Mare, Martha who was made to carry her own husband to the fire. We conquered him, but she died in the fray; they stabbed her to death in the water as men stab an otter. As we rowed away from the battle with Count Montalvo as our captive, he awoke and stabbed his own son, Heer Adrian, with a knife from behind, and he lies here in this house dead or dying.

"My master and I, we brought this man, who today is called Ramiro to be judged by the woman whose husband and son he slew. But she would not judge him. She has said, 'Take him to the people, let them judge.' So judge now, ye people," and with a show of his mighty strength, Martin swung the struggling body of Ramiro over the parapet of the balcony and let him hang there above their heads.

They yelled, they screamed in their ravenous hate and rage. They leapt up as hounds leap at a wolf upon a wall.

"Give him to us, give him to us!" That was their cry. "He is guilty of murder and worthy of death."

Martin nodded his head in acknowledgment of their ruling. "Take him then," he said. "Take him, ye people, and judge him as you will," and with one great heave he hurled the murderer that writhed between his hands far out into the center of the street.

The crowd below gathered themselves into a heap like water above a boat sinking in the heart of a whirlpool. For a minute or more, they snarled and surged and twisted. Then they broke up and went away, talking in short, eager sentences. And there, small and dreadful on the stones, lay something that once had been a man.

Thus did the burghers of Leyden pass judgment and execute it upon the wicked Spaniard, the Count Juan de Montalvo.

Chapter xxx
Two Scenes

Scene One

Some months had gone by, and Alkmaar, that heroic little city of the north, had turned the tide of Spanish victory. Full of shame and rage, the armies of Philip and of Valdez marched upon Leyden, and from November 1573, to the end of March 1574, the town was besieged. Then the soldiers were called away to fight Louis of Nassau, and the leaguer was raised until, on the fatal field of Mock Heath, the gallant Louis, with his brother Henry and four thousand of their soldiers, perished, defeated by D'Avila. Now once more the victorious Spaniards threatened Leyden.

In a large bare room of the Stadthuis of that city, at the beginning of the month of May, a man of middle-aged might have been seen one morning walking up and down, murmuring to himself as he walked. He was not a tall man and rather thin in figure, with brown eyes and beard, hair tinged with grey, and a wide brow lined by thought. This was William of Orange, called the Silent, one of the greatest and most noble of human beings who ever lived in any age; the man called forth by God to whom Holland owes its liberties, and who forever broke the hideous yoke of religious fanaticism among the Teuton races.

Deep was his trouble on this May morning. Only last month, two more of his brothers had found death beneath the sword of the Spaniard, and now this same Spaniard, with whom he had struggled for all these weary years, was marching in his thousands upon Leyden.

"Gold," he was whispering to himself. "Give me gold, and

with the Almighty's help, I will save the city yet. With finances ships can be built, more men can be raised, powder can be bought. My country stands in a desperate state—and I have not a ducat! All gone, everything, even to my mother's trinkets and the plate upon my table. Nothing is left, no, not the credit to buy a dozen geldings."

As he thought after this fashion, one of his secretaries entered the room.

"Well, Count," said the Prince, "have you been to them all?"

"Yes, sir."

"And with what success?"

"The Burgemeester, van de Werff, promises to do everything he can, and will, for he is a man to lean on, but money is short. It has all left the country and there is not much to get."

"I know it," groaned Prince William, "you can't make a loaf from the crumbs beneath the table. Is the proclamation put up inviting all good citizens to give or lend in this hour of their country's need?

"Yes, Sir."

"Thank you, Count, you can go; there is nothing more to do. We will ride for Delft tonight."

"Sir," said the secretary, "there are two men in the courtyard who wish to see you."

"Are they known?" asked the Prince called Silent.

"Oh yes, perfectly. One is Foy van Goorl, who went through the siege of Haarlem and escaped, the son of the worthy burgher, Dirk van Goorl, whom they did to death yonder in the Gravensteen. And the other a Friesland giant of a man called Red Martin, his servant, of whose feats of arms you may have heard. The two of them held a shot tower in this town against forty or fifty Spaniards, and killed I don't know how many."

The Prince nodded. "I know. This Red Martin is a giant, a patriot, and a brave fellow. What do they want?"

"I am not sure," said the secretary with a smile, "but they have brought a herring cart here, the Frisian in the shafts for a horse, and the Heer van Goorl pushing behind. They say that it is laden with ammunition for the service of their country."

"Then why do they not take it to the burgemeester, or some-body in authority?" asked the prince.

"I don't know, but they declare that they will only deliver it to you in person."

"You are sure of your men, Count? You know," he added, with a smile, "I have to be careful."

"Quite, they were identified by several of the people in the other room."

"Then admit them, they may have something to say," remarked Prince William of Orange.

"But, Sir, they wish to bring in their cart."

"Very well, let them bring it in if it will come through the door," answered the Prince, with a sigh, for his thoughts were far from these worthy citizens and their cart.

It was not long before the wide double doors were opened, and Red Martin appeared, not as he was after the siege of Haarlem, but as he used to be, well-clothed and robust, with a beard even longer and more fiery than of yore. At the moment he was strangely employed, for across his great breast lay the broad belly-band of a horse, and by its means, harnessed between the shafts, he dragged a laden cart covered with an old sail. Moreover, the load must have been heavy, for notwithstanding his strength and that of Foy, who pushed behind, they had trouble in getting the wheels up a little rise at the threshold.

Foy shut the doors, then they trundled their cart into the middle of the great room, halted and saluted. So curious was the sight, and so inexplicable, that the Prince, forgetting his troubles for a minute, burst out laughing.

"I daresay it looks strange, Sir," said Foy, hotly, the color rising to the roots of his fair hair, "but when you have heard our story I am quite sure that you will laugh with us."

"Mynheer van Goorl," said the Prince with earnest courtesy, "be assured that I laugh at no true men such as yourself and your servant, Martin the Frisian, and least of all at men who could hold yonder shot tower against fifty Spaniards, who could escape out of Haarlem and bring home with them the greatest devil in Don Frederic's army. It was your equipage I laughed at, not yourselves," and he bowed slightly first to the one and then to the other.

"His Highness thinks perhaps," said Martin, "that the man who does a donkey's work must necessarily be a donkey," at which point the Prince laughed again.

"Sir," said Foy, "I crave your patience for a while, and on no small matter. Your Highness has heard, perhaps, of one Hendrik Brant, who perished in the Inquisition."

"Do you mean the goldsmith and banker who was said to be the richest man in the Netherlands?"

"Yes, Sir, the man whose treasure was lost."

"I remember, whose treasure was lost, though it was reported that some of our own people got away with it," and his eyes wandered wonderingly to the sail that hid the burden on the cart.

"Sir," went on Foy, "you heard right; Red Martin and I, with a pilot man who was killed, were they who got away with it, and by the help of the waterwife, who now is dead, and who was known as Mother Martha, or the Mare, we hid it in the Haarlemer Meer, whence we recovered it after we escaped from Haarlem. If you care to know how, I will tell you later, but the tale is long and strange. Elsa Brant was with us at the time—"

"She is Hendrik Brant's only child, and therefore the owner of his wealth, I believe?" interrupted the Prince.

"Yes, Sir, and my betrothed wife," responded Foy.

"I have heard of the young lady, and I congratulate you. Is she in Leyden?"

"No, Sir, her strength and mind were much broken by the horrors she passed through in the siege of Haarlem, and by other events more personal to her. Therefore, when the Spaniards threatened their first leaguer against this place, I sent her and my mother to Norwich in England, where they may sleep in peace."

"You were wise indeed, Heer van Goorl," replied the Prince with a sigh, "but it seems that you stayed behind?"

"Yes, Sir, Martin and I thought it our duty to see this war out. When Leyden is safe from the Spaniards, then we go to England, not before."

"When Leyden is safe from the Spaniards," and again the Prince sighed adding, "well, you have a true heart, young sir, and a right spirit, for which I honor both of you. But I fear that things being thus the Jufvrouw, cannot sleep so very peacefully in Norwich after all."

"We must each bear our share of the load," answered Foy sadly. "I must do the fighting and she the watching."

"It is so, I know it, who have both fought and watched. Well, I hope that a time will come when you will both do the loving. And now for the rest of the story."

"Sir, it is very short. We read your proclamation in the streets this morning and learned from it, for certain what we have heard before, that you are in great need of money for the defense of Leyden, and the war at large. Therefore, hearing that you were still in the city and believing this proclamation of yours to be the summons and clear command for which we waited, we have brought you Hendrik Brant's treasure. It is there upon the cart."

The Prince put his hand to his forehead and reeled back a step.

"You do not jest with me, Foy van Goorl?" he said.

"Indeed no."

"Well, are you confident that this treasure is yours to give, I thought it belonged to Elsa Brant?" questioned the Prince.

"Sir, the legal title to it is in my name, for my father was Brant's lawful heir and executor, and I inherit his rights. Moreover, although a provision for Elsa and Red Martin is charged upon it, it is both of their desires that the money should be used, every ducat of it, for the service of the country in such way as I might deem proper. Lastly, Elsa's father, Hendrik Brant, always believed that this wealth of his would in due season be of such service. Here is a copy of his will, in which he directs that we act to apply the money for the defense of our country, the freedom of the Christian Faith, and the destruction of the Spaniards in such fashion and at such time or times as God shall reveal to us. When he gave us charge of it also, his words to me were: 'I am certain that thousands and tens of thousands of our folk will live to bless the gold of Hendrik Brant.' On that belief too, thinking that God put it into his mind and would reveal His purpose in His own hour, we have acted all of us and therefore for the sake of this stuff we and others have risked death and torture. Now it has come about as Brant foretold. Now we understand why all these things have happened, and why we live, this man and I, to stand before you today with this treasure."

Foy made a sign, and Martin going to the cart, pulled off the sail-cloth, revealing the five mud-stained barrels painted, each of them, with the mark "B." There, too, ready for the purpose, were a hammer, mallet, and chisel. Resting the shafts of the cart upon a table, Martin climbed into it, and with a few great blows of the mallet, drove in the head of a cask selected at random. Beneath appeared wool, which he removed, not without fear lest there might be some mistake. Then, as he could wait no longer, he tilted the barrel up and poured its contents out upon the cart.

As it turned out, this was the keg that contained the jewels which Heer Brant had wisely store up from the majority of his massive wealth. Now in one glittering stream of red and white and blue and green, breaking from their cases and wrappings that the damp had rotted—save for those pearls, the most valuable of them all, which were in a watertight copper box—they fell jingling to the open deck of the cart.

"Forgive me men for being slow of heart to comprehend this gift for what it is—an answer to prayer!" said Prince William of Orange.

"I think there is only this one tub of jewels," said Foy quietly. "The rest, which are much heavier, are full of gold coin. Here, Sir, is the inventory so that you may check the list and see that we have kept back nothing."

But William of Orange heeded him not, only he looked at the priceless gems and stated, "Fleets of ships, armies of men, convoys of food, means to sway the powerful and buy good-will—aye, and the Netherlands themselves wrung from the grip of Spain, the Netherlands free and holy and happy! O God! I thank Thee Who thus hast moved the hearts of men to the salvation of this Thy people from sore danger!"

Then in the sudden surge of relief and joy, the great Prince hid his face in his hands and wept. After several moments, the godly prince took the time to petition the Lord for the wisdom necessary to utilize the riches he now possessed.

Thus it came about that the riches of Hendrik Brant, when Leyden lay at her last gasp, paid the soldiers and built the fleets that, in due time, driven by a great wind sent suddenly from heaven across the flooded meadows, broke the dreadful siege and signed the doom of Spanish rule in Holland. Therefore it would seem that it was no mere coincidence that Hendrik Brant was stubbornly courageous and foresighted, that his life and the life of Dirk van Goorl were not lost in vain. We may also conclude that it was not in vain for Elsa to suffer the worst torments of a woman's fear in the Red Mill on the marshes; for Foy and Martin to play their parts like men in the shot-tower, the Gravensteen, and the siege, and for Mother Martha the Sword to have found a grave and rest in the waters of the Haarlem Meer.

Quite some time past before William of Orange was able to assemble a fleet and device a plan for the liberation of Leyden and much of the Netherlands. Eventually, Prince William and his men attacked Leyden, and broke down the dykes, causing a great flood which destroyed many of the Spanish strongholds. Foy and Martin were with the rescuing ships, and sailed shouting and victorious into her famine-stricken canals. For the Spaniards, those that were left of them, fled away from their broken forts and flooded trenches.

Scene Two

So the scene changes from warring, blood-stained, triumphant Holland to the quiet city of Norwich and a quaint gabled house in the Tombland district almost beneath the shadow of the tall spire of the cathedral. This house, for about a year had been the home of Lysbeth van Goorl and Elsa Brant. Here to Norwich they had come in safety in the autumn of 1573 just before the first siege of Leyden was begun, and here they had dwelt for twelve long, doubtful, anxious months. News, or rather rumors, of what was passing in the Netherlands reached them from time to time; twice even there came letters from Foy himself, but the last of these had been received many weeks ago just as the iron grip of the second siege was closing round the city. Then Foy and Martin, so they learned from the letter, were not in the town but with the Prince of Orange at Delft, working hard with the fleet that was being built and armed for its relief.

After this, there was a long silence, and none could tell what had happened, although a horrible report reached them that Leyden had been taken, sacked, and burnt, and all its inhabitants massacred. They lived in comfort here in Norwich, for the firm of Munt and Brown, Dirk van Goorl's agents, were honest, and the fortune he had sent over when the clouds were gathering thick, had been well invested by them and produced an ample revenue. Notwithstanding their physical comforts, however, these women struggled daily with emotional and spiritual burdens, which were only alleviated through the instrumentality of prayer.

One evening, they sat in the parlor on the ground floor of the house, or rather Lysbeth sat, for Elsa knelt by her, her tear-stained head resting upon the arm of the chair.

"Oh! It is cruel," she sobbed, "it is too much to bear. How can you be so calm, Mother, when perhaps Foy is dead?"

"If my son is dead, Elsa, that is God's will, and I am calm, because now, as many a time before, I resign myself to the will of God, not because I have closed my heart to suffering. Mothers can feel, my child, as well as sweethearts."

"Would that I had never left him," moaned Elsa.

"You asked to leave, child. For my part I would probably have preferred to weather the best or the worst in Leyden."

"It is true, it is because I am a coward; yet Foy did seem to think my plan was sound."

"He wished it, Elsa, therefore it is for the best. Let us await the issue in patience. Come, our meal is set."

They sat themselves down to eat, these two lonely women,

but at their table were laid four settings as though there were expected guests. Yet none were bidden—this was Elsa's habit.

"Foy and Martin might come," she said, "and be vexed if it seemed that we did not expect them. Besides, I think it is a fitting act of faith to demonstrate to the Lord that we believe He will answer our prayers." So for the last three months or more she had always put four settings at the table, and Lysbeth did not discourage her. In her heart she too hoped that Foy might come.

In answer to her prayer, that very night Foy came, and with him Red Martin, the great sword Silence still strapped about his middle.

"Hark!" said Lysbeth suddenly, "I hear my son's footstep at the door. It seems, Elsa, that, after all, the ears of a mother are quicker than those of a lover."

But Elsa never heard her, for she was already wrapped in the arms of Foy; the same Foy, but grown older and with a long pale scar across his forehead.

"Yet," went on Lysbeth to herself, with a faint smile on her white and stately face, "the son's lips are for the lover first."

An hour later, or two, or three, for who reckoned time that night when there was so much to hear and tell, while Foy, Elsa, and Martin knelt before her, Lysbeth put up her evening prayer of praise and thanksgiving.

"Almighty God," she said in her slow, earnest voice, "Thy awful Hand that by my own faithless sin took from me my husband, hath given back his son and mine who shall be to Elsa a husband. Thanks be to you Lord for this reunion, and for your goodness to our country over the sea. Above us throughout the years is Thy everlasting will, beneath us when our years are done, shall be Thy everlasting arms. So for the bitter and the sweet, for the evil and the good, for the past and for the present, we, Thy servants, render Thee glory, thanks, and praise, O God of our fathers. It is You that fashioneth us and all according to Thy desire, remembering those things that we have forgotten and foreknowing those things that are not yet. Therefore to Thee, Who through so many dreadful days hast led us to this

hour of joy, be glory and thanks, O Lord of the living and the dead. Amen."

And the others echoed "To Thee be glory and thanks, O Lord of the living and the dead. Amen."

Then, after the prayer ended, Foy and Elsa stood up, and, with separations behind them and fears appeased at last, embraced each other in the love and hope of their common faith.

But Lysbeth sat silent in the new home, far from the land where she was born, and turned her stricken heart towards the dead.

Finis.

EPILOGUE

Many lessons can be drawn from the story of the Netherland's struggle for the liberty to serve God, among them are that there is no freedom without sacrifice, and no triumph without loss.

Another lesson that flows out of this story is that the victory for religious liberty that was won at such a high price by the Dutch Protestants benefited more than just the Netherlands. In the early seventeenth century, Holland became a place of extended refuge for the Pilgrims, who eventually sailed in 1620 to North America. The Mayflower Pilgrims, who resided in Holland for over ten years, would never have been able to utilize this land as their temporary haven had not Almighty God, in His sovereign mercy and perfect timing, freed the Netherlands from Roman Catholic domination in the late 1500s. It is probably not too much to state, that if the Lord did not grant freedom to the Dutch when He did, then the whole scope of early American history would have been dramatically altered. Indeed, it is probable that North America would never have become a stronghold of Protestant Christianity and a beacon for virtuous liberty.

Peter, an apostle of Jesus Christ, to the strangers scattered throughout Pontus, Galatia, Cappadocia, Asia, and Bithynia, Elect according to the foreknowledge of God the Father, through sanctification of the Spirit, unto obedience and sprinkling of the blood of Jesus Christ: Grace unto you, and peace, be multiplied.

Blessed be the God and Father of our Lord Jesus Christ, which according to his abundant mercy hath begotten us again unto a lively hope by the resurrection of Jesus Christ from the dead, To an inheritance incorruptible, and undefiled, and that fadeth not away, reserved in heaven for you, Who are kept by the power of God through faith unto salvation ready to be revealed in the last time.

Wherein ye greatly rejoice, though now for a season, if need be, ye are in heaviness through manifold temptations: That the trial of your faith, being much more precious than of gold that perisheth, though it be tried with fire, might be found unto praise and honour and glory at the appearing of Jesus Christ: Whom having not seen, ye love; in whom, though now ye see him not, yet believing, ye rejoice with joy unspeakable and full of glory: Receiving the end of your faith, even the salvation of your souls.

 *1 Peter 1:1-9*

I believed, therefore have I spoken: I was greatly afflicted: I said in my haste, All men are liars. What shall I render unto the LORD for all his benefits toward me? I will take the cup of salvation, and call upon the name of the LORD. I will pay my vows unto the LORD now in the presence of all his people. Precious in the sight of the LORD is the death of his saints.

Psalm 116:10-15

Also by H. Rider Haggard,
from Christian Liberty Press . . .

. . . comes this classic adventure of Miriam, a young Christian woman living in the Roman Empire during the first century after Christ, and Marcus, the Roman officer who desired to win her hand. As Miriam faces hardships and fiery trials, her faith is continually strengthened by the Lord. The historic events portrayed in Pearl Maiden culminate in the Roman siege and destruction of Jerusalem and its Temple in A.D. 70.

Now in a newly revised and updated Centennial Edition, Pearl Maiden continues to be a wonderful story of faith for modern readers. Stirring events, captivating characters, and careful attention to historical detail are seamlessly blended here to produce a truly uplifting novel.

For more information visit
www.christianlibertypress.com and
search for *Pearl Maiden.*